THE REALITY OF WANTING MY BULLY

LOVE WITHOUT LABELS

BOOK TWO

LEXI AMBER

BEC BENSON

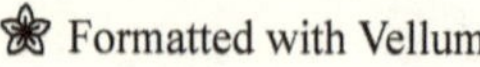 Formatted with Vellum

For anyone who needs the reminder that your past does not define your future.

CONTENT WARNING

- Homophobic bullying, including from the point-of-view of a teenage bully
- Teenager implying that the way someone dresses gives others permission to harass them
- Disordered eating: really shitty parent who calls their child fat, forces them to workout and restrict their diet under the excuse that they're helping them be healthy, parent pressures child to pursue an athletic career,
- Homophobic parents
- Emotional abuse from a parent
- Use of "gay" as an insult
- Bullying based on appearance/self-expression (including name calling: weirdo/freak, etc. but NO f-slur!)
- Gender stereotyping
- Physical arguments between teenagers
- Internalized homophobia + fear of being outed
- Physical harm to a MC
- Hospitalization (off page) and concussion as a result of homophobic bullying

- Being disowned for being queer
- Degradation
- Online bullying
- Unintentional misgendering from a side character
- On page sex between 18-year-old high school students
- Last minute wedding cancellation for secondary characters

AUTHOR'S NOTE

A few notes before we begin. First, this is NOT a dark romance, it is a bully romance that is set in 2010-2012 based on bullying and situations that WE witnessed during those years.

Please know that part one may be painful at time for all of the characters. They are teenagers, they make mistakes, they are not perfect (or close to it). We hope you can remember how deeply things like popularity, belonging, and acceptance mattered in those years, and how sometimes we let those things cloud our judgement.

These characters are messy and complicated, but they do eventually get it right. We hope you love them as much as we do by the end.

PROLOGUE

Jace
Present Day
January 2025

I'm about to meet my future spouse.
At least, I hope I am.

Somehow, KD agreed to move in with me despite the fact that we've never met in person, and I don't know if I've ever been this excited about anything before. I have no idea what they look or sound like, how old they are, or even their gender, but none of that matters to me. I know who they are as a person.

We've been dating on *Love Without Labels* for the last week, which might not seem like a lot of time, but somehow the connection I feel with K seems more meaningful than any other connection I've had in the past.

I'll be the first to admit I was skeptical about the whole process when I signed up for a "label-free dating show," but I needed a change. Something—anything really—to distract me from the pattern of failed relationships I've fallen into. I know it's my own damn fault that no one can ever live up to the version of *him* I've built up in my head over the years, but I can't help making the comparisons.

For as long as I can remember, Kieran Delaney has been the ideal person to me, and I don't know how to quit my obsession; I don't know how to stop measuring everyone I date against him. I watch every video, like every post, know about every public appearance, product launch, and endorsement deal. Sometimes it feels like I still know him—even if I use a fan account he wouldn't recognize—while he probably wishes we'd never met in the first place. It's been over a decade since I've seen him in person, and Kieran has probably forgotten all about me. *I need to try to forget about him, too.*

When my last girlfriend dumped me, claiming "I cared more about some stranger on the internet than her," I knew I needed a dramatic change. I tried to delete all of my social media apps and quit cold turkey, but that only lasted a few hours. I've never had the best self-control, and after I'd updated myself on everything "Sparkles" that I'd missed, I was doomscrolling when I saw the ad for *Love Without Labels*.

Something, maybe fate, maybe because I was overtired and should have been sleeping hours before, made me want to know more. I followed the link to the application and saw contestants would be isolated during the process, cut off from the rest of the world—and more importantly, their phones—to focus on dating other participants on the show.

It seemed perfect. They would literally force me to give up social media, and I could potentially meet someone without being distracted by whatever Kieran was doing that day. Even if it seemed unlikely that I would actually get chosen for the show at all—let alone match with anyone I could spend the rest of my life with—I knew I had to try.

Maybe it isn't fair for me to have signed up for the show when a part of my heart will always belong to him. It's not like anything could ever happen between us anyway, especially given how I treated him and how things ended between us.

Now here I am, pulling my suitcase behind me as I follow one of the show's producers, Jay, as he escorts me to the new apartment I'll be sharing with KD. This whole process has been kind of surreal, and there's a part of me that hasn't quite accepted that I'm actually a contestant on a reality show at all. But I'm embracing this once-in-a-lifetime experience, and I'm so excited to meet the one person here who's captured my interest.

I follow Jay into the elevator, leaving the anonymous part of the show behind, ready to jump into this next chapter. I'm taking deep, measured breaths, trying to calm my racing heart as I wonder—for probably the last time—who it is I've been bonding with over the countless messages and hours talking through the show's distorted voice technology.

What if it's him? the annoying voice in my head asks for the millionth time.

I'm not proud of the fact that all I could think about during my first date with KD was that they share the same initials as Kieran. But I'm not a complete idiot, I know there are probably tens of thousands of people in New York whose first and last names also start with K and D.

This KD is by far the coolest person I've talked to in years. We clicked right away, and despite the short amount of time we've been dating, I do feel like we have a real shot at a future together. Talking with K has been so easy; they're really fucking funny, kind, and there hasn't been a single moment of awkward silence or tension between us like I experienced in some of the other dates early on.

I'm so relieved and excited they also like me enough to have agreed to move in with me and enter the next phase of the show together. If the next week of sharing an apartment goes well, we might even be engaged soon. I feel like I might actually be ready to build a life with someone without constantly wondering about what might've been if things didn't end the way they did back then. *K could be it for me.*

Jay motions for me to get off the elevator first. "Apartment 13 on your left. KD should already be in there."

Kind of an ominous number to include on a dating show, but thirteen was also my jersey number in high school, so what might seem like an unlucky sign to most feels like confirmation that I'm exactly where I should be. I run my fingers through my unruly hair like that might somehow tame the mess of curls.

I push open the door, eager to meet the person who I could spend the rest of my life with… and my heart shatters.

It's like I can feel it being ripped apart in my chest, splitting right down the middle as I'm torn in two. Half of me is elated, overwhelmed by the person standing in front of me, because I was right. We are perfect for each other, and no one else could ever compare.

But the other half of me, the more logical, rational part, is shattering in a way I know I'll never recover from. It doesn't matter what happens after this; no one will ever be able to help me fit all the broken pieces of who I was before this moment back together.

Because it wasn't just a silly crush that turned into an embarrassing obsession—there really might have been a chance for something real between us. This moment proves it.

But I fucked that possibility up years ago.

PART I

1

KIERAN

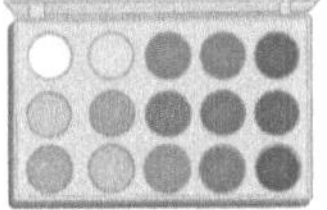

Junior Year
September 2010

kay, deep breath. Time to do this.

I smooth down the front of my jacket one more time before adjusting the car mirror to check that my mascara is still perfect—and it is.

My stomach is doing somersaults, but I open the door anyway, because I really have no other choice now.

"Love you!" Mom calls out.

"Love you," I echo, slamming the door behind me before she can add something mom-ish like "don't let them get to you."

I've already spent way too many hours stressed about how today could go, so her pep talk won't help, though I am grateful for her support. I decided over the summer that I'm sick of hiding who I am to make other people "happy" or "comfortable" —especially when they've never once cared whether I'm comfortable, too.

I sling my backpack over one shoulder and start walking toward the school. My palms are already sweaty from the stress even though, realistically, I'm wearing so little makeup no one should even notice. Which is intentional for school. I've always been a creative person who enjoyed expressing myself through art, and makeup allows me to do that in a whole new way, but I'm still nervous to wear it here for the first time.

As soon as I walk through the doors, I make my way to where Olivia is waiting for me at her locker. Liv has been my best friend since fourth grade when she moved to my school. She didn't know anyone, and since I didn't have many friends, and she was nice, we clicked instantly.

"Kieran!" she calls when she looks up and sees me, flipping her phone closed as her face breaks into a smile. "You look so good! Wait, turn, I need to see the back!"

I laugh and spin for her, showing off my dark jeans and black tank top, layered with a black zip-up jacket that has sparkly vertical stripes down the front.

"You look so cute, K! I'm so excited you're finally doing this!" she exclaims.

"Thank you. Honestly, I need the vote of confidence today. I keep telling myself I don't care what anyone else thinks, but I'm only human," I admit. She knows how hard it's been hiding so much of myself, and has been encouraging me to stop shrinking just to fit in, which has been the push I needed.

She nods in understanding. "Same. I barely slept last night. I kept imagining every worst-case scenario. You'd think, by junior year, starting your first day of high school wouldn't be so hard, but it's still nerve-racking. Like what if I get stuck sitting next to someone who smells way too strongly of Axe body spray?" She visibly shudders before mumbling, "I seriously hate that stuff. But I'm also so sick of being single. This needs to be the year we get boyfriends and become cool. I think I'm going to join the yearbook club, too. I'm ready for us to go all in on what we want this year."

I laugh and shake my head. Her being so over-the-top is exactly why we get along so well.

"Kieran, I'm serious!" she pouts, adjusting the headband that's holding back her curls. She went with light-wash jeans, and a cute top with an infinity scarf for the first day, and looks as great as she always does.

"Too bad there's, like, two out gay guys in this school that I know of, and I don't want to date either of them."

"You never know: it's a new year. Maybe some hot guy just moved here."

"Are you done at your locker?" I ask, brushing off her comment.

"Yeah, let's go."

We walk down the hall, and my nerves begin to trickle in more and more, even with her by my side. *You can do this, you are confident and strong,* I remind myself.

I open my locker and put the magnetic mirror on the inside, just like last year. I also set up my bookshelf and decorate the space with some photos of Liv and me. I'll definitely add more, but this felt like a good starting point. Before I'm ready to walk to my first class, I take a moment to check my makeup again— my foundation still looks good, and there are no mascara smudges.

Honestly, it's so subtle, I'll be surprised if anyone even notices besides Liv. I doubt they'd be looking at me that closely. No one has paid that much attention to me the last two years of high school; I don't know why they'd start now.

Liv leans in beside me and fluffs her curls in my mirror.

"You look great, too, Liv." I smile.

"You know," she says, smiling back at me in the mirror, "if this whole school thing doesn't work out, we could totally start a glam squad. Do makeup professionally, travel the world, become famous."

"Tempting, but let's see if I can make it through today first," I say, only half joking.

2

JACE

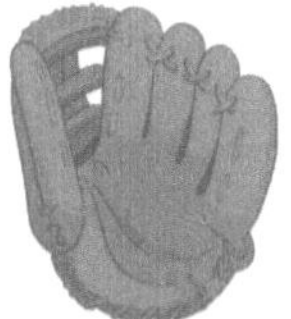

"Are you planning to spend another year hanging out in the hallway, or are you going to go to class and actually learn something?"

That over-the-top friendly voice immediately has my spine straightening in annoyance as my dad claps a heavy hand on my shoulder, like we're best buds and he's not going to rip into me later when we're alone.

I don't understand how I'm the only person who notices how condescending and rude my dad is despite his upbeat and cheery tone. Everyone else hears encouragement; I hear the unspoken warning injected into every word.

"Jace doesn't need to know math, Coach," David, my best friend, jokes. He's also on the team and as obsessed with my dad as everyone else in this town seems to be. "Once he's in the MLB, he can pay people to know it for him."

They both laugh, but I fail to see what's funny. Especially because I'm actually smart. Not that it matters to my dad, though. The only reason he cares about my grades is to keep me eligible and on the field, which has never been a problem.

My dad squeezes my shoulder in an unnecessarily aggressive

grip. Not enough to leave a mark, but enough to remind me that he's in charge and not to fuck with him. "Get to class, boys." He finally lets go after his obvious warning, nodding and flashing his fake smile at us both before he continues down the hall toward his office.

David is as oblivious as he always seems to be about how tense that interaction actually was and calls out after him, "See ya at practice, Coach!"

I don't bother to hide my eyeroll. Everyone loves my father. He's basically a legend around our town. Jesse Ryan made it all the way to the MLB… *for a whole four games.*

He was never signed long-term to any of the major teams, but he spent a few years playing AAA and bouncing around to any team who'd take him so he could chase his dream. Then he got my mom pregnant, which was definitely not part of his plan. They were only dating at the time but quickly got married. Mom wanted a more stable life for her kid—or so she claimed—and he's never let me forget that I'm the reason he had to give up his major league aspirations.

He blames me like I ever had a say in choosing to be born.

Now he's "Coach Ryan," teaching gym class and in charge of the whole baseball program at the only high school in our New Jersey town. Which means he's at *my* high school. And that failed dream of his? That's now mine too. According to him, at least.

For as long as I can remember, all he's ever talked about is getting me to the MLB. Which means every second of my life has been about baseball. I've been on travel teams since I was seven. He's made me custom workout plans with special diets to stay fit. I wasn't allowed sleepovers or ice cream or fun. Nothing that could distract from the future he planned for me was allowed. You'd think my mom would have something to say about it, but she's content to go along with whatever my dad wants. All she's focused on is my little sister, Molly.

I've missed out on a lot of what my friends have gotten to experience as a sixteen, almost seventeen, year old because of it. But my dad doesn't care about fun I'm missing out on, because his number one rule for me is staying out of trouble "for the sake of my future." He controls my life, and there's no escaping him, especially when he's everywhere I am—at home, school, baseball.

Even though he isn't physically in every classroom, he might as well be. He's friends with all the teachers and employees, and they all know about his big plans for me and my future. They all "help" to keep me in line and make sure I don't screw it all up… not that I've ever given any of them a reason to doubt me.

I try to shake off the bad mood my dad's presence always puts me in as we head into our final class of the day. A minute or two after I'm settled at a desk—not even close to being late—the classroom door opens and in walks a guy I've never seen before.

He's… impossible to miss.

He's wearing a sparkly jacket for god's sake, but somehow that's not even the most noticeable thing. His hair is styled perfectly like he hasn't been at school all day. He isn't small, maybe only a couple of inches shorter than me, but he's slender.

I bet his dad's never dragged him out of bed before sunrise to lift weights in the freezing garage. Never made him run sprints until he puked "just to prove he wanted it badly enough."

Then there are his eyes. I've never seen a guy with such pretty eyes before.

Wait, what?

I quickly shut down that line of thinking because that sounds like I'm describing a girl. It's just… they stand out against his fair complexion. That's all. Probably because his eyelashes are so dark and long, almost like he's wearing makeup.

Holy shit.

"Are you wearing makeup?" I blurt out without thinking as he walks past me.

He freezes where he's standing just in front of me now, and his shoulders lift then fall like he's taken a deep breath before he turns back to face me. I can't help scanning the rest of his face now that he's so close. He's totally wearing makeup, and I can't stop staring at his eyes.

Not in a weird way.

More in a *what-the-fuck* kind of way.

I've never seen a guy look so feminine before, and it's... confusing me.

"Makeup isn't gender exclusive," he answers boldly.

His full lips are glossy too, and they momentarily distract me from the challenge clearly shining in his bright eyes. *I seriously need to stop looking at him. Any second now. Turn away, Jace. Jesus, people are going to wonder why you're staring at him.*

"Whatever you say, Sparkles," I finally mutter, shaking my head as I tear my gaze away.

Except, maybe I didn't say it as quietly as I thought, because everyone around me laughs, and David echoes, "Yeah, bye, Sparkles." Then fake-coughs "loser" in his hand as the guy storms away with a huff and an eye roll.

Dramatic much? I only asked him a question. You don't do something *that* out of the ordinary if you don't want the extra attention. Honestly, it's rude to get all offended when I was only playing into what he so clearly wants.

To my complete shock, he sits directly across from me. The desks in this room face each other with an aisle down the middle. I don't understand why he'd sit there after seeming so pissed off at my comment, but as I look around the room, I realize almost every desk is full since he got here so late. *Sucks to suck.*

He looks up to shoot another glare my way before pulling a notebook out of his bag. I can't help but laugh when I see it because even that has sparkles on it. Seriously, who does this guy think he is, and why does he need attention this badly?

The bell rings to start class, and the teacher starts the same boring monologue I've heard in every class now. I quickly skim the syllabus and mentally note the important info so I can block it out and turn my attention back to Sparkles.

I wonder what his real name is? Is he new here? Where does a sixteen-year-old boy even learn to put on makeup? Or get it?

My dad would lose his fucking mind if I asked him to buy me anything girly. Not that it takes much to piss him off or that I'd ever want to wear makeup. But I've spent so much of my life being told "no" or that things weren't allowed, I wouldn't even attempt to ask for anything outside the norm.

And then there's this guy—walking in with a sparkly jacket, makeup on his eyes, and shiny pink lips—who obviously wants people to notice him. Almost like he's asking to be made fun of.

He's doing the exact opposite of everything I've ever been taught.

I don't think I've ever seen anyone try harder to stand out than a *guy* wearing makeup. It's pathetic. Who shows up on the first day of school like that? Isn't the whole point of high school to try to fit in? Make friends and be likeable? Not paint a target on your back?

I've spent my whole life learning how to follow the rules, how to keep my mouth shut, and how to keep my image clean. My dad's favorite stories are warnings about the guys who blew their shot in the majors over one minor scandal or one bad decision. Every story ends the same way: "He could've made it if he didn't..." followed by whatever lesson he thought I needed to hear. It's the reason his favorite phrase is: "It only takes a few seconds to ruin your whole future." Not that it's hard to forget when my dad reminds me every day that my existence ruined his.

And Sparkles is just doing whatever the hell he wants, like there are no consequences.

I have so many questions, and the most annoying one is *why the hell is this weirdo taking up so much of my thoughts?*

When the bell rings, dismissing us for the day, I'm not in any hurry to rush out of here since practice doesn't start for thirty minutes. Sparkles ends up right in front of me and David as we exit the room into the hall of lockers, and the glitter, or whatever is covering this guy's jacket, is once again distracting as hell. David bumps my arm, waggling his eyebrows toward the outfit as he silently laughs.

But ya know what? I don't think laughing behind his back is enough. This guy obviously wants attention, so why bother holding back? Something about him is really pissing me off, and I can't seem to let it go.

Before I even think it through, I grab the strap of the backpack he's wearing so it jerks him back a step.

He spins around fast, eyes wide with panic.

Good. Maybe that'll teach him to stop wearing all this crap.

"What's with the makeup? Do you want to be a girl or something?" I taunt. "Or are you just a freak?"

A few people slow down, and there's a small crowd forming around us all, and I'm aware I need to hurry this along. The last thing I need is to get caught up in something that makes its way back to my dad. He's already got a laundry list of what I'm apparently doing wrong—I don't need to add "starting fights in the hallway" to it.

"No, I don't want to be a girl," Sparkles spits out, glaring at me with those bright blue eyes again. "And I don't see why you care so much. Me wearing makeup has absolutely nothing to do with you."

He's still holding that ridiculous glittery notebook, so I grab it out of his hand and dangle it between us.

"Come on, Sparkles. You shouldn't flash gay stuff like this around."

"Well, I *am* gay, sequins or not," he huffs out, completely unashamed.

I still, not expecting him to admit to that so freely.

Especially not in front of everyone.

I don't think I've ever met a queer person before. Definitely not anyone who was so vocal about it.

He's acting like being gay is no big deal, like he wouldn't get destroyed in the locker room or at home because of his admission.

Do his parents not care?

They must not because he's wearing makeup, and they'd have to know about that, right?

He clearly doesn't give a shit about fitting in or being liked. Just walks around like it's okay to be different, without a worry in the world.

How can his life be that easy?

My dad would lose it if I ever said something like that. Not that I would, I'm definitely straight, but my dad and the other coaches always make little comments that've made it more than clear that being gay isn't something you should be proud to advertise.

But Sparkles seems to have missed the memo—once again.

"All this sparkly crap is distracting," I say, louder than I need to. "It's like you're asking for people to make fun of you, dressing like that."

He narrows his eyes. "Like you? Why don't you just leave me alone?"

"Can't," I snap. I don't know why the thought of ignoring him sounds so impossible. "Someone's gotta teach you not to be so fucking weird," I add, grasping for a reason that makes sense. "I'm trying to help you out here. Ditch the makeup and shiny clothes, and we'll leave you alone. Simple as that. No one wants to see a boy dressed like this. My sister doesn't even wear that much makeup."

My dad doesn't actually let my sister, Molly, wear any makeup. Granted she's in middle school, but still.

"Do we need to teach him a lesson?" David asks, crossing his arms and flexing like he's trying to appear even more menacing than he normally is. The threat is clear in his tone. David's very competitive, which makes him a great teammate, but he's always taken things a little too far when joking around with the other players or heckling the other teams.

David doesn't understand that I don't really want him to hurt Sparkles—just like he always misses my dad's condescending comments—but I'm also very aware of everyone looking on. I know it's only a matter of time before a teacher comes to investigate, so I need to shut this down in a way that appeases the crowd and David's desire to put this guy in his place without escalating things too much.

"Nah, not today," I answer. "Let's get to practice. This weirdo isn't worth our time." I knock into him with my shoulder as I walk past, trying to give a little warning that this could have been way worse.

"I've never seen you try to put losers in their place before. Finally grew some balls, huh?" David taunts as we walk to the locker room.

"Shut up, you know I can't get in trouble."

"Yeah, yeah, don't forget about me when you go pro. But if that freak gets too distracting, let me know. I'll take care of him."

"I don't think that'll be a problem," I assure him, because for whatever reason, I really don't want David to fuck with him.

If it comes to that, I'll be the one to do it.

It isn't until we're nearly at the locker room that I realize I'm still holding onto his notebook. I should probably throw it away, but at the last second, I slip it into my bag instead.

I never got Sparkle's real name, and all throughout practice, my thoughts keep drifting to him. The way his makeup made his eyes look so bright or the shiny way his lips looked.

Such a freak.

"Ryan! What the hell was that? You call that a throw?" my dad shouts at me from the dugout, loud enough for the whole team to hear. "Smith could've crawled to second and still made it."

Today is our first unofficial practice of the year. On the first day of school, no less. Baseball is a spring sport, but for any guys who aren't in other sports, he expects us to show up nearly every day of the week for practice or weight training. And no matter how brutal he gets with me on the field, everyone just shrugs it off as his coaching style. Just Coach Ryan doing his thing.

Except no one seems to realize the insults don't end when we're at home.

He's right, though. I'm the school's best catcher, and I should be more focused. There are other guys on the team, but I can't count on them to cover for me if I want to be great.

This is why distractions are dangerous.

"Sorry, Coach," I yell back, adjusting my helmet and settling into my stance to call the next pitch.

"Sorrys are for losers. You're better than that," he barks.

I nod sharply again and lock-in to practice.

3

KIERAN

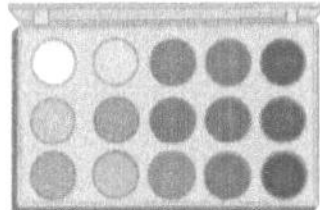

Of course some jock assholes had to pick on me on day one.

As much as I'm trying not to let it get to me… it is. When they had me circled in the hallway, all I could think was: Maybe being myself isn't worth it, and maybe I shouldn't have worn makeup. I could just wait two more years until I get to college. People would be more accepting there, right?

It's not that I didn't expect comments. I just don't understand why *I* need to be the one who hides or changes who I am. Why couldn't they just let it go?

I've known Jace Ryan since elementary school, even though he seems to have no idea who I am.

From what I've noticed over the years, most popular guys love all the eyes on them, but not him. He's always been kind of cold and standoff-ish in comparison. When his friends were obnoxious, he'd tend to hold back. Looks like he's finally given up because he was a complete dick today when he decided to make me his target.

I slowly make my way to my locker to grab what I need to head home, then meet Olivia at hers. She perks up when she sees me. "How was your last class?" she asks, and there's no point in sugarcoating it. She saw me a few hours ago when I was going on and on about how great my painting class is going to be, so my shift in mood is obvious.

"Not great," I admit with a sigh. "Apparently, Jace Ryan decided to drop the nice-guy act and embrace the popular kid bully cliché this year. His little sidekick, David, was there encouraging him, too. Jace called me out about wearing makeup in front of the whole class, then called me Sparkles." I shake my head, trying to keep my complaint light so I don't start crying. "Oh! And he thought calling me gay was an insult. Fucking idiots. I knew this"—I motion to my outfit and face—"was a risk, but if they weren't such assholes, today would've been perfectly fine. No one else seemed to care, and if they did, they didn't say anything."

"That's so weird, Jace has always seemed so nice to me," Liv comments. "Sparkles doesn't sound too bad though: we love sparkles! Don't let them get to you, they'll probably move on by tomorrow."

I shrug, not really wanting to go into it more. It's hard feeling so different from my peers, and sometimes I wonder why I can't just be like everyone else. But that wouldn't make me happy, and I've always hated hiding and pretending to blend in.

Since discovering makeup a few years ago, when I first played around with my mom's eyeliner, I've felt more myself than ever before. It's taken time for me to get to the point where I was confident enough to wear it in public, and other than that last class, I've felt amazing all day. I just wish the version of me that made me the happiest didn't naturally attract assholes.

"Let's get out of here. I'm ready to go home." I sigh, turning to walk out the doors and head to the pick-up area. She loops her arm through mine, completely unashamed to be seen with me as we leave. Even if she doesn't seem to understand how the interaction with Jace and David left me feeling, her acceptance of who I am settles some of my anxiety.

Today might have ended on a low note, but the first day of junior year is officially over, and I'm proud of myself for staying true to what makes me happy.

IT'S FINALLY FRIDAY. The first week of school is almost behind me, and I only have one more class to go before the weekend I desperately need.

Because I cut it close on the first day of class, and with Jace stopping me to harass me, the only open seat left was on the side of the aisle facing him. And, of course, our teacher made us keep those seats. *Lucky me.*

Now, all I have to do is try to ignore Jace once more while he attempts to burn a hole through my head with his eyes, then I get a two-day break. Well, that, and shrug off whatever insult he has waiting for me today.

Every time I've walked into class this week, Jace has glared at me and made some comment about my outfit or makeup. To make matters worse, they've all been completely unoriginal.

If he's going to be mean, he should at least be clever.

I truly don't understand his weird obsession with me or why he refuses to leave me alone. I wonder if he spends all day trying to come up with his snide comments to try to get a laugh out of his dickhead friends.

Probably.

Any other attractive guy looking at me as much as Jace does might be a good thing, but he's such an asshole that his appearance doesn't even matter; especially when I know he's doing it because he hates the way I look.

And, the cherry on top of my not-so-great week is that I

learned I have gym with him—and his dad—every other day. As if gym wasn't already hell on its own. I'm pretty sure his dad hates me too, probably because I'm not athletic enough to exist in his sacred sports temple of a class.

Stepping up to the classroom door, I take a deep breath and steady myself for whatever is about to come my way. I walk in, and Jace is already at his usual desk. As I make my way past him, he says, "Don't you know it's not Halloween, Sparkles?"

I don't even bother stopping, I just roll my eyes and keep walking to my seat, eagerly waiting for the final bell to ring so I can go home where I know I won't have to see Jace Ryan for two whole days.

Despite how much of a bully he's been, I'm proud of myself because all week I've worn what I've wanted and haven't let his harassment stop me from being myself.

After a boring lecture that I half pay attention to, the bell finally rings. All I'm focused on is getting out of here. I grab my backpack and quickly make my way toward the hallway, but as soon as I'm in the doorway, I feel my backpack being yanked again.

"Let go," I hiss.

"Shut up," the voice behind me says, and no surprise, it's Jace.

He shoves me forward down the hall before stopping and slamming me into a wall of lockers.

My heart rate instantly skyrockets.

Shit.

He hasn't laid a hand on me before now. My chest is tight, and my skin's buzzing with panic. The verbal crap sucks, but I can handle it. This, though? This feels unpredictable and dangerous. I'm not built for fights, and I have no idea how far he's willing to take things.

"Sparkles, I've been so patient, but it's time to cut the crap," he snaps angrily.

I'm still struggling to understand how my outfit choices are so personally offensive to him. He's a lot stronger than I am, though, and the way he has me backed up against the locker is intimidating. "I told you to stop wearing the girly shit. A bunch of people heard me give you that warning. Yet here we are a week later, and you're still dressed like this," he says, grabbing the rhinestone collar of the shirt I'm wearing. "Are you doing it to piss me off?"

Jesus. Is he really that fucking conceited?

"What? No. Believe it or not, Jace, but not everything is about you," I spit out, hoping I hid the tremble in my voice because I refuse to let him see how rattled he has me.

He glares at me for a long moment; acting as if staring at the makeup on my face hard enough will make it disappear. Finally, he smirks, which only makes the fear in my gut amplify. What could this asshole possibly have to smile about?

"Fine, if you can't handle it on your own, I'll help you out," he offers, and before I process what's happening, he yanks the collar of my shirt hard enough for the seam to rip. He tears until that side is hanging completely off, effectively ruining it. He steps back quickly, looking smug as I try to slow my rapid breathing.

"You're welcome," he taunts before turning and storming away.

Did that really just happen? It all happened so quickly. My heart is still pounding in my chest, and I'm frozen in place as I try to convince my panicked body the threat is gone. I stare at the spot Jace walked off to, blinking hard to stop my eyes from burning.

I lift my hand up and confirm he really did just rip my shirt. This wasn't a nightmare. I'm awake, and he ripped my shirt like he had a right to touch me because he didn't like my outfit.

My fingers twitch with leftover adrenaline as I force myself to peel away from the lockers behind me. I feel sick and exposed, and I can't go home looking like this.

I hurry to my locker and yank open the door to grab my scissors. My hands are shaking as I bring them up to the mirror, slicing through the rest of the ruined collar while trying not to picture his face when he did it.

I'm not ready to explain any of this to my mom, so once it looks normal enough, I run outside and get in the car with her.

"Hi, honey! How was your day?"

"Hey, Mom. It was fine," I brush her off. Landing on the half-truth like I have all week. I don't want her to worry, so I haven't mentioned the unwanted negative attention. "Can Liv come over tonight?" I ask.

"Of course." Mom smiles at me. I knew she'd say yes; she always does where Liv is concerned.

As soon as we get home, I head straight upstairs to my room to get on my MacBook to decompress from the week. Most kids my age don't have computers in their rooms, let alone a laptop, but my dad is very into getting the latest technology. I got his old one when he bought the new MacBook Air that recently came out. It's been amazing to be able to watch YouTube videos and learn new makeup techniques in the privacy of my room instead of at the built-in desk where our family computer is in the kitchen.

Liv won't be over for a few hours, so I spend some time on Tumblr before I start watching videos. After I'm caught up on my favorite creators' latest posts, I check Facebook, but there must be some kind of glitch because there's no way I'm actually staring at a friend request from Jace Ryan right now.

What the hell? Why can't he just leave me alone?

He's tormented me all week, and now he wants to bring that online too? Is he running out of insults and looking for more material to make fun of? Maybe he's hoping I'll accept so he can scroll through my posts and find more things to rip me apart for. God forbid he misses a detail of my life he can weaponize.

I click on his name, fully expecting to see a wall of shirtless mirror selfies and baseball team photos, but his profile's practically empty. It's a brand-new account with only eighteen friends so far.

Why is he adding me as one of his first friends?

Does he think this is funny? Like some cruel prank to top off an already miserable week? Seriously, what is wrong with him?

I walk away from my computer, shaking my head, and plop down on my bed. I don't accept the request. *Obviously.*

But I don't delete it either.

Not because I'm interested. I'm not. I just… I don't know. Maybe because letting it sit there feels like a silent middle finger to him and gives me the smallest feeling of control knowing he's waiting for me to respond.

Seconds later, there's a knock on my bedroom door, and Olivia walks in, freezing when she sees my face. "Why do you look like you just saw a ghost?"

I blink at her. "Jace just tried to add me as a friend on Facebook."

She snorts loudly in disbelief. "You're kidding."

"Nope." I grab my pillow and yell into it. "Why can't he leave me alone? He literally goes out of his way to make my life hell at school, and then sends me a friend request? It doesn't make sense. The other day he said if I want to hide my face, I should just wear a mask, that it'd be better for everyone, Liv."

"He said that to you?" She crosses her arms, looking more confused than I've ever seen her. "I don't get it. He's always seemed like the nicest of the popular guys. And he's so hot too. Why does he have to single you out so much?"

"Yup. Jace acts like me wearing makeup as self-expression is a crime, but David bleaching his tips? Totally fine. Guess that doesn't count since all the 'cool guys' decide dark roots and fried blond ends are suddenly in. Fucking hypocrites."

She comes to sit beside me on the bed, pulling me into a hug. "I'm sorry, K. I wish they would just leave you alone." Now I'm the one snorting. *If only.* "Do you think he's trying to harass you online, too?"

"I'm not about to give him the opportunity to see what I post, even if I am a little curious about what he has on his page," I admit. "It seems like nothing yet though, he only had eighteen friends, so he must've just created it."

"Do you want me to add him so we can look at it?"

I pick at my blue nail polish as I consider. I know that Liv has some photos of us on her profile, but I doubt he'd go through the effort of making fun of me on someone else's page. That seems like way more work than the half-assed insults he aims at me in class. "Go for it," I finally agree, and her face lights up with a wicked grin.

She sits at my desk and easily enters my password, logging out of my Facebook to go into her own account. "Okay, I sent the request. I'll let you know later tonight if he ends up… Just kidding, he already accepted."

"Eager," I mutter as I jump up to peer over her shoulder at the screen. It looks like all he has is his profile picture he just added of him in his baseball uniform. "It's a shame he's such an asshole because these uniforms could definitely convince me to go to a game. But I would never risk letting him see me there. Besides, it's so boring."

Liv nods in agreement. "He really is attractive," she says on a sigh. Other than the baseball picture and some general info about what town he lives in and the name of our school, the rest of his profile is pretty bare. "I'll keep an eye on it and let you know if he posts anything interesting," she promises.

"You're the best."

She lets me practice a gold smoky eye on her using the new palette I just got, and for a few hours, I manage to forget about the weirdest Facebook notification of my life.

JACE

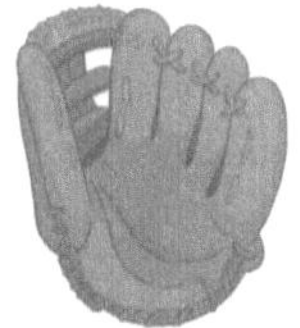

October 2010

J grit my teeth, reading the text under the table even though we're not supposed to have phones out in school—which he knows since he's a teacher. But rules don't apply when he's the one breaking them.

I already know what he wants to hear, and as much as it pains me, I respond.

Doesn't matter that I was one of the first guys to finish on the track. If I don't meet his impossible standards, I'm a letdown.

"Did you see this shit?" Leo, one of my teammates, asks, as

he slides me his phone, pulling me back into the conversation. The screen's small, but it doesn't matter; it's unmistakably Kieran. I could spot him from anywhere.

He's in a fully sparkly—I think I've heard my sister call them sequins—shirt, and his face is covered in very glittery makeup too. In the photo, he's with Olivia, who's in a sequin dress with similar makeup, so they probably coordinated.

Sparkles thinks he's hilarious, picking the loudest, most in-your-face outfits he can find and posting them online. Doesn't he know that's permanent? Once it's online, it's out there for good. I'd think someone would've explained that to him, like my dad's drilled it into me.

I've had my Facebook account for a month, and my dad's already made me untag myself from three pictures and change my privacy settings twice. He checks my account like it's his job. Says scouts are watching and colleges check, that one post could tank everything I've worked for. He flipped out over a comment from David that said "ur dumb" and told me not to let people make me look weak publicly. I asked for almost a year if I could create an account like all my friends and I thought he'd actually make me delete my profile over that. I never got to have a MySpace, and I really didn't want to miss this either.

And yet Sparkles is out here willingly uploading photos that are basically the embodiment of the nickname he pretends to be so bothered by, and no one is stopping him. He walks into school every day dressed like he's daring someone to say something—and somehow, I'm the only one who ever does.

Then he acts like *I'm* the problem.

If he really didn't want the attention, he'd knock it off and would have quit wearing that crap by now. I've made it so clear, and yet, he doesn't care. I don't know how many more times I can shove him into a locker, but if I have to keep doing it, I will.

I haven't got in any trouble yet, but there's only so far I can escalate things. Getting into a fight wouldn't look good to the

MLB, and I've spent my whole life trying to be the kind of guy scouts want to sign, whether I like it or not. But something about Sparkles sends me from zero to one hundred so quickly that I can't hold myself back. No one has ever caused this type of visceral reaction in me or made me feel this out of control before.

I hate it, and I don't understand it.

My anger used to stay focused on my dad. On how he's always breathing down my neck about every single thing I do—what I eat, how I play, how I walk, even how I talk when I'm around coaches and other adults. He's never like that with my sister. She gets everything so damn easy, which only pisses me off more. When I asked why she didn't have to wake up early and work out, he said it's because she can't get into the MLB, and Mom wants her to focus on other things. Whatever that means.

But now, Sparkles has all my attention.

At this point, every girly thing he wears, every bit of makeup he puts on, and every time he shows up with painted nails, it feels like he's taunting me personally. He knows it pisses me off, and it's like he's seeing how far he can push me before I completely snap.

Everyone else in this school tries to suck up to me, either because of my dad or just because I'm friends with the other popular kids, but not him. Not Sparkles. He acts like the rules don't apply to him.

It's infuriating.

He's driving me crazy, consuming way too many of my thoughts as I consider ways to get him to fall in line without risking my father's wrath if I'm caught.

"Hey, that guy's in our math class," David comments, looking over my shoulder at the phone.

"What's his deal?" Leo asks with a laugh, looking at the picture again after we hand back his phone.

"He wears shit like that all the time," David explains.

"Even the makeup," I clarify.

"Wow, so he's basically asking to get harassed?"

David and I both nod our heads. "Yup."

"Does he think he's a girl?" Leo asks with another laugh.

"I asked him that on the first day, and he tried to tell me makeup was for guys too. I'm pretty sure he likes the attention," I sneer, loving the excuse to finally voice my frustrations and talk about him with my friends. Shit talking Kieran has quickly become my favorite topic.

"You know what would be funny?" Leo prompts, already looking smug.

"What?" I ask, desperate for a way to mess with him that won't end up with me in the principal's office or worse, my father's.

"What if you borrowed your dad's master key to the locker room and swapped his gym uniform for a girl's? I can give you my sister's old one."

Well, shit, that might actually work. David is already cracking up over the idea, smacking my arm and insisting that "You gotta do it, bro" as I consider the specifics of pulling it off.

We have uniforms for gym class so people can't complain about getting in trouble for breaking the dress code. We purchase them at the beginning of the year and are responsible for taking them home and washing them ourselves. If someone's went missing, it's not like they could just grab a different one. It would be a pretty good prank, actually.

We have the same gym period, so I doubt it would be hard to watch him put his locker combo in and swap his uniform before school the next day. I probably wouldn't even need my dad's keys for this; I could just say I forgot something in the locker room during our weights session. He has keys for a lot of things around the school though… Maybe there's more I could do. Eh, I'll save that thought for another day if this doesn't work.

Maybe switching his uniform will be enough to finally teach him to stop being so obnoxious and distracting all the time. He's the reason I can't focus this year, doesn't he get that? He could potentially fuck up my future, and that's why I can't leave him alone.

The more I think about this prank, the more I like it because the odds of me getting in trouble are pretty slim. Even if another teacher caught me, they'd start by telling my dad, and honestly, with how much he complains about the gay kids at our school, this would be one of the few rule-breaking activities he'd probably approve of, maybe even laugh about.

"Hey, isn't that him?" Leo asks, tipping his chin up to where I already knew Kieran was sitting a couple of tables away from ours. He's standing up, gathering his things even though we have a few minutes before the period is over. He always leaves lunch early, which is weird. *And a totally normal thing for me to notice.*

"Bring the uniform tomorrow, and I'll let you know when I do it," I murmur to Leo right before Kieran turns our way. He's on the path to walk right past me to exit the cafeteria.

God, he looks so obnoxious. Is he somehow wearing more makeup today than he normally does? I attempt to focus on Leo's reply, but the thought of Kieran taunting me with even more girly shit has my blood boiling. At the last second, I stick my foot out from under the table to trip him as he walks past. He falls to his hands and knees, and the water bottle that had been in his hand rolls under our table after he drops it.

"Ow, what the fuck?" he gasps.

I bend down to grab the bottle as he quickly scrambles to stand again, cheeks red, eyes darting around to see who just witnessed his fall.

A few people are staring at him, but it's so loud and packed in the lunchroom, it seems like a majority of the people didn't notice. But my table clearly did with the laughter behind me.

His gaze locks on mine, and I can see the moment he realizes what actually happened. I extend my arm, offering his water back to him. "You should really be more careful," I warn with false concern.

"God, can't you just leave me alone, Jace?" he says, snatching the drink and storming off without a word as my friends all burst into more laughter around me.

"Make sure you film his reaction to the uniform thing." Leo laughs, and I nod. I'm sure it will be funny, but I also hope it's enough to finally convince Kieran to just blend in.

Maybe then I can finally focus on something other than him.

5

KIERAN

Gym days are the worst because it means I have to do physical activity in front of Jace. Him and his friends are always laughing at me, and his dad doesn't say a damn word about it.

To make today worse, we have to run the mile, which is an awful thing to make teenagers do in the first place. I'm creative; can't I paint something instead? Jace Ryan doesn't have to prove he understands color theory to graduate. So I don't understand why I need to complete a timed run in front of everyone. It's not like a college won't accept me because I'm not "fast enough."

I pass Jace as I enter the locker room, and he's once again staring at me like I'm a zoo animal. Seriously, has he never seen someone mildly different from him? I stop at my locker and enter my combination, but when I open it, my gut immediately drops. A feeling of icy dread spreads throughout my whole body as I realize what's in there isn't my usual navy blue uniform. It's a girl's light blue one. I pick it up to double check, but as expected, it's the only one in there.

I try to stay calm and not cry because I know the person who did this is in the locker room right now, waiting for my reaction.

I tell myself to breathe, but it's so hard. My throat feels tight, and my eyes are stinging. I don't understand why he can't just leave me alone. I shove the clothes back in my locker, and that's when I hear his falsely pleasant voice.

"What's wrong, Sparkles? Isn't that the uniform you'd prefer anyway? You're always trying to dress like a girl. Just thought I'd help you out."

"Yeah, you should be thanking us, you freak," I hear David add behind me, but I still don't turn around.

I can usually brush off their ignorant and hateful comments, but this feels so much more violating. Breaking into my locker and stealing my clothes is a line I don't know how to come back from. This is cruel and calculated. Even worse than when he shoved me into the lockers and ripped my shirt or tripped me in front of the whole cafeteria.

I try to force in another deep breath, to bury the emotions I always hide from them... but I don't think I can do it today. They've been chipping away at my shield of false confidence, and apparently this is my breaking point. I can't keep pretending to be unaffected. My eyes are stinging with tears I'm trying to hold back. My lip is trembling, and my own throat feels like it's suffocating me with how tight it is.

I need to get out of here.

Now.

"Go ahead, put it on. I bet you wish it had a skirt, though," Jace taunts. "Don't you, Sparkles?"

I slam my locker shut and run past them, out of the locker room and into the hallway. I can't deal with this right now. I can't breathe in there. I have to get away.

As soon as I see the bathroom, I shove the door open and hurry into a stall, locking it behind me. My tears finally fall as I gasp for air, still unable to take a full breath.

Jace broke into my personal space and stole my clothes, all while relentlessly trying to make me feel bad about who I am.

And for what? For fun? To feel better about himself? I don't get why he's so focused on harassing me.

The door to the bathroom opens, and I quickly pull my feet up on the toilet and try to hold my breath so whoever walks in can't hear me cry.

"I swear he went in here," the voice says, and my gut sinks when I realize it's David. "What a loser, hiding in the bathroom."

"Seriously," Jace scoffs. "All we did was try to give him what he clearly wants." They both crack up at that, but after another endless moment, he speaks again. "Come on, we can't be late for gym. You know my dad will freak."

Just as quickly as they came in, they leave. Only their taunts remain hanging in the air while I finally suck in what feels like the first full breath I've managed since entering the locker room.

I don't care if the school calls home, or I get detention for skipping—there's no way I'm going to gym today. I'll fake being sick or say I forgot my uniform if anyone asks, because the last thing I need is my parents finding out about the bully-ing. If they step in, I'm sure we'd all get called to the princi-pal's office, Jace and his dad included. And if he thinks I ran to Mommy and Daddy? He'll make sure I regret it, I just know it.

Skipping class won't fix anything, but right now, not walking into that locker room feels like the best decision I can make for myself, so I take out my phone and text Liv.

KIERAN

It's an emergency.

Can you skip?

Meet me in the library?

LIV:

Yeah, give me a min

I wipe my face with my sleeves and make the short walk to

the library right in time for the bell to ring. Liv walks in a second later.

"What happened? Come here," she says immediately, grabbing my hand and dragging me to the back corner of the library where we're a little more secluded. As soon as we stop walking, she turns to me.

"Oh, K, tell me what happened," she prompts again before pulling me into a hug, and more tears start to fall.

"Jace switched my uniform for gym with a girl's and said he did me a favor. When I ran out of there, I hid in the bathroom, and he and David followed me in there," I confess.

"Don't let them get to you. I know you're strong enough to get through their pranks," Liv encourages.

Pranks? That sounds way more innocent than how today felt, but I don't want to get into a fight with Liv on top of everything else, so I don't correct her. "I don't even know what I did to them besides express myself. Which literally doesn't affect them at all," I say even though she's heard this exact complaint from me before.

"I know. I'm sorry, I wish they'd move on."

I wipe under my eyes with the sleeve of my jacket, careful not to smudge what's left of my mascara. "He's never going to stop. It doesn't matter if I ignore him or try to stand up for myself. It's like… existing in the same room as him is a crime."

"Is there anything I can do?"

"Do you want to come over after school?" I ask, hating that there's really nothing else she can do to help. There's nothing anyone can do to help.

"Oh, um," she starts, and I have a feeling I know what's coming. "I actually have plans tonight with the girls from yearbook club. We're going to Jess's house for dinner, and I can't bail."

Knew it.

I hate that it feels like I'm losing her to her new friends.

Especially now when it feels like Jace Ryan is trying to ruin me, and most days, it feels like he's succeeding.

But my brain catches on the word "try." Because that's really all he can do, isn't it? He can call me names. He can bully me. He can glare and shove me into lockers. But he doesn't get to decide who I am.

As much as I hate the negative attention and bullying, the thought of giving into his peer pressure, of showing up to school on Monday without any makeup on or wearing the same boring clothes as the other guys do, sounds equally painful. I'm not going to fold: that isn't who I am.

I'm not changing who I am for anyone.

Especially not Jace-fucking-Ryan.

6

JACE

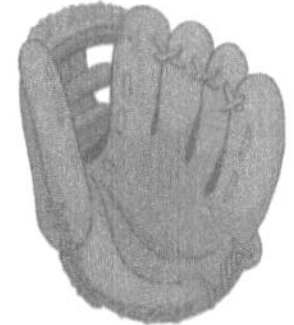

November 2010

*S*wapping Kieran's uniform wasn't enough. It's been weeks since I did that, and Kieran hasn't wavered at all. All he did that day was skip gym, and when he showed up to math class a couple of hours later, he seemed completely fine. Including his makeup.

Either David lied about seeing Sparkles crying or he reapplied that crap on his face because I can still remember how bright his blue eyes looked in contrast with his black lashes.

It was embarrassing because I'd claimed the stunt in front of the whole locker room, and he barely cared. It's making me look weak. Pathetic. Just like my dad always tells me I am.

Thank god he doesn't know I've made getting Sparkles to fall in line my personal mission, or he'd be even more disappointed in me.

I've spent every day since then trying to think of what else I can do that pushes the limits without going too far, and I've got nothing.

All it's done is manage to piss off my dad more than normal

because "I've got my head up my ass" according to him. He lectured-slash-yelled at me for an hour last week in the car after practice, about how I've been playing like shit and no pro team would want me if I keep it up. We're not even in season right now; it's just fall ball for the guys on the team who aren't playing other sports right now. Oh, and it was my seventeenth birthday. *Happy freaking birthday to me, I guess.*

If Kieran could just stop dressing so girly, I'd be able to focus on baseball again. I could simply move on and forget about him.

But, no, he refuses. I swear he's doing it just to make my life harder at this point.

My phone vibrates in class, pulling me out of my thought spiral that's once again all about Kieran. I look up to see our teacher absorbed in grading papers while we work on our group project, so I pull my phone out and see the message my dad just sent to the team.

DAD

> The pep rally tomorrow might not be for baseball, but that doesn't mean there won't be eyes on you all. So let's set a good example. We're the best team at this school, so it's important to be the leaders I know you all are. See you bright and early in the weight room.

Another text follows that's just for me.

DAD

> Don't embarrass me again by being late to the assembly tomorrow.

I grunt under my breath at that. I showed up late to one meeting freshman year, and now every time there's an important event—if you can even count a pep rally as important—he reminds me of my single fuck-up two years ago.

There's no point in responding now. He knows I'm in class,

so if I respond before the bell, he'll ask me why I wasn't paying attention. It's always a mind game with him. I shove my phone back in my pocket and try to focus on the group project in front of me.

"So, Danny, did you and your boyfriend really break up?" one of the girls in our group asks the guy next to me.

"Yeah, but he was kind of a jerk, so I'm over it." He shrugs. "Better this way."

"Well, then, I'm glad. Good for you." She laughs and they move on, returning their attention to the project while I sit here, mind reeling with this new information.

Because there's another gay kid in our class.

Does Kieran know this?

Does Kieran know Danny?

If not, he should take a page out of Danny's book, because he's blending in so well I had no idea he existed or that he was gay. No makeup or sequins to be seen. I take in the rest of him, and the jeans and long-sleeved shirt he's wearing with our school's logo on it don't stand out at all.

See? This guy's not making me mad or forcing my attention at all.

That's what Kieran doesn't get. If he would just stop being so damn obnoxious, then I wouldn't have to bother him anymore.

But he doesn't listen.

Danny turns to whisper something in the girl's ear, and I read the back of his shirt. It says "marching band 2009" on it, so he must be in the school band, but he doesn't seem especially dorky.

I bet Kieran doesn't know he's newly single, even if he does know him.

Hmm.

The uniform swap might not have been enough to convince Kieran to stop taunting me with his makeup, but maybe now my dad's keys could come in handy after all.

7

————

KIERAN

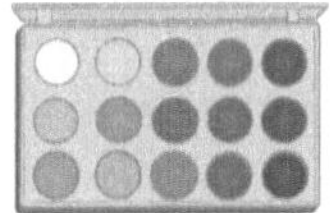

I stare at the note in my hand, rereading it for probably the tenth time since I found it in my locker.

Kieran,

Hey! I hung out by your locker for a bit since I don't have your number, but must've missed you. I've been wanting to talk to you for a while, but have always been a little intimidated by how confident you are.

I broke up with my boyfriend recently, and figured now's the time to try to work on my own confidence.

I'd hoped this would be more casual in person but I'm planning to ditch the pep rally because I've always hated sitting through those things. I usually hang out in the big equipment shed behind the away bleachers (they never lock it) and was wondering if you'd want to join?

Hope to see you there.

XO Danny

I know of Danny; we've had a couple of classes together throughout the years, but we've never really talked. I did hear he was dating someone from the neighboring town, though. People love to gossip, especially because, like me, he's one of the few students who are out at our school. At least, that I know of. It's not like there's a school club for the LGBT kids or anything.

My eyes keep catching on the XO in his note.

Does he want to date me now that he's single? He wrote he wanted to be more confident, but he's the one with experience.

God, I would love to kiss someone. I don't even really want a relationship—despite what Liv said about getting boyfriends—but I'm sick of feeling like the only person left at this school who still hasn't had their first kiss.

The pep rally is in the football stadium after my next class. It's supposed to be in the gym, but it's an unseasonably warm day so they announced yesterday we'd be moving to the field. I don't particularly have any desire to sit through it, and it should be easy enough to slip away from the crowds behind the away bleachers as the rest of the school files into the stadium. If anyone does say anything, I'll claim I'm looking for a bathroom or something.

Even if Danny just wants to ditch together and isn't interested in anything more than friendship, I could definitely use more of those too. He might think I'm "confident," but most of the time, I feel like I'm barely holding it together. That false self-assurance is the armor I barely keep in place but need to get through a day of school.

Olivia and I have been best friends for so long, and until recently, that friendship has felt like all I really needed. But as much as I've tried to ignore it, things have been changing between us for a while now. She joined the yearbook club and has been hanging out with the other girls from that more and more. I didn't think she cared about who was popular, but now all she wants to do is gossip about who's dating who and what popular guys have talked to her or added her as a friend on Facebook.

Maybe I should join a club. Make some more friends too. Is there an art club? I know my art teacher has asked if I'd be interested in helping paint the sets for the musical in the spring, but I don't think that lasts more than a couple of weeks.

Whatever. I can worry about that later. Maybe I'll have a new friend by the end of the day.

When it's time to head to the pep rally, I ditch my backpack at my locker on the way out of the school. I know it's silly, but I can't calm the nervous fluttering in my stomach as I approach the stadium. I really doubt we would just start making out when we've never even talked, but it still feels like this could be an important moment, the start of something more.

Teachers are in the parking lot we cross to get to the field, and there are more at the gate. No one is paying any attention to me as I make like I'm heading to the bathrooms, but I continue to walk past them behind the away bleachers toward the equipment shed. The door is ajar, and the light is already on as I push it open further to slip inside.

"Danny?" I call out quietly, looking around. The shed is pretty big, and it feels much more spacious than my parents' two-car garage, even if it is full of football and marching band equipment. Walking in further, I peer around a row of what look like punching bags, but I think they're the things the football team practices tackling on. "Danny?" I try again a little louder. Maybe I beat him here?

The lights cut out suddenly and the door slams. My stomach drops.

Fuck. *I am such an idiot.*

I spin around to face the direction I just came in, and the light from the gap under the door is just enough of a guide to find my way back to it. I try to push it back open, but nothing. Fuuuck.

I shove my shoulder into it, attempting to force the flimsy door to move, but it's no use. It won't budge. I try a few more times, and nothing.

"Ha ha. Very funny. Open the door," I demand, pretty sure I know who's on the other side and that he's waiting for a reaction.

"Are you going to stop wearing makeup?" Jace asks. "Finally ready to blend in and stop taunting me with your girly shit?"

"Taunting you? Jace, wearing makeup has literally nothing to do with you. It never has."

"That didn't sound like a yes." His sidekick, David, snickers.

"It sounds like you need some time in there to think about your answer," Jace adds, and they both laugh. But the sound seems to grow quieter too quickly.

"Jace?" I yell, wanting to stop them from walking away. "Wait! Are you seriously going to leave me in here?" I bang my fist on the door. "Jace!"

There's no answer. I try to make as much noise as I can, not caring about who finds me at this point as long as I get out of this shed.

The shadows the equipment cast in the already dark space stretch ominously, playing tricks on my vision as I try to calm my racing heart. I can't find the light switch, and at this point, does it even matter?

I'm alone. Nothing is moving. Deep breaths, and this will be over soon. The sounds of the pep rally starting don't quite manage to drown out the pounding in my ears. I know any chance of someone hearing me is gone as the noise of the marching band starting to play combines with the already loud cheers of the students.

I'm stuck here; locked in the equipment shed.

I slide down to the floor, shutting my eyes and leaning my head back against the door as I take a moment to scold myself for letting this happen. I should have been more careful. I knew the uniform swap wouldn't be the last thing Jace did to try to bully me into blending in more. It's not like my makeup is even extreme. I've kept it nearly as minimal as day one, but Jace can't let it go. I should have questioned the note, should have tried to talk to Danny in person before blindly walking into this creepy shed.

I wonder if Danny even broke up with his boyfriend. Did he help Jace and David set me up? Ugh. I was so excited about the possibility of being friends with another gay guy at school. Of maybe doing *more*. I'm assuming he wasn't actually involved… but what if he was? How many people know I'm trapped in here right now?

The thought of everyone out there whispering about me, laughing, is mortifying. But it still isn't enough for me to want to give into Jace's demands, especially because they don't make any sense. My decision to wear makeup or clothes he wouldn't wear should have no effect on him. He's the one who chooses to get so pissed off at me for no reason. For fucks sake, I'm wearing black jeans and a hoodie today. I'm not even dressed any differently from the rest of the school.

At this point, after how much shit he's given me, even if I had a desire to stop wearing those things, I don't think I'd want to.

Especially now. Fuck him.

Expressing myself definitely didn't start off as a way to spite Jace—it was fully for me—but he's the one who's turned it into that very thing. I like who I am. And he doesn't get to bully me into changing.

I take another deep breath in, and as I exhale, something settles inside me. I can't stop Jace from harassing me, but I can control how I let it affect me. I'm allowed to be angry and annoyed, and yeah, I'm also definitely embarrassed, but if I let him see any of those things, it will only feel like he's winning.

The best thing I can do now is act like none of it bothers me.

Luckily the pep rally doesn't last too long. When the structured cheers shift to the murmurs of a crowd, I stand back up and resume banging on the door as I shout. "Can anyone hear me? Hello, I need some help!"

It isn't long before the football coach is unlocking the door, dragging a podium and a microphone behind him, probably to put back in here.

"What the hell are you doing locked in here?" he demands, looking around, no doubt for something to help my situation make more sense.

I shrug, not wanting to get in trouble for ditching, or give Jace the satisfaction of knowing how bothered I was by ratting him out. "One of the teachers asked me to check if they'd turned the light off in here, but when I came in, it must have locked behind me."

"Which teacher? It's a physical lock, someone locked you in here," he tells me like I don't already know that.

But I shrug again. "Bad timing. They must not have known I was inside."

He looks at me skeptically, but I'm sure he doesn't want to deal with the process of reporting he found a student locked in his equipment shed anymore than I do. Finally, he shakes his head. "Well, I'm sorry that happened, kid. Are you alright?"

"Yeah, I'm fine," I assure him, flashing what I hope looks like a normal smile. "Thanks for letting me out." Then I slip past him. I'd rather not give him time to change his mind.

I rush back toward the school. Honestly, I'm kind of used to Jace and his friend's bullshit at this point. The thing I can't stop thinking about is if Danny helped them. The lockers are assigned by last name, and I might not know him, but I know his last name is Rodriguez so I head straight to where I think the *R* last names would be.

I'm not sure if I should be relieved or more nervous when I

see Danny still standing at his locker, but at this point, I've hyped myself up enough about confronting him that I don't slow down until I'm right next to his locker.

"Hey, Danny," I start, slightly out of breath from my rush to find him. He looks up at me with obvious confusion. But is he confused I'm randomly talking to him for the first time, or is he confused I'm not locked in the shed? Only one way to find out.

"Listen, I know this probably didn't involve you at all, but I need to hear from you that you didn't write that note. I need to know if Jace just used your name to trick me into going into the equipment shed or if you helped him lock me in there," I ramble quickly before I can lose my nerve.

He blinks up at me, still looking confused before his expression slowly shifts from concern into a smile. He turns to face me fully and offers his hand. "Hey, Kieran. Nice to officially meet you. I have no idea what you're talking about, but if I understood correctly, Jace locked you in a shed? I am so sorry that happened to you."

He sounds genuine enough, so I reluctantly shake his hand and mutter, "Nice to meet you too."

"So, wait. There was a note that you thought was from me?" he asks.

Maybe I didn't think this plan through. But at this point, I don't think there's any turning back as embarrassing as it might be to admit to him. "Yeah, there was a note in my locker that said it was from you asking if I wanted to hang out in the equipment shed and ditch the pep rally."

"What did you think we were going to do in the shed, Kieran?" he teases suggestively.

I groan, covering my face with my hands so I can only see his amused expression from between my fingers. Shaking my head, I drop my hands. "Ugh. This was a horrible idea. You clearly didn't help Jace. Please forget this conversation ever happened. Sorry to have bothered you." I try to spin away, but

Danny sticks his arm out to block my path. He's a couple of inches shorter than I am, and I could easily move around him if I needed to, but I don't.

"You're not bothering me, Kieran. I was just going to suggest that we exchange phone numbers, so you'll know for sure it's me when I actually ask you to hang out."

Well, damn. I wasn't expecting us to bond over this. "Oh. Uh, yeah. That would be cool," I agree as I pull out my phone. He rattles off his number, and I text him my name, half expecting it to be fake, but his phone buzzes on the shelf in his locker. He immediately picks it up, taking a moment to type out a response.

DANNY:

> Hey, would you want to hang out? I still haven't seen the Facebook movie if you'd want to see that. Or there's some horror movies out too, but they might have creepy storage sheds so probably better to avoid those.

I snort a laugh at the storage shed comment before responding aloud. "I haven't seen the Facebook one yet, either. I don't have any plans this weekend, if you're free."

"Awesome, I'll text you tonight after I look up the times for tomorrow. Want to grab food too or just the movie?"

"I'm always down to get food." We smile at each other for a moment before I realize what we just planned. "Wait, is this a date? Or are we just hanging out as friends?" I ask, then immediately regret it, because I sound so uncool. Good thing he didn't actually write the note because I'm not giving off confidence at all right now.

But Danny's smile grows even bigger. "Do you want it to be a date?"

Do I? The last hour of my life has been a whirlwind. But when I first thought the note was from Danny, I'd been excited about the possibility of spending time with him. I've never been on a real date. Dinner and a movie sounds nice.

"I think I want it to be a date," I admit with a nod.

"Good."

I give him a smile and turn to leave school for the day, feeling excited about this possibility.

Danny is cute. He's got dark hair, bright brown eyes, and a warm complexion, and he seems naturally confident. Unlike Jace's fake note.

And as promised, he texts me later that night to confirm the details. My dad lets me borrow his car, so I offer to drive us. We get tacos before the movie, and conversation comes easily. Danny's fun, and I'm really enjoying myself, but I don't think I actually want him to be my boyfriend. It feels more like I'm hanging out with the old Liv.

When we're heading to the car after the movie, Danny stops before he gets in, turning to me. He looks at me curiously, and I give him a small nod. Maybe this is where the spark will come from. He reaches up and cups my face, guiding me to kiss him, and it's… nice.

A perfect first date ending with a lovely first kiss.

But there's no spark.

Nothing like I've been waiting for or heard the other kids at school describe when they kiss someone they like.

When we part, he gives me a crooked grin, like he's thinking the same thing too.

"Well," he starts. "Maybe I'm not ready to…"

"Better off as friends?" I add, cutting off his trailing thought. There might not be chemistry between us, and I'm not desperate for more in the way I think I'd like to be with someone I'm dating, but I think we could be really good friends.

He lets out a relieved chuckle, nodding. "Yeah. I'm glad we gave it a shot, though. Now we know. I really would like to keep hanging out as friends."

"Me too."

We make plans to see another movie next weekend, and I can't help feeling a little smug at the way things turned out. Jace might have wanted to embarrass or scare me into blending in more, but his plan led to me making a new friend.

I even got my first date and my first kiss out of it too.

I can't wait to tell Liv.

8

JACE

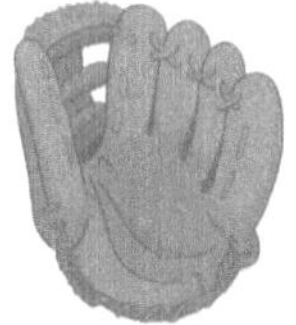

March 2011

"I thought you were supposed to be doing homework?" my dad questions as I scramble to switch back to the tab with my history project's research on it before he can see who's profile I was looking at.

"I am," I lie, trying to slow my heart rate down.

"Do your fucking homework or I turn off the internet, got it? Good luck researching then. You'd have to use a goddamn book like I did. So fucking easy for kids these days," my dad mutters before slamming the door to the home office.

Fuck. Of course he walks in right when I had decided to take a little brain break and check Facebook. I don't know why I'm still dumb enough to let my guard down when I know he has a habit of walking in without knocking.

Once I'm sure he's gone, I click back to the other tab—the one I've been staring at for the last fifteen minutes.

It's been *months* and Kieran still hasn't accepted my friend request. He thinks he's so special, refusing to accept. Or decline. Just letting it sit there. It's distracting as hell, and it's been on my mind every single time I see him and Danny laughing in the hall. I still can't believe they actually became friends after we locked him in the shed. Are they just friends? Or are they dating? None of my friends seem to care, and I can't look online because Danny won't accept my friend request either.

Locking him in there didn't seem to bother him. Once again. He's always completely unbothered, and it's impossible to get a rise out of him. I haven't been able to think of anything big to attempt since then, so I've stuck to what I was doing before: shoving him into lockers, tripping him when I can get away with it, calling him Sparkles, and trying to get him alone so I can get in his face to threaten him.

He irritates me to the point I can't stop thinking about him.

Why does he have to be so… him?

Every time I think about the unanswered request, I get even more annoyed. I know he uses his account because his friend Olivia added me. I accepted, of course, because it's what you're supposed to do on Facebook. And now I can see even more photos of Kieran. There are albums on there of them doing makeup and other girly shit I definitely haven't gone back and looked at. There are also tons of photos with her, him, and Danny too. The three of them must just be the best of friends. How annoying.

For some reason, it's worse that he's ignored the request than if he had just denied it, because then I could move on. Yes or no; it's easy. I could forget about it. But it *still* says pending, and surely if he'd declined, the website would give me the option to send another, right?

Maybe I should cancel my request and send another one so he sees it? Maybe he forgot. Because if he's just pretending it doesn't exist… That's a power move I didn't expect from him.

I hate being ignored, and once again, it's like he knows exactly how to push my buttons and piss me off.

Kieran is dutifully watching the teacher drone on and on about polynomials, but this is easy, and I don't need to listen to the lesson to understand something so simple.

Technically, my teachers have been recommending me for advanced and honors classes for years, but my dad says the same thing whenever I ask: "It'll take away from baseball. You don't need to be smart to go pro. Just stay eligible."

Great advice from him as always.

He seems to forget I still need good grades to get into college. Not that he cares about college; he thinks I'm bound for the MLB as soon as I graduate high school, but I'm not as sure. You'd think he'd be more practical about my future and encourage college seeing as how his future in the pros didn't work out according to his plan.

Even with his lack of support, school isn't something I need to work that hard at. He'll yell at me to study when I'm home, then refuse to acknowledge how smart I am. He acts like I'm a dumb jock and has never once been proud of me for my report card or even the elite schools who've been recruiting me because of my grades and athletic abilities. I want to go to college, but since it isn't in his plans for me, I haven't been able to seriously consider any of the schools that've been asking me to come for a visit.

When the bell rings, I close my notebook and sling my bag over my shoulder, pausing at my desk until Kieran stands to leave, too, so I can fall into step beside him.

He doesn't acknowledge me, so I say the first thing I can think of to get a rise out of him.

"Hey, Sparkles, you too good to come to a baseball game?"

"Do you really know everyone who comes to your games or are you just that obsessed with me?" he snorts. I hate how he always manages to twist what I say around and make it seem like I give a shit about him.

I clearly don't. How can he not tell that? How is he still so confident after everything I've done to try to get him to fall in line? Any other student would have given up that first week. Or after tripping him in the cafeteria. Or after the gym uniform swap. Or trapping him in a fucking shed.

But not Kieran.

He was gone by the time I got back to let him out after the pep rally. I hoped he might finally listen to me, but he came back that next Monday in even more makeup than before, adding bright eyeshadow. It was so obnoxious. I wanted to punch the smug look off his face when he saw me glaring during class, but that's not something I could risk.

"I'm not obsessed with you," I scoff. "I just figured you'd want to show off your makeup to as many people as you can. Isn't that your whole thing? You want everyone to look at you."

"I think you've got that covered. You always seem to be looking enough for everyone."

"Shut the fuck up." I seethe as I shove him into the alcove of a closed classroom door. I swear to God, if anyone heard him say shit like that to me and it got back to my dad… Nope, I'd rather not even think about it.

His eyes go wide the way they always do when I put my hands on him.

"Can't you just leave me alone, Jace? Jesus." His voice catches, full of nerves, and yet, somehow, he also sounds exhausted by this interaction. But he made this personal a long time ago by repeatedly ignoring my advice and warnings, so no, I can't leave him alone. And I don't buy that he even wants me to.

"Where's the fun in that?" I taunt, unable to help myself as I try to regain control of this conversation. At this point, I think I might be addicted to getting a rise out of him, even if he makes it hard to do sometimes. If he won't do what I've asked—and he won't even accept my stupid friend request online—then I'll continue to point out how irritating he is face-to-face when he can't ignore me. "Come on, everyone comes to the baseball games. We're probably the best team on the East Coast this year. Where's your school spirit? Or is it because you don't have any friends?"

"I have friends," he assures me, sounding offended.

"You have two friends," I correct. "And I bet Danny and Olivia would love to come to one of the games."

He huffs, finally fully looking up at me, and for a moment, I forget the pissed off glare he's aiming my way as our gazes meet, and his captivating blue eyes steal my full attention.

"How do you know who I'm friends with?" he demands, drawing my focus instead to his pouty lips. They really do look like they belong on a girl, with how full and shiny they are.

"I've seen you and Danny hanging out at school together," I finally answer. "And Olivia's always posting pictures with you two, but I never see anyone else do that. So, they must be your only friends. I would know for sure if you ever accepted my friend request," I mutter under my breath.

Or maybe it wasn't as quiet as I intended, because when he responds, he's way more upset than I'm expecting. He's usually so frustratingly calm. "Why would I accept your request? We hate each other!" he insists, practically yelling now.

"It's just Facebook," I dismiss. "I'm pretty sure I'm friends with everyone else in our grade." *Except Danny. And you.*

"You harass me every day! If you think I'd give you more access to my life, then you're dumber than I've been giving you credit for." He scoffs before storming off toward the front exit of the school.

"Ugh, what did you say this time?" a girl asks behind me, and I turn to see Olivia looking at me expectantly. I've known Olivia since she moved here, but we've never really interacted before. *She's actually gotten very pretty.* Her warm brown eyes are nothing like Kieran's, but the makeup looks similar and it looks great on her. *See, that makes sense to me: makeup on an attractive girl.* No confusion with her.

"We were actually talking about you," I answer excitedly, flashing her my most charming smile. That clearly isn't what she's expecting, and her whole face scrunches up in confusion. "I was asking Kieran if you might want to come to one of my games?" I bite my lip as I wait for her answer and catch her gaze dropping to look at my mouth. *Does Kieran's friend like me?*

Now *that* could be a fun way to mess with him without getting into any actual trouble.

"No. Why would I come to one of your games?" she asks hesitantly.

Alright, I understand Kieran hating me, but does Olivia hate me too? Has she really let him poison her opinion of me so drastically? Plenty of people think I'm a great guy. I'm basically the most popular person in our grade, so she should be excited to talk to me.

"Because I asked you to?" What other reason does she need?

"You're mean to my friend," she points out.

"Kieran dresses like that because he wants attention. I'm just giving him what he wants," I counter.

"That's not true," she insists, rolling her eyes at me as she crosses her arms. But she does it in a way that sort of pushes her boobs up, like there's a chance she wants me to think she's attractive, even if she's mad.

Maybe all hope isn't lost for my new idea.

"If he ever showed up without makeup, I'd have no reason to talk to him," I say in a gentle tone. "I've told him that, and he continues to taunt me by wearing it. It looks really pretty on you, though."

"Oh, um… really?" she asks, looking away as her cheeks darken.

"Yeah," I confirm with a chuckle. "I'd love to hangout sometime," I add, stepping a little closer to her as people move around us to try to leave the school. She's at least half a foot shorter than I am, and the hesitance in her expression is obvious as she tilts her head back to look up at me.

The more I think about it, the more spending time with Olivia sounds like it could be a really good thing. A lot of guys on the team have girlfriends, and my dad's been asking me if any of the girls who come to the games are there for me. You'd think he'd consider dating a distraction, but he's also obsessed with image, and to him, being popular isn't enough—I also need a pretty girl on my arm to fit his stereotypical idea of what my life should look like. And I don't want him to think there's a reason I don't have a girlfriend. *Not that there is a reason.* I just haven't thought about it much until right now.

Baseball takes up so much of my time, and at school, I'm usually with my friends or distracted by whatever weird crap Sparkles is wearing.

This could be perfect.

Olivia is beautiful, and I would love to have someone consistent to hook up with. It's not like I'm at parties every weekend with my baseball schedule and my dad's need to control my life. Plus having a girlfriend would probably help me avoid getting in any kind of trouble. She seems nice, and maybe if we were dating, she could get Kieran to tone down his obnoxious girly shit too. Then I wouldn't need to keep harassing him about it.

Win-win.

Olivia hasn't answered me yet, so I decide to just go for it. "Maybe we could even go on a date?" I suggest. "I promise I'm not the villain Kieran's probably made me out to be." I offer her a crooked smile and shrug, hoping I've done enough to win her over.

Finally, her annoyance melts away entirely. "You want to take me on a date?"

"Of course," I confirm easily. "We don't have a game this Friday, so maybe we could go to a movie or get dinner?"

She doesn't answer right away, looking around at the people walking past us. After what feels like a way longer pause than necessary—where I start to worry she might actually turn me down—she takes a deep breath and finally offers me a soft smile.

"Okay, Friday works for me."

"Perfect."

9

KIERAN

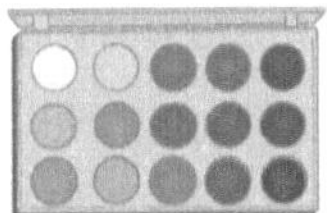

"*I* think I misheard you, Liv. There's no way you just told me you can't hang out because you're going on a date with Jace-fucking-Ryan? Are you fucking kidding me?"

I hear her gulp on the other end of the phone. She has to know she's fucking up. She's heard me complain about Jace and his bullshit almost every day this year, and now she's going to ignore all that and go on a date with him? I knew things were changing between us, and she's been more and more obsessed with being popular, but I had no idea she was capable of this.

"No, no, it's not like that!" she insists. "It could be like *Mean Girls*, but instead of doing what Cady did, I could hang out with the popular mean person, actually figure out what Jace wants with you, and tell you. It's not like I actually like him or anything!"

"Whatever," I mutter and hang up on her.

I swear to God if I lose my oldest friend because of that asshole, I'll never get over it. I don't understand why he can't just leave me alone. Then he has to go ask Liv on a date after pointing out she's one of my only friends? I fucking hate him.

I get a text from Liv saying she'll call me when it's over, and all I can do is distract myself with YouTube videos while I wait.

It's nine-thirty when my phone rings, and Liv's name lights up my screen.

"How was it?" I ask in a monotone voice, completely skipping pleasantries and really hoping she tells me it was awful. I'm still mad at her, but I've also been dying to know what was happening the entire time she's been gone.

"K, hear me out. He's actually really nice, and I think you'd like him if you got to know him—"

"No! What the fuck is happening right now?" I cut her off, not believing what I'm hearing. Again. "Did you really just tell me the guy who nicknamed me 'Sparkles' and insults me every single day is *nice* and misunderstood? What the fuck, Liv?"

"I know how it sounds, but he was so sweet. We met at that nice Italian restaurant by the theater. He was waiting outside so he could open the door for me, and he paid for dinner. Then he let me choose the movie and bought my ticket. Afterward, we even walked to get ice cream, and he asked me a lot about you. It was in a nice way because he knows we're friends. He didn't say anything bad. I don't think he's trying to be mean, K."

"Um, no, that's *exactly* what he's doing. I can't believe you're defending him right now because he used his dad's money to buy you dinner!"

I can't believe any of this is happening. Panic is rising in my chest, and I need to know. "Are you going to go out with him again? Don't lie to me."

I can hear her slow breathing on the other end of the line and brace myself for the inevitable. Jace's taunt earlier this week wasn't inaccurate, she's one of my only friends. One of two. And in a fucked-up way, Danny and I are only even friends because of Jace, and that's so new. The bond Liv and I have is different. We've been friends for almost as long as I can remember.

But, obviously, she's changed. I know I can't be friends with her anymore if she's going to willingly date the person who gets joy out of bullying me. She might not see it as choosing him over me, but she is. That's exactly what it would be.

"Um, don't hate me… but… I think I like him, K. But I'm still your best friend!" she assures me, as if I'd forget all my self-respect and everything I've worked so hard to accomplish accepting who I am just to keep her as a friend. Nope. Not happening.

"Well, you're not mine. This friendship is dead to me," I say and hang up as I hear her start to say, "K, no, this doesn't…"

It might be petty, but I'm not above it. She was *my* best friend for years, my *only* true friend for most of that time. She might have been a little distant recently, hanging out with girls from her yearbook club, but she never made me feel weird or feel like my interests needed to change or conform to everyone else's. She's been there for every breakdown and moment of self-doubt, even if she didn't know the perfect thing to say.

But now she's ignoring that Jace has been taunting me for months because she wants a boyfriend?

Obviously, I'm not as important to her as I thought I was.

I squeeze my eyes shut and try not to cry, but it doesn't work. The tears stream silently down my cheeks as I mourn our friendship.

If Liv had met literally any other guy, I'd be so excited and supportive of her. But she isn't falling for just any guy. She chose my bully, then tried to convince me *I'm* the problem. Just like Jace has been doing all along.

Fuck her.

And fuck him.

Maybe they deserve each other.

I should delete her number. Maybe that would make me feel better. Or, at the very least, write a Tumblr post about backstabbers and fake friends. She knows my profile, so I bet she'd read it, and maybe it would make her realize why I'm so upset right now since she clearly can't figure it out on her own.

I crawl into bed and pull the covers over my head as I let myself feel every emotion running through me. I can't believe she picked him over me so easily, especially after everything we've been through.

My heart hurts, and I'm so pissed off. I feel discarded, and the thought of going into school without her on Monday feels like a punch to the gut. I text Danny but he must already be asleep because there's no reply.

I have to do something to make myself feel better. I can't just sit around in my anger all weekend. I'm pissed off and feeling especially petty as I try to think of anything that might make me feel better. Less alone.

I wish I had my sketchbook. Although, anything I drew right now would probably be really dark. The last time I attempted to sketch while I was in a bad mood, I kept snapping the pencils. I have an easel and some blank canvases in the corner of my room, but I left almost all my other art stuff at school. And the thought of starting a new painting right now sounds daunting when I haven't been doing it as much outside of class projects. My gaze lands on the makeup scattered across my vanity, and I realize exactly what I can do instead.

Liv said *we* should go for glam and fame? Well, sucks to be her now. I'll do it on my own without help from anyone. She can kiss my ass when I become famous.

I've watched enough of my favorite content creators to know what makes a good video, and I've even thought about what I would do differently if I made my own.

What better time than now?

I'm going to create a YouTube channel.

10

———

JACE

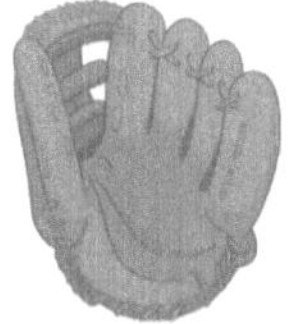

May 2011

"*J*ace Jesse Ryan, get your fat ass in the car before I bench you for the rest of the season!" my dad yells, before slamming the door that leads into our garage. The sound echoes throughout the house, and I can't help but flinch. I'm sure I'll get blamed for waking up Mom and Molly. *Must be nice to get to sleep in all the time.*

I'm also not fat. I'm a catcher for god's sake, my ass is big, but it's muscle from all the damn squatting I have to do behind home plate.

I was running late because I dropped my contact in the sink and it took forever to find it, then I had to run back into my room for my cell phone, but there's no way I'm telling my dad that. He hates how much time I spend on it now that I have an iPhone and am dating Liv. He seriously doesn't understand how high maintenance a girlfriend can be. She's constantly texting me, and if I don't let her know I'm on my way to the game, she'll think I'm ignoring her and be pissed. I get that her and Kieran's friendship ended, but I swear she wants my attention constantly. I feel like it's been never-ending in the two months we've been dating.

At least my dad likes Liv. After we went on a few dates, my batting average went up, and he was quick to comment that I should've gotten a girlfriend sooner because I was "actually playing well for the first time all season," then he told me he had started to worry I was "one of those queers."

Which, obviously, I'm not.

I rush downstairs and jump in my dad's SUV. I hate Saturday games because there's no buffer from him. At least on the weekdays, I get a few hours in classes with people who aren't on the baseball team to distract me. Weekend games mean I'm with my dad for the entire day, and I'm already in a bad mood thinking about it. I can't even be excited about summer either because he'll be breathing down my neck every day since he'll be off too. I never get a fucking break from him.

"Can I go out with Liv tonight?" I ask, hoping to get some time away from his harsh post-game analysis. Even when I play well, I expect him to spend the whole car ride home yelling at me and picking apart everything I did wrong. And when he's really in a mood, we just sit there in the driveway after getting home while he keeps tearing into me.

"How about you focus on winning before you worry about getting your dick wet."

"I just wanted to go get ice cream or something," I clarify.

"Maybe I should bench you if you're that eager to put sugary shit into your body. No wonder you're so fat."

Whatever. My dad is just jealous because my recent growth spurt resulted in me passing him in height, and my shoulders are broader than his now too. I'd probably be grounded for a month if I "disrespected my elder" by pointing that out, though. My dad's never hit me, even though he's seemed pretty close a few times. His anger has only gotten worse the older I get, but I don't think he'd go there now that I'm bigger than him.

For now, though, I shut up like I always do and try to tune out his pregame "pep talk" that sounds a lot more like threats than encouragement. The rest of our drive is filled with tense silence as I try to focus on deep breathing and shifting my attitude so I'm not pissed off for the rest of the day.

I do like playing baseball. I've always been good at it, and I like the physicality and mental focus my position requires. Plus, winning is great. But my dad's attempt to push me to be the best is starting to make me resent even the parts of it I've always loved. I wish I could have one day where every decision and moment wasn't already planned out for me. Just one day where everything I did didn't relate back to baseball.

We're still the first people to arrive despite my "fat ass" delaying us, and I help my dad bring everything out for warmups before heading to the locker room to change into my uniform and grab all my catcher's equipment.

Despite my dad's constant threats to bench me, I'm definitely the best catcher at our school, even as a junior. My pop times are way faster than everyone else's, and the guy who's probably our second-best option can't frame a pitch for shit. I swear anything in the shadow zone gets called a ball whenever he sees game time.

The school we're up against today sucks, and after the first four innings, we're already winning by seven. A normal game is seven innings, but if either team is up by ten or more after the first five innings, it can end early.

I really love when we get to end games early.

Our pitcher, Aaron, must be on the same page because despite our lead, he isn't holding back. He strikes out the first two players, and when the third batter clips a foul down the third base line, our guy manages to catch it for the out.

I'm not up for another six batters, so I don't completely unclip my gear as I watch the first few at-bats. We get two players on base before the first out: a fly ball right to their left fielder. I'm quickly ditching my equipment and grabbing my batting helmet when our next batter hits one straight at their second baseman for another out. I rush out to the on-deck circle before my dad can scream at me for not being ready, and our next batter hits the second pitch just past their shortstop, making it to the base and successfully advancing the runners.

We officially have bases loaded with two outs as I approach the plate. If I can avoid the out, there's a chance we could continue the inning to score enough points to end the game soon.

But where's the fun in that?

I haven't had batting coaches since I could hold a bat to just *get on base.*

I take a centering breath and put on my cockiest smile as I stare down their pitcher. He winds up, and I lock in on the ball as it leaves his grip, letting my instincts take over. As soon as my bat connects, I know it hit the sweet spot, but my dad will be pissed if I stand here and wait to watch the ball, so I take off toward first just like I would with any other hit. The first base coach already has a huge grin, signaling me to round the base, and I'm distantly aware of the crowd's cheers. I glance at third to confirm what I suspect, and our coach there is waving me through, shouting "home run," so I slow down and let my smile grow.

Game fucking over.

This is the part of baseball I love—the high of an exciting win, the team coming together to celebrate our shared victory. The other guys rush out as I cross home plate, surrounding me as everyone pats my back and helmet, celebrating the grand slam. This game might not have mattered as far as standings go since we're leading in our league, but a win is a win, and I just got everyone a couple extra hours on their Saturday.

"You really wanted to go out with your girlfriend tonight, huh?" my dad comments with a laugh when I finally make it back into the dugout. *No congrats from him.* But I'm not going to complain when I'm getting what I want.

"Could I borrow your car and take her out to dinner?" I ask, adding, "No ice cream" when I remember his sugar comments.

"Yeah, whatever," he agrees, handing me his keys. "I'll find your mom and sister and go home with them. Just make sure you use a condom. Even if she says she's on birth control, that shit isn't a guarantee. Don't make the same mistakes I did," he grumbles before plastering on a big fake smile as the other coaches join us to congratulate me on the winning hit. *God forbid we go a day without mentioning what a huge mistake my existence is.*

I excuse myself as soon as they lose interest in me, and make my way over to where Liv is sitting with my mom and sister. In the two months since we started dating, Molly's come to idolize her, so Liv usually sits with my family.

She spent the whole first month talking about Kieran. He stopped talking to her because of our relationship, and I only wanted to annoy him, but he had to make us dating about him by completely cutting her off. She tried to talk to him at school since he wouldn't answer her texts or calls, but he's so damn stubborn, he wouldn't even hear her out. It's ridiculous, really.

Being able to talk about him with Liv was fun, we really bonded over it until she decided to move on and focus on me and her new friends. She's pretending like it doesn't still bother her, but I haven't been able to do the same.

Despite losing his supposed best friend, and my constant taunts, he still hasn't toned anything down. He makes it impossible for me to ignore him. Every day, he shows up wearing something that makes me feel like I'm going to physically explode, so every day, I have to try to get him to stop. Now I have to do it away from Olivia, which is fine because I prefer taunting him when no one else is around anyway. Especially David. He follows me everywhere and always pushes too far where Kieran's concerned. He's given me a little more space since I started dating Liv, but he still drives me crazy—and not in the same way Kieran does.

"There's our superstar," my mom says as I approach them in the stands.

"Congrats, baby." Liv jumps up to kiss me, and Molly, who's in seventh grade and is obsessed with romcoms, "awws" as we do.

THERE'S one Mexican restaurant in our town that is way better than any of the others, and it's become our go-to meal spot when Liv and I get to go out. It's always packed, so I'm not surprised when we have to wait in a line to order.

"Oh, shit," Liv hisses, grabbing my arm and huddling into me like she's hiding from someone.

"What's wrong?" I ask, pulling her closer even though I'm confused who we're hiding from.

"The Delaneys are here," she whispers, and it takes me a moment to figure out who she's talking about. Kieran is standing a few groups ahead of us, currently ordering with two people who look a few years older than my parents. The man who I'm assuming is his dad is pretty tall, but Kieran looks more like his mom. She's very pretty, and they have the same blue eyes with dark brown hair and slight builds. He turns around, immediately meeting my gaze as if he could feel me staring at him.

Kieran's as sparkly as ever with purple eyeshadow as he glares at me from the front of the line. Eventually, he turns back to say something to his parents before walking away in the direction of the bathrooms as his parents pay and move down to the pickup counter.

"I don't think his parents saw us," I point out because Liv still looks worried.

"Yeah, hopefully not," she agrees, still hiding behind me.

We're able to order without incident, but the only route through the restaurant is to the pickup counter where his parents are still standing. Liv tries to hide behind me, but they spot her anyway.

"Olivia! Oh, hi, honey, it's been so long. We miss having you around the house," his mom gushes, rushing to give her a hug. Liv returns the gesture, but she's shrinking into herself in a way that makes it obvious she doesn't know how to respond to her warm greeting. Kieran's dad says hello to us both, and I have a feeling Kieran hasn't mentioned why Liv no longer hangs out at their house based on this interaction.

Kieran probably knows his overreaction to us dating was dramatic, and he's embarrassed to admit to them how shitty of a friend he was to Liv.

His mom steps closer to Olivia, looking at me curiously before lowering her voice to ask, "What happened? He still won't tell us. You know how he is. Always trying to be so strong and shoulder everything himself."

"Oh, um… I don't know that I should say if he hasn't—"

"He was upset we started dating," I interrupt. There's no use sugarcoating their son's choices; he should own up to hurting Olivia for basically no reason.

His parents look to each other, faces scrunched in confusion.

"Is he jealous? Did he want to date you?" his mom guesses, and it takes me a moment to realize she's aiming the question at me, not Liv. She's definitely looking me in the eyes.

She thinks Kieran wanted to date me?

And she's cool with the fact Kieran wants to date a man?

I can't help but laugh through my confusion. "No. Definitely not."

They look even more confused now, but Kieran must have given up hiding in the bathroom because he walks up from behind his parents and responds before I can explain. "I wouldn't be caught dead dating this asshole. I didn't realize Liv cared more about popularity than being a good friend, that's why."

"Come on, K, it wasn't like that at all," Liv tries to insist, but he's shaking his head now with his arms crossed in front of his chest, glaring at the two of us.

Finally, the Delaney's number is called, breaking up the very awkward tension of our group. His parents don't say anything else, focusing their concerned attention on Kieran, who isn't answering them either, as they quickly take their food and go.

"Well, that was awkward," Liv finally says on an exhale, and I pull her in for a quick hug.

"I can't believe they're so chill about him being gay," I comment, thinking over how his mom's assumption was that he was jealous of Liv for dating me. They seemed totally unfazed that he's gay, or about the clothes and makeup.

My dad would actually kick my ass. I think that would be his breaking point. I truly can't comprehend having that kind of loving and supportive family. All my dad cares about is baseball, and all my mom cares about is Molly and making sure we come across as some perfect, stereotypical suburban family.

"Yeah, they've always been amazing. That's why I was so worried about seeing them. They used to be like my second parents. I miss them, but I wasn't sure what he would have told them. I don't want them to hate me too."

"I'm sure they don't hate you. Kieran's just being a bitch about us dating, that isn't your fault," I try to console her, but then my mind jumps to another thought. "Wait, do you think they think I'm gay?"

"Why would they think you're gay?" she asks.

"Because of that comment about Kieran wanting to date me."

"No, Jace. You're literally dating me. I think it was just a question, and she assumed because they know Kieran is into guys."

"I'm just saying, if he made me out to be, like, gay or something, I swear, I'll have to say something. I'll have to—"

"Oh my god," Olivia cuts in. "Can you go one conversation without making it about him? Please. You are always talking about him! Seriously, Jace. Can we focus on me for once? That question had nothing to do with you."

That shuts me up because it's not like I mean to talk about Kieran all the time. It's just... he gets under my skin and stays there. It doesn't matter if I'm making out with Liv or trying to fall asleep or get through class, he's always there—annoying the shit out of me. I just want him to stop; doesn't she get that?

"I always focus on you. We spend all of our free time together, and I text you constantly," I say back with a forced smile. I really do like her, but being a boyfriend is way more work than I was expecting.

"Whatever. But if this is going to work—and it has to because I lost my best friend because of you—then I need you to be obsessed with me the same way you are with him. Got it?"

I'm not obsessed with him so that should be easy. "You got it, babe."

Our number's called so we grab our food before we find an open table. I talk about the game today and how my dad was such a dick this morning, and she tells me about how Molly asked her to do her makeup for some middle school dance that's coming up.

Her smile never quite reaches her eyes, though, and I can't help but wonder if she's thinking about Sparkles as much as I am despite her requesting my attention be fully on her.

11

KIERAN

"I had no idea editing the videos would take so much longer than filming them," Danny comments.

"Filming is the easiest part, in my opinion," I share, before the rest of my thoughts catch up. "Well, actually, I don't know if easy is the word, but definitely the most fun. Coming up with the ideas and editing everything to be exactly how I want it feels like work most days."

He nods, flashing me the smile he always seems to have. "It's so cool that you do all this. I'm impressed."

"Thanks, Danny." I return his smile before turning back to the screen, feeling proud of myself for doing this and sharing it with someone.

At first, I wasn't sure if I should tell Danny about my YouTube channel or if it was something I wanted to keep for myself. Obviously, it's public so it isn't a secret, but I don't think he would have found it on his own. We've been spending a lot of time together now that Liv and I are no longer speaking, and he's an awesome friend. I'm so glad our failed date didn't prevent us from continuing to hang out.

Every time I upload a new video, he watches it and texts me

all the things he enjoyed about it, even though makeup isn't his thing. He asked if he could see behind the scenes of the next one —which is what we're currently doing—and it's been fun to share the process with him.

"You know what would be a cool content idea?" Danny asks.

"Please don't say fake freckles, I'm so bad at them," I say with a laugh.

"Is that a thing?" He looks puzzled. "But, no. I was going to say prom makeup."

I think about his suggestion and nod. "Yeah, that could be good. I've done some full glam looks before, but I could talk about coordinating makeup with your outfit and what products to use to get the best pictures."

"Do you know what you're going to wear?" he asks.

"What to wear? For what?"

"To prom," he answers like it should be obvious.

I snort a laugh and shake my head. "Nothing? I'm not going to prom," I dismiss without any heat.

Danny is staring at me like I've suddenly grown wings with how confused he looks. "Why the hell not? You have to go!"

"Why would I possibly want to go to a school dance? Isn't it for couples anyway?" I protest, because I am very, very single, as he knows.

"Because it's prom!" he insists. "It's, like, a requirement of the high school experience. We can go together if you're worried about not having a date," he offers, sounding even more excited at that idea. "Wait, we should totally do that! Will you be my prom date? We can coordinate our suits and rent a limo and do the whole thing. Pleaseeeee, Kieran. Come to prom with me!"

"Aren't you going with your band friends?" I ask, searching for more reasons this wouldn't work.

"If you want to take pictures with a big group, most of them are going, yeah. And we could definitely join in their prom weekend plans after, but you're right, I think they've all coupled up. I was fine tagging along with all of them, but this sounds way more fun. I can't believe I didn't think of us going together sooner."

He's practically bouncing in his seat with how excited he clearly is. I honestly have no desire to go to a dance. I'm sure Jace and his friends will love the opportunity to harass me outside of normal school hours. And I don't really want to see Liv and Jace dancing or making out or whatever people do at those things.

But Danny is right, prom is kind of a big deal. I've told myself not to let Jace stop me from doing what makes me happy so many times, why should this be any different? Plus, Danny looks way too into this idea for me to turn him down. Still, I want to make sure he's thought it through before I agree.

"I don't think I've ever heard of a queer couple going to prom together at our school. Would you really want to be the first? We aren't even dating."

"Fuck yeah, I want to be the first. It doesn't matter that we'd be going as friends, I think it'll be so fun," he insists, looking up at me with so much hope shining in his eyes.

I sigh dramatically, roll my eyes, and play up my reluctance a bit even though I'm also starting to like the idea. "Fiiiine. I can't say no to you," I finally agree, laughing as he leans over from his chair next to me to throw his arms around my shoulders in a hug.

"Hell yes! We're going to have so much fun."

JACE

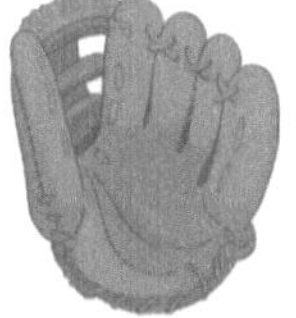

June 2011

"I don't care if all your friends are doing it, no drinking in the limo," my dad reminds us for what feels like the tenth time as we get ready to leave. He's going to be there as a fucking chaperone—surprise, surprise—with the other teachers, so obviously I won't be drinking.

We just spent over an hour taking pictures. We started at Liv's house, then went to the country club where my teammate Tom's dad is a member, to meet some of the guys on the team and their girlfriends for more photos.

Liv looks amazing in her light blue dress with sparkles. The combination immediately reminds me of Kieran's eyes, and I wonder if she thought the same thing when she picked it out, but I refrain from asking. She still complains whenever I bring him up, so I'm trying to be better about not doing it.

I'm wearing a matching light blue vest under my black jacket. We're definitely the hottest couple in our group, and if we were seniors, I think we'd have a good shot at being voted prom king and queen. People at school are always commenting on how we make such a great couple, and Liv said we were nominated for some "Most Likely to Marry Their High School Sweetheart" award in the yearbook.

I doubt we'll get married, but it's cool that people like us together.

"Alright, let's go!" Tom yells as everyone piles into the party bus we rented even though I won't be doing any real partying.

Leo has the aux cord and is blasting music, and I'm trying to hype myself up about going to prom, but for some reason, it all feels like I'm just here to perform. For my dad. For Olivia. For my friends.

By the time we get to the event venue our school rented for tonight, we have to wait in line for even more pictures before we can go inside. *How many damn photos do we need? Seriously.* Liv is commenting on other people's dresses and who is here with who, when I glance over at who's currently getting their picture taken ahead of us.

My whole body feels like it's submerged in ice with how quickly I freeze.

Kieran is standing behind Danny Rodriguez with his arms wrapped around him as Danny holds onto his arms, looking up at him over his shoulder. They're both laughing as they hold eye contact for the picture. They're in coordinated navy suits because, of course, Kieran couldn't be normal and wear black like everyone else. His dark blue eye makeup matches his outfit, making his eyes look even lighter than they normally do, like the moon lit up against the dark night's sky. *Or just like blue eyes; what the fuck was that thought?*

I knew he and Danny had become friends since the shed incident backfired, but I haven't heard if they are actually dating. Kieran looks so happy. I don't think I've ever seen him smile like that, so free and open. His whole face is lit up, and I can't look away.

They move into another pose holding hands and facing each

other, still laughing the whole time. *What the fuck is so hilarious?* Kieran has never laughed at anything I've said, and I'm really funny.

"Ugh, Vanessa is wearing the same dress as me," Liv says, pulling on my arm as she points toward the end of the line. I turn my head in that direction long enough to mutter "That sucks, but you're way hotter" before turning back to face Sparkles and his boyfriend, but they're already gone.

I don't know why I hate the idea of them dating so much. It must be because it feels like the ultimate "fuck you" that Kieran once again came out on top. He must know Danny didn't write that note, but he was still able to take what I did and use it to date the guy. Pretending he didn't care that we locked him in there was annoying enough, but to spin the whole thing into something that helped him? It's infuriating.

Eventually, we make it through the line, pose for our own cheesy photos, and find a table in the ballroom to ditch our stuff. There's a buffet set up on the edge of the room, but most people seem to be ignoring it in favor of the dance floor. Liv drags me out there toward some of her yearbook friends, and we join the crowd for a few upbeat, popular songs without incident.

"Isn't this so much fun?" Liv smiles at me, and I nod before hearing a slow song start playing.

"Oh, we have to dance to this!" she pleads, so I put my hands on her hips as she wraps her arms around my shoulders and we sway to the beat.

But I hate it.

This is so awkward. Why do people like this shit?

I have no idea if I'm doing it correctly, and I'm worried I'll step on her feet or bump into another couple. And where the hell am I supposed to be looking? Into her eyes? For a whole three-minute song? No, thank you. That's far too much eye contact. I look over her shoulder at the other guys who are still dancing to see what they're doing, but Kieran's blue suit steals all my attention.

He and Danny are slow dancing.

In front of everyone.

"Are you okay?" Liv asks, looking up at me with concern. "Why did you stop?"

Did I stop? "Oh, sorry. I guess I was distracted."

"By what?" she demands, sounding even more annoyed.

"Over there." I nod in Kieran's direction as I spin us so we can both see him to our left. "Kieran is here with Danny. Look at how obnoxious they are, hanging all over each other like that. We get it, he likes guys, but do they really need to rub it in everyone's faces like that?" I scoff, expecting her to agree with me.

But instead of laughing along with me, she shakes her head, staring at me with furrowed brows and a disapproving look. "They're here together. They aren't being obnoxious. And you seem to be the only one who cares! Stop fucking staring at them," she scolds in a harsh whisper.

"I'm not staring at them," I insist in the same quiet tone as we continue our awkward slow dance.

"You're always staring at him. Why do you even care if they're dating?"

"I don't," I argue weakly, but I think we both know it's a lie. It's only because he flaunts how different he is so openly—it's got to be. He shows up in makeup and clothes no other guy would wear, poses with his boyfriend in public in front of everyone, and does it all without a single ounce of shame. It drives me insane.

I hate it because he doesn't care, and I can't understand how that's possible.

After a long moment of tension, she finally sighs. "Can we please just have one night where we don't talk about him?"

"Of course," I quickly agree.

But I really should know better by now—ignoring Kieran is never easy.

I do it, though. I manage not to talk about him for the rest of the night, even if he's all I can think about. Every time my eyes wander to him, I bite my tongue. My thoughts circle on him and Danny and how frustrating their relationship is, and how obnoxious they look all cuddled up together.

They're so annoying that I don't even care when my dad insists on taking me home instead of letting me go to the party at Tom's with everyone else. I'm aware Liv is pissed, but I'm not surprised by his demand.

My dad spends the drive commenting on how awful a dancer I am, but all I can think about is the way Kieran's whole expression lit up when he was looking at Danny.

When I attempt to sleep, his face is all I can see. Eventually, I give up and find myself in the office. The rest of my family is asleep, so I don't even bother with turning on the lights. I just sit here alone, staring at his new Facebook profile picture. He looks so happy, smiling with Danny. Have I ever looked like that?

The pending request still taunts me.

1 3

KIERAN

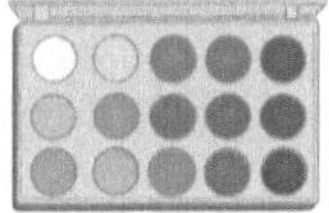

Summer Before Senior Year
July 2011

I scroll past Liv's latest post without spending too much time looking at it. She's tagged at the lake with Jace again, both of them in matching sunglasses, grinning at the camera.

It bugs me more than it should.

I know that I should just unfriend her. But the petty part of me wants to follow their relationship. They might have won some stupid best couple's award in the yearbook—*the club she's a part of, just saying*—but I'm definitely waiting for the day he suddenly disappears from her profile.

That's the only reason.

I'm definitely not still sentimental about losing my oldest friend. The girl who showed up at my house with a bag full of brand-new makeup when I finally admitted to her that I'd tried using some of my mother's. She was at my side for so many big moments: every birthday, when my grandparents passed, and our families even went on vacations together.

Not talking to her is one thing—she definitely deserves my anger after she chose Jace over me—but for some reason, unfriending her feels like the final nail in the coffin of our friendship, and I can't bring myself to follow through.

I hate that I miss her, but I'm only human.

I toss my phone onto the bed and sit at my desk, moving the mouse until the screen lights up, showing the new comments that are still coming in on my "Pride Month Glitter Eyeshadow Tutorial" I posted a few weeks ago.

And, unfortunately, most of them are exactly what I expect:

@CARSANDCHICKS85

Freak.

@U_SUCK77

This is why society's doomed.

@SPORTZ6969

You'll never be a real man lol.

It feels like I set myself up to be bullied even more online than I did in real life. But, still, every week, I tell the camera I don't care what people think. Some days it's harder to believe than others, and most days I need a reminder that I'm doing something that matters. I scroll faster and don't stop until I see something positive.

@RAWR_MAKEUP20

I showed this to my brother, and he lit up watching you. He's thirteen and just started playing with makeup. Thank you!"

I let out a sigh of relief. That's what I needed to see. It's so hard to block out the negative comments, but I try to by reading the positive ones again and again and again. They make me feel less alone and more like my art and self-expression is worth sharing.

The one other comment that keeps playing over and over in my head, though, is the one my mom made to Olivia and Jace.

There's no way I'm jealous of her. For dating him.

No way.

I hate her *because* she's dating him.

Because she chose him over me. Chose her image and her desire for a boyfriend over our friendship.

It's that simple.

No part of me wants to be the one dating Jace.

The same guy who's spent the last year making me his favorite target. It's so embarrassing that my mom jumped to that conclusion and said it to his face. I bet he thinks I told her I wanted to date him because that's how self-centered he is. I didn't give her a play-by-play of the bullying or why Liv and I are no longer friends, but it's ridiculous that's where her mind went.

If anything, the only thing I'm jealous of is that they have each other, and I'm going into my senior year single as ever. I've still only had that one kiss with Danny, and I'm sure that's all I will have when I go to college. It's just... I want to make out with someone I'm actually attracted to. I want passion, to feel connected to another person in the way I've only ever seen on screens or read about in books. But I doubt I'll find that in this town.

Now that it's summer, I feel even more isolated.

Danny went away to band camp after the first couple of weeks. I thought it sounded kind of dorky, but honestly, his texts make it seem like a great time. I almost wish I knew how to play an instrument, or that I'd looked into some sort of art camp even though I've hardly been painting and drawing now that I have my YouTube channel.

I spend most days and nights alone in my room, trying not to cringe at my voice as I edit my videos. Danny can only have his phone on him at certain points throughout the day, so with him unavailable, I've been turning more and more to the community growing in my comment section. Once I weed out all the negative ones, they're the closest thing I've got to feeling like someone other than my parents cares about me. There are slowly more and more people who are finding me who love what I'm doing, instead of just the ones hating me from behind their screens.

To be honest, I'm not even sure how the haters find me. The only way I'd show up in their feed is if they searched makeup tutorials, I think, and then the more interactions my videos get, the higher up I would be in what's recommended. So, my understanding is they seek me out, then comment how much they hate what I'm doing. It reminds me of Jace, and it only makes me hate him more. Especially because I have nothing but time to internalize every negative comment.

I don't want to bring Danny down when all his updates have been so positive. He still texts me and celebrates every time I post a new video, but he has so little time available for us to actually talk, I don't want to spend it venting about online trolls. The other person I'd really love to vent to is obviously no longer an option, and every time I have that thought, it pisses me off even more.

Ugh, I can't stand Olivia and Jace.

At least I don't have to watch them kiss and hold hands in the hall for another few weeks. *And I'm back to feeling sorry about my love life.* It's just that, I'll be eighteen in September, and realistically I don't think I'll be meeting anyone new anytime soon. I'm scared that when I go to college—even if there are cool, new people who I can form connections with—I'll have no idea what I'm doing and will probably mess up any chance I have with them since I'll be fumbling around because it's my first time.

If I really wanted to, I'm sure Danny would be down to experiment with me, but I don't want to do more just because he's there and also interested in men. It's not fair to him.

That's it. I need to get out of this room before I lose it.

I push off the bed, slide on my shoes, and head for the hall-way, calling out, "Mom?"

She's in the living room, folding laundry, with one of her talk shows playing in the background. She looks up, eyebrows raised. "Yeah?"

"Can you drive me to the mall?"

"Sure. Now?"

"Yeah, if you're not busy. I need to get new makeup."

She tosses a shirt onto the pile. "Give me two minutes to find my shoes."

As soon as we walk into the mall, my mom pulls out her phone. "I'm going to check the department store. Your dad needs a tie. Text me when you're done?"

"I will," I say, already turning toward the makeup store. I head straight there, and when the store comes into view, I stop in my tracks.

"Shit, sorry," I mutter to the person who just ran into me when I abruptly stopped.

"Mm-hmm," they hum as they walk around me, but I don't actually see them. My eyes lock on one thing, and one thing only: the "Now Hiring" sign in the window of the store I love. This feels like exactly what I needed today after sulking about being so alone.

I walk into the store and am met by a girl with teal eyeshadow who's organizing a lipstick display. "Hey there," she says. "Need help finding something?"

I swallow. "Actually, yeah, I saw the sign out front. You're hiring?"

Her expression shifts slightly as she eyes my eyeliner and the shimmer on my cheekbones.

"Yeah." She smiles. "You got a minute?"

I nod, trying to play it cool and not come across as too eager. "Yes."

"Cool. Wait here," she says as she walks away, disappearing into the back.

A minute later, a woman in head-to-toe black with a blonde bob and light makeup appears. "Hi, I'm Rochelle," she says, already assessing me. I definitely didn't dress to impress today. I'm wearing a black and grey striped shirt with black jeans and my Vans. I'm definitely giving more "emo" vibes today—which fits my mood much better than anything else—but I have makeup on, at least, and blue nail polish to hopefully show I'm serious about working here. "You're here for the job?"

"I am," I say quickly. "I don't have retail experience, but I know the product. I do tutorials on YouTube and—"

"Oh, tell me about that!" she says, perking up as she cuts me off.

"Well, I just started a couple of months ago. I have a few hundred followers right now, but it seems to be gaining traction. I do different styles and tutorials, mostly."

"That's so fun!" She grins. "Are you reliable? Can you get here for your shifts?"

"Yes, I am. And I can."

"We're looking for mostly evening and weekend coverage. I assume you're still in school?"

"I am, but I'm not in any sports or anything. I'd much rather spend my evenings and weekends here," I admit. "And now that it's summer, I'm free whenever until school starts again in September."

She gives me another head-to-toe assessment before nodding sharply. "Alright, then. You're hired. The pay is standard minimum wage, but you'll get a discount on anything in the store which is the best part of the job."

My mouth opens, but nothing comes out.

"I'll give you an application to fill out for our records, but I feel like you'll fit in here. What do you say?"

"I'd love to!" I respond eagerly, already feeling like senior year will be better than I'd been imagining only an hour ago. This feels like exactly what I need. Plus getting paid to talk about makeup *and* getting a discount on my favorite products? This is literally a dream.

I fill out the application she gives me, and we go over when I can start and my school schedule. I'm sure my mom won't mind me borrowing her car to drive here myself. I can't wait to tell her. I'm so excited.

I don't realize I'm still grinning like an idiot until I get back to the food court where I agreed to meet my mom. She's sitting at a table with a coffee. "Find that eyeliner?" she asks as I approach.

"No," I say, still buzzing. "But I got a job at the store, so I'll wait to buy it with my employee discount."

She nearly spills her coffee. "Wait—what?!"

"I'm so excited!" My cheeks are already sore from how much I'm smiling. "There was a sign in the window, and I asked about it, and they hired me on the spot."

"Oh, that's amazing, Kieran! I'm so proud of you!"

"I was hoping I could borrow the car more to get here after school and on weekends so you don't have to drive me."

She's nodding at me. "Yes, of course, we'll figure it out."

I THOUGHT "we'll figure it out" meant switching off between her and Dad lending me their cars a few nights a week or maybe dropping me off.

Definitely not this.

Never did I think *this* would be their solution. I'm standing in the driveway, staring at a brand-new 2011 Toyota Corolla. It's black, shiny, and definitely not the kind of car I ever imagined myself getting *as a surprise.*

"Are you serious?" I ask my parents, mouth still hanging open.

My dad tosses the keys up and catches them with a little smirk. "You'll need it to get to work."

I blink. "Wait, seriously?" I repeat, still waiting for them to explain what's actually happening. "You're being serious? You bought me a brand-new car?"

He nods. "Seriously. We're really proud of you for taking initiative with the job, and how you've embraced what makes you happy, spreading your joy with others online too. We know it can't always be easy, but you continue to amaze us with your resilience."

My mom's got that look on her face like she's probably been dying to spill the secret, and I just can't believe this.

"We're so proud of you, sweetie," my mom echoes. "We were going to wait until you started senior year, but after you got the job, we thought that now made more sense. You've worked so hard in school, creating your videos, and now you got a job. We're happy to do this."

I don't know what to say, truly. My parents have always been supportive and incredible, but this just added an entirely new layer.

School might suck, I might be lonely, and Jace Ryan is definitely a pain in my ass, but those things are temporary. I'm so lucky to have the family I do, and I know their support is something I'll always be able to count on.

1 4

JACE

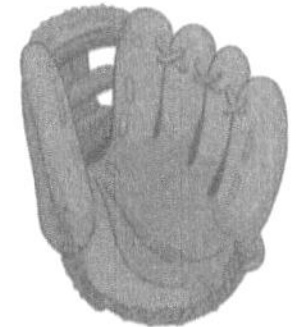

August 2011

"That's way too tight. You seriously don't have anything bigger?" my dad asks, obviously trying to cover up some of his annoyance in front of Liv.

She came over for breakfast, and now I'm trying on the only suit I own in the kitchen for everyone to critique. I rented the one for prom, and admittedly, it did fit way better than this one, but I've grown so much since I needed it two years ago for my cousin's wedding.

"We can go to the mall and pick up something else," Liv suggests. "You were so smart to suggest he try it on now," she adds to my dad. *Fucking kiss ass.*

I wish just one person in this town would realize what a dick my father is. With how much I complain to Liv about him, and the fact that she's my girlfriend, I would have thought she'd be on my side, but apparently even that's too much to hope for. She's always trying to get me to see things from his perspective, pointing out that he just wants what's best for me and that his controlling nature is because he cares.

She's caught under his spell just like the rest of the world seems to be. His fake charm and charisma, on top of another winning season, have even earned him a stupid "New Jersey Public Teacher of the Year" award. The ceremony is tonight, and he insisted I try on my suit to make sure it still fits.

Of course, Liv wasn't here for his comments about "how fat my ass has gotten," though.

"What would he do without you?" my dad asks, smiling at Liv, and she lights up at his praise.

"Make sure you don't clash with what your father is wearing," my mother adds. "Olivia, I'll text you a photo of what the rest of us will be in so that you can find him something that matches."

"Isn't my dress pretty?" Molly asks, jumping up to point it out in the photo my mom just sent her.

They're talking about me like I'm not *right here*. I'm sure I'd be perfectly capable of getting my own clothes, thank you very much. But I'll take any excuse to spend the day with my girlfriend away from my parents.

"It's so pretty," she coos, and Molly lights up.

"Ready?" I prompt her so we can get out of here.

"Yeah. See you all tonight." Liv beams as we walk outside toward her car.

"I wish I had my own car," I complain for the millionth time as I get into Liv's.

"I don't mind driving," she insists with a laugh.

"Thanks, babe. I just wish you didn't have to drive *every* time. I swear I'm, like, the only one in our year who still doesn't have a car."

"Most people's dads don't work at the same school they go to or have the same sports schedule," she teases as she adjusts the radio.

If only I was so lucky.

"Did you see Kieran's new car?" I ask. "It's brand new too,

not even used. Why does he need one, anyway? Where's he going?" I wonder aloud.

"I think he's working at the mall now actually," she mumbles, her mood shifting at his mention. "Saw it on Facebook."

"Really? What store? We should check if he's there," I suggest, perking up at the idea.

"I doubt he wants to see either of us," she points out sadly. "You know how much I've tried with him."

"Do you still want to be his friend?" I ask, trying a different route to talk about him.

After the first month or so, she stopped seeming so bummed when we'd talk about him and more annoyed. Mostly at me and how much I apparently talk about him. I've tried to be better, but it's like word vomit where he's concerned. Maybe if I ask her about missing him, she'll change her tone.

"You know I do, Jace." She sighs, and I give her a small smile. "I wish there was a way for you two to stop hating each other, so him and I could become friends again."

Yeah right.

"Well, maybe he's missing you too. He's just stubborn. Never listened to me, either. It's weird he'd throw away all the years of your friendship so easily. Maybe you should try talking to him? He might've cooled off now that it's been longer?" I suggest even though I doubt he has. No amount of my relentless persuasion has made any difference.

"You think so?" she asks, sounding so hopeful that it makes me feel even guiltier. But I try to shake off the twisting sensation in my gut, reminding myself that he's the one who chose to stop talking to her. And that maybe he really does miss her too.

"If he cares about you, he should want you to be happy," I remind her. "Where's he working anyway?"

"Promise you won't be mean?" she asks hesitantly.

I take her hand and give it a quick kiss, very curious now.

"I'll be on my best behavior, promise," I agree playfully, earning a smile from her.

"He works at the makeup store." She sighs. "Do you still want to go?"

Of course he does.

I should have known, except I also didn't think they let guys work there, so I probably wouldn't have guessed. "Obviously," I confirm. "You can even pick out something for me to get you as a thank you for always driving my ass around."

"Shit, he's here," Liv whispers, stopping so quickly when she sees Kieran through the window of his store that I nearly fall over as she yanks me back with the hand she was holding.

"That's good, right? I thought you wanted to see him so you could talk."

She runs her hand through her hair. "Uh. I don't know. I do miss him, but I don't want to piss him off more…" She trails off, but the unspoken "by showing up with you" is obvious.

I get that he doesn't like me because I call him out for wearing makeup, but I stand by the fact that I'm only giving him the attention he so clearly wants since he's continued to wear it. "What do you want me to get you? I can find it while you talk to him and give you guys some privacy," I suggest.

She relaxes at my suggestion and texts me the name of some new eyeshadow palette she wants. When we enter the store, she points me in the right direction and heads over to where Kieran is behind the register. The store is empty so there's no one else in the line, and they immediately start talking. I'm too far away to hear anything, but I keep an eye on them the entire time I hunt down the correct colors.

Kieran looks pissed. Underneath all his usual makeup, he's

got on the same fake smile my dad always does when we're in public, but the fury behind his eyes is unmistakable. He's obviously trying to remain professional at work, but I don't think the conversation is going well.

Before I can debate if I should step in, Liv throws her arms up in frustration and turns to storm out of the store.

Well, there's my answer.

I have the eyeshadow in my hand already, and confronting Kieran myself is too damn tempting to pass up, so I might as well still buy it.

"Have you finally decided to try some makeup for yourself after harassing me for so long about it?" Kieran sarcastically asks when I get to his register.

"Fuck off, Sparkles," I scoff. "You know it's for Liv. I can't believe this place lets guys work here. Or were they confused enough by your appearance during the interview that they assumed you were a girl?"

He rolls his eyes so dramatically that I think they might be stuck for a moment before he shakes his head like he's trying to clear away how he'd like to respond.

"That will be forty-eight dollars."

"For one fucking thing?" I gawk. But he just points to the sticker, confirming the price I must've missed while I was focused on him and Liv. I swipe my card anyway, thankful my uncle still sends me money on holidays and birthdays even though he and my dad don't talk to each other. *Fuck, I wish I could get a job and have real money too.*

I return my attention to Kieran. "You're telling me you're so desperate for attention that you not only put all that shit on your face every day but that it costs hundreds of dollars to do it?" Must be so nice to be able to throw away money like that. I try to save every dollar I can, especially since my dad has no idea his brother even sends me any in the first place.

"I'm not desperate for—ugh." He groans, cutting himself off. "Just leave, Jace."

"What did you say to Liv?" I push, not quite ready for this interaction to be over. I know I shouldn't, but I love seeing how easily I can get him so worked up.

"Go ask her yourself." He's openly glaring at me now, arms crossed, not bothering to maintain the happy facade that he was earlier.

"Careful, Sparkles, I'm sure your boss would love to hear about how you've treated your customers today," I taunt. Even with all the makeup he's wearing, it doesn't hide how he blanches at the threat. As much as I would love to stay and continue to make him squirm, I should probably go check on Liv.

Still, I can't stop myself from adding "You should really get a different job" as I turn to leave. "No one will take this seriously," I warn him.

He rolls his eyes again, *the little shit.* "Leave, Jace."

I flip him off as I do, finding Liv on a bench outside the store. I hand her the bag with the eyeshadow in it and pull her in for a hug. "It's his loss, babe."

15

KIERAN

Senior Year
September 2011

"*T*hank you for watching, and don't forget to like and subscribe! And remember, never dim your sparkle for anyone! Bye, loves, see you next time." I wave at my computer and hit stop on the recording.

In the last few months, my account has started gaining traction, and I think I have the potential to grow it into something special. But at the same time, I'd love for that to happen *after* I graduate. I get bullied enough as it is; I don't need the whole school to find out about it and team up with Jace and his never-ending taunts. If anyone other than Danny has seen my videos, no one's said anything to me, and I'd like to keep it that way.

I double-check my video is saved and start getting ready for my shift.

As predicted, working has been amazing. I love the employee discounts, and I've been able to learn even more about makeup application, trends, and the things people care about when they're purchasing their beauty supplies. It's also helped with content since I always know the new products. It's even made me start quietly dreaming about my own products in the future.

By the time I park and get into the mall, I walk into the store right on time. "Hey, Casey," I greet my co-worker as I pass her to drop my stuff off in the back.

"Hey, Kieran," she replies before approaching a new customer that just walked in.

The girls I work with are all nice, but they're work friends; I don't talk to any of them outside of my shifts. Most of them go to a different school or are older, and since Danny is back, he's who I spend most of my free time with.

If I wasn't heading to college next summer, I'd definitely want to learn an instrument just so I could tag along to band camp with him. The stories he shared sound every bit as wild as the movies make it out to be. He told me he gave his first blowjob this summer, and hearing about it only makes me want my own experience even more.

God, I feel like that's all I can think about these days.

After putting my coat into my locker, I head back out onto the sales floor, and my pleasant mood immediately sours because Olivia is standing in the middle of the store, looking right in my direction like she was expecting me to appear.

"K, can we talk?" she pleads, coming right into my personal space.

"No." I attempt to dismiss her and walk around her, but she sidesteps to block my path.

"Please, Kieran, I'm so sorry. We really need to talk. Just for a minute, please," she practically begs. Some of my coworkers are looking at us now, and this is not the type of attention I want, so I huff out a big sigh and motion for her to follow me, attempting to move her drama to the back corner of the store.

"What do you want, Olivia? You're causing a scene at my work," I sneer at her. I don't understand why she thinks any of this is okay. We haven't talked to each other recently, other than when she came in here with Jace last month. And the time when my mom very embarrassingly thought I'd want to date Jace. *I still can't believe she said that.*

"You were right, K, and I'm so sorry," she says with tears in her eyes. "Jace and I broke up, and I really miss you. I never should have dated him in the first place."

It takes everything in me not to roll my eyes. What does she think? I'm just going to forget everything and accept her apology? Jace probably broke up with her, and she immediately came running back to me.

"You know he's made my life hell, Liv," I remind her. "And he never stopped. He's continued to harass me while you've dated him, even if he only did it while you weren't around. You think I'm just going to accept you back in my life? No way. You screwed that up. You can go now. I have a job I'd really like to keep," I say with a huff.

Even if it does feel really good that she came here, begging to be friends again.

"I'm sorry, K, I'll go. But I just want you to know that you're right. Jace is obsessed with you. Other than baseball and his dad, you're basically all he talked about the whole time we were together."

That snaps my focus back to her. "Seriously?"

"That's why he dumped me. I was sick of him bringing you up all the time, so I finally suggested that if he wanted to talk about you so much, maybe he should be dating you and not me." She sighs. "It must've really pissed him off because he said 'I'm not gay, why would you even say that shit? We're literally dating.' " Her impression of his voice is pretty funny, but I don't react. "Then he said we were done. He was way angrier than I'd ever seen him."

I can barely process what she's telling me right now. Jace broke up with her because she suggested that he date me?

He was obviously pissed if he ended things with her over it, but the idea is absurd. I know there's no way he could ever want me. Jace Ryan is straight.

Not like I even care; I definitely don't want him either.

Despite my best efforts to ignore him when he's harassing me, he can't seem to leave me alone. He used to do it around his friends, I guess for laughs, but lately, he's been doing it in more isolated places—cornering me when I'm alone in the hallway and following me into the bathroom or library.

Their breakup scares me. What if he ups the ante to get back at me for something that's not even my fault?

I swallow my new panic and take another look at Olivia, thinking about all the times I had to face Jace's wrath alone, and harden my resolve. "That sucks, but you need to leave. I'm not getting fired over this," I say, not letting that final bit of information she slipped change anything.

I don't know what to do with her comment, but I'm not going to accept her half-assed apology, either. I bet if Jace reached out and said he wanted to get back together with her after this "breakup" that she'd go back to him in a heartbeat.

If she wants to be my friend again, she needs to prove it, and even then, I'm not sure I'll forgive her.

16

JACE

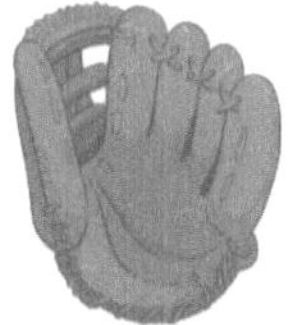

October 2011

"Is that really the only weight you can handle?" my dad asks, not bothering to wait for an answer as he adds more. He finally walks away to comment on another player's form, and I fight the urge to flip him off behind his back.

"Are you going to Cameron's party tomorrow?" David whispers so my dad can't hear.

Today's my eighteenth birthday, but I was still up at fucking five a.m. to be here lifting weights before school. It's not even baseball season, but god forbid I have one day to sleep in.

I'm supposed to be an adult now. I'd think maybe I could start to make some of my own decisions, but when I suggested skipping this morning's session, my dad lost his shit and spent a solid twenty minutes screaming at me about how I'm throwing my life away and how I don't appreciate everything he's sacrificed for my future.

At this point, I'm really struggling to remember why I even bother to stay out of trouble if he's going to tell me whatever I'm doing is wrong regardless of how "well behaved" I am. I get it, the MLB has standards, and a team isn't going to want me if I royally fuck up, but never having any fun, living my entire life focused only on baseball and what my father says I need to do to play, has me really resenting the game lately.

It wasn't as bad when I was dating Liv and she could distract me from it all, but obviously I couldn't keep dating someone who implied I'm gay. Seriously, who says that about their boyfriend? She should have known more than anyone just how *not gay* I am.

She still isn't friends with Kieran, though. I've seen her following him around at school, but it seems like he's being as stubborn as before by continuing to shut her out. He and Danny seem as solid as ever though. Every time I see them laughing in the cafeteria or hanging out at each other's locker after school, it continues to aggravate me.

"I know you normally skip them, but everyone's going to be there since his parents are out of town. It's your birthday, and it's Halloween, man, you can't miss the costumes," David continues when I don't respond. "You gotta go to a party at least once in high school. You're eighteen now, dude."

You know what? A party actually sounds like a great idea. "Yeah, I'll be there," I confirm. I won't drink because my psycho dad likes to randomly drug test me to "prepare me for the majors," and I don't feel like dealing with that fallout. But just getting out of the house and feeling like a normal teenager for a night is exactly what I need. "I'll drive if you want, but if my dad asks, I'm spending the night at your place," I tell him.

"Hell yeah! I even have an extra costume if you want it," he offers. "The guys on the team are all going as superheroes, but the first one I ordered was too big. I couldn't see my muscles at all. Should fit you though."

"Sounds good."

I SHIFT UNCOMFORTABLY, trying to readjust myself *again*. This costume might technically fit me, but I'm pretty sure the whole outline of the superhero's dick isn't on display in the movies. My muscles do look great though.

"Your games are, like, my favorite part of the year," some girl from my Spanish class is slurring as she grips my forearm. I lost David a few minutes ago, he said something about a bathroom, but he probably went to get another drink by now. I'm really regretting offering to be the designated driver tonight. Why did I think it would be fun to be at a party with a bunch of drunk people while I'm sober?

I excuse myself from the cleat chaser to try to find David again. He isn't in the kitchen or the hall outside the downstairs bathroom. I swear to god, if that asshole is hooking up while I'm standing out here getting bumped into by what feels like every dumbass in our grade, I'm going to lose my shit. Seriously, can no one walk in a straight line? I'm not about to go banging on the bedroom doors or anything, but I'm too annoyed with everyone to just stand here. I might as well make sure he isn't vomiting in one of the bathrooms, so I head upstairs.

Cameron's house is huge, and I don't actually know where I'm going. There's a bunch of abstract art on the wall as I continue down the hall, and I'm distracted looking at it as someone opens a door, running right into me. "Oh shit, sorry," I start but stop when I see who it is. "What the fuck are you doing here, Sparkles?" He's dressed up like an '80s rockstar with dark makeup that makes his normally bright blues eyes somehow look even bigger. It's more than he normally wears to school, but the way he has the bandana tied around his forehead, paired with an open leather vest with nothing underneath it and tight black pants, it's somehow less feminine than his daily looks too.

What the fuck is his problem? Is he trying to prove he can wear makeup and still look like a man? Because the whole vibe is just confusing.

"It's a party," he responds flatly, rolling his eyes. He doesn't have a drink, and he's missing that intoxicated glassy look that so many of our classmates currently have, though, so maybe I'm not the only person who's sober tonight.

"No shit," I spit out. "I meant, why are you at a party? I didn't think you had any friends besides Danny, and you don't even seem to be drinking."

He crosses his arms, standing up a bit straighter, but he still needs to look up at me. "If you must know, Cameron is my lab partner, and he invited me. Danny also wanted to come and coordinate costumes," he huffs out. He's still standing inside the doorway to what I can now see is a bathroom, but I'm blocking his path out.

I don't really know what to say, but I'm not ready to walk away, so I blurt out the first thing I can think of. "I saw Liv was downstairs. Are you here with her too?"

"Definitely not," he scoffs.

What is his problem? I might not want to date her, but I don't think Liv deserves to be ignored by her oldest friend either. "I don't get why you've been so shitty to her," I mutter.

"*I* was shitty to her?" he repeats, eyes wide like he can't possibly understand why I'd think that.

"Yeah, you ended your friendship because she got a boyfriend. That's super possessive and weird."

"I wasn't mad she had a boyfriend. I stopped talking to her because she started dating *you,* " he practically yells in response, stepping closer as he does. "The guy who's been harassing me for a year for no fucking reason!"

"No reason?" I repeat back. "You're the one who's continued to show up in fucking makeup and glitter after I warned you against it in front of my friends," I seethe. "You wanted attention so desperately, you got it. It's your fucking fault."

"Are you fucking serious right now?" Kieran huffs. "It's my fault for not fitting into *your* idea of who a high school guy should be? That's a you problem! And you let it get under your skin so badly that you have to constantly remind me that I'm a freak and a weirdo. Does that make you feel good? Do you feel better about yourself when you make comments about how my only future is in the circus?" he rants, throwing his arms out in his frustration, fighting back way more than he ever does at school.

And as funny as that comment was, I'm too pissed off right now to even snicker. "You have no idea how good you have it," I sneer. "You could be living such an easy life with your nice, supportive parents. If you didn't cover your face in that shit and wore normal clothes, you'd probably have way more friends," I continue, unable to stop myself from matching his loud volume. "Was that too boring or something? Do you really need attention so badly that you have to be so fucking confusing all the damn time?"

"Confusing?" He arches one of his perfectly groomed eyebrows. "What does that even mean? How am I confusing, Jace?"

Is he fucking kidding? "Because all the makeup is so distracting!" I explain even louder, gesturing to his current look as evidence. "Guys aren't supposed to be pretty."

We both freeze at that word.

Icy dread spreads throughout my veins as what I just said settles between us. Neither one of us moves or speaks, we just stare at each other in silence. His jaw is hanging open slightly, but I didn't mean...

He slowly smiles. "You think I'm pretty, Jace?" he finally taunts, a wicked glint in his eyes that I've never seen before.

That smug expression is too much.

I'm done being on my best behavior around this freak. I shove him hard with both hands firmly on his bare chest, forcing him back into the bathroom. Storming in after him, I kick the door shut and quickly lock it behind us. He's lucky no one heard him say that shit, but I'm not taking any more chances.

I walk right up to him, forcing him back until he hits the back wall. His body language confirms he's intimidated with the way he's shaking as I bring my face right in front of his. "You need to shut the fuck up. I didn't say that," I hiss.

He sucks in a sharp breath, glancing down. And then this fucking asshole has the balls to smirk as he looks back up at me, holding eye contact. He swallows and stands to his full height before he confidently replies. "Holy shit. Is that what this has been about the entire time? Have you been lying, Jace? Are you gay?" Each question sounds more and more amused.

What the actual fuck? First Olivia and now Kieran? These assholes don't know what they're talking about. "I'm not gay," I insist, trying to shove him back again, but he's already pinned against the wall. Kieran reaches up and grabs my wrists instead, gripping them tightly so I can't pull my hands away from where they rest on his bare chest. *How is he that strong?*

"Does it piss you off that I'm pretty?" he taunts again, obnoxiously enunciating each word.

I'm shaking now too, vibrating with anger. I don't know that I've ever been this pissed off in my entire life, and my dad has really set the bar high for that. My heart is racing as my body goes into full fight-or-flight mode, ready to eliminate the threat of his unfounded accusation.

"Shut the fuck up!" I repeat harshly. "I'm not gay." I'm attracted to women. I've hooked up with his best friend for fuck's sake.

"Then why are you hard, Jace?" he asks, maintaining eye contact as he uses his grip on my wrists to tug me forward. I'm not anticipating the move and stumble into him. As I do, our hips align in a way that has my cock rubbing against his erection. I swallow back a groan that threatens to leave my throat.

Fuck. Why did that feel so good?

This stupid fucking costume makes everything perfectly visible, and it's probably making me more sensitive than normal.

I'm just angry. It doesn't mean anything that I'm harder than I can remember ever being. My heart rate is elevated, and my blood flow is all messed up. That's probably why he's hard too. Plus, Kieran is so fucking confusing with his makeup and his… well, I guess his clothes aren't exactly feminine right now, but I've seen him in enough girly shit that my dick is probably permanently confused.

His grip on my wrists isn't actually that tight. I should pull away. Remove myself from this freak's presence and forget all about whatever is happening right now.

But then he fucking taunts me again.

"Go ahead, Jace, tell me again how you think I'm weird. A freak. What was the word? *Distracting?* Lie to my face and tell me you're not attracted to me right now as your *hard* cock rubs against me," he dares, shifting again to emphasize the contact.

Fuck, that feels amazing.

"I said *shut up*," I demand, voice still harsh as I try to remember how to move. I need to walk away, but my fingers are digging into his pecs now, and I hope they bruise. I hope he has to stare at the reminder of me hurting him for days.

But fuuuck, why does that feel so good?

Did I just grind into him? *No. Absolutely not.*

"Or what, Jace?" he goads, looking so fucking smug. I'd love to wipe that cocky grin off his face. My gaze locks on his mouth. The full lips that are shiny and red, and would look so much better wrapped around my—

Nope. I shake my head, attempting to clear away that completely uncalled for image.

"Or I'll shut you up myself!" I finally answer.

But he seems completely unaffected by my threats, and his smile only grows as he stares me in the eyes.

"Your dick twitched there, big guy. Whatcha thinking about?" he teases.

And I don't know if it's just how blunt he's being or if I want him to feel as flustered as I do, maybe I'm just sick of listening to him, but even I'm surprised when I answer honestly. "A much better way you could be using your mouth, one where I wouldn't have to hear the annoying sound of your voice."

I'm expecting him to finally push me away, to insult me or threaten to spread lies about me being into men.

But no, in true Kieran fashion, he completely shocks me with his response.

"Okay."

17

KIERAN

"**O**kay?" He repeats it like it's a question because he clearly doesn't believe I actually said it.

I don't know what possessed me to say that, either.

Maybe it's because I want to finally be the one with the power, want to watch his confidence crack, watch his denial about being attracted to me slip away until he gives in. Olivia said I'm all he talks about. Maybe it's time to see how true that is —to see just how deep this obsession of his really runs.

Jace's jaw is clenched so tight, I can see his muscles flexing beneath his skin, but no matter what his face conveys, he can't hide his obvious erection in his superhero costume. And that alone has me considering something I'd never imagined doing with him.

He makes my life hell at school, mocks how I look, and I hate him for it. But god, I'm also eighteen, inexperienced, and so sick of wanting something I've never had.

As much as I don't want to admit it, even to myself, I'm attracted to Jace in a way that I've never been with anyone else. I wanted passion and connection, and if nothing else, I'm certainly passionate about how much I hate him.

He's always held the power between us. But right now, his shocked expression makes it clear I'm the one in control as I call his bluff and agree to his suggestion. I want to do this. Badly. I just can't tell if I want to do more *for me*... or to prove something to myself about him. "Yeah," I say, still taunting him. "You wanna shut me up, right? Then do it."

I'm not convinced he'll actually go through with it, but the panic warring in his eyes gives me a sick sense of satisfaction. Mr. Popular Star Athlete isn't so confident now, and it's all because of me. I might be the one offering to drop to my knees, but knowing him, he'll be the one begging for more.

He finally pulls his arms from my hold, I assume to storm off, but then he lifts them to grip my shoulders and shoves me down to my knees. Anticipation is building in my chest—a mix of nerves and excitement about the possibility of hooking up with someone, even if it is him.

His hands remain on my shoulders, and he squeezes tighter. His chest is rising and falling quickly. He looks pissed and terrified and way too turned on for someone who supposedly hates me.

"You want my mouth on you? Take it out, Jace," I goad, looking up at him through my dark lashes, his big hands still gripping my shoulders.

He mutters something under his breath that sounds a lot like "fuck it" and reaches for the waistband of his costume, yanking it down just enough to free his straining cock.

My mouth waters at the sight of his dick inches from my face. I've pictured doing this a million times. Tried to imagine how sucking a dick would feel and taste. If I'd like it. I'm not sure if it's my position on the floor, how close I am, or if Jace just has a huge cock, but it's bigger than I imagined. There's a prominent vein drawing my attention, and I want to lick it, trace it with my tongue until I can suck on his dark swollen tip.

But he doesn't move forward, so neither do I. I want him to

make this decision. He needs to be the one to shove his dick into my mouth while I'm willing and waiting on my knees.

"You've been obsessing over me for months," I sneer. "And now you finally get to use me the way you've wanted to. Go on. Be the big man. Shut me up the way you said you would, hotshot."

That finally does it. His hand leaves my shoulder to grip my jaw, and I drop it open for him. Tongue out, eager for a taste. His hips press forward, nudging the tip into my mouth, and I close my lips around him. I hollow my cheeks and breathe through my nose, just like the internet articles said to do, and he pushes deeper.

And holy fuck, it's a lot. He's huge, hot and heavy on my tongue. I try not to gag when he advances, more than half of his dick in my mouth now, but I can't help it. My eyes water a little, but I keep going, determined to make this good.

He hisses through his teeth and lets out a little groan when I swirl my tongue and suck a little harder. Which definitely means I'm doing it right. Or so I tell myself.

"Fuck," he mutters, barely audible. "Fuck, fuck—"

The sounds of him losing it over me encourage me to keep going. To keep swirling my tongue around his tip as I bob my head up and down, trying to take him even deeper.

I want him to lose control.

Want him to always think of this moment when he thinks of me.

I sloppily suck as much of him into my mouth as I can, and he swears again, louder this time. For a guy who claims he's not into me, he sure seems to be enjoying having his cock in my mouth.

Tears are running down my cheeks, and I gag again, pausing to look up at him until he meets my gaze. If this is a first for him, if he's struggling with being attracted to men like I suspect, I don't want him to be able to excuse it as any mouth on his dick. I want him to remember *I* was the one who made his knees weak if he tries to pretend this didn't happen. I want him to look at me while I do this so he can't pretend I'm someone else. It's me he shoved down to suck his cock—the glitter-wearing, makeup-loving *freak* he's spent the last year trying to humiliate.

He's trying to restrain his moans, probably thinking if I can't hear him, if I don't know how much he's enjoying it, then it doesn't count.

But I hear him, and I want him to know.

I pull back slightly. "Still think I'm disgusting?"

He chokes on a breath at my taunt. "Shut the fuck up," he growls, grabbing my hair and pushing his cock back into my mouth.

Sucking and swirling my tongue, I feel his thighs start to shake, and next thing I know, I'm met with hot bursts of cum. I choke, given the lack of warning, and attempt to swallow the saltiness down, but some of it spills out of my mouth. I pop off, wiping it with the back of my arm.

Before I can catch my breath or look up, he shoves me.

Hard.

Like a fucking asshole.

I fall back onto the tile, arm scraping against the edge of the cabinet as I catch myself. "Ow, fuck," I mutter, blinking up at him from the floor.

He hurriedly tucks himself back into his costume, refusing to look at me.

"What the hell is your problem, Jace? Refuse to believe you just came down *my* throat? A *guy's* throat?" I spit as I stand up to get in front of him and the door, rubbing my arm.

"Get the fuck out of my way," he grits out. "That didn't happen." Then he's shoving me out of his way again before he's out the door and slamming it shut behind him, leaving me in the bathroom.

Alone.

I turn to the mirror to look at myself. My own cock is still hard from the encounter.

What the fuck is wrong with me? After how he just treated me, how could my body still be so turned on?

I brace my hands on the edge of the vanity, trying to breathe. My lips are red, spit-slicked, and my makeup is smeared. I should've known what to expect: he's Jace-fucking-Ryan after all.

But as much as I hate to admit it, there was some tiny part of me that hoped it wouldn't end that way. That, maybe, he'd have some big moment of realization, and he'd confide in me. And the most fucked-up thing is, even though I knew he'd probably freak out and deny everything, I still wanted it. I asked for it. I got on my knees and opened my mouth for a guy who's spent every possible moment of the last year calling me names.

And I don't regret it.

Because I sucked my first dick tonight. And I think I loved it.

It felt like, for once, I was the one making him unravel, not the other way around. I can still taste him on my tongue, still hear the sound he made right before he came. I did that. I made him feel that way.

Still riding that high, I take a moment to compose myself, then walk back out into the party.

JACE

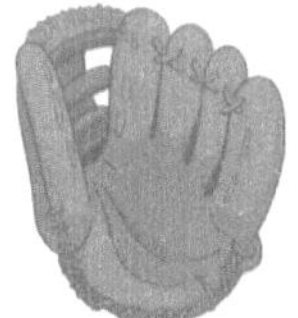

"*D*avid, I don't care where you are or how much fucking fun you're having, if you aren't in the car in the next sixty seconds, I'm leaving your ass here," I practically shout into my phone as I run out of the party.

I have to bail. I can't stay. I need to be far away from whatever the fuck just happened.

My breaths are shallow and way faster than they should be as I bump into people while trying to make my quick exit. I throw the front door open and rush outside, ignoring someone who calls my name as I suck in a deep breath.

I need to get my shit together. But even the crisp fall air isn't calming me down like I'd hoped it would. When I get to the car, I pull out my phone again and see a text from David.

DAVID:

One more min! Don't leave!!!

I try to count to ten, to take a deep breath, but finally I give up on being calm and put on some alt rock-metal music in an attempt to drown out my thoughts. I close my eyes and let my head fall back against the headrest of David's car that I'm in charge of driving. It doesn't actually work, though; my thoughts are still racing, louder than ever.

What the actual fuck just happened?

One minute I was commenting on Kieran's makeup like I always do, and the next he was swallowing my cock like it was the best thing he'd ever tasted. Has he done that to a lot of guys? Shit, did he just cheat on Danny with me?

Fuck! *That is so not the point.*

But it could be if he fucking tells him he cheated on him with me.

I slam my head back against the seat.

Fuck, fuck, fuck!

It was just a blowjob. Any mouth around my dick would feel great. It's been so long too; I haven't hooked up with anyone since Liv and I broke up. That has to be why it felt so good. It wasn't actually the best blowjob of my life. I was just desperate.

I'm not gay.

I would know if I was attracted to guys. I'm around my teammates changing all the time, and I've never been turned on by any of them.

None of them look like Kieran though.

Fuck! I'm not attracted to him either.

Despite the amount of makeup and sparkly clothes he wears, he is a man. It doesn't matter that tonight with his open vest and darker, edgier makeup he looked less feminine than usual or that he seemed determined to hold eye contact while he... *nope.* I'm not even going to think about it.

I am not gay.

I'm not.

Someone sucked my dick in the bathroom at a party, and I came. Those are the only details that matter. No big deal. No dick went near my mouth.

"I'm here!" David shouts as he throws the door open, startling me as he quickly climbs in. I'm already pulling away before he clicks his seatbelt. "Whoa, man, where's the fire? Why did you need to leave so quickly?"

Damn it, I didn't think this through. I have no idea what to tell him. "It's nothing," I stammer, glancing his way before returning my focus to the road. He's staring at me with obvious concern. Was there also suspicion? Does he know what happened? Did Kieran run out after me and announce to everyone who he'd just been in the bathroom with?

Fuck, fuck, fuck. I'd just have to deny it. No one would believe him over me anyway. God-fucking-damn it, what did I do?

I crank up the air in the car. Even though it's cold out, I'm sweating. Fuck. I should have stayed longer, warned Kieran against telling anyone. Holy shit, he wouldn't have actually done that, right?

"Are you sure you're okay? Was it Olivia?" he asks, and his suggestion calms me down just a bit. There's no way Kieran said anything. Even if he did, everyone knows I've given him a hard time about the makeup. There's no way they'd believe *that* if he ever said it.

But he can't say it, because I can't even risk a rumor or my dad will beat my ass. Maybe worse.

David continues when I don't respond. "I saw that she was talking to that guy on the football team, did you see them kissing or something?"

I let out a relieved sigh. Seeing my ex with another guy sounds like a much better excuse for why I'm freaking out. "Yeah, I saw them together and had to get out of there," I agree.

"Sorry, man, that sucks." He lets out a big yawn and rests his head back. "You need a rebound," he slurs, and for the first time during this conversation, I remember that he's probably wasted and won't even remember how weird I'm being.

I let out a deep exhale, finally relaxing further. No one is ever going to know what happened tonight.

No one ever has to know that Kieran deepthroated my cock like a fucking porn star. My dick starts to thicken again at the memory, but I am not entertaining those thoughts. It was a warm, wet mouth. That's all.

I'm attracted to women.

I'm not gay.

He's not going to say anything. *He's not going to say anything.*

I should have stayed home today. I should have insisted I'm sick even though my dad equates being sick with being weak. In all my life, he only let me skip school one time in eighth grade when I was damn near dying with the flu.

But today, it wouldn't even be a lie because I feel like I'm about to throw up as I glance around the cafeteria nervously.

I've managed to avoid seeing Kieran so far today, but it's inevitable… unless he skipped school. We have lunch and math together again this year. So even if he ditches lunch this period to spend it in the library or the art room, *or wherever*, I'll see him in my next class.

I wish I could say I've moved on from what happened at the party on Saturday, but it's all I've been able to think about. Sparkles must have a magic mouth because I get instantly hard whenever I remember it wrapped around me. I've basically been walking around with a semi since then, and I really need to get my shit together. I'm not into him. I'm not gay. I like women. Maybe seeing him will be a good thing, a reminder that he's just a freak in makeup, and I was only confused by all the girly shit he wears. It was a slip up during a weak moment. I would have let anyone blow me that night with how horny I was and how sensitive the costume made me.

"Ready to go, man?" David nudges me with his elbow, and I look up, realizing most of the cafeteria has cleared out.

"Yeah," I mumble, hurrying to pack up my stuff and follow him.

"I'm worried about this math quiz, too," he says, and I nod, going along with his assumption of what has me so distracted.

I've debated if I should try to talk to Sparkles, to make sure he doesn't say anything to anyone, but I've decided my best bet is to ignore him. Talking to Kieran usually ends with him spewing some bullshit at me, and while that normally amuses me, I don't need to give him any excuses to open his mouth… Unless he's putting it to work again.

Nope. Not thinking about that.

Ignoring him is definitely the best way forward. I can't risk him even insinuating anything. The possibility of it getting back to my dad is far too dangerous.

"Doesn't he realize Halloween is over?" David scoffs as we take our seats, and I'm right back to feeling nauseous. No need to ask who he's talking about, but I also can't stop my gaze from shooting over to Sparkles to confirm.

What the actual fuck?

Is he taunting me?

His normal makeup that resembles what the popular girls at our school wear has been replaced with a much darker look. Is he trying to remind me of his Halloween costume? Is he trying to rub it in my face that he isn't a girl and prove that he doesn't look like one so I can't excuse what happened?

My jaw is clenched so tightly I'll be lucky if I don't permanently mess up my teeth. My eye won't stop twitching as I glare at him, unable to look away. His bright eyes are the only thing sparkling today, full of amusement as he holds my gaze. Finally,

I manage to mutter "what a freak," hoping he can read my lips from across the room.

The way his smile grows makes me believe he can, and that he knows every panicked thought running through my mind.

I'm pretty sure I failed the math quiz.

All I know is that I need to stay far away from Kieran and forget all about that stupid party.

19

KIERAN

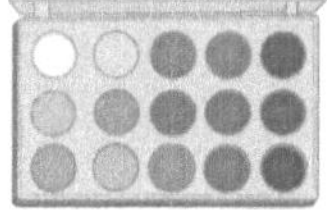

November 2011

"Finally," I mutter to myself as my latest YouTube video uploads. Feels like that took way longer than usual.

My focus has been shit—and yes, a certain baseball-playing asshole is to blame.

It's been over a week and Jace Ryan still hasn't said a single word to me.

Not one.

As much as I hate to admit it, something about being iced out by him feels worse than all the insults combined. I got used to his attention… as twisted as that is. Now the silence is louder than anything he's ever said. He doesn't look at me in math. Doesn't shoulder check me in the hallway or pull me alone into a corner with him. Doesn't call me Sparkles or ask if I got dressed in the dark or mutter something cruel just loud enough for everyone to hear.

I overheard David ask him why he hasn't said anything to me lately, and Jace threw him some excuse about his dad saying he couldn't risk getting in trouble now that he's so close to the MLB draft.

Which would be great. *It should be great.*

Except my brain won't shut up about him. Because it's not that he's ignoring me—it's that he's ignoring me after *that.*

After I got on my knees at a Halloween party, let him tug my hair and use me, and whisper "fuck" in that voice that still runs laps in my head when I try to sleep.

I wish I could say I regret it. That I hated every moment. That I haven't spent the last week trying to think of excuses to do it again. Even the way he was so rough with me only made it hotter. He was my first hookup, and I'll always remember it. Even if he's acting like it didn't happen.

His full-on avoidance makes me feel like I don't even exist. Or maybe he's just so ashamed of what he did with another man… or maybe it was so bad he can't even look at me.

I haven't told anyone, including Danny. I don't even know how I'd admit I sucked off the guy I've been complaining about since we met. Especially after Jace used Danny as a ploy to lock me in the storage shed. Absolutely fucking not.

I don't even know why I did it. Why I said yes. Why I let it happen. Why I wanted it so badly. Why a part of me still wants it to happen again. Or for him to at least acknowledge me.

Every part of me feels desperate for his attention, and I hate it.

God, I hate him. I hate him so much.

This feels like another layer of the fucked-up game he's been playing since I started wearing makeup.

I don't know if the silence means he's planning something worse or if he's waiting for his next opportunity to humiliate me all over again. But it's got me far more on edge than if things had carried on the way they were before Halloween.

I force myself to stop wasting any more mental energy on

Jace and look at my screen as I refresh it and glance at my notifications.

Another hundred subscribers overnight. It's unreal to me how everything on my page is picking up. My "Vampire Smokey Eye Tutorial" is pushing 30k views, and people are messaging me requests for other tutorials they'd like me to do.

I should be riding a high because people are actually enjoying what I'm creating. But instead, I'm sitting here, wondering why the guy who literally came in my mouth a few days ago won't even look at me in math class.

And it's not like I'm dying for his attention. I'm not. But it's still messing with me in that ugly, squirmy way that feels way closer to shame and self-doubt than I'd care to admit.

I've got to stop thinking about him.

Danny walks into my room and flops onto my bed beside me, eating watermelon Sour Patch Kids. "K, you're almost at ten thousand subscribers," he points out excitedly. "What should we do? You have to celebrate!"

I smile at his enthusiasm for me. His support has been awesome.

"No idea, but I think I want to start posting some more of the darker makeup I've been wearing lately. I hope my subscribers like that," I worry out loud.

These past couple of weeks, I've been experimenting with darker looks in public—thicker black eyeliner, matte shadows, deeper tones. The styles are far more noticeable than my usual light and minimal makeup approach, but also feels far more natural. More masculine and more like me.

For a long time, I thought being a makeup creator meant sticking to whatever is trending in magazines or what's popular online for other creators. But playing around with the darker, rocker-inspired makeup—and with how many compliments I got from people at that party who usually don't say anything to me— made me realize I can do whatever I want.

My employee discount has been put to good use lately with my new purchases, and I know this is the direction I want to keep going in.

"They will," Danny says easily, smiling at me.

I click on the latest video I just uploaded and see comments already starting to come in. The more time I spend on my channel, the more comfortable I've become interacting with people, and it's been really fun.

It's easier to feel like I'm not a freak when people are hyping up the things that make me different. The same things that get me shoved into lockers at school are what make strangers hit subscribe.

Here, I'm not too much. The thing that brings me joy doesn't make me a freak.

There are plenty of days at school I wanted to break, but online—in my videos with my little growing crew of internet weirdos who get it—it's so validating. Each positive comment is proof I'm not imagining things, that I'm not the problem. I love knowing I'm helping people embrace themselves as well.

It doesn't fix the way Jace looks through me like I don't exist. But it helps me feel like I'm making a difference, just like they're helping my confidence grow even more.

JACE

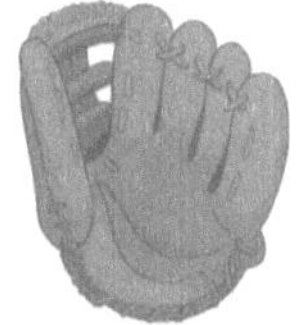

March 2012

*S*parkles cut his hair.

That's the first thing I noticed today and it's all I can think about when I see him in the hallway now. I'm not watching him. I've been doing a phenomenal job of ignoring him since *that night* where *the thing* definitely didn't happen. Haven't said a word to him in months. Haven't so much as looked at him. I dropped the nickname, stopped calling him out on his clothing preferences, and stopped trying to get a rise out of him altogether.

Because if I'm not provoking him, then there's nothing he can let slip.

My encouragement never got him to stop wearing makeup anyway, so I quit giving him the attention he clearly desires. If anything, he leaned more into it with the way he's kept wearing darker makeup since Halloween.

It feels like a taunt to me. I've refused to let myself engage with him even though I want to so badly. He just makes it so hard to ignore him, but I can't risk it. If he ever did start any rumors and they got back to my dad... Nope, there's no use thinking about it. It's been months, and obviously neither of us is going to say anything so I should stop obsessing.

Except now he's gone and cut off half his hair, and I can't seem to look away.

Why is he even still at school when classes ended almost half an hour ago? As far as I know, he isn't in any clubs. He does art classes during the day, but I don't think he sticks around to do anything extra. Did he get detention or something?

I'm still here waiting for our final preseason practice to start in half an hour. It was delayed for some faculty meeting my dad had to go to, and he was not happy about that.

But now that the hallway is empty, I have a clear view of Kieran, standing in front of his locker, looking at something on his phone.

Before, he had the boy-band, skater-kid hairstyle that so many people wore for way too long. Now, he's shaved the sides down in a fade, leaving some length on top, styled like he's on a red carpet and not finishing up a day of high school.

Who does he think he is? And who is he putting in all this effort for anyway? I still haven't figured out if he and Danny are together. They hang out a lot, but other than prom, I haven't noticed any physical contact. He sure didn't act like he was seeing someone when he dropped to his knees for me, but maybe they aren't exclusive. Maybe they wait until no one can see them and fool around. Is he sucking Danny's cock like his life depends on it whenever they're alone?

Fuck.

I don't care!

Kieran can do whatever the hell he wants with whomever he wants, and it's none of my goddamn business. He's certainly never doing anything with me again.

It doesn't matter that, when I tried to hook up with a girl who's in my Spanish class over winter break, I saw Sparkles when I closed my eyes. The fact that his mouth is all I can picture when I jerk off is completely irrelevant.

He finally closes his locker and turns toward the bathrooms when I see it.

There's a huge hickey on his neck.

I don't even realize I've stormed after him until I'm throwing open the bathroom door.

"Who did that to you?" I hear myself demand as soon as we make eye contact. He's washing his hands, and he waits until he's done to bother responding.

"Oh, are you talking to me again?" he deadpans.

I roll my eyes. Is he trying to be cute or something? "Answer the fucking question, Sparkles."

"Did what to me? What have I possibly done to piss you off after *months* of ignoring me, Jace."

I wish I could ignore him, but apparently, I've hit my limit. "Don't play dumb," I scoff. "What, you can show up to school in makeup every day, but you can't be bothered to cover up a giant hickey? Are you trying to show off that someone actually wants you?"

He slowly turns to face me, leaning casually against the sink as a smug smile takes over his face. "What is it, Jace? Are you jealous? You don't want to admit how much you want me, but no one else can be with me either?" he taunts, and I freeze before he spits out, "Fuck off."

How dare he. I'm not fucking jealous. "I'm not gay," I remind him. "I don't want to be with you."

He shakes his head, giving my whole body a once-over as he walks closer to where I'm still standing by the door. "Fine, you might not be gay, but you could be bi or pan."

Did he just say *pan*? Like a pot?

And bi? I didn't even realize guys could be bi. But it's not like I know any queer people other than him and Danny.

I've spent the last few months clinging to the fact that I'm attracted to women. To the fact that *I'm not gay*. Because I'm not. All my other hookups have been with women, and I enjoyed every moment of those. I know I'm not gay.

I can't be gay.

Gay men don't get drafted to the MLB. The word "gay" is a negative descriptor when my friends say it, and it's meant as one of the worst insults when my father uses it.

But the words he's using… I don't really want to think about what they mean.

How they might apply to me and the super fucking annoying thoughts I can't seem to stop having about *him*. Or the even more infuriating way my body seems to react to his. Even now. All because he's pretty in a way boys shouldn't be, and I still don't know what the fuck to do with that.

Hopefully I've managed to maintain my general pissed off expression so he can't see how confused I am.

"Are you really telling me you'd say no if I offered to suck your dick again?" he continues to taunt me. "You're hard right now, Jace," he points out, close enough to me now to reach out and run his finger over the obvious bulge in my sweatpants I somehow got just from talking to him.

Fuck.

This isn't happening. I can't do this again. And at school, where my dad is? Absolutely not.

Except my traitorous dick only seems to be more turned on by the fact we're in a public bathroom at our school right now. And that he skimmed his fingers over my hard dick. And, fuck, that hickey on his neck is mocking me, reminding me while I haven't been able to stop thinking about what happened at that party, Kieran has obviously moved on.

Fuck, was it Danny? Is he his boyfriend?

"Are you cheating on Danny?" I blurt out.

"No" is all he says.

But, fuck, that doesn't really give me an answer. Did Danny

give him that mark and they're just friends with benefits or did some other asshole do it?

Either way, I bet it'd piss off whoever gave him that mark to see a new one put there by someone else. The heat in my gut intensifies at the idea of marking him myself. Any thoughts of labels and what any of this means is easily pushed to the side when I imagine looking over during class and seeing a bruise that *I* left on him. That no one else would know was put there by me.

"Swear you won't tell anyone?" I hear myself asking in a rough tone that betrays how gone I already am.

"Wait, seriously?" Kieran asks, voice no longer cruel. I might even dare to say he sounds hopeful.

I back up a few steps so I'm leaning against the main door, preventing anyone else from coming in.

"You said it yourself, I'm obviously horny," I say, already attempting to excuse what I so desperately want to happen. "Your mouth is as good as any." I shrug, trying to cover up the fact that I'm shaking with anticipation.

I can't believe I'm doing this. Again.

But the thought of walking away right now, when Kieran's offering another chance at his perfect mouth, feels absolutely impossible.

"Are you going to keep ignoring me?" he asks as he steps closer, unzipping the jacket he's wearing and shrugging it off before dropping it on the floor in front of me. "Was my mouth wrapped around you so good that you knew you wouldn't be able to stay away if you talked to me again?" he asks as he lowers himself to kneel on his jacket, pulling my sweats and underwear down with him. My dick is already leaking as he exposes it.

"No," I grit out, reaching out to thread my fingers through what's left of his hair, pulling tight to try to feel like I have any sliver of control in this situation. I might not be the one on my knees, but the way Kieran is taunting me, that smug expression as he reaches out to steady my dick in his hand before he licks up my shaft like it's a damn lollipop, has me reeling. God, normally I hate how fucking pretty he is, but right now, all I can think about is how he's even prettier when he's on his knees for me.

"I've thought about that night a lot," he admits, licking me again. I thrust my hips toward him as I try to pull his head closer to me, but he only chuckles, still in control.

"Were you thinking about me when that guy attacked your neck?" I question.

He lets out a short laugh before finally swallowing my cock. I swear his throat was made to perfectly fit around my dick because he manages to go way deeper than anyone else ever has. It's so warm and wet as he swallows around me, squeezing impossibly tighter.

"Fuuuck," I groan out, using my grip on his hair to hold him in place. I make the mistake of looking down, and our gazes lock. His bright blue eyes might be lined with black, but with his shorter brown hair and the stubble on his strong jaw that looks sharp enough to cut glass, there's no mistaking my cock is in the mouth of another man.

In public. At our school. Where my dad works.

A part of me wants to freak out, to use my hold of Kieran's head to shove him off me, to yell and smash something, because this shouldn't be happening, and it really shouldn't be happening somewhere where we could so easily get caught.

But the part of me that seems to be in control of my movement focuses on keeping him where he is. Focuses on the tear escaping from Sparkle's eye as he chokes and gags on my cock. I finally force myself to pull back just a bit, letting him breathe. As he sucks in a deep breath through his nose, I don't even realize I've used my thumb to wipe the tear before it could fall until I've already done it.

What the fuck.

I'm not being gentle here. That isn't what this is.

"God, you look so happy to be gagging on my dick," I mock, needing to distract him from whatever the fuck that was. "Is that why you didn't cover up that mark on your neck? You want everyone to know what a cockslut you are?"

He moans around me, the vibration nearly sending me over the edge with how absolutely incredible it feels. That moan was straight from a cheesy porno. Did he actually like me calling him a cockslut? I look down again and realize he's fumbling with his other hand to free himself from his pants.

His dick looks painfully hard, and maybe only an inch shorter than mine. The swollen purple tip is leaking precum that he's desperately spreading as he works himself with rough strokes.

My cock is down his throat again, but I'm not the only one enjoying it.

I didn't see his dick at all the first time, and I can't look away now as his hand moves up and down his shaft. I've obviously never seen another hard dick in person before. I wish I could say I hated it. I wish I could say it confirmed everything I've been telling myself for months about how straight I am and the sight of Kieran's erection completely turns me off.

But all I can think about is what it would be like if it was my hand wrapped around him instead.

I don't get a chance to warn him as that thought sends me over the edge. I come down Kieran's throat as the high of my orgasm overwhelms me. The pleasure is so intense that I struggle to stay standing. Kieran gags around me as he swallows, blue eyes watering, and the sight alone sends another wave of heat tearing through me. A second later, his own release hits him just as hard and thick ropes of cum paint the floor. Both of our orgasms seem to go on and on for an endless moment while I stare at him kneeling below me, warring over how incredible this was, again, and how much I can't believe it actually happened.

When I finally recover, I quickly pull up my pants, straightening myself before stepping around him to look in the mirror. I splash some water on my flushed face and try to calm my racing heart.

It'll be fine.

No one will know.

It'll never happen again.

I turn to find Kieran wiping up the evidence of his release with a paper towel, clothes already back in place.

"No one can know," I tell him harshly.

For a moment something raw flashes behind his eyes, almost like he's hurt by my reminder, but he quickly nods his confirmation, and it's gone.

"Don't leave right after me," I warn, this time not waiting for a response before I rush out of the bathroom.

It'll be fine. He didn't tell anyone the first time.

And it will never happen again.

No one will ever know.

KIERAN

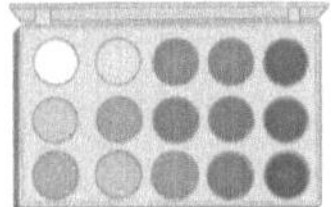

*O*f course, the only time Jace has willingly talked to me since Halloween is because he thought I'd hooked up with someone else... and I went right back to swallowing his cum in the same interaction.

What is wrong with me?

I didn't correct him, either. It isn't a hickey. It's a burn mark from a video Danny and I tried to record before I cut my hair. Danny had never used a curling iron before and he burned my neck on the first attempt. Needless to say, that video never happened.

Jace is confusing. Nothing about his behavior makes sense. It's kind of funny, in a fucked-up way, how he went from obsessively tormenting me to pretending I didn't exist. He gave me the cold shoulder for months, refusing to acknowledge me, and then he gets... jealous? He lost it at the thought of someone else touching me while simultaneously getting hard as steel.

It's confusing. He's confusing.

I've had a growing suspicion after what happened at the Halloween party that Jace's previous attention might have been to cover up his attraction toward me. Or maybe he didn't even realize why he was doing it, and the makeup was an easy scapegoat. Even though he didn't touch me during either blowjob, I can't shake Liv's comment that Jace is obsessed with me. For the first time, I'm starting to think she might be right.

"Earth to Kieran," my coworker calls, and I realize I've been lost in thought about Jace. Again.

He's been consuming every thought I've had, and no matter how much I tell myself to move on, I can't stop my brain from defaulting back to thinking about him.

"Sorry, what's up?" I ask Lilly, who I'm sure has been saying my name for a minute based on how annoyed she seems.

"You were just so spaced out. You good?"

"Yeah, my bad, just distracted."

"Mm-hmm." She nods, but I know I'm not fooling anyone. "You've only got, like, thirty minutes left in your shift, so can you go out on the floor and help customers?"

"Yep, of course." I nod and close the half-unpacked box in front of me and push it off to the side, knowing I absolutely butchered the organization of whatever shipment I was supposed to be working on.

As I step out into the store, I slip into my customer service autopilot. Smile, nod, be helpful, and don't think about Jace Ryan's moans or his weird shift in behavior. Don't think about the way he tasted or the ridiculous fact that I still want him, even though I know I shouldn't.

Nope, I don't have time for that.

Instead, I help a mom pick out a birthday gift for her daughter, then show a teenage girl where the makeup brush sets are stocked. The last fifteen minutes crawl by, and I swear I check the clock at least seven times before I'm finally released. I head to the back, grab my bag from my locker, and pull my hoodie on as I leave the store. With how distracted I've been today, it's a miracle I remembered my stuff at all. I can't wait to get home and shift my focus to this week's video content and forget all about the asshole jock with a nice dick and even nicer butt, not that I'd ever be touching that. I'm sure that'd send him into a complete meltdown.

I turn toward the parking garage, and any hopes of a chill evening vanish because Jace is sitting on a bench, eyes already locked on me.

Of course he's somehow here. I can't escape him. He makes that impossible.

I debate ignoring him entirely, showing him how it feels, but decide against it, walking right up to him instead. I want to know why he's here. If it's for me.

"What do you want?"

"I thought you'd be at work," he says, standing up. "Didn't know when your shift ended."

"So you sat here, waiting for me."

It's not a question, but he answers anyway.

"Yeah."

I let out a humorless laugh and glance around to make sure no one is nearby, especially no one we know. "You've got a weird way of showing interest, you know that?"

"Shut up. I'm not—" He cuts himself off, then huffs as he drags a hand through his curly brown hair. "I just wanted to talk."

"Then talk, Jace. I want to go home."

There's a pause long enough to make me think maybe he's changed his mind.

Then, like he didn't just spend five months pretending I didn't exist until I blew him the other day, he says, "Can you actually drive me home? I need a ride."

I blink at him in complete disbelief. "You're kidding."

"Please? I need to talk to you."

I roll my eyes. "Fine, let's go," I cave, motioning toward the mall exit and not stopping to see if he's following.

We walk in silence, and he seems to hang back a few steps behind me. When we get to the car, I don't say a word as I unlock it and slide into the driver's seat, feeling more nervous than I'd like to admit about this "talk."

When I pull out of the garage, he keeps glancing at me, and I ignore every single one. If he wants to talk, he can open his mouth and speak.

"So... that day in the bathroom," he says finally, voice low like someone could overhear, even though it's just us in the car. "At school," he clarifies, because there have now been two bathroom hookups. *So classy.* "The next day, I had two home runs, got multiple people out who were trying to steal home, and even tagged someone out."

"None of that means anything to me," I remind him as I continue to focus on the road.

"It was one of the best games I've ever had."

"Congratulations?" I say, like it's a question. I have no idea where he's going with any of this.

"Thanks," he says automatically, and I almost laugh at how clueless he can be, but he keeps talking. "But then yesterday's game was shit. I couldn't focus, and I fucked up, like, three different plays. I barely made it on base."

"Jace, I don't know why you think I would care about any of that."

"Because what we did in the bathroom obviously had a positive effect on my game. Sports superstitions are real. I need you to blow me again so I have a good game tomorrow," he says, in a completely serious tone.

I glance at him again while I'm stopped at a red light. There's a part of me that loves seeing him look so distraught, even if another part of me thinks his pinched eyebrows and big, brown, pleading puppy-dog eyes are kind of cute.

His request finally registers, and this time I do laugh. I might have been thinking about what we did more than I'd care to admit, but I also need to have some self-respect. "This is the first somewhat normal conversation we've ever had. You've been a complete asshole to me for over a year. What we did was fun, I'm not denying that, but it was also my decision. You can't just demand I get you off. I was the one doing all the work. I'm not going to keep hooking up with someone who won't even touch me."

Jace looks devastated. His expression shifts, eyes losing focus as he looks out the window like he's so deep in thought that he's unaware of his surroundings. I return my focus to the road as the light turns green, and he's quiet for another minute.

"Okay," he finally says.

"It's for the best," I agree, adding, "Superstitions aren't real anyway."

"Yes, they are," he insists. "And I meant okay, I'll touch you." My mouth falls open in disbelief.

I'd been driving in the general direction of my house, waiting for Jace to correct me with where he lived, but I decide to pull over. There's an office building that looks like it's closed for the day just ahead, so I park in the back of the lot next to a big tree, hoping we don't look too suspicious. I need to focus on this conversation.

"You'll touch me?" I repeat back. "I need you to be more specific than that." I'm not about to suck his dick again if he thinks holding my hand is going to be enough.

"What do you want me to say?" he huffs out, crossing his muscular arms over his broad chest.

I take a moment to consider what I think he might agree to. I'm not opposed to sucking his cock again—it really was hot—I just hated feeling like it was so one-sided afterward. But do I actually think Jace is about to put my dick in his mouth? Probably not.

"A handjob," I offer, proud of how confident I manage to sound. "I'll blow you, but only after you've made me come." His Adam's apple bobs as he swallows, gaze stuck on my crotch where my cock has started to thicken at the possibility that this might actually happen. "You don't have to," I remind him. "I can drive you home, and we can pretend like none of this ever happened. But if you're that worried about your game tomorrow, you know what to do, and your dick looks pretty eager already." I nod to his obvious erection, biting my tongue so I don't add "as usual." He seems to always be hard when it's just the two of us, his loose grey sweats hiding nothing.

"Fine. Get in the backseat," he demands, already moving to open his door.

"Wait, here?"

"Do you have a better idea? The trees are blocking the main street, and it doesn't look like anyone else is around," he points out.

I shrug and open my door, moving to the back before Jace can change his mind. As much as I didn't want to fold to his demand before, I feel like I've taken control with my offer. I love the sense of power I feel, knowing he's going to get me off first. I don't bother to be shy and pull down my pants and underwear as soon as I've closed the door to the back seat.

I jump when my door opens again. "Scoot over," Jace says harshly, following me into the car behind the driver's seat. He reaches under the seat in front of us to move it all the way forward as I awkwardly scoot over to the other side.

"What was wrong with this side?" I demand.

"I'm right-handed," he says simply. I arch a brow, unsure what that has to do with anything. "I'm not going to use my non-dominant hand for a handjob," he explains, in a tone like it should have been obvious.

Oh. That was surprisingly well thought out.

"Alright, Ryan, let's see if you can actually get another guy off," I prompt, attempting to project confidence even though I'm kind of freaking out. This whole night has been so unexpected.

"Don't call me that," he says seriously, looking right at me.

"Ryan?" I check. "Isn't the dude-bro-last-name thing what all your jock friends call you?"

"Yeah, but just… can *you* not?" he asks. I'm not sure why that seems so important to him, but I nod anyway.

"Cool," he responds quietly, then he continues talking, almost to himself. "This is fine. No big deal, really. Do it all the time to myself. And then I get a lucky blowjob. Fair trade."

"I'm not sure if I should interrupt this little pep talk, but the longer you wait the less hard I'm getting," I point out.

He huffs out a deep breath before spitting in his hand and confidently scooting so he's right next to me, our thighs touching as he reaches out to wrap his hand around my cock.

I'm not sure what I was expecting exactly, maybe for it to feel the exact same as if I was jerking off, but this is a completely new experience. I've never had anyone else touch my dick before, and it feels incredible.

Even though Jace has also never done this before, his strokes are confident as he moves his large, calloused hand up and down my shaft, using more pressure than I'm used to, but the foreign sensation only makes everything so much better.

He leans over me for a moment, and I swear my heart stops beating as Jace spits right onto the tip of my dick.

Oh fuck. Why was that so hot?

The added lubrication increases the pleasure, and a deep moan escapes from my throat as I lean back, fully resting against the backseat, back slightly arched. "You like that?" he asks, turning his attention to my face.

I think he meant the question as a taunt, but his tone betrays his genuine curiosity.

"Obviously," I respond, keeping my eyes locked on his hand, working my cock, and how the tip disappears and pushes back through his fist each time he changes direction. It's so hot. Way better than any porn I've seen.

"God, you're such a slut," he murmurs. "The way you're thrusting up into my hand like you can't get enough." The words may not be kind, but there's no malice in his comment. If I didn't know any better, I might even mistake his tone for fondness.

"You're the one who was so desperate for my mouth that you stalked me at my job," I remind him, voice coming out breathier than I've ever heard it.

He doesn't respond, but increases the speed of his movement, wiping his thumb over the tip as he twists his wrist then adds more spit. Every stroke feels so good, and I know I won't last much longer, already on the edge of bliss. "I'm going to—" I start to warn, but it's too late. That moment where everything feels indescribable slams into me, and my cock jerks in Jace's grip, shooting my release all over his fist. The sight only seems to draw out my orgasm as I continue to come, surprised that he hasn't pulled away.

Eventually, when everything becomes overly sensitive, I push him off me and lean over to grab napkins out of the center console of my car, handing some to Jace so he can clean up.

That was… amazing.

I don't know how I'm supposed to go back to being happy with my own hand after experiencing his. I was lucky he even agreed to this one time; I highly doubt it'll be happening again.

Neither of us say anything as we quickly clean up, and when Jace is done, he frees his straining erection. A deal's a deal, so I move to try to kneel on the floor in front of him. Even with the seats moved up all the way, I don't really fit, so he ends up leaning back at an angle to prop his bent right leg up on the backseat, turning his body slightly, giving me just enough space between his legs from the side.

He's already leaking, and I use one hand to grip the base of his shaft before licking up his cock to lap at the tip like it's candy. "Fuuuck, Sparkles," he groans, lifting his hips toward my mouth. I don't know if it's because I've already reclaimed the name with my YouTube channel or if it's the reverent tone he uses, but I don't hate his nickname for me like I used to.

I attempt to relax my throat and focus on breathing through my nose to try to take him as deeply as I can. I use a hand to work what I can't fit, fascinated with how different his dick feels in my hand than my own would.

"Oh fuck, I'm gonna—"

Before I can even try to show off with my tongue or any of the other skills I'd like to think I have, Jace is shooting down my throat, a deep moan escaping from him as his hips jerk.

That certainly didn't last long. Maybe someone enjoyed giving their first handjob as much as I enjoyed receiving it.

I doubt Jace would ever admit to that though.

I do a slightly better job this time of swallowing, but I still use the napkin to clean up the dribbles of his cum that spilled down my chin.

When we're both settled back into our clothes, we silently return to the front seats and sit here without speaking for a moment. I feel like we should probably talk about what we did. I know Jace has never been with a guy before, and for all I know, this is all completely new to him. But I also don't know where to even begin, and I'm a little worried he's about to freak out, so I don't want to set him off.

"So where do you live?" I finally ask, pulling out of the spot and moving back toward the main road.

"You can just drive to your neighborhood. I'll walk home from the entrance."

Ah yes, what a lovely reminder that despite what just happened between us, Jace is still very against being seen with me in public. He probably also doesn't want me to know exactly where he lives as if I'd ever do anything with that information.

When we get to my neighborhood, I pull over, and Jace quickly moves to get out. "Have a good game," I say awkwardly before he can shut the door.

He nods briefly in acknowledgment, which I guess is better than ignoring me like I'm sure he'll do at school tomorrow.

JACE

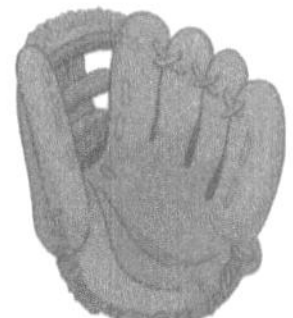

$\mathcal{I}$ run a hand through my hair as I stare at myself in the mirror after my postgame shower, watching a droplet of water journey down my bare chest. It collides with the towel wrapped around my waist before it could come into contact with my dick, but it's like the water wanted to draw my attention to the traitorous appendage.

A grand slam in the third. A home run again in the sixth that brought in two more runs. Not a single runner on the other team stole a base.

Another amazing game… after Kieran blew me.

He barely even did anything, but his mouth wrapped around my dick was enough to send me over the edge with how turned on I was after getting him off.

I'd expected to hate it. I had approached the handjob as a transaction, a trade to get me the blowjob I was after.

But hate isn't the word that comes to mind when I remember the feel of him in my hand.

I think it might be time to admit, to myself at least, that I'm attracted to Kieran. That it wasn't some fluke because of his makeup or the situation.

It's just… him.

I'd gotten David to drop me off at the mall after practice, telling my dad I needed to get a new shirt to wear for Easter this weekend. He'd warned me not to get any bright colors that would make me "look gay," and then I'd sat on that bench for hours obsessing over if I might *actually* be gay. I'd made every excuse to myself about how I was doing it for the win, how it wasn't gay if he was the one blowing me—it's not like I'd had his dick in my mouth.

After thinking about Kieran and his mouth for so long, I'd gotten myself so worked up that I could barely walk to his car with how uncomfortably hard I'd gotten at the sight of him. And then when he almost turned me down, I learned just how desperate I was when I willingly agreed to touch his dick. Not just to touch it, but to make him come.

And it was so fucking hot.

I can't keep pretending like it means nothing if all I've been able to think about was the way his release coated my hand. How I wished I had licked it off instead of using that napkin so I could know what he tastes like.

So, am I bi?

The question has been driving me out of my mind since the car hookup.

"Hey, David," I call out as I head back into the main area of the locker room. "Could you drive me to the mall again?"

We have another game tomorrow, and I need to see Kieran again today. Maybe he can help me figure out what's going on with me and keep up my streak.

"Sure, man," he responds easily. "Did you forget something yesterday?"

"Yeah, but I'll catch a ride home if you drop me off." I try to say it as casually as I can.

"Nah, I'll stay and hang out," David says, looking at me funny. Why does he want to come with me?

"It's really okay, man. Just gotta grab something quick," I insist.

"Exactly, shouldn't be long, so it's no big deal. I feel like we haven't hung out much lately. Besides, who else will bring you home?" he pushes.

Am I paranoid or is he suspicious? Does he know something? How would he know? And if he did, would he say something? He would, right? He's got too big of a mouth to keep it shut.

"My mom's meeting me there," I lie through my teeth. His eye twitches, and I keep burying myself deeper in the hole. "She hated what I got yesterday, so she wants to help me pick something out she approves of. I figured you'd drop me off on your way home, so I said I'd meet her there."

"Whatever you say, man," David concedes. Finally.

"Be right back, I'm just gonna tell my dad we're taking off," I say, hoping to god David doesn't follow me.

"Alright, I'll meet you at my car."

I smile and nod, waiting until he's out of sight to heave out a sigh in relief before I go tell my next lie.

My dad is in his office, reviewing stats, when I tell him David and I need to work on our psych project tonight. He glares at me, but when I start rambling about the different parts of the brain, he waves me off, warning me to be home before curfew.

I'M WAITING on the same bench when Kieran approaches me, scowling once again. The dark makeup around his eyes actually makes him look pretty intimidating with the artsy-slash-emo-slash-rock-band style, but I won't be deterred from why I'm here.

"I need another ride home," I say with a shrug, offering him a lopsided grin.

"Is that what you're calling it? I'm not your chauffeur." He huffs, turning toward the parking garage, so I grab my bag and jump up to follow.

"I need to talk to you," I insist once again, and he rolls his eyes, but he doesn't complain any further when I round his car to open the passenger's side door. He's quiet as he starts driving, and I know I only have so much time to start this conversation, but I'm even more nervous to bring this up than I was to ask about a good luck blowjob.

It's now or never though, so I force myself to go for it, blurting out the thing I've been obsessing over. "You said I might be bi. Or pan."

He keeps his eyes on the road as he answers. "Yeah."

I nod, unsure what to say next. I fold my arms over my chest, shrinking into the seat as much as I can. This is so uncomfortable to talk about. "What's the difference?" I ask quietly.

He glances over at me. Probably confirming I'm asking seriously and not looking for things to give him a hard time about. "You could've Googled it."

"Fuck that," I respond quickly. "I can't risk my dad seeing it in the search history. We only have a shared computer."

He tilts his head considering that for a moment. "So, instead, you waited for the guy who's now blown you in multiple bathrooms and the back seat of a car to finish his shift and hoped he'd drive you home *again* and define your sexuality for you?" he deadpans.

I groan. "God, don't say it like that."

"Which part? The blowjobs or your sexuality?"

"Kieran." I don't think I've ever called him by his actual name before, and it seems to surprise him.

"Okay, okay." He's clearly biting back a grin, but he finally answers. "I'm sure other people might define it a little differently, but my understanding is that bisexual means you're attracted to more than one gender. Pansexual means you're attracted to people regardless of gender. The nuance kinda depends on the person, but that's the gist." I'm not sure how to respond to that, and he must see my trying to work it out in my head because he adds, "And no, they're not the same thing."

I stare out the window, trying to think about what's happened between us, and what that means for me. I've never been attracted to another guy before. But I also didn't realize I could be attracted to Kieran until we were alone in that bathroom on Halloween. It was like all the tension since the first day of junior year leading up to that night, and all the taunting and heated arguments, had come crashing into a violent realization that I was drawn to him. Not because he wore makeup and that made him different from other guys in our school, but because I was attracted to *him*.

"But you're gay, right?" I ask, still trying to wrap my head around what label I must be if all I've been able to think about is hooking up with him again.

"Actually, no," he answers, surprising me. I turn more fully to face him as he continues, eyes still on the road. "I used to think I was, because I'd been primarily attracted to guys, and I thought that made me gay. But as time has gone on, and I've learned more about myself and the different labels, I've realized I'm pan."

"So, you'd date a girl?" I ask, unable to hide my shock, but genuinely wanting to understand him.

"If I liked her, yeah," he says simply. "I'm drawn to people's vibe, and I'm definitely drawn toward masculinity, but it's not about gender for me. It's about the person. I've mostly liked guys, but that doesn't mean I wouldn't date a girl if the connection was there."

I realize I'm gnawing on the edge of my thumbnail as I consider if that means he's met a girl he's into. Could it have been a girl who gave him that hickey? "But you don't? Like a girl?" I can't stop myself from asking. I need to know.

"Not right now, no," he says, glancing at me. "Why? You planning to introduce me to your cousin or something?"

"No," I say quickly, scrunching up my face. "Gross." I don't want to picture Kieran with anyone else, let alone someone related to me.

"Relax. I'm not interested. I have no plans to date anyone until I go to college. Maybe I'll find someone in New York City."

He rolls to a stop at a red light and glances over again, continuing. "So, what is this anyway? You've been a huge fucking asshole to me for over a year. Are you implying that was all because you didn't know how to handle being attracted to another guy? And now you're finally open to accepting that you're not straight?"

"I don't know," I admit.

"Well, just because we hooked up a couple of times doesn't mean we're friends." He pauses, and I'm not sure how I'm supposed to respond to that. Obviously we aren't friends. "But I'm a much nicer person than you are, so if you want help figuring out your sexuality, we're gonna have to talk about the parts you want to stay hidden."

I'm quiet for a long moment, trying to decide how to explain everything I've been thinking since Halloween. Finally, I blurt, "I think about that night. A lot."

A slow grin curls at the corner of his mouth, but he keeps his eyes on the road. "Yeah?"

"You don't have to be a dick about it."

"I'm not. I'm flattered." His tone is teasing but isn't cruel, and I let out a groan. "What's wrong?" he asks.

I shift again. "I can't stop thinking about it. What we did."

"You literally just said that."

"Yeah, well"—I look over at him, waving a hand in his direction—"you seem totally fine. Like you don't care, and it has had no effect on your life."

"Should I be spiraling?" he asks dryly. "You're the one who spent five months pretending I didn't exist after I sucked your dick, not me."

I wince. "I... I didn't know what to do," I admit. "I've never been into another guy. I didn't even think I was attracted to you until Halloween when we were in that bathroom, and I was trying to tell myself it was a one-time thing. A fluke." Apparently now that I've started admitting the truth, I can't stop. "I was terrified if I'd spoken to you, you'd say something, and if my dad had found out..." I trail off, shuddering at the thought before I continue. "But then it happened again, and I haven't been able to stop thinking about it. This has never happened with any of the girls I've hooked up with. What's wrong with me?"

"From the one and only, very brief, real conversation we've had, I'd say you have daddy issues." He laughs.

"*Kieran*," I whine his name again, and he smiles, looking all kinds of smug.

"Fine. Nothing is wrong with you for being attracted to me, Jace."

"Then why does it feel like there is?" I can't help sounding frustrated, hopefully he won't be too offended, but it's not making sense to me. "Why does it feel like I'm going to lose my shit every time I think about you?"

He shrugs. "Because you want me, and you hate that you want me," he answers, easily, like it's all so simple.

If I'm being honest, I've thought that very same thing, but I've been trying to ignore just how much I want him. "Fuck," I groan, covering my eyes with my palms as I lean my head back against the headrest.

"I don't know for sure, but it sounds like you were taught that liking another guy is wrong. That's not true, Jace."

We're well past the office we stopped at yesterday, but I feel the car roll to a stop and realize Kieran's parked next to a nature trail a bit closer to our houses. I turn to look at him, and he's leaning in toward me. What the fuck is he doing? I'm frozen in place as he continues to inch closer and closer to me. I gasp a short breath when he's mere inches from my face. Oh god, is he going to—?

"Relax, I'm not gonna kiss you, if that's what you're hoping for," he murmurs with a smirk. "Not after the way you've treated me."

I swallow, unsure if I'm relieved or maybe disappointed. He does have plump, pink lips that my eyes always seem to be drawn to. "I wasn't—"

"But I will let *you* suck *me* off," he goads me. "If you ask nicely."

My breath shudders out of me. "You're such a dick."

"Yeah," he agrees, leaning back, arms crossing. "But so are you. And I'm not the only one who's hard right now, am I?"

I curse under my breath, shifting again, trying to adjust myself.

"You want it?" he asks quietly. "Then you have to admit it."

I can't believe this is happening. The handjob was one thing, but to actually put his dick inside my mouth? There are so many emotions flashing through me; I'm furious and humiliated, but more than anything, I can't deny how turned on I am by the thought.

Could I actually do it though?

For so long, I've equated being gay, being attracted to another man, as a negative thing. I think back on all the times my dad has used "gay" as an insult. Having a bad game? Not running fast enough? Wearing something that was a little too bright, hell even getting too excited about something, I was told to "quit acting gay."

Now I'm here, seriously debating sucking Kieran's cock because I liked what we did last time.

And the world hasn't ended.

We've hooked up three times now, and I'm still the same person.

Being around Kieran makes me feel more free.

But it's one thing to logically acknowledge that inside my head and it's a whole other to work past the fear of embracing the fact that I *want* to do this.

That's all that should really matter though, right?

Labels and what I grew up believing don't matter in this moment because I *want* to do this.

I swallow down my fear, and take in a final deep breath before I admit the truth. "I want it."

I don't give myself any time to second-guess my decision. I open the car door, grab my bag, and start down the path, trusting that Kieran will follow. This path isn't far from my house. I've been on it before, and the sun has almost set, so I know it'll likely be empty. Still, when I hear Kieran's footsteps just behind me, I veer off from the worn path, finding a more secluded, covered area. When I'm confident we won't be seen even if someone walks past, I spin to face him. He stops and leans casually against a thick tree, arms crossed, and I finally admit to myself how hot he is.

I've always been drawn to Kieran's appearance. I blamed the makeup, claiming he was trying to get attention. But maybe, this whole time, I've just thought he was beautiful, and I didn't know how to apply that word to a man.

I don't know about the whole "attracted to someone *regardless* of gender" thing he said applies to him, but in this moment, I think I have to accept I'm attracted to more than one gender.

Because I want him.

With his sharp jaw that occasionally has a little stubble, his smooth skin that's always glowing, and his blue eyes that constantly draw me in with the way they stand out against his dark eyebrows and hair, he's… fuck. He's… undoubtedly pretty.

And I want those pretty lips wrapped around my cock, just like I think I actually really want to taste him.

"So did you lead me out here to kill me?" he asks skeptically. "Or are you actually going to blow me?"

"I have another game tomorrow," I say in answer as I walk even closer until I'm right in front of him. I waste no time as I drop to my knees in front of him as he works to unbutton and pull down his jeans.

"Ah, anything for the win, right? My magical mouth is going to make you a better player?" he taunts. I think we both know that's not why I'm actually doing this, but I'm grateful that he isn't making me admit to more.

When his hard cock is finally freed, I stare at it for a moment. It seems so much larger from down here, right in front of my face, than it did in my hand. I study it, the slight curve, the flushed tip. It might seem bigger than I remember, but I've gotten this far, and I still want to do this.

My mouth is watering as I think about what it'll feel like to trace the veins with my tongue. I want to wrap my lips around the head and suck, see what noises I can draw out of him. I want to taste his cum before I swallow it down, to go to sleep tonight knowing his load is inside me.

All these thoughts will probably freak me out again later, but for now, with my cock aching for attention, I decide I'm over just wanting this.

I'm doing it.

I reach out to grip the base like he did when our positions were reversed. The weight of him in my hand is just as intoxicating as it was in his car the other day. Knowing what it must feel like as I rub my thumb over one of the veins gives me such a rush.

Tentatively, I lick up his shaft like I remember him doing to me before swirling my tongue around the head of his cock, a little surprised by the salty taste of what's already leaking from the tip. It's not my new favorite flavor or anything, but I don't hate it.

So far so good, but I still need to actually suck his dick.

I can totally do this.

I take a deep breath and lean in, wrapping my lips around his cock. Despite how hard he is, the smooth sensation against my tongue is kind of fascinating as I suck more of him into my mouth.

"Oh my god," he groans, shifting his hips forward. That sounded like a happy noise, so I must be doing something right. I try to use my tongue as I attempt to take him even deeper, but I must be a little too ambitious because I end up gagging.

I pull off him for a moment to catch my breath, and when I recover, I look up at him. "What the fuck, how did you go so deep?"

He shrugs. "I relax my throat and breathe through my nose."

I wonder how many dicks he had to suck to figure that out. That thought only pisses me off though. If I'm doing this, which I obviously am, I don't want to be bad at it. I don't want him to be comparing me to whoever was before me. I spit into my hand and move it back to work what I can't fit into my mouth. I suck him down with renewed determination. I want this to drive him as wild as he's been driving me.

Focusing on keeping my throat relaxed, and breathing through my nose when I can, I suck and lick and twist my hand up and down his cock. My knees are digging into the rocks and branches, but the pain is probably the only thing keeping me focused enough to be present and in the moment.

My cock is aching, begging for friction as I pour all my attention into him. This whole experience is turning me on more than I ever would've thought possible, and as tempted as I am to pull myself out, I know my turn will come. I need to focus on him first.

"Fuck," he says sounding breathless. "You think I'm a cockslut? You should see how hot you look down there, muscles flexing, expression all blissed out as you swallow my dick, hotshot."

I don't want to pull away to scold him, so I reach up to slap the side of his ass in warning. His cock jerks in my mouth, and another deep moan escapes from his throat.

Guess my little cockslut likes spanking.

What the fuck? Not mine. He's not my anything.

"Keep going," he demands when I slow my movements, freaked out by that errant thought. "I'm right there."

Should I actually swallow? Pull off him and finish with just my hand? Kieran swallowed, and even when he didn't catch it all, it was super hot to watch my release drip from his mouth.

Before I can panic and pull away, his cock is thickening, jerking again as warm cum fills my mouth. I only gag a little and manage to swallow almost all of it.

I stand up and brush the dirt from my pants. Kieran has his eyes closed and his head rested back against the tree while he appears to be catching his breath. He looks like he needs a minute to recover, but I don't think I have that long.

There's an embarrassing wet patch on my sweats from how much I'm already leaking. "My turn," I announce. I don't wait for him to tuck himself away, just put my hands on his shoulders and push him down to his knees. He doesn't protest, and when he opens his eyes, there's obvious hunger in them as he pushes my pants down to free my erection.

I stretch an arm over him to lean against the tree, gripping his hair with the other as he swallows my cock. "Damn, Sparkles, how is your mouth somehow better each time?" He hums around me, and as much as I would love to draw this out, I know I won't last long. I try to think about anything other than how amazing Kieran is at this, but it's no use. The pleasure builds at the base of my spine, and my balls are tight, ready to give in to that feeling of euphoria that I know is coming.

Kieran moves his free hand to my balls, and I'm done for,

shooting down his throat as my orgasm crashes into me. I think I black out for a second as I enjoy one of the best orgasms I've ever had.

When I come down from my high, Kieran is standing again, still between me and the tree with my outstretched arm over his shoulder. For an insane second, I can't pull my gaze away from his wet lips, and I wonder what it would be like to kiss him; to taste us together.

But I shake that image from my mind, stepping back to tuck myself away. That isn't what this is. I guess I don't know exactly what's going on between us, just that I'm glad it keeps happening. These secret exchanges have been so much better than any other hookups I've had, even if I stress about anyone else finding out.

We stand here for another moment in silence, staring at each other, before he turns back to the path. I follow, grabbing my bag, grateful I have a change of clothes and some mouthwash in there so I don't need to walk into my house with a cum stain on my pants and smelling like god knows what.

"Need a ride?" he checks when we make it back to his car, and I don't make a move to get in.

"Nah, I can walk from here," I confirm.

"Have a good game tomorrow," he says slowly.

Right. I need to focus on things other than hooking up with Kieran. I still have baseball, and I really need to get home. "Thanks," I finally mutter. It doesn't feel like enough, but I have no idea what else to say.

KIERAN

*H*e isn't coming.

And I have no idea why that thought makes me so upset. I should just leave.

I'm leaning against a tree in what I think is the same spot in the woods as last time, feeling like a complete idiot. This is probably some sort of setup. Another way for Jace Ryan to humiliate me.

Walking into class yesterday, he dropped a folded piece of paper into my open backpack. I knew better than to open it then, so I waited until I got to my car after school. The outside had a poorly drawn tree on it, and the sheet itself was a printed schedule of the baseball team's games.

There was no time. No handwritten note stating we should meet again.

A part of me hopes that I *was* wrong, and that Jace and I aren't already so on the same page that I understood his cryptic message like I'd thought.

He used the excuse that our previous hookups were for good luck, so I assumed he wanted a repeat and that the tree meant to meet here before his next game. *Rather bold to include the whole season.*

So here I am, after my shift just like the last two times. But Jace is nowhere to be seen. Whatever, it's probably for the best. Just because the other hookups have been so hot doesn't mean we should keep—

"Hey." His deep voice interrupts my thoughts, and the relief I feel is embarrassing. *I'm just horny.* It doesn't mean anything. "I wasn't sure if you'd show up," he adds, sounding nervous.

The vindictive part of me loves it, knowing I'm the one making him nervous after everything he's done to me, and revels in the memory of how eager he looked on his knees for me. But there's another part, a much softer part, that's such a sucker for his warm brown eyes, and remembers how vulnerable he was asking me about his sexuality.

"Well, I like getting my dick sucked as much as any other guy," I say dismissively, trying not to reveal my own nerves. Today is different. We both chose to come here, to meet—there was no cornering in a bathroom or sexually charged conversation in a small car. We both showed up on our own, planning to blow each other.

"Should I, uh… Do you want me to go first again?" he asks, stumbling over the question.

I bite my lip in an attempt to hide how cute I think him fumbling around is. "Yeah, you can suck my dick first," I say plainly, loving the way his eyes flare and his cheeks heat at my words.

It's just as satisfying seeing him on his knees below me as it was the first time.

The orgasm is amazing.

And I have to admit, at least to myself, that I enjoy being on my knees for him just as much.

Early April

EVERY TIME JACE sucks my dick, he gets even better.

I have his schedule memorized at this point, and without fail, on the nights before his games, we both end up in this same spot and take turns dropping to our knees.

He swears it's helping him win games, and I don't care enough to fact-check him because he's actually become… nicer.

Not in public. There, he still ignores me completely.

But when we're here alone?

He's different.

There's still no kissing or texting or any interaction at all outside of these woods, but when we're here, it's like the outside world doesn't exist.

We're both fully dressed again after swapping orgasms. I've honestly lost track of how many times it's been. But, the last few, we haven't been in the same hurry as we were during our early exchanges. He's standing across from me now, still leaning against our tree, but he's looking at me when he'd normally be turning back toward the path.

"So I've, uh, I still haven't seen you and Liv together this year. It seemed like she really wanted to be your friend, though, when we were dating," he finally mutters.

Somehow I manage to hold in my laugh. Seriously? He's going to bring up his ex-girlfriend after that?

"What, are my blowjob skills lacking?" I ask dramatically. "Ready to run back to your ex?"

His eyes are comically wide as he hurries to respond. "What? No. No, I never said that."

"I'm just teasing." I brush him off with a grin. "Yeah, she's tried talking to me. But we still aren't friends."

"Oh. I just thought that maybe since you and I have been…" he trails off.

Well, shit.

I hadn't really considered that I ended my friendship with Liv because she wanted to date him, and now I'm… Well, we're sure as hell not dating, but we've been consistently hooking up. *Am I a hypocrite?*

"You're friends with Danny, though, right?" he asks, distracting me from that concerning realization.

"Yeah."

"But you guys aren't… more than friends, right?"

I scoff. "No. We did kiss once, but it only confirmed that there was nothing more between us," I admit, not really sure why I told him all that, but he visibly relaxes at my answer.

"You kissed him? Does he like you then?" he asks curiously.

"No, but it's kind of fun for me to see you all jealous like this," I joke.

"I'm not jealous!" he huffs, crossing his arms "I just… Does he know about…?" He motions between us.

I laugh. "Does Danny know that, a few times a week, I'm meeting up to exchange good luck blowjobs with the person who drove us to become friends after pretending to be him to lock me in a storage shed? No. I'm not an idiot. And I wouldn't out you. I know you're not about to admit what we're doing to anyone."

His shoulders sag in relief as he lets out a big breath, but his expression still looks… concerned, maybe. "Shit, I didn't think you would. That's not why I asked." He rubs his hands over his eyes for a moment. "I wanted to say that I hope you and Liv work it out, but I'm glad you have a friend."

My jaw falls open as I blink at him. It wasn't an apology. But it was… something. An acknowledgement of guilt from a man I didn't think was capable of the emotion. I have to force myself to school my expression before I agree. "Yeah, I'm happy to have Danny in my life."

End of April

SINCE THEN, we've lingered every time.

Nothing too deep. But today he's hesitating again, biting his thumbnail like he does when he's nervous, and he looks like he might want to say more.

So, I wait for him to say what's on his mind.

"Your, uh, your parents seemed cool that one time at the Mexican restaurant. And Liv talked highly of them. Are they always like that?"

I chuckle at how nervous he seems to ask such an easy question. "Yeah, they're the best. Why?"

"I'm just… glad that you have that," he responds with a shrug. And, like I've come to learn he does when things get a little too real, he turns to leave.

Early May

AFTER OUR HOOKUP, I'm ready with my question. "What are your parents like? Everyone seems to love Coach Ryan."

He visibly freezes, his whole body tensing.

Shit. I wasn't expecting that. He's made some comments that've confirmed my suspicions that Jace has some problems with his dad, but that reaction was far more than I expected.

He shifts his weight, glancing around the clearing before he finally scoffs. "My dad's really great at playing his role."

"Of coach?" I clarify, not understanding why he sounds so annoyed by that.

"Of the town's 'golden boy,' " he says in a louder tone. "People idolize him because he was *almost* successful, but they have no idea what he's really like."

I suck in a sharp breath at his change in demeanor, but remind myself that I'm not the one he's mad at. "What's he really like?" I ask softly, hoping he'll talk to me.

He shakes his head dismissively. "Let's just say all the yelling he does on the field that people so easily dismiss as his 'coaching style,' all the slurs and insults he uses, sound like praise compared to what he's like at home."

Fuck. "I'm so sorry, Jace, no one deserves—"

"It's fine, we're not here to talk about that," he interrupts as he picks up his bag. "I've got to go anyway."

Early May

I SPEND the next two days kicking myself for putting my foot in my mouth. Jace was obviously pissed I asked about his dad. I can't believe I pushed and ruined what was beginning to be a pretty good thing. And even though I'm convinced he won't show up, that I made him too uncomfortable, I still go to the woods the night before his next game.

I'm shocked to find him already there. Like always, we get right to blowjobs, and like every other time he's on his knees with his lips wrapped around my dick, he seems to be in a competition with himself to make it better than all the others. Somehow, he always does.

And I try my best to be even better.

When we're dressed, and he moves to his bag, I think he's reverted back to the way things were in the beginning. I'm not even mad because I'm relieved I didn't scare him away completely.

The very last thing I'm expecting is for him to pull out cupcakes.

"I got them at the bake sale the band was having today," he explains with a shrug. "My dad would be pissed if he saw me eating sugar, so I'm going to have it now, if you want the other one," he says, holding it out in offering.

I take the delicious-looking red velvet cupcake, trying to ignore the fact that it's individually packaged and that he must have specifically purchased it for me with this moment in mind. "Thanks, red velvet is my favorite," I mutter, hoping that he ignores how hot my cheeks suddenly are.

"Yeah, I remember Liv mentioning that," he says casually, like that's a totally normal thing to remember about your ex-girl-friend's ex-best friend.

Doesn't mean a thing.

And it certainly doesn't mean anything that we sit down to eat them or that we continue chatting long after the cupcakes are gone.

When we can barely see each other with how dark it's gotten, Jace slowly stands, surprising me once again when he holds out his hand to help me get up.

"Hey, about last time…" He trails off, and I rush to apologize.

"I'm sorry, I didn't mean to pry about your dad."

"No, it's not that, you didn't," he reassures me, and I exhale a breath I didn't realize I was holding, still relieved he's not ending this. "It's just… No one's ever really asked me about him. Everyone assumes it must be so great to be his kid. They have no idea. And my mom doesn't care that he treats me like he does. All she cares about is Molly and her image."

"That sounds really lonely and hard. I hate that you've had to go through that, Jace," I add, and he scrunches his brows together.

"Well, it's not like I can change it. I just meant that I'm not used to talking about it, but I appreciate you asking and not fighting back about how great he is."

"Of course," I reply easily.

"Okay. Um… see you tomorrow."

"Have a good game."

And I try really, really hard to tell myself it doesn't mean anything that Jace opened up to talk to me about personal things he's never shared with anyone else before. I'll just continue to ignore the way my stomach flutters when I think about it.

Doesn't mean a thing.

End of May

I'M RUNNING late today and hope Jace has stuck around to wait for me since I got stuck talking to my boss about my summer schedule even though I still have a few weeks until graduation.

My stomach twists at the thought of Jace not being there, but as soon as I get into the line of sight of our tree, I let out a deep breath as I see him sitting there with his headphones in.

He seems so at ease, not paying attention to anything specific, but when I make my way closer, he looks up at me and smiles softly. I drop down next to him, leaning against the tree.

"Whatcha listening to?" I ask.

" 'Writing on The Walls' by Underoath," he says. "Do you know them?" He laughs and shakes his head. "Even if you don't, you'll probably like them since you dress like… that, now," he says as he waves a hand in my direction.

I smirk, looking down at my band tee, black jeans, and combat boots. My style has geared more toward blacks, whites, and grays since I started embracing the edgier makeup and realized there was no "right way" to be queer. I don't need to be in bright colors or sequins all the time, though I'm not afraid of color. "Let me listen," I say as he hands me the left headphone from the cord plugged into his iPod, keeping the right one in his ear, and he scoots even closer.

I know the cord isn't that long, but we're shoulder to shoulder as he hits play on the song, and it's hard to focus on anything other than how close we are, how intimate this moment feels, despite it being one of the most innocent we've shared. I've definitely heard this before, and I do like it, but I didn't realize Jace would. I don't know why, maybe I associated his popularity with only liking top 100 radio hits.

"Do you always listen to this kind of music?" I ask, staring straight ahead.

"Yeah."

"I didn't peg you for being an emo music enthusiast. You do know most of those guys wear eyeliner, right?"

"Not really. I don't sit around watching music videos," he mutters. Then, quieter, he adds, "Besides, my dad would freak out if I was watching a bunch of boys dancing on my screen."

I want to pry *so badly*, but after last time, I refrain. "What's your favorite song?" I ask instead.

"Hmm, probably 'Numb' by Linkin Park," he says sheepishly. "I guess it's helped me feel less alone."

I briefly run through the lyrics, and how that song is about the pressure to mold yourself into what someone else wants and the loneliness of never being accepted as you are. Jace might not have told me much about his dad, but him saying that just revealed a lot. More than he probably intended.

He shifts to look at me, almost like he's surprised he said that out loud, like maybe he's realizing he confessed something bigger than just his taste in music.

"That's a good song." I whisper unintentionally. "When Liv and I stopped talking and Danny was away at camp, I listened to 'Boulevard of Broken Dreams' by Green Day a lot." I give him another piece of me in return.

He's still watching me, and I hold his gaze, catching him glancing down at my lips, and I swallow.

Is he going to kiss me?

The moment feels heavy and charged, intimate in a way we've never experienced.

Instead of leaning forward though, I feel his hand shift as he lays his fingers on top of mine. We're not holding hands exactly, but it's definitely intentional. The heat of his palm on the back of my hand as his pinky brushes my thumb makes me feel connected to him in an entirely new, nerve-racking way. I can't look away, can't even breathe, even as Silverstein screams through the earbuds between us.

"What are you doing?" I whisper.

"I don't know," he whispers back.

I don't know what to do either, but I'm oddly turned on by the subtle touches. He tears his gaze from my lips and rakes his eyes down my body, until they land on my lap.

"You're hard," he mutters.

"You're staring," I shoot back even though he's right.

His mouth curves into the faintest, most dangerous smile I've ever seen. "So, are you gonna do something about it?"

I nod. The intimate tension snaps, and we're defaulting to our normal. I should be relieved. But, instead, I'm oddly disappointed that that kiss probably won't ever happen.

"Let's try something different this time," I prompt, trying to ignore how let down I feel about not kissing him. I tug the earbud free and roll onto my side so I'm eye-level with his dick, my face close to his bulge.

"Oh, you wanna sixty-nine?" He laughs, nervous and cocky all at once. "Let's do it. Let's see who can make the other come first."

"You're on."

Before I can overthink it, we're both moving—fumbling and laughing as we both try to undress the other in the grass until we get each other's jeans shoved down just enough. The moment his cock is inches from my mouth, I suck him down my throat.

The first taste of him is salty, familiar now, and I moan around his cock when the vibration of his groan runs straight through me.

"Fuck," I mumble, pulling off for a second before taking him deeper, just to hear him break like that again.

It's messy as spit drips down my cheek, and his fingers clutch at my thighs hard enough to bruise before moving to grab my ass and squeeze. *Fuck, that feels good.* I pull back to suck the head of his cock, tonguing the slit just to hear him gasp. He retaliates by swallowing me down to the base, and my whole body jerks.

He pulls off me long enough to pant, "Gonna lose, K—fuck—you're already shaking."

"Shut up," I hiss, but my voice cracks because he's right. My hips buck into his mouth anyway, chasing the heat.

He laughs around me—actually laughs—and the vibrations send me right to the edge. I try to focus, hollowing my cheeks around his cock and pumping the base with my hand, desperate to drag him down with me.

We're both sucking each other's cocks like this competition is life-altering. Gagging and gasping and fighting not to give in first until I feel him twitch on my tongue at the same time my vision goes white.

We come together, choking on each other's moans, muffling the sound with spit and desperation until we collapse, coughing and laughing against each other's thighs.

"Guess we both lose that one," Jace says through laughs.

"I guess," I say, smiling as we continue to lie there.

Did we really lose though? Tonight was different. Things between us feel different.

Tonight felt like… like what I'd imagine being in a relationship might feel like. Hanging out with someone I enjoy spending time with, sharing parts of ourselves we might not with other people. Joking around, laughing, smiling, hooking up because we can, because we want to.

As sad as it might be to admit, tonight might have been one of the best nights of my life. I've been trying to ignore exactly how things have changed between us for a while now. I've always been attracted to Jace. I obviously hated the way he treated me last year. But his confidence is hot, the way he seems to command the attention of everyone in a room when he enters it, both with his physical presence—he's larger than most people our age—and with his charisma. The easy charm he's never bothered to turn on for me has had countless girls tripping over themselves to talk to him.

He's also objectively the most attractive student at our school with his cut jawline, his broad shoulders, his muscles, and his perfect, round butt from all the squatting he does as a catcher. *Yes, I know what position he is, even if I've still never been to a game.* His warm brown eyes, the curly brown hair. He's gorgeous.

But now, when I think about how hot he is, I'm not immediately following that thought with "but I hate him so much" like I used to.

Because I don't. I can't.

I hate the things he did to me in the past.

But I've gotten to know Jace over the last couple of months in a way I never imagined I would. And the more that I do get to know him, the more I'm worried I might even like him.

But the school year is almost over, and I have no idea what that means for us. If there will still even be an us. I think I desperately want there to be.

I'm too afraid to ruin tonight by asking though. So, for now, I can only hope we have more moments like this ahead.

JACE

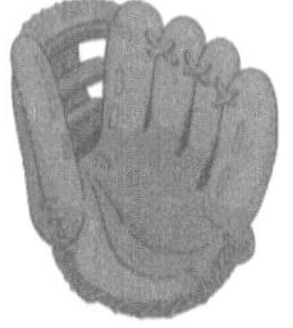

June 2012

"Final game tomorrow!" David reminds me as we get ready for our last practice, like I'm not well aware tomorrow is our championship game. We made it all the way to State, and it'll be tough, but we can probably pull off the win. It's also the last game I'll ever play with my dad as my coach. *Thank fuck.*

While I can't wait to be done with him, I'm also far more concerned about tonight than anything baseball related.

It's the final night I have the excuse of needing a "good luck" blowjob from Kieran. Part of me feels like maybe I've been playing so well just so I can keep meeting up with him, but I can't go further than the state championship, and I'm still not ready for things to end.

The regular orgasms are amazing. By far the best sex I've ever had even if we've only been using our hands and mouths. But it's also become so much more than that. Our time hiding out in the woods, pretending like the real world doesn't exist, has felt like the first time in my entire life that I get to be Jace. Not

Coach Ryan's son or the popular kid. Not a top draft prospect or future MLB player.

Just me. Jace.

Kieran came into our arrangement already hating me, and in a weird way, that was freeing. It allowed me to act however I wanted. He couldn't hate me any more than he already did, so I didn't have to work to maintain my image. I'd never been in a situation where I wasn't hyperaware of how the people around me would judge me, or how my actions would be perceived and if others would approve—or if my father would approve.

But in our woods, when it's just the two of us, I get to be whoever I want. Who I really am. And I think I like that version of me more than I ever expected. With Kieran, I'm lighter. Kinder. More fun. A better version of myself than the one most people in my life know. Somehow, he brings out the best parts of me, and I've connected with him more deeply than I ever have with anyone else.

I'm not ready to say goodbye, and I have no idea if Kieran feels the same way. But I want tonight to be different. I have to at least try. Instead of our usual blowjob exchange and making excuses to stay there longer and longer to talk, I want to finally kiss him.

I've thought about doing it countless times now. Wondered what his lips would taste like. If it would feel different to kiss a man. But not just any man—Kieran.

I want to know what his body feels like pressed up against mine.

I want to do so much more with him.

But a kiss would be enough.

Kissing him is all I've been able to think about lately. I've caught myself staring at his mouth so many times in class, it's amazing he hasn't called me out on it yet. I don't even care if we blow each other tonight. I'm done hesitating. As soon as we're there, I'm going to make my move.

I DON'T KNOW who I'm more pissed off at, David or my father.

Just as practice was finishing up, David *had* to make a comment about how I should really be helping our backup catcher more since he'll be starting next year. And, of course my dad had to hear him and insist the two of us stay late for extra practice. My dad stayed the entire time, and despite my very best efforts to end things so I could leave, I'm almost two hours late to meet Kieran.

It's not like I could've said "Hey, Coach, I actually have to go trade good luck blowjobs in the woods for the game tomorrow" or even what I really wanted to do and say "Sorry, Coach, I was really hoping to kiss a guy for the first time tonight." I can't even imagine what my dad would do if he found out about Kieran and me.

Ever since I started sneaking around with Kieran, David's been far more overbearing, and tonight's just another example of it. Sure, we haven't been hanging out as much, but he never cared this much before when I'd tell him I was busy.

I can't believe tonight, of all nights, I'm this fucking late. We've both been a little late before, but never two whole hours. I'm sure I've missed him since it's nearly dark now, but I have to make sure he isn't still waiting. I really wish we had exchanged phone numbers. We still aren't even friends on any socials for me to message him either. I'll have to bring that up next.

I get to our spot, shining the flashlight of my phone around to confirm, but he's not here.

Of course he wouldn't have waited.

He had no idea I wanted tonight to be different. That I wanted more.

And now, he's probably mad I didn't show. I can explain in

class Monday, but will it even matter? There are no more games after tomorrow. No more excuses.

I feel like tonight was my final chance with him, and I blew it. I sink down to the ground, leaning against our tree, and let my head fall back as I picture what I wanted to have happen tonight.

Maybe in another life, I wasn't late.

Maybe there, I'm not so afraid of what my feelings for him mean. Of what would happen if I acted on them outside of our little bubble here in the woods.

Maybe in that other life, we kiss all the time.

Maybe we're even together.

Maybe there, I'm actually happy.

25

KIERAN

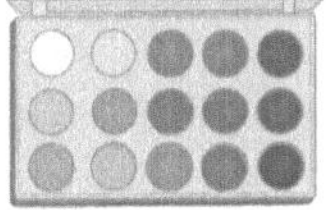

Two Hours Before

Graduation is so close I can taste it, but I can't help but wonder what'll happen this summer when Jace doesn't have baseball as an excuse for us to hook up anymore.

I don't think he's going to suddenly want to be my boyfriend or anything, but meeting up with him has quickly become the best part of my day, and I'm dreading that tomorrow is his last game.

It's hard to think of letting go of something that makes me feel so wanted, even if it's mostly just physical release with someone who spent over a year making my life hell and still chooses to ignore me in public. Because when he's kneeling in front of me, lips wrapped around my cock, it's so easy to forget how much I used to hate him.

I haven't hated him for a while now.

In the short, post-orgasm conversations we've shared, we've maybe even become—I don't know that friends is the right word —but something close to a friend.

I even sort of like him.

A lot.

Maybe tonight I can bring up how I feel. Tell him I'm okay with keeping this going until college, even if we no longer have the guise of good luck to hide behind.

I still don't know what his plans are. I've heard people say he's going pro, but we've never talked about his future, and I'm too scared to ask. I'm afraid of pushing too hard and potentially ruining what little we have like the day he ran after I brought up his parents.

But every time we're together, it feels like he lets me in a little more. Like I'm uncovering pieces of him he doesn't show anyone else.

As much as I hate to admit it, it makes me feel special. Seen. Important.

This was never supposed to mean anything. It was a way for me to get experience and for him to come to terms with being attracted to another guy.

I'm not an idiot, I know we don't have a future together.

I'm just not ready to say goodbye.

I've been telling myself that I'll be fine, even if tonight is the last night we hook up. When it ends, it ends, and I have to accept that. It's not like I'm sticking around our small New Jersey town forever. I won't be heartbroken, pining after MLB star Jace Ryan.

Nope. I'll be going to New York City soon, and I'll finally be around people who didn't bully me because they unknowingly wanted me. It'll be so much better than whatever Jace and I are doing.

Ugh. Why does that sound so unconvincing even in my head? I should be way more excited. I want to be wanted out in the open.

I know drawing out our arrangement will only make things harder when we do go our separate ways, but I still want to offer to continue meeting up. I can't help the hold he has on me.

I get to the spot in the woods where Jace and I usually meet the night before his games. He's not here yet, so I wait, trying not to fidget or think too hard about what this is or isn't. But my brain's a traitor and keeps rewinding to the way he grabbed my ass last time and how good his hands felt there.

After a few minutes, I hear the crunch of footsteps behind me, and my dick immediately perks up knowing he's here.

"Finally," I say, repeating my thought out loud.

"I wouldn't get too excited there, Kieran," the voice calls back, but it's not the playful one I'm expecting. It's dark and full of malice.

My dick deflates, and my stomach sinks at the sound of David's voice.

What the fuck is he doing here?

Did Jace send him? How else would he know where to find me? How else would he know that Jace was supposed to meet me?

But why did Jace tell him?

He steps right into my line of sight, and my heart rate skyrockets when I see his angry expression. David has always scared me far more than Jace, but David listens to him, always following Jace's lead, doing what he says. The few times David has tried to escalate things, Jace has brushed it off, effectively shutting it down.

But Jace isn't here right now. At least, I don't see him.

David is walking toward me with an obvious look of disgust on his face.

"What are you doing here?" I ask, trying to steady my voice.

He stops a few feet away and looks me up and down, shaking his head. "Waiting for someone?"

I clench my jaw. "No, I was just—"

"Don't bother." His voice sharpens. "He's not coming."

Something cold seeps through me as I mutter, "What?"

Jace told him. And I don't understand why he would have possibly done that.

My fear heightens.

"You have some fucking nerve," he snarls.

I swallow my panic down at how angry he seems at me. I'm not even sure what I did.

"I know what you've been doing with him. It's sick," David spits.

Oh my god, Jace must've told him everything. Why? Why would he do that?

"You tricked him," he accuses, voice full of venom. "You made him think he wanted you by dressing up like a girl, but makeup doesn't change the fact that you're a guy, and Jace isn't gay. He doesn't like you, and I'll make sure you never do it again."

My mouth is dry at his threat. "I didn't make him do anything."

"You think this is a game?" David snaps. "That you can just dig your little gay claws in him and make him gay too?"

"I never—"

"You did!" he shouts. "And what? Manipulating Jace wasn't enough? You trying to infect other people with your videos?" My face falls, and he lets out a dry, humorless laugh. "Yeah, that's right. Imagine my surprise when I stumbled onto your little YouTube channel."

My stomach drops. *No, no, no.*

" 'Boys can wear makeup too.' Real inspiring shit." He shakes his head. "I watched every fucking video."

I take a small step back, but he mirrors it, closing the distance again.

"You're pathetic," he spits out, his smile finally showing, but it's wicked. My pulse is hammering now because his threat is laced in every word, even if I don't know what he's capable of.

He steps even closer to me, reaching his hand out like he's

going to grab my arm, and I stumble back to avoid it. My shoulder slams into the tree, and, *damn*, that hurt. I almost trip on the uneven ground beneath me, but I'm able to steady myself.

"Stay the fuck away from him," David growls.

"Or what?" I snap back even though I know I shouldn't. But I'm fucking sick of being treated like I'm wrong for being who I am. "You'll post my videos? Out me? Go ahead. Not like people don't already know I wear makeup and am into guys."

David manages to step closer to me, face tight with rage. This time, when he reaches out, I'm not able to move away before he manages to grab my wrist, squeezing tightly.

"I won't let you fuck-up Jace's future. You should've left him alone. You think he wants to date some emo, sparkly freak who talks about his feelings on the internet? He. Doesn't. Want. You."

I don't care what he thinks he needs to say to me, I've heard enough. I yank my wrist free from his hold, trying to turn away from him, but when I do, I lose my footing. I reach out to grab at nothing as I start to fall. My other hand hits the ground first at an awkward angle and a sharp pain shoots up my wrist right before my head manages to collide with a tree. Hard.

I think I black out for a second. I'm not sure exactly what happened, but I'm aware of a throbbing pain in my skull as David towers over me where I'm lying on the forest floor, head and arm demanding my attention with how much pain I'm in.

"Fucking stay away from him," David snarls. "I don't want to see you so much as look at him ever again, you fucking freak," he says before finally backing away. "This is your warning. Next time, it'll be much worse. I fucking promise you that."

I hear his footsteps backing away, and I let out a shaky breath, trying to steady my breathing. I attempt to roll to my side, to push myself up into a standing position, but the moment I even try to lay my hand on the ground, that sharp pain is returning tenfold. My vision spins with the pain. I'm dizzy even though I'm positive I'm still on the ground.

What am I even doing? Why am I on the ground?

Right. David.

Jace sent David to scare me. Maybe even to hurt me.

I think I'm going to be sick. My stomach is turning, my head is pounding, and my heart is beating rapidly. I use the arm that doesn't feel like it's on fire to finally push myself into a seated position before I manage to stand. But the room is spinning.

Not the room… the forest? Why am I here alone?

Why is the sun so bright, isn't it late? I try to raise my arm to block it out but that only makes the pain in my wrist worse.

Fuck. Something is definitely wrong with me. I can't think over the pain in my head.

I need to get help.

26

JACE

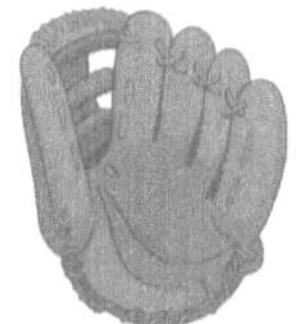

here the fuck is Sparkles? Why isn't he at school *again* today?

He must be sick. I don't think he would ditch school over me missing a hookup five days ago that was never even confirmed. He knows how careful I've been to make sure no one finds out about what we've been doing, and up until now, that's been working really well for us.

At least I think it has been.

I should be focused on finals or celebrating that we won the championship on Saturday.

But honestly, right now, when Kieran's chair is empty, I don't give a shit that we won, even if I didn't play that well. I don't give a shit about anything other than the fact he's not here.

His absence is distracting me from any hope of paying attention to anything. I'm really regretting not having his phone number. He's probably just home with the flu or something. Maybe it's a good thing I missed that hookup after all.

Can you get the flu from cum?

I wanted to do more than that though. *Ugh.* I'm still so upset

I didn't get to kiss him like I'd planned. And I haven't even been able to explain why I wasn't there, because he's not here.

Even though I can logically acknowledge that Kieran missing two days of school isn't the end of the world, I'm not able to think of anything else. By the end of our usual class together, I'm driving myself crazy with all my questions I don't know the answer to.

When almost everyone has left for their next class, I walk up to our teacher's desk. "Hey, Mrs. Carson, I was just wondering if you knew anything about why Kieran has missed school the last couple of days? I thought I might be able to pass on some of the work we've been doing."

"Sorry, Jace, the attendance office deals with absences, so I don't know any more than you," she apologizes.

"Cool. Yeah, no big deal." I shrug. *That didn't help me at all.* Now all I can do is hope she doesn't talk to my dad about my offer. I don't need him prying into why I care about "the gay kid" missing school. I probably should have thought about that before I asked, but Kieran's absence has my judgment all scrambled.

I'm still trying to think of another way I can find out what's going on with him as I exit the classroom and nearly knock David over because I'm too in my head to even notice him. Apparently he waited for me, because he can't seem to do anything without following me around like a lost puppy.

"Seriously, man, stop thinking about that fucking loser," he insists. Shit. I didn't think about anyone else hearing me ask either. I'm really off my game today. "You don't have to worry about him anymore," David continues in a reassuring tone that immediately has my stomach plummeting as we start to walk toward our next class.

"What the fuck does that mean?" I push, praying that my concern is unfounded. David can be a real asshole sometimes, but surely I'm jumping to the wrong conclusion here. He wouldn't actually hurt him, right?

Fuck. What did he do?

He looks at me with a smug expression. "Your baseball stats might have been great this season, but you haven't been acting like yourself," he starts, and my whole body goes cold. What does he know? How can I spin this? I fight to keep a blank expression on my face as he continues, but I feel like I'm going to throw up.

"I thought that maybe the stress of the draft coming up had gotten to you, that you had turned to drugs or something because you've been so shifty and secretive," he explains. "But when I followed you, I found out it was so much worse than that." His smile grows, but there's a wicked glint in his eyes. "So, I took care of it," he brags, clearly proud of himself. I still don't know what he's saying. Did he see Kieran and I together? What could he possibly have *taken care of*?

I can't take the suspense any longer. I'm already on edge, worrying about Kieran and why he isn't at school. "Jesus, David, spit it out! What the fuck did you do?" I demand, unable to control my volume.

He quirks a brow, folding his arms across his chest as he slows to a stop at the end of a row of lockers, staring at me knowingly. "Jace, I don't think you want me to talk about this here."

"Enough with riddles, you fucking asshole, just tell me. Spit it out," I insist.

He tilts his head to the side, studying me with that cocky grin. My heartrate feels dangerously fast as I wait with bated breath for him to finally explain himself.

But when he does, time slows. "I saw you, dude. I know what he's been doing to you in the woods. It looked like you were enjoying yourself, and I get it, it looked kind of hot, but still. I couldn't let him derail your dreams with his gay shit." With each word out of his mouth, the world as I know it seems to crash down around me. The blood drains from my face as he confirms my greatest fear. I thought I was careful. I thought no one would ever know. I thought this would stay a secret.

I'm an idiot. A complete fool who acted like I was immune to the consequences of my actions.

This is the end.

My life is over.

Who else knows?

What is my dad going to do when he finds out?

David didn't specify what he saw, though. Maybe there's still a chance I could fix this, explain it away and make sure he never tells a soul. "I don't know what you're talking about." I attempt to argue, but it's weak.

To my surprise, David doesn't challenge my answer, instead nodding along. "Exactly, it never happened," he agrees in a reassuring tone. "I'm the only one who knows, so there's no need for you to worry anymore. I didn't record it or anything."

I can't tell what the fuck is going on, and I think I might get whiplash from the warring emotions I've dealt with in the last few minutes. At first, I feel an extreme sense of relief that he's promising not to tell anyone else. Maybe it isn't too late and my dad won't find out.

But then he keeps talking. "I reminded Kieran that you're not gay like he is and warned him to stop trying to force himself on you."

And I'm back to freaking out.

Only now, I'm not thinking about my future. I've entered a state of full-blown panic over what he did to Kieran. "Again, David, what the fuck does that mean?" I beg, anger and fear fighting for dominance in my tone.

"Don't worry about it," he dismisses with a shrug. "I just threatened him. If he says otherwise, it's a lie. He tripped over a branch or something all on his own. I don't think he even got that hurt."

My worst fear is realized as the pieces start to fall into place.

"He got hurt?" I repeat, yelling in the middle of the hallway. "He's missed the last two days of school! What aren't you telling me?"

Time stops completely as I wait for his reply.

Kieran has grown to mean so much to me over the last few months. Not just because we exchange regular orgasms, and he's helped me accept the whole part of myself that's attracted to other guys that I'd obviously been suppressing. But because he's the brightest part of my day, even on the days we don't hook up.

Seeing him across the classroom, and the dark, edgy makeup he wears that used to piss me off so much, now has me daydreaming about a world where I could be as carefree as he is. I still have no desire to wear the stuff myself, but I wish I could boldly make decisions without fear of how others would treat me like he does.

If these last few days of freaking out about where he is have taught me anything, it's that I care about Kieran. Not as a hookup or an experiment, but as someone who really knows him. He's someone who makes me feel safe to be myself. Someone who was able to forgive the horrible way I treated him.

Well, maybe not forgive.

Because, shit, I don't think I've ever even apologized. I've been so focused on my own confusion about the way that I feel about him that I haven't taken the time to have that conversation. If I would even be brave enough to. Though, he definitely deserves one. He deserves to know I'm so sorry for all the awful things I said and did. That I wish I could take them all back and start over with him. That I really enjoy spending time with him, and that I wish I had the courage to do it more publicly.

"God, he's such a wimp. I get why you gave in though," David says, drawing me back to the present as he rolls his eyes. Students are still rushing past us to get to their next class, completely unaware of the racing thoughts I'm having about Kieran and how I really feel about him. "I'm sure he's fine though," David adds. "He's probably just embarrassed that I found his YouTube channel. I barely touched him. He didn't even fall that hard."

My rational brain goes offline, and my base instincts take over as I process his words.

I see red.

He touched Kieran? A YouTube channel? He's embarrassed? What is going on?

I try to make sense of what he said, but the thought of David laying a finger on Kieran demands my full attention. This fucking asshole jock who I lift with in the gym almost every day, who probably has at least fifty pounds of muscle on my Sparkles, threatened him, maybe even *attacked* him. After days of worrying about Kieran and where he is, it's too much for me to process.

Before I make any conscious decision to do so, I've grabbed the collar of David's shirt and pushed him back into a locker. My fist connects with his jaw, sending his head back into the metal with a satisfying crash, and the pain in my knuckles only fans the flames of my fury.

How dare he? How dare this complete lowlife, waste of space, think he could hurt Kieran and get away with it? And out of some twisted sense of what? Defending my honor? He deserves to face whatever he did to Kieran tenfold.

I pull my fist back, preparing to punch him again, when a strong grip closes around my wrist, and the grating sound of my father's voice cuts through the static in my mind.

"What the hell are you doing?" he hisses, probably trying to avoid causing an even bigger scene by not yelling. I look around and take in the small crowd of students who have gathered around us.

Fuck.

He flings my arm down, stepping in front of David, running through a quick concussion test that I've seen him do countless times on the field when players have collided or if someone loses a helmet. He seems to be satisfied with David's responses, stepping back.

"You're not going to press charges, right?" my dad asks him.

"Uh, no?" David responds hesitantly.

"Good. I'll walk you to the nurse's office. Jace, we'll drop you off with the principal on the way," he explains in his no-nonsense coach voice. He's pissed.

But not nearly as livid as he'll be if David explains why I attacked him.

I want to protest leaving the two of them alone together, but my father's glare when we arrive in the waiting area outside of the principal's office warns me to keep my mouth shut in a way I'm not strong enough to fight against.

I chew on my thumbnail as I try not to picture how hurt Kieran must be. I don't think anyone was there to pull David off him like my dad just did with me.

I should have been, though, and I'll never forgive myself.

Is he really injured enough to have missed multiple days of school? What exactly did he do to him? Or is it possible that his absence was unrelated and he's fine? He was gone by the time I got there...

My father comes storming into the office, past the reception area I'm in, and heads right to the principal's door. He stops in front of it, taking a deep breath as I see him slip on his mask. The one that he usually keeps on around other people, the false charisma that has everyone falling at his feet. He plasters on a big smile before lifting his fist to the door.

"Juliet, may I come in? It's urgent," he says politely, opening the door as he knocks. He closes it again, leaving me in silence.

I know I should be worried about my punishment, but all I can focus on is my need to know if Kieran is okay. Is he still in the hospital? Would I be allowed to visit? Would his parents even tell me if I showed up at his house?

Finally, the door swings open, and the principal glances at me wearily. "I'll give you two some time alone, feel free to talk in my office," she offers, holding her arm out, gesturing for me to come inside. I reluctantly walk in and take a seat. As soon as my dad closes the door, confirming she's out of earshot, he drops his act.

"What the fuck was that?" he hisses, still attempting to control his volume even though the anger in his eyes is worse than I've seen in awhile. "If you were literally any other kid, you'd be suspended so fast, hell, maybe even expelled. You would've been kicked off the team if the season wasn't already over! What the fuck were you thinking?"

He's firing off his comments and questions far too quickly for me to answer. It doesn't matter though. I know from experience he needs to get them all out before I do or he'll yell at me for interrupting. "I thought David was one of your best friends?" he continues. "Was it over a girl? What could he possibly have done for you to risk the draft? David wouldn't spill so you better open your fucking mouth before I do it for you."

He finally stops on the opposite side of the principal's desk from me, leaning his hands on it to scowl expectantly, finally ready for my answer. I know I should make up an excuse, play along with the one my dad's offering, literally say anything other than what comes out of my mouth, but despite how bad of a situation I've ended up in, I can't seem to move past my own fury, and the truth is all I can think about.

"He attacked Kieran." I hear myself practically growl with how angry I am. "He's missed school now for two days, and I don't know what exactly David did, but I think it was bad."

My dad stares at me blankly for a moment, blinking a few times. Obviously, that wasn't the answer he was expecting, and for a moment, he calms down enough to question me. "Are you talking about that gay kid in your class who always wears makeup?"

I give him a small nod in answer. I already said it, no taking it back now.

"I heard he went to the hospital and won't be returning to school," he says casually, like his words don't feel like knives plunging into my chest. "Are you saying David did that?" he asks, not sounding the least bit upset about it, just curious. "The faculty got an email about it, like, an hour ago. But that kid had it coming. With all the shit he paints on his face, he was asking for it. I'm shocked it took this long, honestly."

Those knives carve deeper, raking down my chest, tearing me completely apart as each word out of my father's mouth echoes those of my past.

I can't believe how wrong I was.

How I let this horrible man, who's taught me nothing but hate and fear, shape me into a copy of him for so long.

The worst part is that I know I'd still be that person if I hadn't met Kieran. I've never been strong enough to break free of my father's mold. I've always done exactly what he wanted because it was easier to give in, to fold myself into what he wanted me to be. I didn't realize how much of myself I've given up over the years to keep my father happy.

But he'll never be happy.

And I don't want to be like him anymore.

I think of all the times I harassed Kieran, bullied him in an attempt to get him to conform to who I wanted him to be—just like my dad did to me—but he never gave in. He kept showing up the way he wanted to.

Because he's free.

I've been trying to be my father for so long because that's what I've been taught. But that's not me. Who I am around Kieran… that's who I want to be. All this other version has done for me is make me feel isolated, disconnected, lonely, and like I'm not good enough. I've never felt like I'm good enough. I've spent my entire life trying to be like my dad, but I think it's time I try to imitate someone else.

Kieran wouldn't hesitate to stand up for himself. But he isn't here, so I need to do it for him.

I take a deep breath, looking my father right in the eye before I argue. "No one asks to be attacked," I say in the most confident voice I can manage. I'm not yelling, but I think the slow controlled tone sounds just as pissed, maybe even more. "He didn't ask to end up in the hospital."

He eyes me skeptically. "Calm down, kid. Don't take me so literally. All I'm saying is that gay kid is practically begging to be bullied with the way he acts."

"Why?" I challenge. "Because of the makeup? It's not even that big of a deal—"

"He's gay," my dad interrupts. "Obviously people are going to target him. It's not right." He shrugs again, unaware of how close I am to my breaking point as he goes on. "I can't believe that kid thinks it's okay to proudly label himself and walk around encouraging other people to be a part of his gay agenda. It's disturbing."

Every word my father says adds fuel to the flames of my rage. "Are you implying he deserves to be attacked because he's attracted to other men?" I grit out. I was trying to be civil. To stand up for Kieran without escalating things to avoid my father as much as possible, but I don't think that was ever really an option.

Fuck it.

If I'm truly done being who this awful man has tried to force me to be, done living my life based on every move he would make, then I need to take a stand. To burn every bridge so there's no room for me to fall back into bad habits. No room for him to keep trying to turn me into the person he wants me to be.

"Well, I guess I belong in the hospital too," I announce,

holding eye contact with the hateful excuse of a man who raised me. "Because I've really enjoyed having his dick in my mouth."

His stare is completely expressionless, blinking a few times before his scowl returns. "Jesus, Jace. What the fuck is wrong with you? Don't make jokes like that, it isn't funny."

I lean back in my chair, trying to project a casual air of confidence as I cross my arms and respond. "I'm not joking. Kieran is one of the best people that I've ever met." Finally admitting the truth feels like a huge weight has been lifted from my chest. I know this is about to get a lot worse when my dad actually reacts, but I can't regret telling him when I already feel so much better. "I can't believe I ever cared about assholes like you and David not finding out that I'm attracted to him when he's such an amazing person."

My father has probably yelled at me thousands of times with varying degrees of intensity. But the few times that I've managed to *really* piss him off, he's remained eerily calm, like he is now as he demands, "Are you being fucking serious right now? Did he infect you with his gay shit?"

"I'm being one hundred percent serious," I reply, echoing his tone. "And you can't make someone gay, that's a ridiculous thing to say."

The office is silent, and I'm not sure either of us are breathing as my dad continues to stare at me. Finally, he gives me a once-over before calmly shaking his head. "My son isn't gay," he insists.

"No. I think I'm bi, actually," I say out loud for the very first time. Honestly, the labels are still kind of confusing to me, but for now, I know I've been attracted to more than one gender, so it feels right.

My comment only seems to piss him off more. "I don't know what the fuck that means, but my son *isn't gay.*"

I think he's waiting for me to laugh this off, to confirm that it's all a joke. So I double down. "Well, no matter the label, I definitely liked having his dick in my mouth. That's what I was actually doing all those times I told you I had to study with David."

He shakes his head again, balling his fists at his side. I'm sure he's weighing the risks of being the one to send me to the hospital right now, but we're at his workplace.

"I'm done with you. You're not my fucking son," he grits out again. "Don't you dare ever set foot in my house again. I mean it, Jace. I'm fucking done with you. I should have let them suspend you, but going back out there to reverse what I did now would only make *me* look bad. I can't believe I wasted my whole fucking life on you, you ungrateful shit. No pro team is going to want a homo on their team. You fucked up everything I worked so hard for!" He throws the door open, storming out of the office, letting it slam closed behind him.

Adrenaline is still coursing through my veins after what just happened. I can't believe I did that. Holy shit.

For a moment, I'm elated. *I'm free.*

I never have to do what that asshole says ever again.

But then the reality of my situation catches up to me.

I have no place to live, no car, and I've never worked a day in my life. The only money I have is the little over a thousand dollars I still have from my uncle.

Going into this, I didn't have a plan, and I never thought past my admission, but I don't regret it. It felt good, really good, to say it out loud. To stop harboring the fear of my secrets getting out and saying them by choice.

I just don't know what to do from here. I attacked my "best friend," and I'm sure he and my dad will warn the rest of the team against helping me. And Kieran. Shit, Kieran. It's not like he'd let me stay with him, but I can't believe he was in the hospital. Or is? Is he still there? He must have been really hurt if he was there. God, I hope he's okay. David tried to play it off like it was nothing, but I know him, and he's always had a way of taking things too far. He had to take it far enough for him to end up in the hospital.

I take a deep breath. *One thing at a time.* The most pressing thing is finding a hotel that I can stay at until graduation. I'm sure the money I have saved can get me through then. And then what? Baseball season is over, and now that I have a choice... I have no desire to follow through with the draft. That was always my dad's dream. I don't want to continue to dedicate my life to the sport that will always be poisoned by the memory of him.

I didn't actually apply to any colleges though. Maybe I can do a year at a community college? I'm smart, I have good grades.

Fuck, my brain is ping-ponging all over the place.

That's not what I really need to be focusing on right now.

I can finish out my senior year, get my diploma, and find a job.

That I can walk to.

Because I don't have a car.

Fuck.

KIERAN

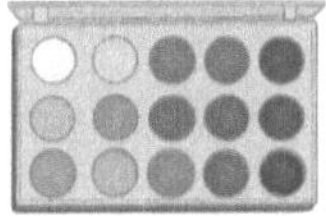

There's still one more week of senior year, but I'm done with that place, done with those people.

Especially Jace.

When I was lying in that hospital bed, hooked up to machines and getting lectured by the nurse about concussions, my mind kept circling back to the one and only conclusion that makes sense to me: Jace told David to go there and threaten me to stay away from him.

My memories of exactly what happened in the woods are a little hazy, which the doctors said was normal after a concussion. But there's no other way David would've shown up at our exact spot, at our exact time, unless Jace told him.

Maybe David suspected us and Jace threw me under the bus to save himself? Or maybe he's more sadistic than I'd thought.

I just wish I understood his plan. Was it to get me to let my guard down, to start... liking him, only to send David in once I was too trusting to see it coming? So Jace didn't have to risk his own reputation by being the one to do it himself? Was he sitting somewhere that night, waiting for a text from David saying it was done? Did he picture me crying in the dirt while he laughed about it with his friends?

It's messed up, but in some ways, that thought hurts more than David's words or the fall did, more than all the pain that's still present in my head and my wrist, even now, days later.

The worst part is, I never saw this coming from Jace. I felt like we had reached a mutual understanding between us. He came out to me, asked questions, started treating me like someone he actually wanted to know, and he opened up to me about his dad. It felt like maybe the walls he kept up in public were starting to crack when it was just the two of us alone.

But I realize now that it was nothing more than a way for him to get off, disguised as a superstition.

And I wonder if he even meant all the stuff about his dad.

Fuck, I hate them both. All three of them.

He never cared. I just made the mistake of thinking he did.

I should've known better. I should've kept my head down, played it safe until graduation, until I was in New York where people wouldn't look twice if I walked into class with a full face of makeup.

Instead, I thought I could survive being myself here—be proud of it, even. And I let myself believe that maybe someone like Jace could learn and change, that he could see me and not hate what he saw, especially once he got to know me.

I mistook the way I'd catch him shyly smiling at me in class the last month or the way his eyes would sometimes flick to my mouth like he was thinking about more than just getting off as proof of that.

But it didn't mean anything.

I'd just told myself it did, because I wanted it to. Because it felt good to believe that the person who spent over a year making me feel small had finally decided to see me.

And knowing that he didn't breaks my heart.

But I was nothing more than a secret. A mouth. A habit that

he could drop as soon as it stopped being convenient. Now that the season is over, Jace sent David to end things for him. He couldn't even face me himself. It only makes sense he sent his dumbass best friend after me to keep his golden boy reputation intact.

My parents were beside themselves when I ended up in the hospital, and in my concussed state, I admitted that someone was threatening me, and when I tried to get away, I fell. But I only told them it was because of my YouTube videos and told them repeatedly I was fine and we didn't need to press charges. They begged me for more, but I couldn't tell them, not if I didn't want everything to be picked apart and dissected and turned into a much larger issue.

Even though I only stayed in the hospital for one night, I agreed with them that going back to finish the final week of school was unnecessary. My doctors wrote me a note explaining my concussion and asking that I be excused from any unnecessary use of my broken wrist. Obviously writing would be difficult even if my brain wasn't injured. But the real reason I'm excused from the final week of school and my finals is because my mom freaked out on the principal, going on about how unsafe school is for queer people, and how they should be encouraging a more accepting and inclusive environment. She demanded to see their anti-bullying policies, and when she found out there weren't any officially in place, she offered to work with them to create a comprehensive plan to prevent what happened to me from happening to anyone else.

David's confrontation didn't happen at school, but my mom can be pretty intimidating when she's standing up for me.

It's weird I won't be going back to school. Danny coordinated with my mom to get the items from my locker, so I really never have to set foot in there again. It's definitely not the ending I pictured.

My parents don't even want me to go to graduation, worried

about what people might say or if I'll see the person who confronted me. They're trying to encourage me to shift my focus to college, and honestly, sitting around for hours, listening to everyone's name being called, sounds like an awful time, so I'm not fighting them on skipping it.

And if we're being really honest, I'd rather not go because I don't want to see Jace. If he was too afraid to end whatever was going on between us face-to-face, then I see no reason to ever be around him again.

I'm also out of work until my concussion symptoms improve. I still have a mild headache, some nausea, and am annoyingly tired. I'm sick of lying around, not doing anything. I can't be on my phone or watch TV, and I'm going crazy with boredom. My mom hasn't been very good about giving me space since this happened, either. She's currently sitting across from me, reading in an armchair, wanting to keep me company.

She thinks I've been so upset about getting hurt, which I am, but I'm more sad about Jace. Mourning what we could've been. Or at least the version of us that I'd built up in my head. It felt real to me—even though I know it wasn't to him.

He hid me away like I was a dirty secret, but he'd also let his guard down. He acted as though I was the first person he could be honest with, the only one who saw past all his walls and the facade he puts on for everyone else.

I let myself believe it meant something. I let myself believe *I* meant something.

I thought that he cared, and I miss the way I felt when he was around.

But now I just feel stupid and heartbroken and angry.

I wish I could brush it all off, move on.

But I'm devastated.

The doorbell rings, distracting me from my seemingly endless thoughts of Jace. Maybe it's Danny? I haven't been on my phone much because it can make the symptoms worse, so I might have missed a message that he was coming over. I sit up, intending to answer it, but my mom stops me. "Stay there. I'll see who it is, honey. You can just rest."

Awesome, more rest.

I offer her a weak smile, but I'm frustrated because I don't need more rest. I need to move on. I need to stop obsessing over the man who sent his best friend to break my heart. It's only fitting I walked away from the exchange with broken bones as well.

My mom returns, eyeing me hesitantly, and my guard is immediately up. If it had been Danny at the door, she would have just let him in. But... who else would it be? It's not like Jace is about to show up here.

I wouldn't want to see him anyway, I try to remind myself.

"Who is it?" I ask.

My mom glances back at the front door, but I can't see it from my spot on the couch. "Olivia," she finally answers, and I let out a sigh of... relief? Definitely relief. I'm not at all disappointed that Jace isn't here.

Because I never want to see him again. *See, that one almost sounded convincing.*

But I actually do want to see Liv. It feels like it's time. Jace's comment about how he hoped I'd forgiven Liv now that he and I were hooking up has been stuck in my head. I've missed her a lot lately, and I don't think he meant to call me out, but he did. He made me realize I was doing the exact thing I'd been so furious at her for. And once it hit me, I felt like a complete asshole.

I sit up fully, nodding to my mom. "Let her in."

My mom smiles and hurries back to the door. A moment later, Olivia slowly enters the room. She's biting her lip, clearly nervous as she approaches.

"Hey, it's good to see you," I greet, hoping my smile is warm.

"Wait, really?" she asks.

"I think it's time we talk," I admit as she takes a seat in the chair my mom had previously been in. She didn't return with Liv so I think she's giving us privacy.

"Okay," she quickly agrees, letting out a relieved exhale. Her foot is bouncing like she can't shake her nervous energy, and seeing that makes me realize how anxious I am too. "Kieran, I really am so sorry," she starts, and I nod.

"I know, Liv. I appreciate you saying that."

"Wait, let me get it all out," she says quickly. "Obviously I'm sorry for dating him, I never should have done that. I knew how mean he was to you, but I was dismissive of it all because of how attracted to him I was and because he was popular." She shakes her head, looking down at her lap where she's picking at a loose thread in her skirt.

"I never should have put my desire for a boyfriend before our friendship, especially when that boyfriend was him. We were friends for so long that I took it for granted, and I'm sorry. And not just with Jace. When the girls from yearbook started inviting me to things, I got swept up in the whole popularity thing. They always seemed like their lives were so perfect, and I don't know… It was nice to feel like I was a part of it. But looking back, I've realized the friendships I thought I had with them are all so shallow compared to how close you and me used to be." Her voice wavers at that, and she glances up at me with tears in her eyes.

"Oh, Liv," I whisper, feeling a little choked up myself.

"I didn't even realize I'd been such a shitty friend to you for as long as I was until after we'd stopped talking. I hate what I did to you and I'm so sorry, Kieran."

She sounds so remorseful, I can't listen to her for any longer. I stand up and open my arms in an invitation. She only hesitates for a second before she's jumping out of her seat and rushing to hug me.

We hold each other tightly for a few minutes, both of us

letting silent tears fall as we mourn the friendship we'd once had. Finally, I pull back. "You weren't the only one who made mistakes," I admit. "I should have heard you out sooner, I was just holding onto resentment, and for that, I'm sorry."

We both settle onto the same couch, turned toward each other as we continue the conversation we should have probably had months ago.

"No, I get it. You had every right to be mad at me," she insists. "Jace was so horrible to you, and I never took it seriously enough. I was so swept up in attention, and then when he asked me out, I was so excited that the hot, popular, probably MLB-bound guy wanted me, I convinced myself it wasn't a big deal. But it was, and I did it anyway. I'm so sorry."

Fuck. Obviously, when she first started dating him that's what I was so mad about. But… I also ignored the way he used to treat me when he started showering me with more positive attention. *And look where that got me.*

Now that Liv is here, and we're finally having this conversation, I'm not sure how honest I should be. I never told anyone about hooking up with him. Should I accept her apology and not give her the full truth? Should I tell her everything even if I'd be outing him?

Liv is looking at me nervously as I consider what to do. Ugh. My brain is still too foggy for this important of a decision, but I know I'll regret delaying this conversation until I'm completely recovered. Liv and I have gone long enough without each other, and I want my best friend back.

I think the only way for us to really recover is if we do so honestly.

Despite our fight, I trust her. I don't believe Olivia would tell anyone else if I ask her not to. So, I take in a deep breath and try to exhale my anxiety and hesitation.

"He is pretty hot," I finally agree with a smirk.

Liv lets out a surprised laugh, obviously not expecting that response.

"In case it wasn't clear, I forgive you," I start. "I'd really like for us to get back the friendship we used to have. And I think the first step to us getting there involves me telling you something kind of big, but I can only do that if you promise not to tell anyone else."

"Of course. Whatever you need to tell me will stay between us," she agrees seriously.

Fuck, where do I even begin? "When you guys broke up, and you tried to apologize, I wasn't ready to hear you out." Now I'm the one nervously bouncing my leg, and I can't seem to stop. "But then a few months later, I kind of did the same thing you had…" I trail off, afraid to say the words.

"Sorry, I don't understand. What did you do?"

She's looking at me expectantly, and I realize that there will never be a perfect way to admit everything, so I go for it, blurting it out quickly so I can't lose my nerve. "I also ignored everything he used to do to me when he gave me attention. It started as more of a taunting, hate-hookup situation, but then it kind of shifted into something else, and I thought it might even mean more. But then he sent David to end things with me in the woods. I ended up in the hospital, and here we are." I shrug, aiming a tentative smile at her. Liv just stares at me, mouth hanging open in what I think is shock for a moment. Did she actually understand any of that? Or is my concussed brain making even less sense than I realize?

Finally, she recovers, expression morphing into one of such joy that I'm convinced she misunderstood until she squeals, "You. Hooked up. With Jace?"

"Shhhh," I remind her, glancing at the hallway.

"Sorry, sorry." She switches to a loud whisper. "I fucking knew it. I told you he was obsessed with you, and then he broke up with me after I said he should date you instead. I can't believe he actually admitted it though. You said it happened more than once?"

I nod. "The first time, we were fighting in the bathroom at Cameron's Halloween party, and then nothing for months. He completely ignored me. Then early this spring, it happened again after school, and then he showed up at the mall and asked me to drive him home." Her eyes go wider with each admission. "And it kept happening. Like, multiple times a week. And I thought we'd even become friends." I rub my temples as I admit the truth. "I thought maybe he liked me, that it could be more…" I trail off.

She sobers a bit. "Did you like him too?"

I hesitate for a moment. "Yeah, ugh, so much. And I should have known better. Obviously it didn't mean anything to him. I was just an experiment or something," I say the words out loud for the first time, and my lip trembles at the admission.

"Fuck, K, I'm so sorry. You don't deserve any of that," she says, and tears start falling down my cheeks.

"I know. But he made me believe he cared about me, and it hurts, Liv. It fucking hurts," I say as she pulls me into a hug.

"I know it does. I'm so sorry, K. You deserve to be with someone who knows how incredible you are, that claims you proudly. Not some asshole jock that's confused about his sexuality."

I let out a surprised laugh at her spot-on description of him. "Thanks, Liv."

"Let it out. I'm sorry you've been through so much," she encourages, keeping her arms wrapped around me. I cry for the time we lost, for what I thought Jace and I could've been, for the pain in my body and heart. I've tried to be so strong over the last two years, to not let anything break me. But I can't keep doing it alone. I sink into her deeper, appreciating that I'm embracing my oldest friend, someone I truly care about, someone I've been through so much with.

When we pull apart, we smirk at each other, and our mirrored expressions give me even more hope that we can move forward together. That we might even be stronger because of it.

"It'll be okay, K. You are going to find someone who loves you and is so proud to be with you."

"Thanks, Liv. God, I've missed you," I say, swiping my sleeve under my eye.

"Do you want me to go, to let you rest?" she offers.

"Hell no," I nearly shout. "I might be tired, but I'm also really sick of thinking about what happened. I'd love for you to update me on everything I've missed in your life," I suggest, moving to get comfortable on the couch. "I apologize in advance if I forget a few details with the concussion though."

Liv smiles, also shifting to settle in deeper. "Let me know when you're ready."

2 8

JACE

I have no idea why my dad and my uncle don't get along, but I really hope he isn't as big of a homophobic asshole as my father.

I'm sitting in the shitty motel room I've been living in for the last few days, biting around my thumbnail as I stare at my phone, trying to hype myself up to call my uncle. It's a miracle my dad hasn't canceled my phone plan yet, but I know it's only a matter of time.

The money I had saved is nearly gone already. Turns out paying for a place to sleep each night and feeding yourself is expensive. Even though I picked this place because it seemed to be the cheapest, and it's only about a mile walk to school.

Thankfully, my little sister isn't as shitty as my parents. She messaged me on Facebook—apparently they blocked my number in her phone—saying she packed a bag full of my clothes and phone charger, and told me there was a convenience store down the street from her friend's house she could meet me at.

Molly and I have never been close, especially with the five-year age gap, so I was shocked she was willing to rebel against

213

my dad to help me. I've always resented how easy her life seemed compared to mine, and I never really gave her a chance.

Add it to the growing list of regrets I have for the first eighteen years of my life.

The last few days of being on my own have led me down a path filled with self-hatred. I hurt so many people, including the one person I care about more than anyone else: Kieran. The shame I feel is overwhelming whenever I picture him in a hospital bed. I was in so much denial about my attraction to him, and I have endless regret for that.

I tried to reach out on social media, but his account has either been deleted or he blocked me. I'm guessing it's the latter. All I want is to talk to him, to explain why I was late that day, how I came out to my dad, to ask him for another chance—a real chance.

But I deserve his hatred and his silence. I might not have been the one to hurt him, but David wouldn't have had the opportunity if it wasn't for the way I handled things. If only I'd come to terms with my sexuality in a healthier way that didn't involve targeting him and sneaking around.

I've thought about showing up at his house, but I don't have a car.

I've spent all my spare time watching his YouTube channel. That first night when I was alone in this creepy room, I was staring at the ceiling, thinking about how much everything had changed in so little time, when I remembered David's comment about his videos. It didn't take long to find his channel; Kieran is apparently kind of a big deal on there.

My stomach twisted when I saw the name of his channel: Sparkle's Makeup Tutorials.

The same name that I gave him as a taunt, the one that's shifted more recently into one of endearment. He's claimed it as his own.

I barely slept that night, only finally passing out mid-video to the sound of his voice. I've watched them all now. I had no idea how much effort went into the makeup he wears, how much skill and talent Kieran has. There are even other people who post their attempts at his looks even though they never look as good.

But he hasn't posted since before David attacked him.

There are so many people in the comments who love, and have been inspired by, his courage.

He can't give all that up.

I even made my own account to join in. I used my first and middle initial so he wouldn't recognize me, and the profile picture is one I took of the sunset over the pier in Atlantic city, so he'd never recognize it as me. Plus, I'm sure there are tons of other JJs.

I should probably accept that he doesn't want me in his life at all and move on, not be making new accounts online to watch his videos without him knowing. But even though I know I don't deserve it, there's still that part of me that hopes he'll be ready to forgive me one day, and I need to see for myself that he's okay. If he puts up a new video, then I'll know he is.

His sparkle might be dimmed right now, but I don't think it's gone.

God, I miss him.

I want to talk to him so badly. Want to pull him into me and hold him while I explain.

I've thought about reaching out to Olivia, but he told me they still aren't friends just a few weeks ago, and I highly doubt she'd give me his number.

But before I can decide to do anything else, there's another call I have to make first.

I finally hit the call button next to my uncle's name on my phone. For a long moment, I'm worried he won't answer and that I really will be all on my own. But he picks up after the third ring.

"Uncle Joey?"

"Jace? Is that really you?" His warm voice feels like a blanket wrapping around me as I exhale in relief. I'm not completely alone yet.

"It's me," I confirm. We've never spoken on the phone, but the birthday cards he sends that never have his info on the envelope—probably so my dad doesn't hide them from me—always have his number in them. I've put a lot of thought into this phone call over the last few days because I really do need help. I have no idea what I'll do if my uncle won't loan me money. But I've also only just freed myself from my father's control, and I don't want to trade one horrible man for another if he's also an asshole. I haven't seen him in years, so I can't be sure.

"Is everything okay? You've never called before."

I need to tell him the truth before anything else. I take in another steadying breath and blurt out everything. "So, it turns out I'm bi, like I'm attracted to both men and women—in case you don't know what that means—and when I told my father, he kicked me out. School ends in a few days, but I'm almost out of the money you've sent me over the years, and I don't really know what to do. I've been trying to find a job, but I haven't heard back yet from anyone." I slow down as I get to the part that I'm really nervous for.

"Is there any way you could loan me some money? Or send my birthday present early or something? If you were even planning to do that anymore," I say, trying my very best to sound casual and not like I'm going to fully break down if he can't help me out.

"Holy shit, Jace. Are you okay? Where are you?"

I appreciate his concern, and I'm hoping that it's a good sign, but I'm nervous he didn't answer about the money right away. "I'm staying in a motel near the school."

"Do you want me to come get you? I can send you money, too, but you don't need to live in a motel when I have a guest room you're welcome to stay in for as long as you need."

I pause for a minute, replaying his words in my head.

I can stay with him? In his guest room? For as long as I need?

Oh, thank fuck.

Relief crashes over me, and I fall back onto the bed, unable to remain upright with how much better I already feel.

"Wait." I pause, worried he might rescind his offer because maybe he didn't catch what I said earlier. "Did you hear the part about why he kicked me out? That I'm bi. Does that bother you?" I check. I refuse to let anyone else control me like my dad did.

"That definitely doesn't bother me, Jace," he reassures me. I think I might actually cry from how much better I feel knowing I still have his support. "Do you remember the last time I saw you?" he continues, confusing me with his change of topic.

"Uh, yeah, I think it was almost five years ago, right? At one of my games?"

"It was. Your dad and I got into a fight. Did he ever tell you why?" he prompts.

Although the memory isn't very clear, I can picture my dad yelling at his brother. "Uh, I think it had something to do with my dad being upset that your friend came with you. My dad said he wasn't invited."

My uncle's sigh is loud through the phone's speaker. "Jace, that friend was my boyfriend. He's now my husband… and, I don't want to make any promises, but he might be able to help you find a union job if that's something that interests you."

"Your husband?" I echo back, unable to form any relevant thoughts about the latter part of what he said.

"Yeah, he's the best," he states, love evident in his tone. "Jace, I'm so sorry you're dealing with all this on your own. When's the last day of school? Do you want me to come down there to help until you're ready to move in with us?"

I'm so relieved by his offer, so grateful he sounds nothing like my father that I easily agree. "If you want to, you can."

"Oh thank god, I don't think I would have been able to stay away knowing what I do now. What's your address?"

I tell him where I am, and he promises to see me in a few hours.

"Thank you so much, Uncle Joey, you're the best." I heave out another relieved sigh and hang up.

My mind is still reeling, processing that call. I can't believe I never knew my uncle is married to a man. And that they're going to let me live with them. Maybe even help me find a job.

It's all so surreal.

My life isn't over.

Maybe it's just beginning.

Fuck. I really need to talk to Kieran before I go anywhere though.

2 9

KIERAN

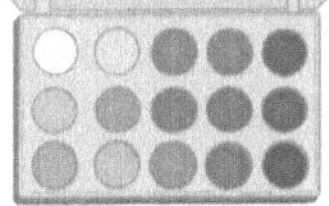

Summer Before College
July 2012

The doorbell rings, and I look around at Liv and Danny, curious as to who it could be. My parents are out, so I'm guessing it's a neighborhood kid with another sport's fundraiser.

It's been amazing to have Liv back in my life. She and Danny have been spending a lot of time hanging out at my house while I've been recovering. They even brought over their robes and caps to take graduation photos with me in my backyard, and my parents absolutely loved them for it.

Olivia was shocked when I showed her my YouTube channel, and she's now completely caught up on my content, claiming to be my biggest fan. Danny might still have her beat—I'm not gonna tell her that, though. She's given me some great ideas for ways to draw in even more views and offered to help in any way she can if I ever need it.

It feels like a big step for her that she isn't asking to be in the videos. The Liv of two years ago would have been after the spot-

219

light. Not that that's necessarily a bad thing, especially since I am the one filming myself and posting it for the world to see, but the fact that she's content to help me behind the scenes in a way that isn't self-serving gives me a lot of hope for our friendship going forward.

"One second," I call out as I make my way out of the kitchen and toward the front door. There have been so many fundraisers lately, and my parents sign up for all of them, but I really hope whoever this is has either the bucket of fancy popcorn or cookie dough.

I pull open the door, and the smile on my face immediately drops. My whole body freezes as I make eye contact with Jace.

What the hell is he doing here?

And how did he figure out where I live?

I blocked him on Facebook, finally. Him and David. I wanted to just move on from this mess and work on getting over him, but now he's standing on my doorstep, daring to look nervous.

"Kieran—" he starts.

I start to close the door, uninterested in hearing him out.

"Kieran, just let me explain, please." He sticks his arm out, preventing me from slamming it in his face.

"Explain?" I scoff. "What's there to explain? I've torn apart every interaction we've ever had, and none of it makes sense. You're clearly a skilled liar, and I can't trust a word out of your mouth. There's no need to explain yourself now." I attempt to push the door closed again. The idea of hearing Jace's new version of the "truth," whatever twisted excuses he's come up with, makes me want to throw up.

"Kieran, please?"

"No." I move to shut the door again, but his hand is still there.

"You're… you're not wearing makeup," he says quietly. "You always—"

"God, Jace, you already hurt me so much. Can't you just leave?"

"It's just… I've never seen you without makeup on." He really is a way better actor than I'd given him credit for. He looks genuinely concerned. No wonder I'd believed his lies. "I don't like it, K," he adds, calling me a fucking nickname like we're friends.

"Seriously?" I bite out, my voice sharp. It's not like I've been in a hurry to do my makeup with my wrist still in a cast, but he's too self-centered to make that connection. "You think that's what we need to talk about? My face? I'm done wearing makeup in this stupid town. You fucking win, Jace. You got what you wanted. Now *go.*"

"Kieran, please can I come in so we can talk?" he begs.

My mind is warring between rage and hurt, and my defenses are slipping the longer I look at him. I rake my lips against my teeth, trying to calm myself down. "No. I don't want to hear your excuses. You hurt me enough, Jace. You broke my fucking heart and that's on me for falling for your lies. Can't you just let me get over you in peace?" My voice cracks, and I hate that I sound as weak as I feel. I gave him more of me than I planned when he showed up here, but I felt like I was moving on. Or starting to, and despite myself, a tear rolls down my cheek and I quickly wipe it away.

He opens his mouth like he's going to say something, but nothing comes out. He just stands there for a second, jaw parted, looking completely helpless, like he isn't the one who ripped out my heart and stomped it into the ground.

Did I think I was starting to heal? Because that wound feels fresher than ever. "You okay, K?" I turn back. Liv and Danny both approach the front door, probably concerned about what was taking so long.

Liv sees Jace first. "What the fuck are you doing here?" she demands.

"I need to explain, I didn't—"

"Explain, what?" she challenges. "How you're a selfish asshole who hurt my best friend?"

I glance at Danny, who's looking between the three of us, very confused.

"You need to go, Jace," I say, holding my ground.

"I'm leaving town today, this is my last chance to explain," he tries.

"He told you to leave," Liv repeats.

Finally, Jace drops his arm, looking utterly devastated. I have no idea if this is another act, but if, on the off chance, my not following whatever script he's prepared is upsetting him, *good*. Fuck him.

"I'm sorry, Sparkles. I'm so fucking sorry," he mutters, and with that, he finally turns to leave, approaching the waiting car in my driveway. There are two men waiting for him, and he shakes his head as he gets into the back of the car.

My pulse is hammering in my ears from, once again, having to stand up to him.

Did he really think it would be a good idea to come here? Was he trying to make himself feel better about the way things ended? Did he really think, after everything he'd done to me, that I'd be in a full face of makeup at my own house? He spent months threatening me to try to get me to stop. And now he's going to stand here and complain that I'm not wearing any?

He and David can get fucked.

If David wants to post all about my YouTube channel and talk shit, then that's what he'll do. Maybe I'll get new followers.

I'm done caring. Next month, I'll finally be at a school where nobody knows me as "the freak who wears makeup." There, surrounded by millions of people, I get to start over.

I'll probably even start wearing makeup again in public.

It's been weeks, at this point, since I posted a new video. As much as I hate to admit it, being so blindsided by Jace and ending up in the hospital did break my spirits and my confidence.

At first, I told myself it was practical because my wrist was broken, and holding a brush steady sent pain shooting up my arm. But, even if I could've pushed through, I didn't want to give anyone another reason to look at me. I'm done being a punching bag for shitty people.

But now, after seeing Jace again, the urge to create a new video is at an all-time high. Inspiration is coursing through me as I storm away from the door and go to my bedroom computer. When I log in, I'm met with thousands of comments. People asking me where I've been, telling me they miss my videos, that my tutorials are helping them get through their own rough days. Some are even defending me against trolls.

It's weird to me how these people don't know me, and yet they feel safer than most of the ones who do.

I think I'm ready to do this. For them. And for me.

I set up my tripod, turn on my light, and start digging through my palettes.

If they want another video, I'll give them one. And this time, it's not just about makeup—it's about showing up, even after my bully tried to break me.

PART II

30

KIERAN

Present Day
January 2025

Producer: "What are you hoping to find in a partner?"

Kieran: "I've gotten to a point in my life where I've accomplished a lot, but at the end of the day, there's no one to share it with. I'd love to meet someone who can handle the attention I get from fans, my busy schedule, and that part of my life will always be public. But who also gives me space to be vulnerable when we're alone. Someone who loves *me*, not their online perception of me."

This is going to be the longest I've been without my phone since I first got one in high school.

It feels melodramatic to even be thinking about it while I'm here, preparing to begin filming *Love Without Labels,* the reality TV show I signed up for. I should be focused on what's happening around me or if I'll meet *the one,* but all I can think about is how much I'm already missing social media.

It will be worth it, I remind myself.

My fans know I'm taking a mini hiatus—I posted about it right before they took my phone. I knew I'd have to give it up to be here, but I feel naked without it as one of the show's producers, Mitch, leads me through the hallway to my new room. We stop in front of a door that's painted like the LGBTQIA+ flag, and he unlocks it to reveal an apartment covered in even more rainbow decor. It's fitting, affirming even, for a queer dating show, but it's definitely not my personal style.

I wouldn't consider myself to be fully emo by any means, but ever since Halloween senior year of high school, I've been drawn to a darker, more masc look. Even when I make videos about other styles, there's usually a masculine undertone that feels like my most authentic form of self-expression.

Still, I've never changed my brand name: Sparkles.

It doesn't really match who I am now—it hasn't for a while —but I like that. I like that it makes people think twice when they see the name, then see me. It challenges their assumptions before I even say a word because you can be grounded and still glitter, dark and soft, confident and healing all at once. That's kind of the point of being alive—to keep evolving, becoming more of who you really are.

Maybe that's why I've kept the name all these years. Because Sparkles reminds me where I came from, who I was when I was with *him*, and who I refuse to stop being now.

"Kieran? Does that sounds good?" Mitch draws my attention back to him.

"Uh, yeah," I confirm.

He jumps right into talking about where my mic pack will go and how he'll grab me to record my intro session after I "settle in," but my brain is still only half here. I think it's finally hitting me that I'm actually on the show. I keep my expression neutral, but my thoughts have officially shifted into "holy shit, I'm actually doing this" territory as I look around the room.

Up until now, I've pretty much just daydreamed about falling in love, especially with someone who doesn't know anything about my career. I've been picturing who I might meet here, and what we can talk about that won't give away any of the "labels" the show wants to remain hidden while we're in the blind dating portion the first week.

I've been so focused on the unique opportunity, after so many failed relationship attempts, that I've kind of ignored how vulnerable this would all make me feel.

It's one thing to sign up for something like this, but it's another to actually be here, talking to producers, being shown my room, noticing the cameras that are strategically "hidden" throughout the space to record every single moment in the place where I might meet my future spouse.

It all has my nerves escalating because if I meet someone on this show, it won't be private. It can't be.

None of what I do or say here will be private.

And that's terrifying.

I may live in the public eye, but I'm used to being the one with all the control. I decide what content makes the final cut in my videos, what events to go to, what products to endorse, just how much of me the internet gets to see. After over a decade of content creation, I've still never put a single relationship online for my followers to dissect. Not once.

Every time I've been asked why, I've claimed it's out of my desire to keep something for myself—and that's true—but the bigger truth is, I've never been confident anyone has actually wanted *me*. Not the version they see on camera or the public name attached to my brand, but *Kieran,* the actual person.

My last partner dumped me because I wouldn't "hard launch" them on my socials. They swore it was about wanting to feel chosen, but deep down, I knew what it was—they wanted the exposure. The clout. They wanted to be the person dating Sparkles, far more than they ever actually wanted to date Kieran.

And when I said not yet, they broke up with me and dated someone they met through me.

Unfortunately, it wasn't the first time.

People assume once someone is successful, that they become somehow untouchable, impervious to negativity. But the bullying never stops online, and, for me at least, the loneliness has never fully gone away.

I've accomplished so many things I never thought would be possible when I started my channel out of spite in my childhood bedroom. I love that I'm able to make a living expressing myself with makeup and fashion, and sharing the joy it's brought me with the world. I live in an incredible four-bedroom condo in New York City, my best friend works with me, so we hang out all the time, and I know I'm biased, but I'm pretty confident I have the cutest cat ever.

I just wish that I had someone to share the life I've built with.

Danny always sends me photos with his husband and their baby, and while I don't want a baby, the husband part seems really nice. He's out in the suburbs, and whenever I get to see them, I can feel how happy they are.

Meanwhile, I've struggled to know who I can trust enough to even try. I learned a long time ago to be suspicious of anyone who suddenly decides they want me around, and the years have only proven I was right to remain cautious.

Jace was my first lesson. I couldn't fully process my feelings for him when I was eighteen, but now that I've had space, I can admit he completely broke my heart. Jace pretended to see me, to want me, only to crush me the second it stopped serving him. It took me longer than I'd like to admit to get over him, which is embarrassing considering how cruel he was before we ever hooked up and that we never even dated.

Now, unlike Jace, instead of people wanting to hide away their connection with me, they're overly eager to smile at my side for the camera. But I know they wouldn't look twice at me if I had twenty followers instead of over twenty million.

That's why I'm here.

Because *Love Without Labels* is anonymous.

The other contestants won't know my name, my handle, or my follower count. No one can look me up before the first date. The people who are on this show are all here seeking a true connection, the same way I am.

It's ironic, really, that I signed up to be filmed even more than usual in an effort to find someone who could love me for who I am off camera. But, I think it might actually work.

I just hope the risk will be worth it. I know the show wants the most entertaining TV, not necessarily the reality of what happens. I can only hope I'm portrayed positively in their editing and that I didn't accidentally dig my own grave for my brand by coming on this show.

Mitch is still talking, and I realize I've completely zoned out, but I had to fill out a novel's worth of paperwork with my lawyer and sit through so many preproduction calls that none of this is new information anyway.

"Any questions?" he asks with a producer's smile that says *don't actually ask me anything that'll make my job harder.*

"I think I'm good," I confirm with a smile, trying to stay on his good side.

"Alright, great! Your show phone is on the coffee table. It's all set up with approved apps you're allowed to use. Right now, it's just the show app with updates and instructions, a weather app, a news app, and our streaming app if you'd like to watch TV. When you reach the point of matching with the other participants, you'll be able to start messaging them. For now, you can start working on your vibe board with the instructions on the TV. We'll approve it before tomorrow, and I'll come get you to do some interview questions shortly. See you soon, Kieran! We're excited to have you here."

I pick up the iPhone the show's set up for me, but the lack of social media makes it feel like a prop and does nothing to ease my withdrawal from the real thing.

Maybe creating this vibe board will be a welcome distraction. I make my way over to the couch, noticing a "hidden" camera over the television, so I make sure to set myself up with flattering angles as I get comfortable. There's a mirror option for the TV I remember Mitch mentioning, so I set that up before clicking into an app with two overlapping hearts for its icon. The instructions appear on the screen, and I read them aloud so that the audience can hear them too, just like I was told to do.

"Welcome to your vibe board. Please take the time to add some information about you for your fellow contestants to see during your blind dates. This can include images of anything you would like to use to describe your 'vibe' that will be shown on your feed. All boards will be approved by the producers prior to the first blind dates to avoid any identifying information being given."

Most people might find it strange to narrate what they're doing, but I've been making content for far too long for any of this to even faze me.

I get to work going through their stock photo options which are pretty basic.

"I definitely need to add makeup on here," I say to the room. "These are all generic but they'll do. Hmm, what else?"

Huh. Without social media to mindlessly scroll or my next video to worry about planning, I'm realizing just how few hobbies I have. I have no idea what else I could possibly add to this vibe board.

"Adding a photo of my cat, or close to it, makes sense," I say out loud, thinking of Freddie.

"Hmm, what else?" I consider out loud. "I should probably add video recording related items too. I could only imagine inviting someone I match with here to my house and them being shocked to see I have a whole recording studio set up."

There aren't many good options, but I do what I can, even though it feels like there's still so much whitespace.

I used to paint in my free time before I really got into makeup. I'd spent a lot of my time sketching and experimenting with different types of acrylics and oil paints. The lighting that I'd obsessed over when I was painting made picking up highlights and contouring a breeze.

I actually have a few sketchbooks and watercolors hidden away in a cabinet in my room. No one knows about that, not even my best friend—I don't want her suggesting I use my art for content. It's something just for me, and I usually only resort to pulling them out when I'm feeling especially alone. With so much of my life online, it feels good to keep it for myself.

But I'm here to find someone to share my life with. And I don't think I can do that if I'm holding even more parts of myself back when so much needs to remain hidden for the show's setup. It doesn't need to be a big deal, I can add it with other things, and no one but me will ever know that this feels like a big moment.

"A couple more makeup items won't hurt. I'll add some art supplies and a photo of New York, too." I step back to look at it and decide it's good enough.

By the time I'm finished, I'm back to being excited about this whole plan. I love the idea of remaining anonymous and building an actual connection with someone, and seeing the ways they're setting us up to do so makes it seem like it's really possible.

I have a good feeling about this. I think I could really leave this show with the partner I've been daydreaming about.

JACE

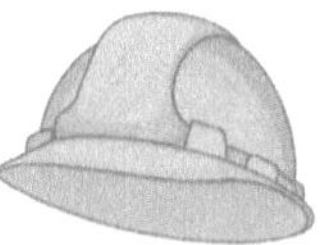

Producer: "Describe your ideal partner in three words."

Jace: *Don't say Kieran "Sparkles" Delaney, don't say it.* "Loyal, kind, steady."

I wish I could text my uncles about Andy.

The show's host is like a cartoon character come to life with how fucking enthusiastic he is, and I could barely hold back my laughter during the welcome interview and promo we had to shoot for the show. Joey would probably roll his eyes at how over-the-top he was during that whole interview, but I know Patrick would have loved every second of it. He would've tried to match his enthusiasm to see if Andy would turn it up even more in response.

Fuck, I miss them already. It's been years since I've lived in their actual apartment, but moving out into my own place in the same building didn't exactly result in seeing them any less. Living on my own just meant that my dates got to sit through their interrogation once we were officially dating instead of over breakfast after the first overnight. I still eat meals with my uncles whenever we're all home, watch sports with them, and wander into their place whenever I'm bored.

Patrick is even my supervisor now. This will be the first real time off I've had since I started as his apprentice all those years ago. I might not have pictured my future as a structural iron and steel worker when I was pulling out of the draft, but I love what I do.

It's a physically demanding job that also requires mental focus, and I always feel accomplished at the end of the day knowing how hard I've worked. Seeing all the finished structures I was a part of building throughout New York City always makes me happy. I love knowing I've contributed to the ever-evolving landscape of such a historic place.

It can be easy to feel insignificant in a city with so many people, to feel lost in a world where so few people really know me. But thinking about families still living and working in buildings I helped create hundreds of years from now or how many people have crossed bridges I worked on, it reminds me that everyone is important, and we might never know exactly how many lives we positively impact, and that's okay.

I am definitely a little homesick right now, eagerly awaiting the dating portion to start.

We're in Atlanta now to film even though the casting was done in New York. If we partner up with someone, we'll continue the second half of filming in New York, but I guess building their studio and filming here was cheaper. Everything is cheaper outside of the city I call home, but I don't see myself ever leaving it.

I've got a great gig with my union. I tend to volunteer for a lot of overtime, and have never taken time off, so I had banked enough hours to be here without risking my job.

I just hope being here works out. I love the idea of the

show. After things settled, and I became more comfortable with my new life in NYC, I *really* embraced my sexual identity.

I'll be the first to admit I have daddy issues, and I'm sure all the men I dated in those early years after coming out would agree. Without my dad's toxic presence, I could finally let loose. I've calmed down quite a bit from my nightclubs and hookups every weekend phase, and eventually remembered I'm attracted to women too.

I was worried that dating a woman would make me less queer somehow. That it would invalidate everything I went through with my dad, and even with Kieran, if I ended up with a woman. But now I know that isn't true. I'm bi, I've always been bi, and I always will be. The gender of my partner doesn't change that fact.

I've wanted to find my person for a while now, and that's why I'm here. I've seen the relationship my uncles have, and I want that too. I'd love to have someone to come home to after a long shift, to just hang out on the couch with. Or to check out a new restaurant or bar with Joey and Patrick instead of third-wheeling all the time.

But wanting something doesn't always mean you're ready for it.

I thought my last partner, Amanda, might be different. We dated for almost a year. But even though she was also a *Sparkle's Tutorials* fan, and she liked that we watched the videos together, she eventually accused me of "caring more about a stranger on the internet" than her.

I probably should've mentioned at some point that I used to know Kieran—that I was the first one who ever called him Sparkles—but I've learned the hard way that if my partner already thinks I'm obsessed with a celebrity, admitting I actually know them only makes it worse.

Sure, maybe if I didn't spend every second of my free time

on his social media, I'd have an easier time staying in a rela-tionship.

But that's easier said than done. I've tried that, I really have. I always fail.

It's just that, none of the people I've dated have compared to the version of Kieran I've built up in my head. I've spent years torturing myself with what-ifs, imagining the way things could have played out differently if they hadn't ended the way they did between us in high school, picturing what could have happened if they hadn't ended at all. That's way more fun than any healthy adult relationship I could have.

Kidding, but this is why I work so much overtime.

And it's also why I'm here. I'm going to get over my obses-sion in a setting that will hopefully help me to make a connection with someone while I'm isolated from the outside world. I can't obsessively check his social media if the show's taken away my phone.

Might have been an extreme way to break the habit, but desperate times and all that.

I need to stop thinking about him now that I'm all settled into my apartment. My vibe board is ready to go, and it's almost time for my first blind date. This is a once-in-a-lifetime experience, and I do want to give it my all.

I'm in my two-bedroom apartment. One room is for sleeping, and the other has been converted into a "date room." The dimly lit room has a loveseat set up in front of a TV screen. There's a desk off to the side with a lamp, a journal with a pen, and water. I grab the bottle, taking a sip as I get settled on the couch. We'll be in here a lot today as we talk with each of the other seventeen contestants, so I'm glad I actually fit comfortably on the couch. I'm a pretty big guy and cramming myself into a tiny chair all day would not have been ideal.

The TV screen lights up with a video of my new favorite TV host, Andy, his comically wide smile still in place. "Welcome to

Love Without Labels!" he starts. "You're about to embark on the most exciting and unique journey of your lives. This isn't just any dating show—this is about making true, lasting connections that go deeper than physical attraction, gender, or age. Are you ready to open your hearts and minds?"

I sure hope so.

"Here's how this works," he continues. "You'll stay in your date rooms for the duration of the morning. Each of you will get ten minutes with every other contestant for a speed date. Your voices will be modified to stay anonymous, and remember, no names or gender-revealing pieces of information. Use only initials and write down notes to help you eventually narrow down your connections."

There's dramatic background music and everything as Andy leans into the camera, dropping into a more serious tone. "Now, a few things to remember for this once-in-a-lifetime opportunity: be open, be vulnerable, and don't hold back. The only way to find a true connection is to be yourself. The producers will be there to support you every step of the way, and I'll be checking in regularly. So... who's ready to fall in love!?" Then Andy throws his arms open, giant smile back in place as he nearly shouts. "Good luck, everyone, and remember: love is love! Now, let's get started!" The video ends with a swirl of rainbow glitter and the show's logo.

This is it. The screen changes to what must be my first date's vibe board.

"Hello?" the robotic voice startles me. I knew they were distorting our voices but it still catches me off guard, and I have trouble focusing on the conversation I'm supposed to be having to quickly "get to know" this other contestant.

But we only have ten minutes, and before I know it, the screen goes back to the show's logo with a two-minute count-down to the next date. I guess I'm supposed to take notes in the journal, so I finally pick it up and try to remember the initials of the person I just talked to… BB? Maybe? Whoever they were, I don't think I'll be ranking them very high if I've already forgotten what we talked about. Not that I did much talking.

After the eighth date that goes pretty much the same way, I'm about ready to give up on this whole experience. I'm almost halfway done, and I can't name a single standout connection. How do they expect us to click with anyone in ten minutes?

The next vibe board comes on the screen, and I laugh at how opposite to mine it looks. There are farm pictures, fruits and vegetables, and a bunch of random seasonal things that make it clear this person is into the fall season.

My board, on the other hand, has a lot of city images, bridges and buildings, some of which I actually worked on. I also put food on there, but none of it is very healthy. I tend to eat out a lot because my uncles and I can't cook. There's also craft beer, and pictures of basketball and hockey, my preferred sports to watch these days. I think their intention was for us to include pictures of our hobbies, but I don't think internet stalking my high school situationship counts as an actual hobby.

"Hey, I'm LM." That distorted voice starts again, and I can't help but comment on it.

"L, are you already as sick of the robot voice as I am or am I just not cut out for this show?"

A strange distorted sound follows that I belatedly realize must be a laugh. "Yeah, this process has been a little overwhelming," L confirms, and I relax a bit. I've already determined that I'm struggling to learn anything about the other participants in the short time we're given, so I might as well just talk about how weird this situation is.

"You could say that again," I agree, sinking further back onto the couch as I set down my notebook I've been struggling to even use. "I'm JR, by the way. Sorry, I know we're supposed to be talking about our interests and stuff, but we're not even halfway done and there's only so many times that I can explain that I like the city."

That laugh sound comes again. "The ten minutes is a bit rushed," L comments. "But I can't imagine this round lasting days if they tried to extend it."

"Shit, that does sound worse. Okay L, it's official—you're smarter than me. I need to stop complaining and remember how happy I am to be here." I say that last part aloud even though I'm mostly reminding myself.

The rest of our conversation is easy and it definitely puts me at ease. I wouldn't say our connection feels romantic in any way, but I'm grateful that L was able to put me in a better headspace. I wouldn't mind talking to them again.

I'm feeling a lot better about the next few people I talk to. The conversations, although still rushed, do feel a bit more like typical first-date small talk than the pained silence I found myself in during a few of the first dates.

The next vibe board pops up and my "don't think about Kieran" plan is immediately abandoned. Not only does this person have the same initials, but there's makeup on their board *and* video icons. It's mixed in with cat pictures, art supplies, and images of New York.

I force myself to take in a deep breath before my thoughts can get carried away with the coincidence. I know that there are probably tens of thousands of people in New York whose first and last names also start with K and D. Plenty of them wear makeup. Art is a very common hobby, and a lot of those people probably know how to record a TikTok.

There's no reason for my heart to be racing or the incessant what-ifs to be running through my mind.

"Hey, JR. I'm KD." That robotic voice is back, but this time, I'm less annoyed. I can't think about anything other than the similarities between this KD and the man I came here to forget.

KIERAN

Producer: "What's your idea of a healthy relationship?"

Kieran: "I love the idea of being in a relationship where we can both breathe comfortably. Where we don't lose ourselves, but we don't feel alone, either. Being each other's safe place when everything else is chaotic. I want trust and laughter and knowing the hard days won't scare them off. Especially because, for me, my fame and the life I've built around it could be gone in an instant. So having someone who shows up and loves me, keeps me steady, reminds me that there's so much more to life than what's posted online, would be amazing."

*E*very time a new vibe board flashes onto the screen, I question every life choice that led me here. Not because the other people are bad, but I'm worried I might have gone into this experience with a little too much hope. I mean, what are the odds that my ideal partner happens to be one of the other seventeen people who were chosen to be on the show?

Not likely, especially because I feel like I'm at a networking event where every conversation sounds exactly the same.

And I have to do it seventeen times.

One date talked excessively about hiking, and the only thing I could think of was that meme about how my idea of being outdoorsy is sitting on a patio with a drink in my hand.

Waking up at five in the morning to go climb a mountain? Not for me. I much prefer to stay *in* the city.

Another talked about football, someone else about photography, then the farm, astrology, and even cars. The closest person I felt a connection to so far was RR because at least we could talk about fashion, but it felt platonic.

They were all… fine, pleasant even.

But it's still a problem because *fine* is forgettable. *Fine* doesn't have me doodling anyone's initials while I imagine our wedding. *Fine* doesn't make me forget the camera in the corner.

It keeps me in my head, feeling far too nervous. I want to be making the most of this opportunity, to really give myself the best chance to connect with someone, but I'm distracted with concern about my reputation and how my answers will be picked apart by my fans.

But I chose to come here for a reason. I can't give up hope when there are still a handful of dates left, so I tell myself to remember how excited I was about this experience and to focus on giving these next dates my all. Whether I feel a connection or not, I need to pick my top people from this first round to continue dating. Maybe that spark will come.

The next vibe board pops up with city skylines, bridges, and buildings. There are basketball and hockey photos on there as well. Then the initials: JR.

It's stupid my mind immediately goes to Jace-fucking-Ryan. Even thirteen years later, I can't seem to forget the first man who broke my heart. The only one I've ever really given a chance, if I'm being completely honest.

Logically, I know the odds of Jace being this JR are slim to none. But knowing that doesn't stop my pulse from kicking up anyway.

I haven't kept up with him at all. I had no reason to. I blocked him that day and was done.

Except "done" hasn't meant forgotten, as much as I wish it did.

Whenever I do think of him, those same feelings of shame and regret I felt all those years ago immediately flood my stomach.

I let Jace in even after he showed me exactly who he was. I let myself believe he wouldn't hurt me. That he might actually like me too. That he wasn't just being nice because I was getting him off regularly. All because I assumed I mattered to him in the same way he mattered to me.

He hurt me in a way I didn't know how to process. He left me feeling used and discarded. The way he dismissed what I thought we had, not even bothering to end things himself, sending David to threaten me that day... Whatever his excuse was, it devastated me that the bond I thought we'd been building had only existed in my head.

It messed with my ability to trust people in ways I'm still unlearning. I know he's why I default to assuming everyone who wants to get close to me is only doing it for their own personal gain.

Knowing that doesn't stop me from making the assumption though. It's only been solidified by a couple of my exes moving from me to other influencers, which really fucking stung.

Thirteen years may have passed since senior year of high school, and in a lot of ways, I've moved on. But I don't think I'll ever truly be able to let it go.

Focus, I remind myself.

There is no possible way this is Jace. Besides, he liked baseball; his whole life was baseball. This has two completely different sports on it, and the initials, JR, are common. There are only so many letters in the alphabet. He's probably still living in Jersey with a life that looks a lot like his dad's did back then, stuck in some dead-end job with a wife and 2.5 kids after a failed baseball career. If he had actually gone pro, I think it would've been unavoidable to hear about, and since I never did, he must not have been as good as he always made it seem.

This person is probably lovely, and I shouldn't judge them for having shitty initials.

I take a deep breath and begin the conversation.

"Hi, I'm KD."

"Hey, I'm JR," the distorted voice says back.

Instead of bringing up the vibe board like most other dates have done, I go for a question. "What is your favorite thing about your day-to-day life?"

"Oh cool. Are we actually going to talk? No one has asked me anything that wasn't on the board yet." They laugh. "Uh, probably spending time with my uncles. I live in the same building as them, and we'll drink our coffee together in the mornings, watch sports together—it doesn't really matter what we're doing, but hanging out with them is always great. They're pretty much my best friends. I even work with one of them."

Before I can even respond, they're speaking again.

"God, that makes me sound really old and boring, doesn't it?" They laugh, but as someone who grew up with a close, supportive family, I love hearing that.

"No, it's sweet," I assure them. "I bet you miss them, huh?" They make what I think is a humming sound in confirmation. "Is it bad to admit the thing I miss the most being here is my phone." I laugh at my own sad reality, and it sounds like they do too.

"You and me both. It's so embarrassing how much I miss being on my phone, too. It's a complete digital detox being here."

My face breaks out into the first real grin I've had during one of these dates at their easy agreement. "You think that's the real reason half the people here signed up?" I joke. Only partly.

"Well, that and the chance to be humiliated on national TV," they add, and I laugh again.

"You're exposing all my deepest fears right now, JR. How are you doing that so quickly?" I tease. I'm smiling like a fool, and that definitely hasn't happened with anyone else today.

"Gifted, I suppose," they say simply. Then, with no warning, they add, "What else are you afraid of?"

"That's a pretty loaded question for a speed date."

"I like loaded questions, I think they tell you a lot about a person."

I wish I could see their face, not even to know what they look like—although, I am curious—but to confirm if their expression matches mine, if they're enjoying this as much as I am. This feels like the first real conversation I've had today, so I don't hold back, giving them the most honest answer I can think of.

"I'm afraid of wasting my time on people who only like the idea of me. Or what I can do for them. Or the version of me they've decided I am in their head."

I don't think they were expecting my answer, and for a moment, I worry I've scared them away already as I wait for their reply.

"Well, shit, K. I can completely understand that," they finally respond, and instead of feeling relief, my nerves spike as I realize that was the first real thing I admitted on this show because I *did* forget all about the cameras.

I quickly move on. "Your turn, what about you?" I hold my breath, wondering if they'll be as honest as I was while they take a moment to consider their response.

"Living my life for someone else. Letting them dictate my choices and make me feel small for what I like and want, and just for who I am as a person, I guess."

Well, that was a very real answer. This is such an unexpectedly raw conversation to have. My heart is pounding, and I feel seen in a way I definitely wasn't expecting today.

"I can also relate to that," I confirm. I don't want this to end, but I know we don't have time to expand on these heavy topics right now. "Maybe a lighter question?" I offer.

"We actually only have about thirty seconds left," JR points out. "This is the first date that hasn't felt long enough."

Something flutters to life in my stomach at their remark. This *was* different than the other dates today. "I feel the same way," I admit. The screen goes back to the show's logo, and I'm excited about how disappointed I am.

Maybe things will be more than fine after all.

3 3

JACE

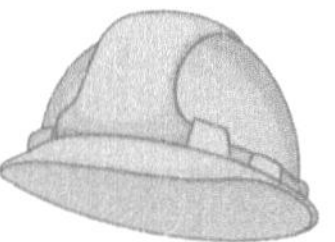

Producer: "What makes you feel loved?"

Jace: "Growing up, I had no idea that love could be offered without expectation. As an adult, I've felt the most loved by the people in my life who offer unconditional support. The people who I know will always be there for me even when I make mistakes."

The last speed date finally finishes, and Andy's excited face is back up on the screen. "You did it! The first round is officially over! Can you believe it? Some of you might have already talked to your future spouse."

Wouldn't that be something? I know it's a long shot, but I fucking hope so. Today has reminded me how much dating sucks.

"Any guesses on who it might be?"

It might sound crazy, considering how little I know about them at this point, but KD immediately pops into my head.

Honestly, they were the only one that I felt that spark with. LM seemed cool, but talking to them felt like I was hanging out with my uncles. I was instantly comfortable, but I'm not nervous that they won't want to talk to me again the way I am with KD.

I think K would be the only one with any chance of distracting me from my Sparkles obsession. Do I really think we'll get married after our first conversation though? Not really. But I guess that's why we're here, right? To see if that's a possibility.

"Here's what happens next," Andy continues. "After you take a break to eat and decompress, spend some time reviewing your notes and thinking about who you'd like to talk to again—and who you're ready to say goodbye to forever. You can request up to ten people to match with for the next round. Make sure to rank your top three for a better chance of connecting with them again."

Ten seems like a lot of people to have connected with. *Wait no, focus.* I'm here to unplug from the outside world, and maybe even find someone who can finally hold a candle to Kieran. I can't do that if no one wants to talk to me again, so I should probably submit a full list.

Andy leans toward the camera as if he wants our full attention before he goes on. "If both of you request each other, you'll be able to directly send messages in our app so you can plan your next date, which could be as soon as tonight. While you absolutely can message whenever you want, we strongly encourage you to plan daily dates if you want to stay matched. If you need prompts, we have some in the rooms, and you can find additional prompts on your app."

Where were the prompts in the first round? I really could have used those.

Andy says something about twists and giving people second chances, but I'm distracted trying to replay the dates from today. Most of them really do blur together in my memory. He claps his hands, drawing my attention back to the screen. "Once everyone's results are submitted on the app, you'll get a message from the producers with your matches." He says something else about the top three, but I'm still stuck on ranking anyone beyond my top two choices.

Andy finally wraps up the video, saying, "Best of luck, everyone! Remember, love is love. Follow your heart, ignore labels, and let's see where it leads you!"

I grab the journal—not that I think my notes will be much help—and head back into the main space to make a late lunch. Pasta is pretty much all I can handle so I start boiling water as I flip through what I wrote down. At least I got everyone's initials. That has to count for something.

The phone they gave us pings—gross, where is the silent option on this thing—and it's a notification stating we can now see other people's vibe boards. Which is admittedly a lot more helpful than most of the notes I took.

After taking a break to focus on making and eating my lunch, I rip out a page from the notebook and write numbers one through ten on a clean page. Obviously, KD goes at the top. LM was cool too and even though I didn't feel a romantic connection, I'll gladly talk to them again. Maybe things will change after more time together.

I take my time going through each of the boards, and with the few things I did have written down, I slowly fill in the rest of the numbers before submitting my final choices in the app.

I'm sure they need time to go through everything, so I consider taking a nap but decide to see if they'll let us watch any sports while we're here instead. I'm surprisingly nervous about the pairings, and I don't think I could actually fall asleep.

What if I don't match with anyone?

That nagging fear grows louder in my head, but I remind myself that KD and I seemed to have a connection, and all I need is for them to have ranked me in their top ten, which seems likely.

I breathe a little easier seeing that the TV does have both NHL and NBA games to stream. I didn't really get into sports other than baseball until I was living with my uncles, so I'm a New York fan and settle in to watch the Dragons hockey game I missed last night.

I'm so focused on the game that I almost jump out of my seat when my phone makes that *ping* sound again. There's a message from the producers, but it's not about the matchings I'm expecting.

PRODUCER JAY

> I know it's day one and it's probably been a lot to take in, but please remember to say as many of your thoughts out loud as possible so the audience can know what's going on.

Riiiiight. The cameras. "Sorry," I say even though I have no idea where the cameras are. When I signed up, excited about the fact that I'd be in the bubble of the show, I never really stopped to consider that I was putting myself in the spotlight to do so.

All my social media accounts are under the name JJ. No one I actually know follows me, and I pretty much only use them to interact with Sparkle's content and his other fans. I'm a moderator in a few fan pages, so I've talked to a lot of people online through that, but I've never met any of them in person or shown my face.

Due to the show trying to gain traction when this is over, I do have to create new public social media accounts so they can tag me in content and fans of the show can find me.

It's kind of wild to think about people I grew up with seeing this. My sister knew I was going on the show, and I gave her the important dates for if I actually make it all the way to getting married, but she's the only person I talk to from *before*.

Most days I feel like a completely different person than the confused asshole teenager I used to be, but I've never been able to close that chapter of my life completely. Not with the way things ended with Kieran. I know he blames me for whatever David said and did in the woods, and even though I would've never instructed David to do what he did, I know my fear and insistence to keep us a secret is what led to David confronting him in the first place, so it is my fault that it happened.

I still hate how much my actions hurt him. I don't think I'll ever be able to move on from it entirely when I'll never be able to properly apologize.

My phone pings again, and this time, it actually is the matches. I see the message from the producers again, so I attempt to react "out loud."

My smile is genuine as I say, "My top choice was KD, and it looks like we've matched." I'm not at all surprised that my list isn't very long when I felt like I was putting people randomly on there toward the end. "I have four matches. LM was also in my top three, and we matched, as well as AP and SJ."

Now that we can message people, I go right to KD's contact and send an invite link where they can see my availability to schedule a date. I think the producers are trying to avoid us talking about the other contestants with each other, so this way, K can just book a date, and I can accept. Easy.

I chew on the corner of my thumbnail as I debate sending an actual message or if I should wait to see if they schedule something. I let out the breath I didn't realize I was holding when the date invitation comes through from KD moments later. They request to have a date in the first available time slot, and I eagerly accept.

I share my calendar with my other matches so they can plan dates if they'd like, but I grab the notebook and head back to the date room. I don't want to be late.

Our first conversation went by so quickly, once I got over the initial shock of their initials matching Kieran and the vibe board having makeup, it was so much better than any of the other dates. Now I'm nervous, worried that I've built it up too much in my head. I've been telling myself to focus on how great being here, away from social media, is. But I think I've been doing that in an attempt to protect myself from being disappointed if I don't meet anyone special. I really would like this social experiment to work. I'm so tired of being alone.

"Hey, JR. Are you there yet?" Their robotic voice comes through the speakers, and I already find myself smiling.

"I am. I'm glad we matched. The first conversation left me wanting more," I admit, but I hurry to continue so they don't feel obligated to agree. "So KD, what's your favorite thing in your day-to-day life?"

They laugh, probably because I've repeated their question from earlier, but I want to know their answer too. "Probably hanging out with my cat. I just have the one, in case you were picturing someone with, like, twenty in their apartment. Although, sometimes I'm jealous of those people." I laugh at the honesty in their answer. "See I made myself sound old there, too. I know we're not supposed to talk ages, but swear I'm not elderly," they add.

I laugh again, feeling very excited about this connection. "I won't get specific either, but I promise I'm around the average age for people on these types of shows."

"I don't know, now I'm starting to worry that I accidentally signed up for one of those 'golden' seasons." I think they're joking around, but the distorted voice makes it a little hard to interpret the tone.

"I have no idea what that is," I admit.

"Well, now I'm worried you're either really old or way too young for me if you've never heard of the *Golden Bachelor*," they say with another laugh.

"Is it bad to admit as a contestant on a reality TV show that

I've never watched any reality TV before?" We both end up laughing at that.

"Why the hell did you sign up then?"

Hmm, what's the Sparkles-free version of this?

"Well, I'd just gotten back from a night out with my uncles, watching them be all cute and coupley for hours while I third-wheeled for the millionth time. I might have been doomscrolling when I saw the application at, like, three a.m., and I started fantasizing about meeting someone without all the distractions of work and social media that have gotten in the way in my past relationships. I never expected them to actually pick me."

"You must be hot. If you don't watch reality shows, you might not know this, but the contestants are always attractive."

"Is that your way of trying to tell me you're attractive? We're really covering everything we're not supposed to talk about," I tease.

"You're right, I won't tell you about how hot I am," they say in what I think is the robotic equivalent of a deadpan.

"Okay, back to safer topics than how gorgeous you must be before we get kicked off the show." I laugh. My cheeks hurt from smiling so much. I don't think our first date was a fluke.

I take a second to remember what else we were talking about… right, their cat. "So, cats. Yeah, I've never had a pet before," I admit. I've never really thought about it, but I guess growing up, we were too busy with baseball. And my uncles didn't have any animals either. "I've never been around an animal enough to confidently want my own."

"My cat is awesome. I'm kind of a workaholic—I don't think I can say what I do based on the show's guidelines to keep things totally blind, and we've probably skated the line enough already —but I do a lot of work at home. My cat keeps me company while I'm endlessly working," they explain.

"I also probably shouldn't say what I do for work, but I can't imagine working at home. My coworkers are pretty much the only people I hang out with besides my uncles, and even then, it's always right after work." Wow, I am not making myself sound cool at all. "Do you ever get lonely?" I ask, eager to learn more about them and distract from how boring I sound.

"That's why I have my cat, duh." I laugh again, already vibing so well with their sense of humor. "But to be a bit more serious, I work with my best friend, and a few other people work with us, so I do talk to some people in real life."

"Is working with your friend fun or does it get awkward if you disagree on something?" I love working with my uncle, but at the end of the day, he's always been my boss, the one teaching me what to do, so there hasn't been a situation for me to disagree with much.

"It's fun," they assure me. "We've been through enough together over the years that we know how to talk things out without taking anything too personally."

"That's really cool you have that."

"You said your uncles are your best friends?" they ask.

"Yeah, so they're kind of stuck with me." *Not that I haven't been abandoned by family before, but I think we can save that for another day.*

"And are they brothers, or…?"

"Husbands," I correct with a smile. "They act more like my big brothers than anything, but they really stepped up to be like parents to me when I needed them. I'm really lucky to have them."

"That's awesome you had positive queer role models, too," KD adds, and, oh, how I wish that had been true. My father did so many things that negatively impacted my life growing up, but keeping my uncles from me was one of the worst. "My parents have always been very supportive," they add. "So it seems like we both really lucked out there."

"Definitely," I agree, but the mention of great parents isn't exactly an easy topic for me, so I switch it up. "So do you have any hobbies?"

"Ummm." They pause to think about it for a while. Maybe I'm not the only one without any. "I used to be more into art, and occasionally I'll draw or paint something. But to be honest, most of the time, I'm either working or on my phone," they finally answer. "God, I need to change that when I get back."

I laugh. "I was thinking the same thing when I was making my mood board. It was surprisingly hard. I even threw food on there to fill space."

It sounds like they laugh, too. "Maybe we can try out a hobby together while we're here," they suggest, and I smile at the implication that we're going to continue to talk.

"That sounds perfect," I agree.

This round of dates are only thirty minutes long, so after a brief brainstorm of some things we might be able to try while we're here, it's over before I'd like it to be.

"So do you want to stick to the formal dates?" KD asks. "Or is texting okay too?"

"Texting is great," I answer, excited to be continuing things with them. "But I'd also like to do this again, if you're up for it."

"I'd like that."

When the date ends, I see LM has scheduled a date with me for tonight as well, so I stay in the room, and we talk for a bit. The conversation is as easy as this morning, and we spend some time talking about the show itself, then exchange bad date stories. There's still no romantic spark, but talking with L makes the time fly, and I probably would have scared KD away if I'd jumped right into texting them, so this was well timed.

But I think I've waited long enough.

3 4

KIERAN

Producer: "Do you prefer to plan a date or be invited on one that's already planned?"

Kieran: "With my job, I'm used to being the one who makes all the decisions. Sometimes it's hard for me to give up that control, but I would really love to be with someone who I could trust to do things like that."

The door between the date room and the rest of my temporary apartment shuts behind me as I make my way into the living room and drop onto the couch. That date with JR went too quickly once again.

I wonder if any of my other dates will ever move from "thank god we're done" to "wow, I wish we had more time," but so far, JR is the only one I feel that way about.

I don't know why I assumed I'd have more connections when I was preparing to come on this show. Yes, I've been picturing falling in love with *the one,* but I kind of thought I'd have to slowly weed down my choices as the filming progressed. I thought seventeen conversations would produce a few solid standouts to capture my attention. Instead, my list ended up looking like JR at the top, a decent gap, and then a scramble to fill the rest.

Second place went to ZM, mostly because they were easy to talk to, even if I couldn't say a single deep thing about them now. Third was PT, who at least made me laugh twice, though I think one of those times was unintentional. The rest of my list felt like picking names out of a hat.

Fine, forgettable, and probably not my perfect match.

Except for JR.

I don't even bother pretending I'm going to wait for them to text me first. The producers gave us the green light to message matches, and I'm not about to make small talk or delay texting just to play it cool.

Normal social standards, like waiting to text someone after a date, seem kind of silly when we're both here with the intention to meet our future spouse. But I could really get in my head if I start thinking about just how soon the show has those weddings planned, and I don't want to end up focusing on the wrong thing.

The connection I already have with JR seems promising, and I want to continue to build it. We haven't even talked that much, but in some ways, I feel like they might know more about me than some of my previous partners ever did. So much of my dating history has played out while I've been creating content, and being here without that as a part of my identity... It's strange.

Especially because I don't know who I am outside of that. I thought I did, but being here, being forced to leave that out of the conversation has made me aware of just how much of my life truly revolves around my work.

Before, I thought the problem with my dating life was that I never knew if people were drawn to *me* or to the version I've carefully put out into the world as Sparkles. Even here though, I'm hyperaware of the cameras, and still feel like I need to be "on" all the time, constantly wondering how my followers will react to what I'm doing or saying when this does eventually air. Hoping I don't let them down.

Joking around with JR has been the only time I'd forgotten about being recorded, when I felt like I was just Kieran, even if I'm still figuring out who that is. I definitely want to talk to them again.

But before I give JR my full attention, I take a few minutes to respond to my other matches about scheduling something tomorrow. I don't want to write everyone else off this early simply because JR is my clear favorite.

I grab a snack before returning to the couch to get comfortable and reach for the show phone I'd left on the coffee table. As soon as I unlock it, I see there's already a message waiting for me. I laugh under my breath, half relieved I don't have to be the one to break the ice. "I was just about to text JR, but it looks like they beat me to it," I say automatically.

I read the message out loud. *"Just checking to make sure my top match survived round two without regret."*

I mirror the texting conversation to the TV like the producers requested, and it hits me again that the cameras are catching all of this. Which means it's not just JR who's going to see how I respond.

It was much easier to stay in the moment when I was in the date room, having a conversation out loud in real time. Now, I'm trying to get out of my head as I think of a response to text back, worried I'll embarrass myself as I attempt to flirt, even if I know they may never use these clips.

The only one who matters right now is JR, I remind myself.

"Guess I don't need to keep talking out loud if you can see what we're saying," I say as I think out a response. I liked the easy teasing we'd fallen into during our date. It made me feel like we skipped the awkward introduction phase when first getting to know someone, instead jumping right in to being comfortable enough with each other to joke around. So I attempt the same tone.

KD

> Wow, two dates in one day and now texting to confirm I still like you enough to keep talking? I must've made quite the impression, huh?

I grin to myself at my reply as I press send. Before I can set my phone down, it buzzes again almost immediately.

JR

> You're still holding on to that top spot in my ranks.

KD

> Good, I'd hate to have peaked before day one ends.

JR

> Guess we'll see if you're still there tomorrow ;)

KD

> Sounds suspiciously like you're saying you want to schedule another date?

JR

> I'd love to

I try not to let myself get too carried away. It's just day one, and I really don't know anything about them—just that talking to them feels easy in a way that nothing else here has. There's a pull I haven't felt in a long time, and it feels good knowing this connection is happening with me—the person—first, and not the creator.

KD

Good answer. I'll schedule one now. See you tomorrow, J.

THE NEXT MORNING, I wake up still thinking about that text exchange, which is annoying because I have another four dates to get through before my date with JR. I make myself breakfast and coffee before getting ready for the day.

Even though my dates can't see me, the cameras can, so I throw on jeans and a black graphic tee with light makeup—a simple foundation, eyeliner, and mascara combo, and fill in my eyebrows. With my eyebrow piercing, I've learned people's eyes go there first, and I have no idea how much the cameras plan on zooming in.

"Alright, let's get these dates started," I say with as much enthusiasm as I can muster up as I walk into the dating room.

Two of the four dates are actually much easier and more natural than the speed dating round, which is understandable since yesterday was a lot. The other two, well, let's just say, I'm grateful for the thirty-minute cap.

Finally, it's JR's turn, and because we already had a "round two date" last night, we're officially onto the less structured part of the show, and it's our first date without a time limit.

"KD?" I hear through the speaker.

"I'm here," I confirm.

"I'm relieved it's finally you," they say, and a smile spreads across my face before I can stop it.

"That bad, huh?"

"I'll just say, I'm glad this one doesn't have a clock."

"Same." I chuckle. "I've needed to use the question cards

this morning, but there are actually some good ones in there, and I kind of want to know your answers if you'll appease me."

"Always," they tease. "Could be fun to mix those in."

I reach for my own stack. "Alright, let's see… First card: What's a random skill you have that most people wouldn't expect?"

There's a couple-second pause before JR answers. "I can fold a fitted sheet."

I burst out laughing. "No, you can't. No one can. That's a myth."

"I swear I can. Corners and all. I'll prove it someday."

That little implication of someday makes hope bloom in my chest, but I play it cool. "I'm holding you to that. I've lived my entire adult life with a fitted-sheet-shaped ball shoved in the closet, and I'm not sure I believe there's another way."

"You're on, K. I'll gladly prove it to you," they reply, and I'm already imagining us folding laundry together in the future. The vision is so much more domestic than any of my other daydreams have been, and that somehow makes it feel even more like a real possibility. "Okay, your turn, what's the best non-appearance-based compliment you've ever gotten?"

I lean back, smiling, thinking about some of my YouTube channel comments when I first started and was questioning everything. "Someone once told me I helped them feel brave enough to be themselves. That one stuck."

"Yeah," JR says. "I get why it would."

Those comments changed so much for me and helped me keep going when I really wanted to give up at the end of senior year, but I don't need to disclose all that right now. I go to reach for another card when JR surprises me with another question.

"So, are you a couch friend?"

I laugh, because I'm almost certain I heard them correctly, but the words don't make sense. "A couch friend?" I repeat in question.

"Yeah, ya know, the type of friend who you don't have to worry about actually doing anything with. You can just hang out on the couch, and it doesn't even matter if you're talking or working on something separately. You can just be with them and feel recharged by their company."

Well, that sounds amazing. "I would love to be a couch friend, but I don't think I've done that with anyone in years," I admit. I think about my friends for a second, and no one comes to mind. "My best friend works with me, so we do work near each other a lot, but we're constantly swapping ideas and trying to solve problems that come up. It very much feels like work, not relaxation." I think back to how I felt yesterday after our dates, hanging out on this couch, and I wonder if maybe JR could be that person for me. "I think I would really love to have a couch friend."

"Well, if the position is open, consider this my official application. I'm an excellent couch friend. If someone invites me to hang out and do nothing, I am so there. I don't love being by myself, which is why I end up hanging out with my uncles so much, but one of the reasons I like living so close to them is that spending time with them doesn't need to be a big production."

"That sounds really nice." I reply, and normally I would stop there, let them continue, keep my own responses more surface level to avoid giving away too much of myself, to avoid giving people things to pick apart. But I want to give JR more, and I know now isn't the time to hold back, so I give in to that feeling.

"I haven't lived with anyone since college," I tell them. "None of my previous relationships have ever progressed to that stage, so I'm used to having my own space. But being that comfortable with someone, having them around without the pressure of being 'on' all the time, sounds exactly like what I came on this show to find."

"Well, you definitely don't have to worry about performing in front of me. I'm pretty chill. And as a bonus for special friends only, I'd like to also offer more perks if you're interested," they say, and I'm confident the robotic tone is covering up a very flirty one.

"Go on," I flirt back.

"I have been told I'm an excellent cuddler. As your first official couch friend, cuddling would be included whenever you'd like."

"I'm sold, you're hired," I agree with a laugh. Cuddling honestly sounds amazing. I obviously have no idea what this person looks like, but I'm picturing strong arms wrapped around me while I get to be the little spoon, and I can't remember the last time I felt like I could really lean on someone like that, soak up their warmth and forget about my worries. I won't be disappointed if JR doesn't actually fit that physical description, but the daydream is really nice.

"Hell yeah," they say, also laughing.

"Ready for another card?" I ask.

"Ready."

"When was the last time you surprised yourself?"

They laugh again. "Signing up for this. I'm not a big risk-taker. I like my predictable routine, but when I saw the ad, it felt like a sign."

"I'm glad you did," I say before I can stop myself.

"Me too or who else would you be talking to right now?" JR jokes, and I'm laughing again, picturing any of the other people I talked to yesterday. "Actually, don't answer that. But I am glad I'm here and it's me that you're talking to."

"So am I," I reply honestly. I try to imagine my day without this date with JR to look forward to, and I wonder if I'd be ready to give up on this whole process already. "Okay, next question. What's your love language?"

"Physical touch," J says quickly. "If the cuddling offer didn't make it obvious, I really do enjoy that connection. It was something I lacked growing up, and now I really embrace it. More than just the cuddling though. I want to hold your hand, put my arm around you, hug you daily. I just like being close."

"I like that too," I confirm, adding those scenarios to my daydreams about what spending time with JR might look like. "Especially when it's consistent." I hesitate for a moment before adding, "And it's even better when it's more at home than for show in public, if that makes sense."

"You mean, like, it feels more real if it's not for anyone else's benefit?"

"Exactly," I agree. I don't know how to tell J how many times I've had the opposite. A partner making sure they were seen holding my hand in public so they could be photographed with "Kieran Delaney" then barely touching me at home when the cameras and eyes were off us. I want someone who's the same with me in private—if not more affectionate—than they are in front of the world. Someone who's holding me because they want to, not because someone might be watching.

"What about you?" JR asks.

"Words of affirmation," I admit, "but only if it's genuine. I don't want filler compliments or someone telling me what they think I want to hear. I want the kind of words you say because you feel them in the moment and you can't not say them, ya know?"

"Yeah, when it's real, you can tell."

For the first time since we sat down, I realize I've completely forgotten about the cameras and layering my answers for the viewers—once again. This is the most honest I've been with no way to redo the filming or the answers, and no editing power. I notice I'm slouched into the couch, smiling, without thinking about how I look, versus my normal intentional posture. This feels so much more like talking to someone I care about in my own living room. It's like it's just me and them and nothing else, and it's so rare for me. Almost impossible.

The fact that JR has made me so comfortable so quickly just

confirms what I've been thinking: this feels right. Maybe they are already my couch friend, and hopefully, they'll become more than that.

We keep pulling question cards, the conversation slipping between playful and personal. We talk about the most ridiculous thing we've each ever done on a dare, the one meal we could eat every day for the rest of our lives, and what a perfect Sunday looks like. Every answer gives me another tiny piece of them—and lets me share more of myself in ways that don't feel forced.

By the time we've run through a stack of cards and a dozen tangents, I know two things: one, this was by far my favorite date yet; and two, I'm not going to be able to wait long before I talk to JR again.

JACE

Producer: "Is there anything about this process that concerns you?"

Jace: "Not really. I'm sure I'll do something embarrassing or that people watching the show won't like, but I willingly came here, and I'm hoping that I can meet someone special, so it is what it is."

KD

So apparently these phones have the voice distortion option too... Would you want to talk on the phone? Or stick to texting?

JR

I was just thinking about how I miss the robotic voice! Lol you can call me

a second later, my phone lights up with KD's initials and I pick up immediately. "Miss me already?" I tease.

"Not sure if I'm supposed to pretend like I just wanted to see if I was still your favorite or if I should be honest and admit that I did."

I smile to myself as I consider their answer. I've been in relationships before, some that I thought might even be serious at the time, but I don't know that I've ever felt like someone else's priority the way I'm starting to with KD. Even with friends, I haven't really had a *best* friend as an adult like so many people do. I have people I can go out with, mostly coworkers, but those invites are all group activities. No one invites *just me* to do anything.

Growing up, my friends were all assholes who only cared about popularity, and after everything that happened with David, I think I've held back from getting too close with people.

Obviously, I have my uncles, but they have each other.

KD deciding to call me tonight, not one of their other matches, makes me feel important in a way I didn't know I needed. It's the feeling I was chasing when I signed up for the show, but I don't think I really believed it could happen until this moment.

"Well, I'll happily confirm that you are, in fact, still my favorite, *and* let you know that I was missing you as well," I reply, my smile still firmly in place.

It might be odd to be so honest about those feelings, but there's something about the anonymity of talking through the voice changer and not actually seeing each other that makes confessions so much easier. Combined with the tight timeline of the show, there's really no room to hold anything back.

I don't mind though. KD's confirmation made me feel special, and I want to make them feel the same way. And I *was* missing them.

I spent so many years ignoring and hiding my true thoughts and feelings. Not only did that end up hurting me more, but worse than that, it hurt the one person I cared about most in my past. I've tried to learn from those mistakes, to grow, and one of the ways I do that is by being as honest as I can. If spending time with KD makes me happy, they should know that.

"It's probably a good thing you can't see how obnoxious my blushing is right now," K says with a laugh.

"Damn, now I really want to see it." As I say that, I realize I haven't given much consideration to the way KD looks. We've joked about our ages, and as long as they aren't older than my parents or still a teenager—and I'm seriously doubting either of those possibilities after how much we've talked over the last couple of days—then their age doesn't actually matter. I also have no idea what their gender identity is but that truly isn't important to me either. I haven't been picturing anything specific when we're talking, they're just *K,* the person I've really enjoyed getting to know, the person I've found myself picturing going through the next steps of this process with.

When we were talking about cuddling, I guess I was picturing myself as the big spoon, but most people are smaller than me, so I didn't even stop to consider another option. Even though I would also be cool with being the little spoon.

"Maybe soon," they tease, but I think we might be on the same page about really wanting that to happen.

"I hope so," I confirm. "So, if you weren't participating on a reality show with your every move being filmed, what would a normal night look like for you, K?"

They laugh at my topic change and take a moment to think. "I'd order in food from my favorite sushi place, then I'd probably spend the night cuddling with my cat while I work."

"I thought I worked a lot, but I'm starting to think it'll seem like nothing compared to you."

"I think one of the things I need to work on after this is my work-life balance," they agree with a laugh.

"Maybe we can message the producers to provide us with supplies for a hobby tomorrow, get started on that."

"Absolutely."

"Um. Is this what you were picturing?" I ask with a laugh as soon as K answers the phone.

They're laughing too hard to respond for a moment. "Did yours have the note on it too?"

"For the 'elderly couple' who almost gave us all heart attacks from nearly revealing your ages. Keep the blind topics blind, please." I double-check, chuckling as I read my note again.

"Yup, same one. And no, this is not what I was picturing, but I'm committed at this point. Let's learn how to fucking cross-stitch," they say, with what I think is fake enthusiasm.

"We're going to be amazing," I agree. They delivered a Learn to Cross-stitch kit to each of us. I'm set up at the kitchen table with all the supplies in front of me, skimming the instructions. "What's yours a picture of?"

"A cat. It's kind of adorable."

"We must have the same one. Okay, it looks like we need to find the center of the Aida first, and then thread two pieces of floss through the eye of the needle," I read aloud.

"I only know, like, half of those words," K says, making me laugh.

"Based on the pictures, I'm guessing the Aida is the fabric with the holes in it, and the floss is the string."

"Are you sure you haven't done this before?" they tease.

"Trust me, I would remember if I'd ever done anything even close to this." I picture my father's reaction if I had ever brought home something I cross-stitched or if I had tried to do it in his house. I'm sure it would've been immediately trashed, and I'd have had to sit through him yelling about me acting gay and how I needed to stay away from girly shit, so people didn't get the wrong impression.

I wish I'd have given people that impression instead of the asshole bully one I actually did.

"Your vibe board had art supplies on it, have you ever done anything like this?" I ask.

"No, but I'm hoping the skills transfer," they say with a laugh. "Growing up, I was into drawing and painting. I never really committed to a favorite medium, it changed every couple of months and even depended on my mood somedays. But I've always liked creating things. I think it'll be fine to say I use my creativity for my job, so that's where a lot of my creative energy goes these days. But sometimes when I'm alone, I still like to sketch, and lately, I've enjoyed using watercolors."

"Nice, is it, like, landscapes or people or…?" I ask.

"Recently it's been a lot of portraits, but abstract ones. I like to make part of the image hyperrealistic and then really use my imagination to try to express what I think the person is feeling in the other part." Even the robotic filter sounds more animated as KD describes their art. I wish I could see them right now, see the way their expression has probably lit up as they've been talking.

"That sounds really, really cool. I would love to see it."

They don't respond right away, and I double-check the call is still going before they finally reply. "I think I'd like to share it with you. I actually haven't shown anyone my art in years, outside of what I do for work," they admit.

Wow. "Well, no pressure, you obviously never have to show me, but if you ever wanted to, I would be honored. It sounds like it's very personal."

"It is. It always has been, I guess. Growing up, I never really felt like I fit in. I didn't feel like who I was would ever be good enough. But when I was drawing or painting, it didn't matter if I was different in school or if I wished I had more friends. Art became my safe space, and eventually the other creative outlets I found did as well."

"Damn, K. I'm sorry you felt that way. It's awesome you found that love for art to distract from it."

"Thanks. It was mostly at school. I know it could have been worse. My parents have always been amazing, and they didn't hesitate to get me whatever latest art supply I needed. What about you? Did your uncles support any hobbies when you were younger?"

"God, I wish," I say. If I had been with them sooner, and I'd expressed any interest in a hobby, I can only imagine how quickly they would have supported it. If I'd decided to take up art, Patrick probably would have come home with bags full of art supplies and insisted on learning how to do it with me.

But that obviously didn't happen, and K was vulnerable with their answer, so I want to give them a bit of my truth too, even if I try not to focus on that time of my life if I can help it. "I, uh, I can actually relate to the whole not feeling like you were good enough thing. Like no matter what I did, it would never be enough, and that the things I wanted were wrong."

"Sorry, J. Did you have any escapes from it?"

Kieran. The memory of sitting with him in the woods all those times pops into my head.

Yeah, I don't want to get into the details of that with KD yet. Maybe one day I can tell them all about what an asshole I was to the first person I ever really cared about, but I'm not ready for that conversation. I also don't want to lie, though, so I go for a general summary. "I was really athletic when I was younger, and I tried to put all my focus into sports, into being the best. When that stopped working though, I did eventually find someone who made me feel like I could be myself for the first time. They didn't give a shit about popularity or if my team was doing well." I smile fondly as I remember the way Kieran was so dismissive about baseball the few times I brought it up, as opposed to everyone else in my life at that point who seemed to only care about the possibility of me going pro. "They changed my life," I add.

"Do you still know them?"

I wish. "No, but I'm so grateful that our paths crossed when they did."

"Sounds like it was at the right time," K says. "I'm glad you had that."

"Me too." I literally can't imagine how different my life could have been if Kieran and I had never met. Would I have gone into the MLB? Would I think I'm straight? Would my father still be trying to control my life?

All those possibilities sound miserable. I'm so glad things turned out the way they did as far as my career and parents are concerned. I just wish Kieran and I could have ended things on better terms… if we had to end them at all.

I need to stop thinking about Kieran Delaney and focus on the new KD in my life. "I feel like I can be myself around you, too," I admit softly, realizing the truth in the words as I say them.

"Good, because I feel the same way, J. And that's kind of a really big deal for me."

"Good," I tease, but then I add, "I really like who you are, K."

"I like you too."

We let the moment hang there, not adding anything else to the silence as we let everything we just said sink in. I know we had joked about being each other's top picks, and even about things we'll do in person, but this felt more like an honest admission of our feelings, like we might both be hoping to move on to the next phase of the show together as actual partners.

I've been trying to go along with the structure of the show and talk to other people, but I don't want to give up any more time to people I don't see myself having a future with. It's KD for me. I can't imagine moving on with anyone else.

I need to enjoy our time together now, but later, I think I need to be honest with the other people I'm still technically dating.

"Okay, are you ready to master cross-stitching?" I ask, attempting to move back into a lighter mood, but grateful that we had that more serious moment and that KD was comfortable enough to share deeper parts of themselves with me.

"Yeah, let's do this," K agrees. "I think I separated the thread correctly but getting it into this tiny hole is way more difficult than I thought it would be."

"That's what he said," I say before I can stop myself. Hanging out with K, even if it's over a voice-distorting phone call, is so easy and comfortable that I don't even think about how a joke like that might come across. I panic for a moment that they'll think I'm immature or crude, but to my relief, they crack up.

I wouldn't want to date someone who I couldn't be this comfortable joking around with, so I guess that ended up being a nice way to accidentally test it.

We spend the rest of the afternoon attempting to finish our patterns, laughing and chatting the entire time. The more I learn about KD, their humor, their general attitude about things, their outlook on life, the more it all confirms how well we really do seem to fit. We even talk about kids. They've never had a strong desire to have them, which is a relief because neither have I. I keep waiting for the other shoe to drop. To learn something about them that's somehow a dealbreaker or for me to say the wrong thing and it results in our connection suddenly becoming awkward. But it never happens.

We both end up with what I'm assuming are technically poorly executed cat cross-stitches, and I know I'll smile every time I look at it remembering today and my time with KD.

We talk through meals and only take a brief break from our call to do short dates with our other matches. After another great day where I felt like I really bonded with KD in a way that I don't see myself doing with my other matches, I go through with my plan and end up telling everyone else that I don't feel a romantic connection with them, and that I think we should put our time and effort into the people we do feel that way about.

Jay messaged me again, reminding me to at least read the texts out loud if I don't explain my thoughts beyond them. AP and SJ are both really nice about it. AP wished me luck with whoever I was vibing with, and I wished them the same. I was surprised that SJ seemed disappointed, telling me that whoever I'd clicked with was a lucky person, but we also wished each other luck and ended things on good terms.

LM surprised me by suggesting we continue to rank each other platonically. They agreed with everything I said, and after confirming we weren't both pursuing the same person, asked if we might want to keep talking for friendly support. I immediately agreed, loving the idea.

KD and I call again after the other dates are wrapped up, but I don't tell them I ended things with everyone else. I don't want them to feel any pressure to continue this process with me, but I feel better knowing my focus can be on the only person I've had any sort of real spark with here.

It really does feel real. We request another cross-stitch pattern the next day and spend the whole day talking. I don't want to assume anything when K's schedule is clear of any other dates, but by the time evening rolls around, and Andy appears on the TV screen informing us that the round is over and it's time to narrow down our connections to our top four, I'm feeling really great about where KD and I are at.

It's only been a few days, but the connection we've made feels real. KD has made me laugh and smile more in that time than I can ever remember with another partner. I've even realized that the constant urge to check my phone for Sparkles updates is nearly gone whenever KD and I are talking.

I think this dating experiment might actually work.

I really want it to.

KIERAN

Producer: "What's the biggest red flag you've ignored in your previous dating life that you're more aware of now?"

Kieran: "Probably not believing people when they show me who they really are."

Somehow, it's already day five, which I'm reminded about because production sent us a message that we have to submit our top two picks by tonight. It's almost funny, because for me, there's no decision to make.

JR is the only person I have left.

When I came here, I thought I'd keep my options open because this was the one place where I could get to know people without questioning their motives. But even with all that freedom, it didn't take long to realize I only had one person I actually want to keep talking to.

Every other conversation felt like small talk. JR was different from the start, and they're the only one I can imagine meeting in two days.

I don't technically know if I'm the only one they're still talking to, but I have a hunch. And if I'm right, I wish the show would bend the rules and let us move in with each other early. I'm over waiting. I want to kiss them, touch them, and see if the chemistry is there physically as well. I want to share our space, attempt cooking together, and cuddle on the couch while we cross-stitch. I want to compare whose is better when we finish, and actually hear their laugh while we joke around.

The thought of another two nights in separate rooms feels like a waste of time, but they structured it this way for a reason, I suppose.

Today's twist is "planning" our own dates. We each get to request props that the producers will deliver to the other person to use during our time together, but since we sort of covered that base early when I asked them for a surprise hobby, I've got a new spin for today.

But first, I need to get ready.

I'd be lying if I said I didn't miss filming, it's such an integral part of who I am at this point. So, when I pitched my date idea to the producers, I also asked them to bring me a camera. I figured I'd give them some bonus footage of a "get ready with me" clip.

Who knows if they'll actually use it, and I really don't care either way. I'm bored and this sounds like a fun way to pass the next hour until I meet with JR for our date. I really do enjoy the full process of putting on makeup, seeing how each new product can change the whole vibe, deciding how I want to present myself to the world for the day, and then bringing that look to life.

I grab all my makeup from the bathroom and bring it into the living room area that has a full-length mirror hanging from the wall. I set up the camera in the best possible spot I can think of before making sure everything I need is in the frame, then I turn it on and sit down cross-legged in front of the mirror.

"Hey, Sparkle's fans," I say, smiling into the lens. "Today we're doing a very special *Love Without Labels*: Isolation Edition look. Step one: bring your entire makeup kit from home. Obviously." I laugh, gesturing to the spread in front of me.

"Now, we all know the real first step is to prep the skin. This is my ride-or-die, my holy grail, my—" I pause mid-sentence and grin as I hold up my favorite moisturizer. "Actually, I probably can't name-drop brands here, so… just moisturize first, okay?"

I add a layer, then start working primer into my skin with practiced motions. "You know, some people here probably pass the time by working out—they even messaged us about a gym we could use—but this sounds like a way more fun thing to spend my time doing."

Talking to the camera and filming myself getting ready is second nature to me, so I move through my routine easily.

When I usually do social media "lives," I typically engage with the audience and their comments, but since I don't have that option, I just talk like I do in prerecorded content. "I wonder what JR will think of my makeup tutorials. I wonder if they've ever seen a video of mine? Heard of me? Or maybe they watch all my videos. Or what if they had an ex who watched my content? Oof, that could get awkward fast." I cringe slightly at the thought as I finish applying my concealer.

"This is *Love Without Labels*, but… I'd be lying if I said I wasn't a little nervous about the makeup thing. I've already decided to go all in on one match, so what if we finally meet in two days and they're turned off by it? I know that wouldn't actually be about me—that would be on them, and they clearly wouldn't be my person—but still. That worry comes from way back, from some of the stuff you long-time followers already know."

I grab one of the eyeshadow palettes I brought with me as I continue. "And if you're new to me, I started wearing makeup my junior year of high school and was bullied relentlessly for it —surprise, surprise. The early 2010s were not friendly to me. It sucked, and when I thought maybe I was past it, things got even worse. I almost quit wearing makeup all together, but the comments I received on my YouTube channel really motivated me to not let some small-minded bullies break me."

Pausing for a moment, I tap the excess off my brush. "This isn't the first time I've told that story—it's become a big part of my brand. I've heard from thousands of other people over the years who've messaged me about how my videos helped them feel seen or gave them the push to try something they'd been afraid to do, and I can't tell you how much that encourages me to keep going, despite all the trolls.

"I've thought about sharing this with JR. I almost did when we were talking about not feeling like we were good enough growing up. But the thing is, telling them why I was bullied likely means saying it was for wearing makeup, which could give away my gender since a woman wearing makeup is far more common and they wouldn't typically get called out for wearing it. And I actually want to stay in this experiment. I like what we have, and I want to see it through. So that means not risking a conversation that could lead to potentially being kicked off." I pause for a moment. "Don't worry, I got you, Andy," I say with a laugh.

I finish the look by filling in my brows, adding eyeliner, mascara, and a touch of chapstick. "Alright, Sparkle's fans, that's today's *Love Without Labels*: Isolation Edition look. Don't forget to like, subscribe and—well—wish me luck. I'll need it." I give the camera a little wave before getting up to hit the power button.

"That was fun," I say into the room and all the other cameras that are filming my every move. I pack up my makeup and check in with the producers to confirm everything's set for the date. They give me the green light, and a minute later, I'm walking toward the date room—feeling both ridiculously excited and nervous. I hope this works out like I'd planned.

"JR?" I ask as I enter the room.

"Hey, K. I'm here," they respond, and I immediately feel at ease about this whole thing.

"Okay, so I might have gotten a little carried away with the whole date-planning thing, but I'm excited. You're going on a scavenger hunt in your apartment," I tell them, not wanting to hold it in any longer.

"No way." They laugh through the voice distortion technology. "I was wondering why the producers told me they needed me to go into the bathroom for five minutes so they could prepare for today's date."

Now I'm laughing too. I hadn't thought through what they'd tell J while they were hiding the clues, but I guess that's one way to do it.

"Do you want to get right into it?" I ask eagerly.

"Of course, sounds fun."

I had hoped they'd like my idea, but hearing they're actually into it is a relief. I know some people might think the whole thing was a little over the top, but J easily going along with my plan feels like yet another confirmation that we're a good fit. "Alright, there are three clues and no help," I say with a smirk, knowing I'd totally help if J needed it, but it's honestly all pretty simple. "There should be an envelope on the table in your date room with the first clue. Also, we might need to be on the phone for this, so I can still hear you when you're in your apartment."

"Okay, I'll read this then go out there and call you," they reply. "The first clue says: Find the thing you'd need if we were going to share our perfect Sunday morning." There's a moment of silence, then I hear them say, "Easy."

Next thing I know, my phone is ringing, and I pick it up.

"I'm heading to the bedroom," they say.

I laugh to myself over how much fun this is already proving to be.

"I'm pulling the covers back, but I'm not seeing anything," they say, walking me through it. "Let me check the pillows, hang on." I hear what I assume is rustling through the pillowcases, looking for a note that's definitely not there.

"Hmm, well, I'm not seeing anything here," they update me, and I can't help but laugh.

"Read it again," I instruct, trying really hard not to give them any additional clues.

"Well, I don't think I can find you, so I went to the next thing I could think of which would be the bed. I'd want to be wrapped around you on a Sunday morning. Hmm, the thing I'd need… in the morning…" They trail off. "Okay. I think I've got something!"

I laugh to myself again. "Care to share with the class?" I prompt. I can't imagine JR talks to the camera much when they're alone, they seem like more of an internal thinker, but I really want to know where their mind just went.

"I'm thinking coffee. We both talked about spending weekends in bed drinking coffee. Is that it?"

"I can't just tell you, are you looking?" I grin, knowing as long as they check the right spot, they'll find exactly what they're looking for. We talked about our mutual love for coffee and staying inside the apartment on the weekends. J talked about working in person and having a commute every day in the city, and that on the weekends they like to take the mornings slow. I told them that since I'm a workaholic, I usually wake up, make coffee, then get back in bed to do some light work.

"Found it!" they confirm excitedly, and my smile somehow grows.

"Awesome. I was thinking when we get to meet, assuming we will, we can spend the morning drinking coffee in bed together. So you easily could've been right when you walked into the bedroom too."

"I'd really like that. It sounds perfect." Every time I talk about what we'll do when we're together, my stomach fills with nervous, excited fluttering, and every time they confirm they're looking forward to it as much as I am, my daydreams about our future feel more and more like plans than fantasies. "The next clue says: Your perfect meal for a rainy fall day. That one is easy."

Since J's already in the kitchen, I know it'll be a matter of seconds before they find the clue.

"Yup, found it!" they say quickly. "Mac and cheese is the perfect comfort food."

"I never disagreed with you." I laugh, remembering our conversation from the other day. "I just said that tomato soup and grilled cheese is also a great choice."

"Tomato soup just doesn't sound good, but I know, I know, I promise I will still try yours." I swore I had the best recipe.

"I'm holding you to that, I swear I have the best recipe. Alright, what does the last clue say?" I prompt.

"Find something that makes you think of me when you see it, hmm… Is this one intentionally vague?"

"It is," I confirm. "You can find anything in your apartment that reminds you of me, and then the production team will bring it to me so I can see it. Then they'll give you the thing I already picked out for you and we can compare."

"Oh, awesome. Umm, what's the perfect thing to pick," JR says, and I am dying to know what they'll choose. "Okay, what screams 'KD'?" they wonder aloud. "Do I go with emotional, random, practical, hmm."

"You can't tell me. That's the fun of the challenge. This is your test, JR," I joke.

"Great, no pressure." I hear movement and what I assume is

some sort of clanking around for a little bit. "Maybe this. Or, wait, no, this. I think I have it."

"Oh, yeah, what is it?" I prod.

"Guess you'll just have to wait and see when production brings it over to you. Maybe I'll hang onto it for just a little longer," they say with a laugh.

"You should know by now I don't have that kind of patience, come on, J," I beg.

"Alright, alright, I'm handing over the goods now. They gave me yours wrapped up, so I'll head back to the date room to open it, and I'll hang up here."

"Okay." The call ends, and it's a moment before JR is back in the room and we're able to talk here. I'm anxiously awaiting the final scavenger hunt item's arrival, though.

A few minutes later, there's a knock on the door to the date room before Mitch comes in holding something behind his back. "Here you go," he says, showing me the item, and I break out into a huge grin. He smiles back at me and walks out of the room, closing the door behind him.

"Oh my god, is this the cat you cross-stitched the other day?" I burst out laughing. We're so in sync already.

"Yeah, I did my best, but I was a little too distracted by the person on the phone to pay too much attention to what I was doing."

"No, this is great, I love it," I confirm, and my face hurts from smiling. It's a lopsided gray cat with a few threads poking out. It's cute and chaotic, and I really do love it. "It's perfect."

"Well, I didn't want to just pick a random object. I figured if you had this, you'd be able to remember our new hobby."

"I'm keeping it forever," I promise, setting it down carefully beside me, my chest buzzing in that way it has been lately with equal parts excitement and disbelief that this is actually happening.

"Did you open yours?"

"One sec… No fucking way, we picked the same thing! That's amazing." They also laugh. "You're definitely the artist in this relationship, mine was not this good."

This relationship. Fuck, I love hearing them say that about us.

Two more days.

That's all we have left before we can both decide to move in together, before I can see them for real, before what feels like the start of my forever.

37

JACE

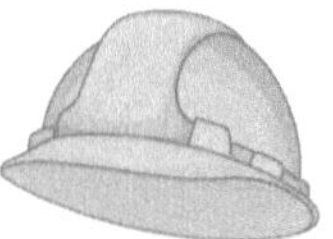

Producer: "What's been missing from your past relationships?"

Jace: "I don't know if this will sound creepy, but I want to be obsessed with my partner. I want to find someone who I look forward to seeing when we're apart, who I want to do the boring parts of life with. I don't think I've ever had that."

"$\mathcal{I}$ apologize in advance if my planned date seems boring in comparison," I warn. "I went a little more traditional."

"I'm sure it'll be great," K assures me with a laugh. "What's our plan?"

"You said your favorite food is sushi, and I'm sure it won't compare to New York, but one of the producers is from Atlanta and assured me that they knew of a place that was great."

"Oh my god, yes! I'm so sick of my own cooking. I'm so excited I'd kiss you if we were actually together."

"Note to self: bring sushi when we meet," I tease, really wishing we could skip to that part now. "Me too, though. Honestly, I can't remember the last time I went multiple days in a row making all my food."

"Does that mean one of us needs to learn how to cook?"

My stomach flutters at the casual implication that we'll be eating together going forward. "Nah, we can just take turns choosing where we get takeout from."

"Okay, perfect. I've already committed to the whole cross-stitch thing, adding learning how to cook would probably be too much," they deadpan.

"Basically impossible," I agree with another laugh. "Do you want to watch a movie after dinner and really round out the stereotypical date night?"

"Obviously. Can we watch a cheesy romcom?"

"Perfect. They should be delivering popcorn and watermelon Sour Patch Kids to your living room during our dinner."

"Bonus points for remembering my favorite candy, too."

I grin, thinking about our favorite snack foods popping up in our lightning question round. "Do I need bonus points? Was my date idea so bad that you're ready to dump me?" I tease.

"Definitely not, just pointing out that you're doing so well I don't think you'll be able to get rid of me even if you wanted to."

The fluttering in my stomach intensifies. "Can I be honest, K?"

"Always."

"I don't think I'll ever want to get rid of you," I admit. If I don't think about how strange this whole situation is, that I have no idea about so many details of who K is, if I only focus on my feelings for them, it's easy to picture more nights like this. The fact that we haven't met doesn't change how much I want K to be a part of my life.

The relief that I feel when they finally respond is overwhelming. "Good answer."

We finish dinner, and it's just as great as the rest of our time has been. We move into our living rooms and switch back to a call as the producers make sure our movies start at the same time. We've both seen the one we chose before, so we make a lot of commentary throughout that's even more entertaining than the film.

It's another great day with KD.

I truly hope they say yes when I ask them to move in with me.

TODAY IS the last day of the "blind" part of the show. *Finally.*

Even though LM and I are technically still matched, we've only been texting each other updates and encouragement. Right now though, we're both freaking out a bit about the possibility of having to go home if the person we want to move in with doesn't feel the same way.

LM

On a scale of "mild anxiety" to "full-blown freak out" how stressed are you about tonight?

JR

LOL, full-blown panic. Who knew only leaving one person as your top pick would be so nerve-racking.

LM

We definitely should have thought of that sooner. Not that I had any other options I actually liked haha. I really don't want to leave here alone. I can't fathom the thought of dating again outside of this experience.

JR

I'm right there with you. At least we formed a solid friendship out of this, right? But from what it sounds like on your end, BB is likely to pick you too.

LM

I really, really hope so. How are things with KD?

JR

Good! I think we've built a really strong connection, it's almost like I've known them for years instead of a few days. But then again, it's my ONLY connection so I hope they feel it as strongly as I do.

LM

I get that. That's how it is with BB for me. I didn't expect it at all, but now I can't imagine leaving here without them.

JR

I feel the same way. Although, KD has been in my top since the beginning, unlike BB for you, haha. But it's terrifying not knowing for sure if you'll be picked and if they feel the same way about us that we feel about them.

LM

Here's to hoping for double dates in the future! Keep me updated on how it goes. I want to know everything.

JR

Same to you!

Any minute now, KD and I will meet in the date room for the last time. We'll either agree to move in together to start the next phase of the show or we'll go home alone. Either way, my bags are packed. I'm just waiting to find out if I might actually have a shot at the kind of relationship I fantasized about when I came here or if I'll be adding another person with the initials of KD to my fantasies of what might have been.

38

KIERAN

Producer: "What do you think people assume about you, and what are they wrong about?"

Kieran: "People think I'm confident all the time. They see the content, the fans, the interviews, and they think I'm untouchable. But I'm definitely not. I get insecure, I overthink, and my feelings get hurt, just like anyone else."

I didn't think I'd be this nervous on day seven, but I'm sort of freaking out. This morning, Andy's bubbly face popped up on the TV, telling us to pack up before our final dates. Dates, plural. I completely forgot some people might have their top two picks that they're still considering.

But JR is it for me. It's that all-your-eggs-in-one-basket thing. I've never actually put eggs in a basket, but I get the metaphor. And right now, the basket feels like it's holding my entire future. I want this to work out with them so badly.

The producers had me do an interview this morning, talking

about the first phase of the show, how excited and nervous I am for my date with JR today, what I think they'll be like in person, and if I had any guesses on the details that have been hidden up until now. I honestly couldn't care less about JR's gender, appearance, age. The only thing I can focus on is hoping they feel as strongly about our potential relationship as I do.

I've been getting ready for nearly an hour now because this could be the day I meet my future spouse, and I want to look my best.

The alarm on my phone goes off and that means it's *finally* time for our last blind date. I'm trying to stay positive and remain confident that we will take the next step together. Every interaction we've had has felt so easy, so right. We've talked about being each other's top matches, so I shouldn't be this nervous.

But I still worry that, despite all that, I won't be good enough, and that JR would rather be done with the show than commit to being my partner.

Nope, only positive thoughts going into this date.

"Alright," I say to the cameras in the room. "My bags are packed. Let's hope I'll be moving into a shared apartment instead of heading to the airport." I flash a weak smile and I really doubt it's doing a damn thing to hide how nervous I am. My stomach feels like it's packed to the brim with butterflies.

I reach for the handle of the date room and walk inside. "J?" I ask weakly.

"Hey, K, I'm here."

"Are you as nervous as I am right now?" I blurt out, unable to stay calm.

"You could say that," they agree, but my nerves are still completely unsettled. "But I think it's a good thing too. That's kind of the point, right? Figuring out if we want to take the next step solely based on our connection. It's a big deal."

"Right," I say, twisting my fingers together in my lap.

There's a pause, and I tense up as panic washes over me. With all my worrying this morning, I never thought that I might actually need to say the words, to be the one to ask if JR wants to live together.

Then JR makes a sound, like maybe they're clearing their throat. "K, I know we still have so much to learn about each other, but I feel like we've built something special. I don't want our connection to end when we leave this room. I want to get to know all of you. I want those lazy Sundays in bed drinking coffee. I want to meet your cat and try your tomato soup and see your artwork if you'd let me. All the other little things we've talked about. I'd really like to continue learning everything about you that I can. So, what do you say, K, will you move in with me?"

It feels like all the air is knocked out of my lungs, only to fill back up with happiness. I laugh, and it's the giddy, can't-contain-it kind of laugh. I truly can't help it with how relieved and excited I am. "Yes! Yes, J, absolutely."

I can't see them or hear their voice yet, but the voice distortion sounds a bit higher, and I have to imagine they're feeling the same way I am right now. "I can't believe we're doing this, I'm so excited," they say.

The knot in my stomach begins to loosen just a little, but my nerves are still at an all-time high because we're going to meet... in person. They're going to be real.

I meant what I said, I don't care what they look like. I've been far too wrapped up in how special they've managed to make me feel. How easy things have been between us and how much fun we have together.

But now that we're actually going to meet, it's impossible not to think about appearances, and it's not them I'm worried about. It's me.

JR is going to see me and decide if I'm their version of attractive. If I'm what they pictured.

And more than that, JR's going to have to decide if being with a man who wears makeup is a deal-breaker.

I keep telling myself the connection we have will outweigh everything else, including what they see when they look at me. But there's still a small part of me that's terrified, reminding me of my past and all the hateful internet trolls I still encounter on a daily basis. There are so many people who hate me for being myself, and I can only hope J isn't one of them.

Ideally, JR doesn't just accept it or tolerate the makeup, but likes it. I had makeup on my vibe board, so maybe it won't be too big of a surprise, but those first few dates already feel like so long ago.

I want them to like me. I want to live up to whatever they've fantasized about when picturing our future together. JR is the first person in a long time who's made me believe I might actually get everything I want, everything I came here to find.

Time feels like it's slowed down as my anticipation only grows.

"I'll see you soon," I finally get out, still shocked that this is actually happening.

"Can't wait," J agrees.

When I get back into my apartment, I take a few deep breaths, looking myself over once more in the mirror. There's a knock at the door and Mitch comes in.

"You ready?" he asks.

"Yeah, I can't wait," I tell him.

"Alright, grab your bags, let's go meet JR."

I pull my bag behind me, following Mitch into the elevator, leaving the blind part of the show behind.

When we get to room 13, Mitch stops outside the door. "JR isn't here yet, so you'll go in first. They'll be here any minute."

"Thanks." *Awesome.* Now I'll get to sit here alone with my racing thoughts and anxiety as I wait.

I pull my bag into the room behind me, and this is already the longest wait of my life. Every second feels like a countdown to a new life—maybe even one that looks like the daydreams I've been obsessing over.

I want it so badly. I want those fantasies to become plans. I want couch snuggles and cross-stitching. I want takeout. I want to meet their uncles. I want to watch them fold a fitted sheet, and I want them to come to events with me because they want to be there for *me*, not just to get ahead by being in the room.

If I thought my anxiety was bad going into the last date, it's got nothing on this moment. My nerves feel like they can choke me, and I'm not really sure where to wait, so I'm just standing in the main living space of this new apartment, far too nervous to take in any of its details, when I hear footsteps outside the door.

My heart is in my throat. I run my hands through my hair and smooth my shirt as I wait for them to step inside.

It all comes down to this one moment.

This is it.

They open the door, step into view... and my heart breaks.

Again.

Because this isn't the first time that this man has utterly devastated me.

I'm shocked, horrified, livid. There are so many emotions competing for my attention, and I'm frozen, completely speechless for a moment as I take in who's standing before me.

The man who used to bully me for wearing makeup. The man who destroyed my self-confidence junior year. The man who I thought I had helped come to terms with his sexuality after he showed me who he really was, only for him to send his best friend to threaten me to stay away from him when he was done using me.

I still have no idea what the extent of that threat was meant to be, if David was sent there to get me to stay away by any means necessary. If he was planning to hurt me. The concussion made my memory hazy, but I'll never forget the anger in his eyes as he grabbed me.

All because this man, who is apparently back in my life and on a queer dating show, couldn't be bothered to end things with me himself.

This man who I blocked and never wanted to see again.

There's no way.

No fucking way.

He's obviously older than the last time I saw him, but his curly brown hair and warm brown eyes that always reminded me of chocolate and seemed so out of place on such an asshole's face are the same, even if they're hiding behind a pair of glasses. And fuck me, because I'm a sucker for glasses. He's always been tall, but he's filled out with a softness that wasn't there when we were in high school. Now, he's got that burly lumberjack look, with a full beard and everything, and he looks fucking delicious. His shoulders and arms are huge, and he really does look like he'd be an amazing cuddler.

Dammit, of course I'm still undoubtably attracted to him, just like I was back then. But it doesn't matter because I obviously won't let myself indulge in *him* again. I learned my lesson the first time.

Finally, I remember how to speak. "Hell fucking no. This has to be some sort of twisted joke, right?"

JACE

Producer 1: "Did he just say 'twisted joke?' What's he talking about, what's the joke?"

Producer 2: "Shit. Do they already know each other?"

Kieran looks just as shocked as I feel, but it's clear he knows exactly who I am. And knowing what I do now, after spending this time talking and falling for who he actually is as a person, it makes it so much worse than if my fascination had remained online because I've officially confirmed that Kieran is the man of my dreams.

But the glare he's aiming my way, framed by edgy, dark purple eyeshadow, makes it clear I could never be that for him.

"Hell fucking no. This has to be some sort of twisted joke, right?" he asks in disbelief, peering around the apartment like he's expecting someone to pop out and yell "gotcha," but there's no one else here. Jay didn't follow me, so it's just Kieran and me standing in the kitchen now.

"Fuck, Kieran, I'm so sorry," I blurt way too loudly, fully panicking that I'll somehow make this worse than it already is. I don't know what to do, but I can't give up yet. I refuse, even though I'm sure he wishes I would just turn around and leave or maybe stay so he can slap me. But I've made that mistake before, and this time, I'm not giving up without a fight. One of my biggest regrets in life was giving up so easily that day when I showed up at Kieran's house to try to apologize.

I knew he would be upset—that David had threatened him away from me before he hurt him—but I didn't realize how broken he would seem until I stood on his front porch, my own heart aching at how shattered he looked. At eighteen, I wasn't prepared for him to tell me how much I'd already hurt him, to ask me to go so he could "get over me in peace."

I'd hoped he might have feelings for me back then, and the confirmation that he did—only after I'd already ruined things— was devastating. I didn't know how to respond, worried that I'd continue to make things even worse. I couldn't handle my own emotions at that point, let alone his. When Liv doubled down, telling me to go, I gave up, offering a weak apology before sulking back to my uncles.

I was immediately comfortable with Joey and Patrick, and I couldn't keep it all in any longer. I spent the entire drive to their place in New York filling them in on what had happened between Kieran and me. I even texted Olivia asking for Kieran's phone number, but she must've blocked me too because she never responded.

I'm not eighteen anymore, and I might still have no idea what the fuck to say or do right now as Kieran glares at me, but I do know I won't be given another opportunity to correct those past mistakes.

This is my one and only chance to fix things with the man I've thought of every single day for thirteen years. I need to do whatever it takes to convince him to let me stay. I can't walk away like I did back then. "Please, is there any way you'll hear me out and give me an opportunity to apologize or explain?"

Kieran looks absolutely pissed, but his eyes are shifting around quickly without focusing on anything, like he's lost in thought, trying to process how he should handle the situation. He spins around again, zeroing in on the open doorway that leads into a bedroom before storming off through it, dragging his bag behind him and waving for me to follow.

Okay. This is good. Following Kieran further into the apartment has to be a good thing, right?

He closes the door the moment I enter. "There are no cameras in here because they can't have footage of people having sex," he explains with a huff as he paces back and forth in front of the bed. "Just give me a minute to think... I'm not going to let you embarrass me on national television. Ugh, I can't believe I wasted an hour getting ready for you," he groans, rolling his eyes before dramatically draping himself across the bed, covering his eyes with his forearm.

"You look amazing," I offer weakly, unable to stop myself from complimenting him because he should know how great he looks. Kieran's easily the most beautiful person I've ever seen, and he's only gotten better with age. His brown hair frames his face perfectly, he's got a sharp jaw, a killer resting bitch face, and it's the first time I've seen his eyebrow piercing and all his new earrings in real life. He's so fucking pretty even when he's glaring at me like he is.

"No need for false compliments," he mumbles, looking at me again. "Spit out whatever you feel like you need to say so we can move on and figure out a story to tell the producers that explains why we're leaving. I'm going to need you to sign an NDA the moment we get our phones back, too. I can't have you making up some awful lie about me to sell to a gossip site for quick cash."

"I'll sign whatever you want," I assure him, happy that we're still talking at all and he didn't slam the bedroom door in my face. "Do people really make up lies about you?"

"All the time." He sighs, sitting up to look at me again. "Fuck, why did you have to get even hotter with age?"

Wait. *What?* "You think I'm hot?" I ask in complete disbelief. Kieran knew me when I was at my physical peak. He was very well acquainted with my abs when they were individually defined and not hidden away under some padding like they are now.

But why the hell would he say that if he didn't think it was true? Is there any chance I might be able to salvage this?

"Don't fish for compliments, you know you've always been hot," he says dismissively like that's not the greatest praise I've heard in my life.

"Kieran, I know I was a complete asshole to you, and I am so sorry. I know you won't believe me, but the way I treated you has been the biggest regret of my life, and not a day goes by I don't wish I would have done things differently back then," I say, holding his bright blue gaze as I pray to a god I don't believe in that he'll somehow forgive me.

"Laying it on a bit thick, don't ya think?"

"Kieran, you have to believe me," I reply honestly.

"You hated me, Jace. Made my life a living hell. And let's not forget how you treated me when you were done with me," he argues, but I can't move past the first statement because it couldn't be further from the truth.

"I never hated you. I liked you too much, that was the problem," I rush to explain with a self-deprecating laugh. "I panicked all those years ago. I was confused about why I couldn't stop thinking about the pretty boy in my class, and I was terrified that someone would find out and tell my dad. There's no justification that would excuse how I treated you, but you deserve to finally know the truth. I was so confused back then, K."

Kieran doesn't respond. He just stares at me, and his squinted gaze feels like it's searching my soul.

"Fine."

"What's fine?" I ask, not wanting to get my hopes up, but obviously it's too late for that.

He crosses his arms, leveling me with another intimidating glare. "I'll be honest, leaving tonight wouldn't look good. Even if I came out with all the truth of the shit you used to do to me, I don't know what you've done on the show so far to win audience support, and I know how powerful editing can be. They could twist our story to make me out to be the villain, and I already lost the future I thought I was building with JR, I'm not risking my career too. My reputation is my livelihood, and I'm not letting you ruin everything I've worked so hard to build. We'll stay in here tonight where there aren't any cameras, and tomorrow morning, when I've had time to think, we'll make a game plan that allows us to remain in control of the narrative."

"Whatever you want me to do, I'll do it," I quickly agree. "I know there's probably no hope of you actually wanting to date me, but the last week talking to you has been amazing. One of the very best weeks of my life. For what it's worth, I don't think I'll ever meet anyone I could like more, and I'll always mourn the life I was picturing with K."

Kieran gives me a disbelieving look before shaking his head and standing up from the bed. He might not believe me, but I'm not going to stop being honest now that I know who he really is. I have so many regrets about the things I didn't say to him back then. I won't make the same mistakes this time around.

I know it's not a second chance. He rightfully hates me, and that will always overshadow what we built over the last week, but maybe there's an opportunity for me to do something right this time around. Whatever he needs from me, I'll do it without hesitation.

He grabs a suitcase from the corner of the room and quickly

unpacks it into the dresser, setting aside what appears to be a silk sleep set and a large toiletry bag. "I'm going to get ready for bed. I sleep on the left side."

Holy shit. *Does that mean he's okay with us sharing the bed?* "My bag is out there, should I go get it? Or did you want us to both stay in here until the morning?" I ask sheepishly, worried that one wrong move will have him kicking me out for good.

Kieran rolls his eyes again, but I don't mind. He has the most fascinating eyes I've ever seen, the makeup only highlighting their beauty.

"Stay in here. I don't want them having any other footage of us to analyze tonight. Our meeting was awkward enough."

"Yeah, that makes sense," I agree, nodding. I can just sleep in my underwear or something. "Thanks for not sending me home tonight," I add with a small smile.

This wasn't what I was expecting when I pictured my first night with KD, but I'm definitely not mad about it when I still get to sleep beside him.

KIERAN

Producer: "What's going on? What was Jace apologizing for?"

Kieran: "Nothing."

Fuck. How is this happening?

How?

How is JR the same guy who used to shove me into lockers? The same guy who called me Sparkles as an insult and switched out my gym uniform and locked me in a fucking shed? The same guy who fooled me into falling for him senior year, only to later break my heart when he was done with trading good luck blowjobs?

And how am I supposed to believe he's the same person who made me laugh so hard my stomach hurt? The one I was picturing my future with. It feels like I'm mourning that life, that future, as anger and heartbreak battle it out in my chest.

It doesn't make sense. When I think of JR, I think of warmth.

I think of someone who is funny, kind, and thoughtful, the person I desperately wanted that imaginary future with.

When I think of *Jace*—who is somehow JR—I think of him laughing at my expense. He tried to make my life smaller, he refused to let me be me, wanting me to fit with his version of what was acceptable. He had his best friend threaten me, maybe even told him to attack me, and I ended up in a hospital bed with a broken wrist and a concussion.

They can't possibly be the same person.

I even had that thought when I met JR. I told myself from the start that there were thousands of people in New York City with those initials. That there was no way in hell Jace Ryan would be on a queer dating show. And yet… here we are.

I try to calm myself down as I grip the vanity, but it isn't working. My breathing is rapid, and my eyes sting. My whole world feels like it's crashing down around me as I try to fuse two truths together that can't possibly coexist: I hate him. And I'm falling for him. *Was falling for him?* I don't know.

The contradiction makes me furious, and I feel like I'm eighteen again. Scared, hurt, heartbroken, and confused.

When I imagined us meeting, I pictured both of us breaking out into huge smiles, feeling instant attraction because of the connection we'd built. I pictured them leaning in to kiss me and feeling like I'd finally found my other half, a sense of being complete in a way I've never experienced.

I could've never imagined what actually happened, and now I don't know how to move forward.

I pace the bathroom, and my jaw aches from how tightly I'm clenching it. I splash water on my face to try to relax, some drips onto my shirt, and I don't even bother wiping it off. My whole body feels hot and tight, and I want to scream.

And underneath it all is the reality that, even if the future I was imagining with JR can never happen, this doesn't just get to end. I can't go home tomorrow without facing the consequences of more than just another broken heart from Jace.

I'm a public figure. I've seen what happens to friends who've gone through public breakups. The constant commentary from strangers who are suddenly experts in your life. People taking sides based on nothing. I've seen the toll it's taken on friends not only trying to grieve their relationship but trying to navigate the comments and the slander without letting it negatively impact their careers, which are unfortunately so rooted in public opinion.

And now, that could be me.

Coming on this show was already a risk. One that I'd hoped would be worth it to meet *the one*. All I want is to find the person I'm meant to share my life with, and yet, somehow, the universe brought me back to Jace-fucking-Ryan.

And somehow, after all this time, and all the pain he's caused me, I'm still attracted to him. Jace is still making me feel things no one else ever has. And yes, one of those things is definitely anger, but apparently all the amazing things I was feeling this morning were also because of him. And there's the smallest, tiniest, quietest part of me that wonders if it's for a reason, wonders if this is how we can rewrite our story.

But I can't fall for that.

Now I'm faced with a situation I never considered, and ending things with JR on television before they even officially start face-to-face would turn me into the villain. Even if I told the truth—that he was my bully in high school—half the internet would say I'm the one bullying him now for not giving him a chance. I would have no control over how they edit the show, over how the world would see me.

Which means leaving immediately isn't an option.

So that means I'm staying… with Jace.

As much as I hate to admit it, the best and safest thing for me to do here, really, is to play along and continue with the process as expected.

My eyes sting even more as my tears start to fall.

I'm so angry at him for hurting me all those years ago. I'm so angry at the show for casting him. I'm so angry at myself for feeling such a strong pull to him. I'm so angry that I'd be the one ripped apart by the media if I walked away. Not him. As far as I know, no one knows who he is. I'll be the self-absorbed celebrity who thinks the "regular person" isn't good enough for him or whatever bullshit headline they come up with. But not Jace. Of course not him.

More tears break free, and I swipe them away as I shake my head. I've cried enough over this man in my lifetime. I'm not going to cry now.

He said he'll do whatever I ask him to. Fine. I'm asking him to be strategic with me. If I can't have the relationships I came here for, the one I'm currently mourning, then I need to shift my focus. There will be a huge audience watching this, some who know me, most who don't. If he's willing to pretend to be my boyfriend, we're going to be the best damn couple this show has ever seen. We'll give them exactly the kind of "look at this perfect romance" footage they love. I might not be in the editing room, but I know how to create good content.

And when it's over, we'll fade out. After Jace signs his NDA, we can have a lowkey mutual breakup. I'll share my side of the story on my terms.

The thought makes me feel a bit more in control for the first time since seeing Jace. This isn't the ending I wanted—it's the furthest thing from it—but at least I have a plan.

I take one last look in the mirror, telling myself to pull it together. I flatten my expression, not wanting Jace to see how much he's wrecked me, and when I open the bathroom door, he's already in bed. On the right side.

His eyes land on me as I cross the room to my side without a word, pulling the covers back and sliding in.

His shirt is off, and I refuse to look at his thick hairy chest. I hate how attracted to him I am.

Jace starts to say something, but I cut him off. I'm so far past what I can handle tonight; I just need today to be done. "We'll talk tomorrow."

I turn off the bedside lamp and attempt to settle in.

My plan might not be perfect, but it's the best I can come up with for now, and that thought allows me to eventually drift off to sleep, even with Jace sleeping beside me.

41

JACE

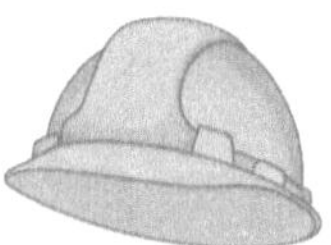

Producer: "Obviously your meeting was not what we were expecting, but it wasn't clear to the audience what happened. Kieran seemed upset. You immediately tried to apologize. What were your initial feelings when you saw him: excited, shocked, maybe even disappointed? Come on, Jace, you've gotta give us something."

Jace: "Uh, shocked, disappointed, and excited all sound accurate."

"Get up." A familiar voice wakes me from the deep sleep I must have been in. *Kieran.* I bolt upright in the bed, nearly colliding with him as I do.

"Shit. Sorry, I'm up! Am I late for something?" I ask through a yawn as I rub my eyes, and everything that happened yesterday comes crashing back. I'm in bed... with Kieran.

Fuck, I wish he wanted to be sharing a bed with me.

I put my glasses on in time to see him roll his eyes, his

makeup already perfectly in place again. *What time did he wake up?* "Nothing specific, but we need to form a plan before we go out there and are on camera again today. We need to make sure we're on the same page," he reminds me.

"Yeah, of course," I quickly agree as I move to stand from the bed. I slept in my underwear, proud I only hesitated for a moment before taking off my shirt in front of Kieran, but this situation doesn't have room for vanity.

I don't usually think of myself as self-conscious. Plenty of people are attracted to bigger guys, and my body more than holds up for my job, which keeps me active and strong.

But being around Kieran again stirs up old high school memories and drags my dad's old insults back to the surface. It took years to eat without hearing his voice in my head, measuring how "healthy" every bite was. But I got there, eventually.

That's what I tried to remind myself of last night. I've still got the catcher's ass from all those years behind home plate, and I'm still strong. I just no longer have a six-pack because I'd rather eat all the good food NYC has to offer.

Even so, I can't help wondering what Kieran really thinks. My physique is so different from the last time I was this exposed around him.

He's always been gorgeous, and looks great in all his videos, but in person, his beauty is radiant. It's hard to tear my eyes away from him. After I put yesterday's outfit back on since I still don't have my luggage in here, I turn back to face him where he's now sitting cross-legged on the bed, staring at me expectantly. I'm not sure what he wants me to say, though. "So, what do you want me to do?"

He continues to stare at me for another moment before taking a deep breath. "I said it last night, but I'd like to emphasize why I didn't storm out of here and take the first flight home. I'm not sure if you know what a beauty influencer is, but I have over twenty million followers on YouTube, and, like, three times that on TikTok. I make a lot of money from my videos, but also from endorsements, appearances, and products."

"I know," I say without thinking, belatedly realizing that maybe I shouldn't have admitted that so readily.

His brows furrow as he gives me a questioning look. Then he shakes his head like he's trying to clear it, muttering, "I guess I was naive to think I'd escaped hometown gossip."

He looks upset by that thought, so I give him a little more of the truth. "Kieran, I haven't been to New Jersey in thirteen years. I know that because I'm a fan. I'm one of those twenty million followers," I admit with a chuckle.

I was hoping that might make him feel better, but he only looks more confused. "You're… a fan?" he repeats like he can't possibly comprehend the idea. I nod, not really sure what else to say. This moment doesn't feel like the right time to admit just how big of a fan I am. "But you used to… never mind." He shakes his head again. "Okay, so you understand why I can't risk the show's editors painting me as a villain, right? If you've earned fans here with your big-cuddly-protector vibe and cute cross-stitching and whatever else you've done. I don't want them to hate me if we break up on the show. "

"Okay. So, you want us to pretend to be together for the cameras?" I clarify. Selfishly, I kind of love this idea, even if it would be pretend. Any time I can get around Kieran feels like a win.

"Exactly. We can make up an excuse about why I freaked out last night and say it in front of the cameras. Then we'll be the cutest couple that we can be to make sure people like us. After the show is over, we'll have control of the narrative again and can decide when it's appropriate to announce that things didn't work out between us in the real world."

It sounds like a decent plan. But as I think through the specifics of what remaining on the show would look like, the reality of what he's asking sinks in. "So, you want to pretend to marry me?" Definitely not the marriage I wish I could have with him, but I'd still do it. Kieran's eyes go wide at my question like maybe he'd forgotten that detail, so I answer before he can change his mind. "Okay."

He stares at me for another moment, eyes even wider, brow quirked. "Okay?" he repeats back, sounding shocked by my answer. "Why in the world would you agree to that?"

"If that's what you want me to do, then I'll do it. I meant what I said about whatever you need."

Kieran runs his hands through the long stands of his dark hair before he starts to twist his earring like he can't sit still. After another moment of silence, he shakes his head again. "Fuck, I forgot that part because I was so surprised it was you. I guess it would have to be an actual marriage. You'd really do it?"

"Of course." I promise. "I'll never make up for what I did back then, but I can at least try to make things easier for you now. I'd love the opportunity to try to repay some of the kindness you showed me. My life is infinitely better because you were a part of it, and I hate that you have the opposite opinion of me. Let me add a positive chapter now."

"See, if you said anything like that, I'm sure the audience loves you," he grumbles.

"I doubt it when the producers kept having to remind me to talk out loud."

Before he can respond, there's a loud knock on our door.

"Hey, it's Jay. I've been sent to remind you to spend as much time as you can in the public spaces where there are cameras. Neither of you answered our texts."

Kieran gives me a final questioning look. "You're sure about this?" I nod. "Okay." His shoulders fall as he lets out a deep breath. "Then it's showtime."

42

KIERAN

Producer: "What's the messiest thing fans don't know about your past?"

Kieran: "Why in the world would I tell you that?"

$\mathcal{I}$ open the door and see an unfamiliar face smiling back at me.

"Hi, Kieran, I'm Jay. I've been the one assigned to Jace this whole time."

"Nice to meet you," I greet, keeping my voice polite but clipped. I'm still distracted, running through my mental checklist of how I want to play today.

"Alright, so… we didn't get the footage we were hoping for last night. We don't know what happened and we kind of need to. Or we need you to redo your meeting so that the viewers aren't left with so many questions."

"I think we'd rather just move forward," I say with a smile, hoping he'll drop it, but that's when Mitch rushes into the apartment too.

"Kieran, we shouldn't have let you just storm into the bedroom and stay there all night, and we're probably going to get our asses chewed out for that. Can you give us something to use? Just a quick interview explaining why you reacted the way you did. If it's good, we won't need to film it again."

Jace is standing quietly beside me, and when I glance at him, he's already looking at me, obviously letting me take the lead. Maybe we can pull off our hastily made plan after all.

"Define good?" I prompt, turning back to the producers, and I'm met with a huff from Mitch.

"Jace, can you tell us anything? What's going on here? You must know each other from somewhere. Hookup gone bad?" Jay prompts.

"What the hell? No." I feign shock at the suggestion, swallowing down the truth that, yeah, that's exactly what happened. But we're not about to share that part of our history.

"Nope," Jace echoes, popping the *p*, still following my lead.

Mitch doesn't blink as he stares me down, but I won't give in that easily, and I only smile even wider.

"Then we'll have to reshoot it," he finally states flatly.

"Of course you will," I murmur with obvious false cheer. *Fucking "reality" TV.*

Jace snickers beside me, and when I turn back to him, he just flashes me a smile before schooling his features.

"Well, go freshen up, and then we'll be waiting for you to pretend it's the first time you're meeting," Jay instructs. "Unless you want to keep the intro and do an interview?" he offers again.

I turn around, heading back into the bedroom. Jace follows me after grabbing his bag that was still out there and shuts the door behind us.

"I can't believe they're making us redo this," I complain, crossing my arms now that there aren't cameras.

"So, what exactly are we going to do when we pretend we're meeting?" he asks, looking at me for direction again, and I can't quite wrap my head around Jace so easily handing me the control.

"Fuck, I don't know. Do we act excited? I think we should. I was so excited yesterday morning, and nervous and hopeful about us." I ramble before I realize what exactly I'm admitting, so I rush to continue. "Normally, I'd think that's how people would act when they're meeting their perceived future spouse."

"Okay, I can do that," Jace confirms easily with a big smile, and I seriously can't get over how weird this is as I go to the bathroom to start getting ready. I pull out the same palettes I used yesterday and recreate the look as closely as I can, and when I'm satisfied and feel steady enough to face the camera, and Jace again, I open the bathroom door. Jace immediately jumps up from the bed where he must have been waiting.

He turns to face me fully, and his jaw falls open as he rakes his eyes over my body.

"Wow," he says on an exhale, and I roll my eyes.

"You don't need to get into character yet. The cameras aren't in here."

"Character? Kieran, I'm being serious. You look incredible." His eyes are pleading for me to believe him. But I remember how convincing he was when we were eighteen, too. A couple of compliments aren't going to prove to me he's changed.

And even if he has, that doesn't erase our past. Jace could be a fucking saint now for all I know, but that doesn't mean I should just give in to him, even if it feels like my body has some invisible tether to his whenever we're in the same room.

Not to mention the annoying and persistent voice in my head, reminding me how only twenty-four hours ago, I was convinced JR could be my future and now I'm throwing it all away.

Fuck.

"K, I have so much I want to say to you whenever you're

ready to hear it," he continues. "You're the most beautiful person I've ever seen." The way his voice catches makes something twist in my stomach.

He sounds genuine, and that's the problem. Because all those times when I thought we were growing closer back then, he proved to me I didn't matter. That's the Jace I have to remember right now, not the one looking at me like I'm the only person in the world. I can't let the hopeless romantic side of me that was planning a wedding yesterday get the best of me.

But I also want to know what he's going to say.

"Jace, I want—"

"Are you ready yet?" Mitch asks through the door, slamming his fists against it.

Right. I need to focus on the filming we're about to do so we can move on from this meeting fiasco and start selling the picture-perfect reality television couple we're planning to be.

"Ready?" I ask, swallowing down the emotions he stirred up.

"Whenever you are."

I open the door into the main living space, and Mitch and Jay are waiting for us, as promised.

"Okay, so, we already got you both walking down the hallway yesterday, so all we really need is for Jace to open the door from outside. Oh, do you have your bag?" Jace goes back to grab it while they continue directing me. "Kieran, you need to stand…" Mitch trails off as he comes to move me back into the kitchen area. "Here."

"Remember, you're excited! You are meeting your future husband after all!" Jay cheers.

"We got it," I assure them.

Jace walks back out into the hallway with Mitch and Jay, and I stand awkwardly in the kitchen, hyping myself up to be *excited* about this.

A second later, the door opens and Jace walks in.

"K?" he questions, immediately slipping into character even if it sounds super fake.

"Yeah, it's me," I exclaim, and cringe because it feels way too forced, and that's going to seem even more weird to the people watching. "Sorry, can we do that again?"

"Yeah, no problem," he agrees easily, turning to walk back into the hallway.

This isn't a big deal, I remind myself. Except it is. Because the second this airs, everyone from our hometown is going to watch it. I can't even begin to imagine how that'll go over. There's no way we can pull off this scripted introduction. Someone from back then will sell their story about what we were like in high school.

Social media warriors will eat up this super-fake meeting.

Fuck.

"Wait," I call out, stopping Jace. "I don't think we can do this. At least, not this fabricated, happy version we're trying to sell… Come back into the bedroom. Quick."

He swiftly follows me into the bedroom with his big, long strides, and the second we're closed in, I rush to explain before Mitch and Jay can yell at us again.

"This whole thing is a disaster, obviously. And I feel like an even bigger mess without Olivia to consult about what to do, but I'm now realizing that once this phony redo of our meeting airs, our hometown is going to bash the hell out of it and it'll probably come back to bite me. I think we need to do the interview instead."

"Okay, sure." He shrugs. "Wait, you and Olivia are still friends?"

"That's what you took from all of what I just said?"

"I heard you, and I'm down to do what you think is best, but that's really cool you're still close after all this time. I'm happy for you."

I stare at him with what I'm sure is a confused expression for another second before reminding myself to focus. "We can talk about that later. Let's go tell them we'll answer their questions." I let out a sigh. "Shit, this is such a mess. I hate not knowing what the right thing to do is, and feeling like no matter what I decide, I'm choosing wrong," I vent out loud to Jace as I'm processing this situation.

I do usually have Liv help me make decisions, but I can't talk to her until the next phase of the show when we go back home, and it's making this whole situation harder and more complicated than it already is.

"You're not choosing wrong," Jace assures me. "But you'll never make everyone happy; it's not possible. So, what do you want to do. What is your gut telling you is the right thing?"

I take in a steadying breath, allowing the exhale to calm my body before I answer. "Let's do the interview; keep it vague. We can just say we know each other and leave it at that. I'm sure people from our hometown will still probably run their mouths about high school, but if anything, that'd just justify the actual meeting. We should focus on moving forward as a united front now."

Jace nods and turns to update Mitch and Jay on the new plan.

As much as I hate the idea of being on the same team, of relying on Jace-fucking-Ryan of all people, thirty-one-year-old Jace does seem to be very different from the Jace I remember.

When I walk out a moment later, I hear Mitch say, "Great, we already have questions prepared just in case the rerecording didn't go well. Follow us."

Jace starts to follow them down the hall, and my eyes—the traitors that they are—go straight to his ass. His thick, perfectly rounded, ass. The kind of plump catcher's butt that makes me feel like it was created for the sole purpose of tormenting me. His jeans cling to him like they were custom fitted, pulling tight with every step.

I should look away, but I don't.

My gaze trails higher, taking in the rest of him. He's every inch the attractive golden boy I remember—just older, thicker, and a hell of a lot more distracting.

The elevator dings, and I remind myself to focus on this interview.

We follow Mitch and Jay onto another floor where a small lounge with a couch and a camera are already set up. The second I sit down, a mic gets clipped to my shirt, and Mitch settles into the chair across from us.

"Alright, lets dive in," he says brightly. "Did you know each other before the show?"

I glance at Jace, just long enough to see him patiently waiting for my answer, then back at Mitch. "Yeah," I say, keeping my voice even and offering the camera a smile.

"Can you tell us more?" he prompts. "Kieran, you seemed upset when you realized JR is Jace."

That's because I was. My smile doesn't falter as I answer in a polite, polished, interview ready tone. "I was surprised, but I'm ready to move on and move forward with him."

Mitch doesn't miss a beat, sounding annoyed. "Could you at least repeat the question back so I have something usable?"

"Yes, we used to know each other. We met before the show," I say with my best camera-ready smile. "I was surprised that JR was Jace, and I handled that initial reaction poorly."

"Well, where do you see this going after such a… memorable introduction?"

"Definitely forward. After we had a moment to let the surprise settle, we decided to start fresh. We reconnected in the blind part of this process for a reason. Whatever's in the past, is in the past, we're here now, so…" I turn to meet Jace's eyes and he gives me a small smile. "I'm ready to move on and give our relationship a real chance."

The lie tastes bitter. I haven't even finished mourning what could've been with JR, and now I'm sitting here pretending to be excited about a future with Jace.

"Yeah, I definitely think we can make it work," he adds with a bright smile back at me, really selling it.

He doesn't appear to be struggling the way I am. Jace seems eager to go along with everything I suggest, as if this performance could somehow make up for everything that came before. Maybe it can make him feel better about himself. But for me, it's just proof he still knows exactly how to pull me back in.

43

JACE

Producer: "So, can you expand on what exactly you were apologizing for? Neither of you have given any details other than that you used to know each other."

Jace: "Oh, that's all there really is to know. It was a misunderstanding. We're all good now."

"Anything else you'd like to add, Jace?" Mitch asks hopefully.

"No, I think that covers it. Can we go back to our apartment now?" I request. Kieran obviously wants to keep this brief, and I have no problem with that plan.

Mitch and Jay don't seem thrilled with our answers, but I decide to take a risk and pull Kieran's hand into mine, resting our locked fingers on my thigh as we wait to be dismissed. There's a flash of surprise in Kieran's expression when he realizes what I'm doing, but he doesn't swat me away, so I'll count it as a win.

He told me he wanted us to basically become "couple goals" on the show, and for me, that means we should be cute and cuddly whenever we're near each other. I know KD had mentioned hating when dates only seemed to want public displays of affection and didn't care as much when they were alone—which makes a hell of a lot more sense now that I actually know who he is—so I'll have to ask him what his boundaries and expectations are about us touching on camera moving forward so I don't trigger those same negative emotions.

Mitch looks at our joined hands and back up at us before rolling his eyes. "Fine. But please stay in the main living spaces as much as possible or we'll have to add cameras in the bedroom, and I really don't want to have footage of what's going to happen when you two give in to whatever tension is happening here," he adds, motioning between us.

"Come on, Mitch, you don't have to lie to us," I tease. "I'd definitely want a copy." Mitch looks completely unamused, but Kieran snorts a surprised laugh next to me, and I feel a sense of pride swell in my chest. I hate that I'm causing stress in his life *again,* so my personal mission for the remainder of our time together is to get as many laughs and smiles from him as possible.

KD and I spent the last week constantly joking around and making the other laugh, I won't be naive and pretend like we can get all the way back to that point with how much he obviously still hates me, but maybe things can be better than they are now.

"We'll give you more cross-stitch materials or more makeup, whatever hobby you need, just stay. Out. Of. The. Bedroom," Mitch reiterates, emphasizing each word.

Kieran perks up at that. "I'll never say no to more makeup and another camera."

"There are cameras all over the main space," Mitch argues.

"I'm used to having a camera set up right in front of me, not the random angles of the ones in the apartment." Kieran shrugs.

I can't wipe the smile from my face. Kieran hasn't dropped my hand this whole time, and I love seeing how confident he is, standing his ground asking for what he wants. He comes across as so poised and sure of himself in his videos, but I've always wondered what he was like off camera. I feel guilty about how excited I am that I get to see it firsthand when I know he'd rather never see me again, but I'm trying not to get lost in negative feelings and enjoy my limited time with Kieran as much as I can. I'll deal with the crash out when it's over.

"We'll get all that to you as soon as we can," Mitch concedes.

Kieran stands from the couch we're on, pulling me up with him as he still doesn't drop my hand. When we're back in the apartment, he finally does, and the loss of his touch is far more upsetting than it should be. "I'm so ready to put on different clothes now that we're not pretending it's yesterday." He cringes slightly and walks toward the bedroom.

"You can go first," I offer, hanging back.

After we're both showered and in new outfits, we both make our way into the kitchen. "Are you hungry?" I ask, realizing we haven't eaten yet today as I open the fridge to see what they've stocked. "I know we've both talked about being bad at cooking, but I can handle scrambled eggs and bacon."

"Extra crispy," he responds, sitting at the kitchen island with a makeup bag and small mirror as I pull out ingredients.

"Whatever you'd like," I remind him with a wink. Maybe if I say that enough, he'll understand just how deep my promise goes.

His makeup came off in the shower, and it looks like he's applying a different look for the "new" day. I get lost watching him for a moment, feeling like I'm the live audience for the show I've only ever seen on my screen.

"So, we should probably go over some things we couldn't say or explain while we were in the blind part of the show," he prompts, pulling me back to the present. "Sounds like you know what I do. Tell me about your life. Baseball didn't work out?"

I can't help but laugh as I get to work cooking. "I never tried. When my dad found out I wasn't straight in senior year of high school, he kicked me out, and I decided that the MLB was his dream, not mine."

"Senior year?" he repeats back, eyes wide. "How did I not know that?"

"It was only the last week or so," I explain, not wanting to remind him on camera that he was in the hospital and never came back to school. "I didn't really tell anyone either."

"So, is that when you went to live with your uncles? When I didn't know who you were, and you said they stepped in, I thought maybe your parents had died and you weren't ready to talk about it."

"As far as I know, they're both still living in that same house, but I haven't been back since. And yeah, I actually hadn't talked to my uncle at that point for years," I tell him, remembering how scared and pissed off I was back then. It's crazy how much better my life became after feeling like it was over.

The only thing I would've changed was the way things ended with Kieran. But it wasn't the end, was it? We're here now, together. Even if he doesn't want to be, we're getting the chance to add to our story. I'm not living under some delusion we'll have some happily ever after together… *but what if?*

At the very least, I'm hoping we part on better terms than last time, which shouldn't be too hard.

"I was living in a crappy motel by the school, trying to make it through graduation, and I was almost out of money, so I called Joey," I tell him. "Turns out the reason I hadn't seen him for so long was because my dad is a homophobic asshole who cut him out of our lives when he tried to introduce us to his boyfriend."

"Shit."

"Yeah. Moving in with him and his husband, Patrick, was

one of the best things that ever happened to me." I manage to stop myself from saying the time we spent together senior year before everything fell apart is also at the top of my list. Followed closely by what's happening right now because I never in a million years thought I'd get to spend time with him again.

"Wait." Kieran pauses, looking confused. "So, when we were talking about not feeling like you were good enough growing up, was that about your dad? I had kind of assumed JR meant with other people their age—"

"That's what you were talking about, right?" I cut in, the truth of what he's about to say is already a painful reminder of the past. "But it wasn't everyone. It was me, wasn't it?" I know it might be stupid to bring this up at all, especially on camera, but I need him to know that I'm not dismissing our past and how cruel I was. I hate the things I did, and I want him to believe me, to somehow make it up to him. "I'm so sorry I ever made you feel that way. I was such an idiot. I wish I had understood back then how special those things I saw as different make you."

He blinks at me a few times, and then shakes his head and smiles, but it doesn't reach his eyes. It's the polished, camera-ready smile he's perfected, and I know before he opens his mouth that his answer is for the audience and our act. It isn't his honest one.

"Thank you for saying that, J, but you don't have to keep apologizing, we've already moved on. I was just wanting to continue to get to know you by asking about things we talked about earlier in the process."

I might as well continue to tell the truth. Maybe Kieran will eventually believe me if I continue to be completely honest at every opportunity. "Well, to answer your question, yeah, I was mostly talking about my dad and how nothing was ever good enough. Do you remember what you asked me next when we were talking about that?"

He takes a moment to consider. "I think I asked if you had any escape from those feelings."

"Do you remember my answer?" I prompt.

He's quiet for a long moment, and then his whole body goes still as his eyes widen. His voice is quiet as he answers. "That you found someone who made you feel like you could be yourself for the first time."

"I don't think I ever properly thanked you for that."

"No need," he whispers, looking very overwhelmed, so I decide to move on. I love that we're actually hanging out, and I don't want it to end because I ruined things by making him uncomfortable.

"Then I found it again with each of my uncles. I'm really lucky to have them. Patrick even took me on as his apprentice when I first moved here. I'm an ironworker in the city now. Not at all what I pictured back then, but I love it."

"Huh," Kieran says, and I turn away from the food for a moment to look at him again. I swear I catch him checking me out before he quickly looks away, but I make sure to flex my arms as I continue, just in case.

"What about you?" I ask.

"You said you've seen my videos. You know what I do."

"Well, yeah, but I mean, tell me about your life. What are the things you love about it or the parts you wish you could change? I had no idea that you and Olivia are still friends. Why isn't she ever in the videos? What should the person you're dating know that other people don't?" I try to tell myself that I'm asking these questions because I want to be a good fake boyfriend, or whatever we are at this point on the show, and not because they're things I've wondered for years.

He's quiet for a moment. And I turn to face him again as I wait for the bacon to finish. His piercing gaze is assessing as it meets mine. I don't think he expected me to ask him anything real, and I hope he isn't upset about it.

"I love all of it," he finally answers on an exhale. "It doesn't matter that I've been doing it for so long now, most days I'm still shocked that people want to watch my videos," he says with a self-deprecating chuckle.

"They're so good." I can't help but tell him.

His mouth twists to the corner like he's holding back a smile as he says, "Thanks." For a moment, I think that's all he'll give me, so I'm thrilled when he goes on. "I think my favorite part will always be the comments from people telling me that I've inspired them to do something that might be scary, but makes them happier. The people who are inspired to embrace their true selves."

He's playing with his ear piercing, twisting it around like I've noticed him doing when he's being vulnerable, like he needs the distraction to put himself out there. "I know some people might look at my channel and think that what I do is silly or pointless, but the people who say I've changed their lives for the better make me so fucking grateful for the life and the job I have."

"You're amazing," I tell him, making sure to hold his gaze as I do. I'm not complimenting him for the cameras or because I think it's what a fake boyfriend would do. And I can only hope he understands how much I mean it.

He bites his lip before shifting his gaze behind me. "I think the food's ready."

I hurry to get everything plated. Kieran managed a totally different makeup look during our conversation, and now has dark navy eyeshadow with a bit of a shine to it, and it makes his eyes really stand out. "I love when you wear that color," I admit when I can no longer take the silence between us as we're eating.

He looks down at his shirt. "Black?"

"No, sorry, I meant your eyeshadow. The deep blue looks great with your eyes."

He looks confused for a moment before he gives me a genuine smile. "Thanks, J."

After our late brunch, Kieran and I move to the living room and turn on the TV. Kieran goes to sit on the opposite end to me, but I push my luck. "Would you want to sit with me? I really have been told I'm a good cuddler."

He hesitates for a moment, probably psyching himself up to play his part. "By who? I need names," Kieran teases as he settles in under my raised arm, leaning against me as he pulls a blanket up to cover us.

"Are you doubting my references or threatening my exes?" I joke back.

"I think you already know the answer to that," he says with a wink that has my stomach doing cartwheels. *This isn't real.* I try to distract myself by pulling up the approved streaming service.

"We have to watch reality TV," Kieran suggests, and we pick the first show that we find. I'm trying to pay attention, but Kieran is cuddled up with me on the couch, and I can't focus on anything other than how perfectly he seems to fit under my arm.

"Was that your phone?" he asks, and I realize my show phone has been vibrating so I pull it out to see a few missed texts from LM. "Who the hell are you texting?" Kieran asks, sounding offended.

"It's one of the other contestants, not anyone outside of the show," I explain with a laugh.

"You're still talking to one of your other dates?" He sounds even more confused now, so I rush to explain.

"No, no, not really. LM and I were never really dating. We clicked platonically right away, and agreed to keep talking so that we weren't going through the process alone."

"And you're sure they're not into you?" he pushes. He's really nailing the jealous partner look, and I wish more than anything that it wasn't for the cameras.

"I'm sure. They're very invested in their partner, BB."

He finally settles back into me. "Huh. That's cool."

I quickly send LM an update about how things are going. That—surprise—I actually knew KD and he's not a fan of me, but we've agreed to move on beyond our past and see where things go. They update me that both he and BB are cis men, but that BB apparently thought he was straight—which, what? Why would you sign up for this show?—and that BB had assumed he was talking to a woman the whole time. But somehow he's still all in and wants to date LM.

I don't think either of our situations were what the producers had in mind for the season, but it'll end up being entertaining, I'm sure. I show Kieran that part of the text, and he bursts out laughing. "Maybe our meeting wasn't the worst one."

4 4

KIERAN

Producer: "Since you won't give us any details on how you two already know each other, what's your favorite thing about Jace that you knew from before the show?"

Kieran: *Don't say his ass from all the catcher's squatting.* "Um, he's always been very passionate."

*J*ace seems like a completely different person than he was in high school. More like the person he was when we were in the woods together, except even more genuine and more comfortably himself.

But I remind myself that I told him to act, and just like back when we were eighteen, he's nailing it.

He's been all over me today.

Every time I sat down, he was there. Reaching for my hand while filming, asking me to cuddle on the couch, thigh pressed against mine while we were eating dinner. All. Damn. Day. And the worst part? I couldn't call him out on it because the cameras were always rolling, and we'd already been warned not to hole up in the bedroom or they'd put cameras in there too.

I forced myself to play nice and pretend it didn't irritate the hell out of me, mostly because if it was anyone else... I think I would love it. But it's Jace. I can't forget that. By the time he wrapped himself around me while I was cleaning up dinner, I was wound so tight I could barely see straight.

I've officially had enough.

"Ready for bed?" I ask him with my best pleasant I'm-on-camera voice.

"I sure am," Jace says with a beaming smile, eyes lit up behind his glasses. And goddamn does he look good with glasses.

He follows as I lead the way, and the second he closes the door, I snap, letting all my pent-up emotions out.

"What the fuck was that?"

Jace stares at me, blinking innocently as if he has no idea what I'm talking about. "What was what?"

I throw my hands up. "You. All over me. All. Day. What was that?"

His eyebrows pull together in mock surprise. "Uh, yeah. That's what couples do. You told me to make us look like 'couple goals,' remember? In my mind, 'couple goals' involves touching. We talked about our love languages, how mine is physical touch. If I'm in a relationship, then I want to be with that person, to touch my partner, and feel the proof of our connection."

"Well, that's not what I meant." Heat prickles the back of my neck. "You don't need to... to—" I gesture vaguely because he should get it. That was too much. Casual contact is one thing, but this was constant.

No one has ever touched me that much at home. Not even the people I've actually dated.

But Jace? He's draping himself all over me and holding my

hand as we walk through the hallways because he wants to? Or because he thinks I want him to? I don't know, and the fact that I'm questioning his motivation at all makes everything even more confusing. *It's for the cameras*, I remind myself.

The fact that he's the first one giving me attention in this way is pissing me off even more though. It feels too easy, too normal —too fucking dangerous when a part of me doesn't hate it at all.

"I didn't ask for all of *that*," I finally huff out after a moment.

"I thought you wanted it to look real. I'm sorry, Kieran. I didn't mean to overstep," he concedes, and it adds another irritating itch under my skin at how apologetic he truly seems.

Fuck, I don't even know what I'm feeling right now.

Am I mad at him or at myself for letting my exes convince me their bare-minimum attention was love? Mad because he got under my skin so fast after nearly thirteen years of not seeing each other? Mad because he's seemed so honest in all his actions and apologies, and I can't help but wonder if he might have really changed? Until I remind myself not to go there again.

"You don't have to touch me that much." My voice comes out sharper than I intend. "Okay?"

"Is it the way I look? I know I've gained some weight since high school," he asks quietly. The steady confidence he's had this whole time is gone as he looks down at the floor.

Heat flares through my body, and I roll my eyes, trying not to look at his perfect body. "No, god. I've already told you how hot you still are. You don't get it."

"Then explain it to me, because I can't know what I'm doing wrong unless you tell me," he pleads, looking back at me.

I hold his gaze, not even sure what I'm hoping to find there. My head's spinning after the day I've had with Jace all over me. "I don't owe you an explanation," I finally huff. "I already said less touching."

"Then stop glaring at me like I crossed some secret line," he demands, and for the first time since the big reveal that JR was

Jace, he isn't tripping over himself to please me. It reminds me of the way things were in the very beginning, back when he was just my bully as he goes on, stepping closer to me.

"You asked me to pretend, and I'm just trying to make *you* happy. You wanted a perfect story for the cameras and your fans. Well, newsflash, K—if we want people to think we're getting married by the end of this, that's going to involve some touching."

Fuck. Him.

Every emotion coursing through me feels like a contradiction, and I don't know what to do with any of them. My chest is heaving as I try to breathe, try to think, but all I can do is hold Jace's molten stare.

We're standing mere inches apart, and I'm brought back to that bathroom at the Halloween party. The bathroom at school when he thought I had a hickey. We're behind another locked door, away from where anyone can see us. The tension between us is a palpable thing, and my control is slipping. I need it back. And the only way I know how to grab it back from him is to fight.

"Just so we're clear—I still hate you, Jace. Cameras or not, I don't suddenly like you just because you're a good actor. What we said out there isn't true, I can't forgive and forget everything you did to me. You're not fooling me this time. Okay? I. Fucking. Hate. You," I seethe.

Even though I don't know if that's true.

It doesn't feel true.

Fuck.

What is he doing to me?

"Kieran—" Something that looks a lot like hurt flashes in his eyes, but I can't even trust that.

"No," I cut him off. "I don't want to talk about it."

His jaw works like he's holding something back as he looks me up and down, but when I think he might finally concede, walk away and end this confrontation, he does the opposite, taking another step even closer.

"You keep saying you hate me," Jace grits out, his own frustration boiling over. "But you don't act like it."

That makes me laugh, harsh and bitter. "Oh, you think you know me? You don't," I spit, stepping closer to him on instinct to show him he can't intimidate me. But he doesn't move back, and suddenly, we feel far too close.

My pulse spikes at the tension between us. I should shove him and walk away. Instead, my hand snags the front of his shirt, twisting the fabric in my fist to keep him there, where I won't admit I want him.

"Oh, but I do," he mutters, and his hand clamps over mine. The heat of his grip shoots straight through me. "Go ahead, Kieran, tell me again how you hate me. Lie to my face and tell me you don't want me."

I tighten my fist in his shirt, pulling him closer even though every nerve in me screams to shove him away. My voice comes out low, ragged. "It isn't a lie. You don't know a damn thing about me."

He smirks. "Then why are you shaking?"

"I'm not," I grit out, though we both feel the tremor in my hand where it's locked against his chest.

"Sure you're not." He's acting smug now. "You can lie about that all you want, but you can't lie about this," he says as he reaches his hand down, his knuckles grazing the front of my jeans. "Why are you hard, Kieran?"

My heart is pounding, and it really is like we're back in the bathroom all those years ago when I was taunting him to give in. I swallow down the emotion in my throat, frozen in place.

"You want me to stop?" he asks, rough and mocking, like he already knows the answer.

I can't think, too overwhelmed by the memories and the lust and the anger warring for my attention now. I'm not capable of conscious decision. The only thing I can do is press harder against him, grinding out the words through clenched teeth. "Fuck you."

"Gladly," he shoots back, squeezing my aching cock.

I attempt to shove him back, but he doesn't budge—and I hate that I'm relieved. Instead, his large hand closes around my wrist and changes our position so my back is now against the wall. He pins that arm above my head as he wedges his thigh between mine. The entire time, our eyes are locked, like he's daring me to look away, to tell him to stop.

"Say it again," he taunts, grinding against me and adding friction exactly where I want him.

"I hate you," I snarl, twisting his shirt in my free fist again. My voice comes out raw, not half as convincing as I want it to be.

"You don't sound so sure," he whispers. His mouth hovers close enough to mine for his exhale to caress my lips. His gaze flicks to my mouth.

"Don't," I say harshly, setting the boundary. Kissing is the line we never crossed, and I'm not going to let him start now.

He chuckles low, shifting his mouth way too close to my ear. "Fine. No kissing." His teeth scrape along my jaw instead. His thigh presses harder between mine, grinding me against the wall, and I can hardly think.

Fuck, he feels good pressed against me.

"What do you need, K?"

"I need you to shut the fuck up," I hiss.

"You have a better way I could be using my mouth? One where you wouldn't have to hear the annoying sound of my voice? Gonna use me, Kieran?" he taunts. "I'd like that; you have no idea how much."

His words make my pulse stutter. How is he using my own words against me all these years later? *Why do we both remember them so clearly?* "God, you talk too much," I complain.

"I think you like it," he whispers, grinding against me again. It feels good, too good. I was already struggling to think, to convince myself that this—doing anything physical with Jace again—is a horrible idea. But the feel of his hard dick rubbing against me is only making me eager for more. I feel like I'm that eighteen-year-old again who secretly enjoyed meeting up with his bully in the woods. Only now, I'm struggling to remember how things ended, because all I can focus on is the want and desire, just like I did all those years ago.

Without my permission, a "fuck" falls from my lips, spurring Jace on.

"That's it, K. Use me. Hate me. Come on. Take what you need." He lets go of my wrist, shifting his hand into my hair, tangling his fingers with the long strands.

I can't take it anymore. My hand shoots down to grip his thick cock through his pants, and I squeeze.

"Fuckkkk," he hisses, and I smirk to myself as I regain some semblance of control. But then he opens his fucking mouth again. "That's it, just like that. Hate me harder. Tell me what you want. My mouth? Want me on my knees for you again?"

"Fine. If you're so desperate to suck my dick again, do it," I seethe, face inches from his. My words sound vicious, but underneath, my nerves are buzzing, just like all those years ago when I challenged him to touch me. Only this time, it isn't fear and anxiety that have me worried about how badly things could end; it's the memories.

I don't know what I'm doing, but I'm well aware I just gave him the power here. He's about to watch my denial about wanting him slip away, but in this moment, I don't care. I want it. Want him. Even if I'll never give him the satisfaction of saying those words out loud.

He's staring at me with wide eyes, and I wonder for a

moment if he'll back out. But I should know better than that. His mouth twists into an infuriating smirk.

"What are you waiting for?" My voice comes out hoarse. "Get on your knees, hot shot. Suck my cock and remind me what your mouth can do besides piss me off."

"Gladly." Jace releases his hold on my hair and drops to his knees, looking up at me. He licks his lips, then scrapes his bottom lip between his teeth before unbuttoning my pants and freeing my straining dick.

"Fuck," he sighs quietly, and the awe in his voice pisses me off even more because that's not what this is. He shouldn't be on his knees looking like he's eager to worship me. This is us giving in to the tension that's always existed between us. The hatred and the satisfaction we get off on knowing we hold this power over the other. That's all this is.

But somehow, he still knows exactly how to get under my skin. I can't let him though. It's just physical. It has to be. Just like it's always been.

"I thought you had a better way to use your mouth?" I taunt.

That finally does it. He grins up at me before licking a long, wet stripe up my cock, then takes me into his mouth. His lips seal tightly around my dick before he sucks me down his throat, and every negative thought I've had about Jace over the last thirteen years disappears.

"Holy fuck," I choke out. Eighteen-year-old Jace could not deepthroat like this. He's confident, skilled, and it's nothing like it was before. His nose is pressed against my stomach as he tries to swallow around me before pulling back for air without ever breaking eye contact. He wraps his large hand around the base of my cock as he rotates his wrist and laps at my tip.

"Jesus fucking Christ," I groan, reaching out and digging my fingers into his hair and pulling tight. "You used to call me a cockslut. Look at you now, Jace. Desperate for a taste of my cum."

He hums around me, popping off then moving his mouth lower. He takes one of my balls into his mouth, then the other, while his fist continues working my shaft. I jolt when his tongue moves a little lower to my taint before he comes back up to suck my dick.

"Fucking hell," I moan.

"Mmm, you like that, K?" Jace grins when he pops off. "I felt the way your body reacted to my tongue going lower. You want my mouth on your hole?"

I choke on a breath at his suggestion. Jace seems determined to convince me he isn't the same Jace I used to know—the one who kept us hidden, the one who only ever wanted blowjobs under the guise of good luck.

This Jace is sure of himself, sure of what he likes, sure of his sexuality.

But I don't want to think about that right now. Thinking leads to feeling, and feeling hurts like hell when it comes to him.

"Shut up," I growl, grabbing his hair and shoving his mouth back on my cock.

He goes eagerly, and that almost makes it worse. His throat opens, and goddamn, is he talented. It's impossible to hold in my moans because Jace's mouth is too good, and he's making me lose control.

"Fuck, almost there," I warn.

He works me relentlessly, hand twisting as he's sucking and swirling his tongue, looking at me with glassy, determined eyes. My thighs start to shake. He keeps bobbing his head, twisting his wrist, and—

"I'm coming," I gasp, refusing to say his name as I fall apart. My chest heaves as I come down his throat. Jace swallows it all, pulling back with his lips wet, and our eyes lock again.

The reality of what just happened catches up to me quickly.

"Fuck you, Jace," I snap, needing to get away from him. I pull my pants back into place and storm out into the living room, leaving Jace there on his knees. He can finish himself off. Or not. It's not like he cared when I didn't come at the Halloween party all those years ago.

God, I hate him.

I hate that I hooked up with him.

I hate the way my body is still trembling from his mouth.

I hate myself for wanting it.

I hate that he's the one person in the world who seems to have this invisible hold on me.

I hate that when he was swallowing me down, I felt eighteen again—reckless, needy, and completely unable to resist him.

I hate that I've never been able to let what happened between us go.

And I hate, absolutely fucking *hate*, how it feels like this thing between us is far from over.

I quickly realize I can't hide out in the main space for long— it wouldn't be very "perfect couple" of me to spend the night on the couch. So I use the first excuse I can think of, filling a glass of water. At the last second I get a second glass for Jace, for the cameras, and mentally prepare myself to face him after storming out like I did.

I should be relieved to find our bed empty, so I ignore my disappointment when I hear the shower on in the en-suite.

And I really shouldn't be ready for another round as I picture what he's probably doing in there.

Fuck.

I seriously need today to be over.

I put his water on his nightstand and force myself to go to sleep, trying to remember why I hate him, even if all I can picture is how happy he looked with his lips wrapped around my cock.

I'm so fucked.

45

JACE

Producer: "Will you tell us what happened with Kieran yet?"

Jace: "No."

LM

You awake yet? B is still out like a baby
despite falling asleep first again last night.

J laugh at the text from L. Kieran was already in the bathroom getting ready when I woke up this morning, but god, I wish I'd woken up with him in my arms. I have a feeling we're going to pretend last night didn't happen even though I know he was only giving in to our insane chemistry and sexual tension, nothing more. So, I'm respecting his privacy and waiting for him in our bedroom while reminding myself that this relationship isn't real.

Still, I can't stop replaying last night in my head and wondering if there's any chance of a repeat. Even if it takes a little fighting to build that tension back up, I want it. He'll deny it meant anything, I'm sure, but I felt something between us.

And I want more.

I thought offering to help him, however I could, would give us the best chance at moving forward—and I still intend to do that—but maybe a little teasing and taunting when we're alone wouldn't be a bad idea either. Kieran has seemed so tense and stressed this entire time, I'd love to be the person he unloads some of his frustrations on. Hell, I'd give him as many orgasms as it takes to finally get him to relax.

God, I hope we hook up again.

JR

Not sure what's worse—finding out you're dating a straight man or finding out you're dating the person who's hated you for the last thirteen years.

OBVIOUSLY, there's no one I'd rather be with than Kieran, but I don't want L to think I'm a total stalker, so I leave out the teeny tiny detail that I might have never gotten over him and very much have followed his every move since high school. I still can't get over the fact that a straight guy signed up for this show, though.

LM

I'll take my relationship, thanks. It actually isn't so bad.

For my friend's sake, I hope that's true. But I've been the supposedly straight guy hooking up with another man before, and I know it's one thing to be with someone privately—even if there are cameras around—and another to actually claim your sexuality in front of the world. I'll definitely be keeping an eye on BB tonight when we meet the other contestants on the show. I just hope that L doesn't get hurt in the process.

JR

We've made it through our first few days, we got this.

LM

Yeah, we do. Excited to finally meet you later! Gonna be so weird but cool, haha. Can't believe I still don't know what you look like.

JR

Big dude, brown hair, and beard.

LM

HA. You just described me too.

I'm looking forward to meeting L, and I guess the other contestants to an extent, but mostly, I'm curious how Kieran will act around me in public. Will he want us to lean into the couple act or pull away? Yesterday he was pissed I touched him, but that ended with his back against the wall and my mouth on his cock, so who knows. He's mentioned feeling like past partners were only into PDA for the perks of being with a celebrity, but I don't give a fuck about that, and I hope he knows that.

I really wish we were in one of those cheesy fake-dating movies where the couple has to kiss in public to sell their fake relationship. At least then I'd get to kiss him for real. Maybe I still will though. Maybe if we make it all the way to the altar like we plan to, I'll get to kiss the man of my dreams then.

Kieran eventually comes out of the bathroom, but the fake smile on his face, even in our room away from the cameras, makes it obvious that he doesn't want to talk about what happened last night.

We quickly move into the main area of the apartment, going

through the motions. I cook like the day before, Kieran puts on his makeup in the kitchen, and we occasionally chat, but none of it is deep or meaningful conversation like it was yesterday when he actually let me in for a while.

If someone didn't know him, they'd think everything was fine. But it's clear to me that he's lost in thought, locked behind the walls I thought I'd started to break down.

The whole time, I can't stop wondering if he's regretting last night. If giving in to the tension between us ruined whatever we had before it even had the chance to become something real. He didn't seem to hate it in the moment—hell, he seemed to really enjoy himself—but now I can't tell if he's frustrated at me, at himself, or both.

I know I can't ask about it on camera, and the wait until we're finally alone again tonight is killing me. We waste the afternoon watching TV, sitting right next to each other but not cuddling like yesterday. The distance between us feels bigger than it should, and I hate it.

THE PRODUCERS DROPPED off name tags to our apartment with our initials and names in bold, black ink before we headed up to the rooftop bar the show created.

We're the first couple to arrive, so we claim a love seat while we wait, continuing our small talk. Yesterday we talked about things that actually mattered, and I don't know how we get back there. Anytime I try to dig deeper, he gives me his polished camera smile and a brush-off answer. I'll keep trying though. Or maybe I just need to stop being so nice when we're alone and call him out again. He seemed to like that last night.

Earlier, when I asked him how he wanted me to approach

touching him for this event, he said "Fine, just don't overdo it," so I've been keeping my hands to myself. For now.

Finally, another couple walks in, and we focus our attention on them.

"Hi, I'm Rachel, or RR," the girl says, smiling. "And this is my partner, Keith. Or KA."

"Nice to meet you, I'm JR or Jace, and this is my partner, Kieran. KD," I say.

Kieran offers her his best on-camera smile, then another couple walks in and we all turn toward them.

Other than LM, I've honestly forgotten everyone else's initials by now. Well, I know BB for Liam's sake, but I'm all in with Kieran, and I haven't thought about anyone else since pretty much day one of this experiment.

Then a third couple walks in, both attractive men who look around our age, and I'm guessing the one in a flannel might be my friend given his hair color and beard when the slightly larger blond man announces himself. "Hey, I'm Blake, also known as BB," he says, flashing a huge smile before slinging an arm around the other's shoulders. "And this is my partner, Liam, or LM as you might know him."

Huh, maybe this straight guy won't be so bad after all. "That's my friend I've been texting. Want to come with me to introduce ourselves?" I ask Kieran. He nods, so we stand and approach Liam. "Hey, man! It's so good to finally meet you." I laugh awkwardly, pointing to my name tag. "I'm Jace."

It's so strange that we've been talking and know so much about each other without ever meeting. I guess that was the whole point of the show, but the moment I saw Kieran waiting for me in our apartment, it was like something clicked, *like, of course it was him,* so the blind aspect of the show seems so distant to me now.

"Liam." He smiles back. I introduce Kieran and start to tell Liam a bit about who Kieran is, but Liam is obviously distracted.

I glance behind me and see an attractive woman, I think her name was Rachel, talking to Blake. They're standing close together, her hand on his arm as she leans in. Liam looks like he's seen a ghost as he mutters, "I'm sorry, one second." Then he's walking away toward them.

Honestly, I get it. I was worried about the "straight" man, too.

"What's going on there?" Kieran asks me in a low tone as we both turn to watch the drama unfold. Liam hasn't quite made it all the way to them when the woman's partner joins their conversation, and I think Blake might be in the clear. But then she quickly dismisses that guy and turns her attention back to Blake.

Liam is probably close enough to overhear them, though they don't seem to have noticed him. He takes a small step back, like he's shocked by something, before turning and quickly storming past us, muttering "I'm not about to be dumped in front of the cameras" before completely leaving the bar.

"Shit, did he really just leave?" Kieran whispers to me.

"I think so. Fuck, I wonder what he overheard."

Blake glances back at us, and I do my very best to glare at him. I'm not sure exactly what was said, but I think it's pretty easy to connect the dots here. The "straight guy" who matched with a man, now found out one of the other people he was talking to earlier in the process is the hot woman he was hoping to meet here. And now, at the first opportunity, he's running to her.

So much for him announcing his partner when he came in. What a jerk.

He looks around the bar before he seems to excuse himself from her and make his way over to us. "Hey, did you see where Liam went?" he asks after looking at my nametag. He seems concerned, but I'm not convinced.

I cross my arms and stand up straighter, trying my very best to look intimidating when I answer. "He said something about not wanting to be dumped in front of the cameras." My anger is obvious in my tone, and I know it might not be my place, but Liam is my friend, and he doesn't deserve to be treated like he's a second choice. "What the fuck were you and Rachel talking about?" I ask. "Are you really planning to dump him for the first girl to throw herself at you? I know you thought you were straight, but that's low."

Blake looks at me like I'm speaking another language.

"What the fuck are you talking about? I don't want her. I want him. Where is he?"

Maybe I'm projecting, picturing my teenage self and feeling guilty about the way I treated Kieran in the past, but I'm just not buying this guy's innocent act. "Probably packing up his things before you humiliate him further," I spit out.

He turns and runs for the door. Maybe he really does care about Liam. I hope I'm wrong about him, but that whole exchange was far more dramatic than I was anticipating for tonight.

"Damn, I know you said reality shows can be really scripted, but I don't think this one is going to need to be," I say with a laugh, turning to Kieran. It takes me a moment to process the look he's giving me, but I think it's... appreciation? And maybe it's wishful thinking but there might even be some heat in his gaze.

4 6

KIERAN

Producer: "Jace told Liam that you used to hate him, is that true?"

Kieran: "It must be if he told Liam."

Ugh. Why was that so hot? The way Jace stood up for Liam was an immediate turn on, and he wasn't even standing up for me. It was another moment where Jace was nothing like the teenager I remember, and it's so fucking confusing.

I want him.

Physically at least.

Our chemistry is off the charts, and the blowjob last night only proved I wasn't misremembering how amazing that part of our relationship was all those years ago.

And now that we went there again, I don't want to stop. I've been distracted all day, replaying last night over and over again in my mind, trying to convince myself that it was a one-time slip. That it won't happen again.

But watching him defend his friend from the straight golden boy? I can't help but feel like he was chastising his former self. That, more than anything he's said or done, felt like proof that he might actually regret what happened between us... even if I'm not ready to forgive him just yet for the very real pain he caused me physically, mentally, and emotionally.

And today, while I was lost in my thoughts, I found a whole new reason to be angry.

Because why did I have to know Jace back when he was a Grade A asshole?

Last week, when it was just JR who I was talking to, I was falling hard and fast. I really believed I'd finally found what I'd been searching for all these years—a partner who actually saw me. Someone loving and supportive, someone who made me laugh and feel comfortable in ways no one else ever had. Our growing relationship felt easy, natural, and I really believed we had a future together.

It's hard though because he does seem like a different person now. Sometimes he's so genuine it almost makes me forget the pain that's lingered in my heart for over a decade. It's embarrassing to admit how often Jace has crossed my mind over the years. People say there's something unforgettable about your first love. Not that I'd call it love exactly. But the feelings and the impact he had on me were bigger than I could ever explain. And so was the pain when things ended.

Which only makes it harder not to wonder—if last week had been the first time we'd ever met, if I didn't have years of scars with his name carved into them—could we have actually been happy together?

Do we still have a chance?

I'm angry that our *now* is so tainted by our past.

But I really enjoyed last night with him, despite my freakout, and I think I want to do it again because I *am* still very into him.

Jace seems to be a little self-conscious about the way he looks, and I've tried to make it clear that he has no fucking reason to be. I'm more attracted to Jace than probably any of my previous partners. But I'm not just going to gush about that when I'm supposed to hate him. No, I *do* hate him... I think.

It doesn't seem to matter that I know better, that history has a way of repeating itself; I can't stop wanting him. I can't erase our past, but I also can't ignore the pull I feel toward him.

With the plan we made, we're going to be spending a lot more time together. And despite the fact that he had my dick in his mouth less than twenty-four hours ago, I'm already desperate for another round. I don't know how I'll be able to hold back from giving in to him the few more days we're here, let alone the duration of the show.

Maybe giving in wouldn't be the worst thing? Jace knows it wouldn't mean anything. I think we were on the same page about that last night, and he's been back to his overly helpful, pretend-perfect-couple routine today without any problems. Maybe I can take what he's offering and, at least physically, enjoy the time we have to spend together.

"Do you think we could leave too?" I ask. After his display, I'm really fucking horny. I don't want to wait until this ends to touch him.

"Like... *leave, leave?*" he whispers, obviously excited by the idea.

Fuck. Is this a horrible idea?

No, I've already resigned myself that this is going to happen. I might as well give in now and enjoy the extra orgasms I know Jace is offering. I bite my lip and give him a quick once over before nodding slowly. "The way you stood up for your friend was really hot," I admit.

"We're definitely leaving," he says, grabbing my hand and

pulling me to the exit, clearly not giving a shit about what the producers expect from us right now.

The second the elevator dings at the end of the hallway, I hear Mitch yell for us. "Kieran! Jace! Where are you going? You can't leave!"

"Oh, shit." I laugh as Jace pays him no attention, hitting the elevator button while also laughing. As soon as we're inside, he's jamming the Close Door button as if that'll actually make it shut any faster. It's such a childish thing, but in a way, it reminds me even more of our past, hiding away from the world to be together.

Not like we were together. God, why can't my brain stop romanticizing everything? We hid our hookups because Jace was in denial about his sexuality and had a shitty dad. It wasn't some epic romance.

Sure, we might be on our way to go hookup for the second night in a row, but that's just sex. We aren't actually together.

"I can't believe we just ran away from the party," I say.

"Me neither, but honestly, I don't think I even like Mitch. He's not very nice."

"I thought that was just me." I grin back.

"Not just you. Come on." Jace smirks, tugging me out of the elevator by our intertwined fingers toward our apartment. When we get inside our bedroom, Jace locks the door and turns to me.

"So, we're here," he says suggestively. "Are you going to use me again?"

I look at his mouth, and part of me wants to kiss him. But the louder part of me is screaming *no* because once we cross that line, I know I'll be in too deep. It's one thing to give in to the chemistry we've always had, but it's something else entirely to break the rule I made for a reason.

The way he's staring at me, the obvious heat and desire in his eyes, only makes it worse. His gaze drops to my lips and lingers before coming back up to meet mine, like he knows exactly what I'm thinking but refuses to be the one to move first.

God, if I kiss him right now, it's over. I know myself. It won't just be a kiss—it'll be everything. And even though he's already chipping away at my walls, I still haven't forgiven him. I can't give him that part of me again. Not until I'm sure he won't break it.

It has to be just sex. Release. Nothing more. I'm sure I'll be able to think more clearly when all my blood isn't being redirected south. All I can focus on is how sexy Jace is, how his glasses and beard make him somehow look so distinguished and rugged at the same time. How I can see a tease of his chest hair where his shirt collar dips, and how soft his brown curls felt between my fingers last night as I guided his mouth onto my cock. How easy it would be for his thick arms to toss me around so he could have his way with me.

Fuck, I can't put this off any longer.

I pop open the button on his pants and shove them down, along with his boxer briefs, until he's standing in front of me with his cock out and pants around his ankles. He's just as stunning as I remember, and I want to hate him more for it.

But I don't. I can't.

I'm not sure I even hate him at all.

But I *can* use him the way he's suggesting.

"Fine, Jace. You want me to use you? Then let's see if you ever learned how to use that thing," I taunt. "Fuck me."

4 7

JACE

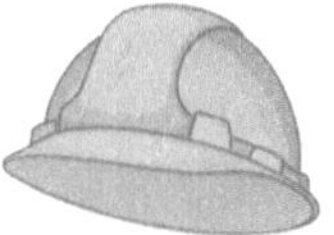

Production: "Do you feel like Kieran brings out a different side of you?"

Jace: "Yeah. He's always had a way of bringing out the real me. Guess some things don't change."

"Fine, Jace. You want me to use you? Then let's see if you ever learned how to use that thing," Kieran taunts. "Fuck me."

I don't think I've dealt with this many conflicting emotions since the last time Kieran was in my life.

I crave him in a way that's so intense, I can barely form a complete thought beyond *mine*. I'd remembered our connection seeming so much stronger than any other relationship I've attempted over the years, but I thought I'd built it up in my head because he was the one that got away and all that. But this, this is real. Kieran just pulled my dick out and told me to fuck him. And the lust coursing through me is all consuming.

Actually, he mocked me first, and as much as I've always thought our back and forth was hot, I don't think he realized how valid his taunt may be.

I haven't topped anyone in years.

My last relationship was with a woman. I had sex with her, but the only anal sex she enjoyed was the kind where she was wearing a strap-on and fucking me, which I was more than happy about. When I first moved to the city and spent every weekend in gay bars and clubs, I participated in all sorts of hookups, but my first official boyfriend preferred to top, and I enjoyed bottoming enough that it became my preference going forward.

It's been a long time since I prepped anyone. But I've been on the other end enough times to know what I'm doing; I'm not worried about hurting him.

I've enjoyed it in the past. I guess, technically, I'd consider myself to be vers. It's not that I don't want to fuck him—because I really do—I'm just worried that he's expecting me to be some burly dominant top because I'm bigger than him. What if, in his eyes, I literally "won't know how to use it" like he teased?

"There are condoms and lube in the front pocket of my suitcase," he informs me, misreading my hesitation.

"Where do you want to do this?" I ask, stepping back to retrieve the supplies. This might not be exactly how I fantasized about having sex with Kieran would be, I wish he wasn't still claiming to hate me so we could talk about our preferences, but I don't think he's ready for that. And I could never say no to him. If he wants me to fuck him tonight—with rules about not kissing and reminders that he hasn't forgiven me—then I need to do a good enough job that he'll want me again and again until maybe, finally, he'll let me kiss him. Just like I wanted to all those years ago.

"Not the bed, that's not what this is," he says dismissively, taking the bottle of lube from my hand as he heads to the vanity.

"This should be a fine height." Then he's shoving his pants and underwear down in one quick motion. I barely have time to process it before he's bent over the dresser, slicking his fingers and starting to work himself open.

"What the fuck are you doing?" I scold, swatting his hand away.

"Prepping myself," he says plainly over his shoulder. "This isn't some dramatic virginal first time. I'm horny, I want your dick in my ass, and it'll be faster if I do it myself."

"Fuck that," I say, grabbing his wrist when he reaches for the lube again. Then I grab his other wrist for good measure until I have them both in one fist, holding them against the small of his back. His perky round ass is taunting me, glistening with the lube he managed to put on his hole before I stopped him.

I lean in so my mouth is right next to his ear. "If you want me to fuck you, Sparkles, then you're going to let me open you up myself."

"Don't call me that," he spits out, turning to glare at me.

"Why not?" I demand as I add more lube onto my free hand and start to work a finger inside him. It's *my* fucking name for him. I should get to call him that more than anyone else. "I thought you liked my nickname?" I accuse. "Made it your whole brand. Everyone else can use it but me? Is that it?"

"It's different coming from you and you know it."

I work a second finger in easily, and despite our supposed anger, he's doing a great job of staying relaxed physically so that I can stretch his hole. He's so tight, so soft and warm, the thought of replacing my fingers with my cock has me ready to burst.

"I still get under your skin after all these years? Huh, K?" I drag my leaking erection against his bare ass as I slowly work him open. I want to take my time with him because I don't know how many chances I'll get to see him pent up and desperate for my cock like this.

"I haven't thought about you in years," he hisses. "You're the *fan*, remember? Do you really watch my videos? Do you stroke yourself to me filming for *millions* of people?"

"Shut up," I grit, pushing a third finger inside, stretching him wider. "Or maybe I should slow down, leave you begging. You might have millions of people who adore you, but *I'm* the only one you're trembling for right now. As much as you might claim to hate me, you still want me to fuck you."

He lets out a broken sound, half laugh, half groan. "Beg? That's rich. Do you remember who was the one choking on the other's dick last night?"

Fuck, he knows I haven't stopped thinking about him, and I don't even care. But if he needs us to keep taunting each other to justify what we're doing, to excuse it, I'll let him think that's all this is. For now.

"Yeah, well, tonight you're the one spread open for me," I snarl, teeth scraping down the back of his neck. God, I wish I could kiss him. "Are you going to take every inch of me, K? No amount of running your mouth can change how much you'll love that."

"You think I can't? Try me," he fires back, but his body clenches around my fingers like it's already bracing. And I know he wants this just as badly as I do. "Fuck me, hot shot."

I yank my fingers free and finally drop his wrists as I reach for the condom, quickly putting it on before slicking myself up and lining my tip up to his waiting hole. I grip the base of my shaft as I push the head of my cock inside him, and I swear I almost black out from how insanely good it feels and I'm hardly inside of him.

I glance at the mirror and nearly freeze. It's everything I used to dream about, everything I ever imagined we could be, everything I thought I'd lost the right to want. And yet, it's even better than I ever let myself hope, because it's real. I'm inside Kieran, the man I've idolized for as long as I can remember, the one no one has been able to compare to. I never, in a million years, thought that I'd get to have sex with him again. That I would actually get to experience what it's like to have him this way.

For a second, it almost feels like he's really letting me back in, but then it hits me that I'm romanticizing what this really is. He isn't forgiving me. He's still angry, and I'm still trying to earn something that was never mine to begin with.

The thought burns through me, and I channel every bit of it into the way I move—into giving him exactly what he wants—as I snap my hips forward.

"Yeah, keep pretending," I growl when I'm fully inside of him. The grunt he makes shoots fire straight down my spine.

"Fuck," he rasps, knuckles gripping the dresser. "That's all you've got? Thought you said every inch."

He wants to really feel me? *Fine.* I'll fuck him harder. I slam forward, burying myself to the hilt in one brutal thrust that knocks the breath from both of us. My hand clamps down on his hip, and I shift the other lower, lifting his leg so it's bent, nearly propped on the dresser as I hold him steady in this new position that allows me even deeper. I drag out slowly, setting a torturous pace with long punishing strokes, each one forcing him to feel exactly how deep I'm inside of him.

"Still talking shit? Going to pretend you're not loving this when those pretty sounds keep coming out of your mouth?" I pant against his ear as he lets out another low noise of pleasure. "Because all I hear is you moaning for my cock like you've been waiting for it for the last thirteen years."

He twists his head, smirking even through the sweat slicking his temple, and drawing my attention to his eyebrow piercing. Why is that so hot? "Keep telling yourself that. You're just here to make me come, hot shot. Same as back then."

His claim hits like a slap to the face, but the way his body clenches around me betrays his words, dragging a groan out of my chest I can't hold back. I thrust harder, chasing that same reaction from him again.

"Yeah?" I rasp, snapping my hips. "The way your ass keeps squeezing me like it's begging to milk my cock for every last drop of my cum feels like you might be enjoying this, K. You might not want to use your words to beg me, but your body seems pretty desperate, and I don't think that's an act."

"Fuck. You," he spits out between pants as I continue to pound into him.

"You already are," I snarl, grinding in deep until he shudders under me. "And you love it. I can feel you shaking." I reach up, thread my hand through his hair, and force his gaze forward toward the mirror. "Look at us. Look at who's inside of you right now, driving you wild with my cock." He locks on our reflection, and the heat in his gaze sends another bolt of lust down my spine. I can't wait any longer. Releasing my hold on his head to reach my arm around him, I finally wrap my hand around his straining erection.

He shudders again as I swipe my thumb over his tip, spreading the precum that's leaking from it. I give him a few rough strokes before removing my hand, and smirk at the sound of protest that escapes him. "Spit," I command in explanation as I hold my hand in front of his mouth. He glares at me through the mirror for a moment, probably struggling between following *my* directions and wanting my hand back on him.

With a roll of his eyes, he concedes, spitting into my palm. "Good boy," I mutter into his ear, and he drives his elbow back into me, but it only makes me chuckle into his neck before I whisper right into his ear again. "I felt the way your ass clenched around me at the praise. You don't need to hide from me, Kieran. I see you."

He shakes his head, but the only thing that comes out are pleading sounds that instantly become my new favorite. His spine bows under me as he takes every brutal thrust. His perfect ass is swallowing my dick like they were made to fit together, the pleasure so much more than I can ever remember from topping.

And even if this is the only time I get to have him like this, I know I'll never move on. This will be burned into my memory forever as the moment I got everything I'd ever wanted, even with the glares and hatred. It'll be the best sex of my life, and I hate knowing that it'll probably never happen again.

"Not so mouthy now, huh?" I taunt, trying to distract myself from how much this actually means to me.

He laughs, a ragged, breathless sound, but still tries to throw it back in my face. "This all you've got? Thought you'd break me by now."

I bare my teeth, driving into him harder, faster, the sound of our skin slapping together loud and filthy. "You want to be broken, K? I'll make sure you feel me every time you sit down tomorrow."

That drags another sound from him—half groan, half moan —that betrays how much he wants it.

"Just as eager as I remember, and it's all for *me*. You're mine like this," I snarl, still holding eye contact in the mirror. "Always have been. You can run your mouth and lie to me all night, but your actions reveal your truth. You want this. Want me."

"I just want to come. You can go to hell for all I care," he snarls, but it breaks on another moan when I slam in deep and hold there, grinding until he's shaking.

"Already there," I growl against his ear, pounding into him like I might just be able to fuck the fight right out of him. "And you're coming with me."

"Fuck—I'm gonna—" he chokes out, but I cut him off by pounding even harder, chasing down his release.

"Come for *me*. Come on *my* cock. Make a mess of yourself."

Seconds later, his hole grips me like a vice, and his dick jerks in my grip as he comes all over the dresser in front of him. The way he squeezes me drags my own orgasm out of me, the pleasure almost painful with how intense it is as I spill into the condom with a groan, grinding through it until every last pulse is wrung out of us both.

When I finally let go, he slumps against the wood, breath ragged, dark hair plastered to his forehead. I pull back slowly, lowering his leg back to the ground, leaving him trembling with his arms shaking where he still clings to the edge.

Kieran doesn't look at me when he pulls himself off the dresser. His thighs are unsteady as he stumbles toward the bathroom, slamming the door behind him.

I stand there, chest heaving, thinking about how badly I wish I could kiss him, but knowing that isn't what this is.

Instead of letting myself get caught up in that fantasy, I close my eyes, replaying the heat of him clenching around me, the way his body gave me everything even while his mouth spit fire. Being buried inside of him like that was enough, even without the intimacy of kissing. It has to be because it was more than I ever dreamed of having again.

The best thing I've had in years. Since *him*.

He's always been it for me.

I came on this show hoping to meet someone who might come close to the version of Kieran I'd built up in my mind. Someone to distract me from my constant thoughts of him. Instead, I ended up with the man himself.

Originally, I thought this might be my opportunity to finally apologize for what happened back then, to make up for my mistakes.

But what if it could be more?

I stand here in the room—*our* room—knowing we'll both pretend tomorrow that this was nothing but rage and old habits.

But we started like this back then too, and there was a time that I believed he might actually like me the way I realized I liked him.

In the short time we've been back together again, we've already given in to the pull between us twice.

Maybe, just maybe, this time we could do more than apologize. Maybe it could be a real second chance for us to get our happy ending.

No matter how small that chance may be, I know I have to try.

KIERAN

Producer: "How do you know when you're actually in love?"

Kieran: "If it ever happens, I'll let you know."

*W*hat is it about Jace I can't resist? I didn't understand it then, and I sure as hell don't understand it now.

We're older, we should be past taunting and degrading each other. But when I'm horny around him, it's like I'm eighteen again. I still want him, no matter how much I shouldn't. I hate how much I was silently begging for him to take it even further. To call me *his* cockslut like he did back then, like I called him last night.

I certainly wasn't expecting him to throw in the praise. Or how much I liked that too.

My thighs are still shaking, body still raw from having him inside me. I hate how well he still seems to know me. Hate that my body betrays me every time he's near. Hate that no matter how much I tell myself this is just a release, I know I'm lying to myself. I still want him. Still ache for him. Still want him to fuck me again.

But I refuse to tell him that.

I'll keep telling myself I hate him, because it's the only thing that even halfway protects me. It was so easy to hate him all those years we were apart. Easy to focus on only the bad things that happened back then, and to build him up as a villain without giving him a chance to redeem himself.

Now, after only a couple of days together, it doesn't seem to matter how many years I swore I'd never let him—or anyone like him—touch me again. I never thought it would even be possible that we'd end up here, but I let him have his way with me. I asked him to.

No one's ever fucked me like that. No one's ever known what I needed without me having to ask. My desires have always been silent, because I've never trusted anyone to keep it between us. I didn't want it blasted on gossip sites that I like to be degraded and taunted while I'm being fucked relentlessly.

Of course, Jace had to go and fuck me damn near perfectly. He's always known exactly what I needed, and when he drove into me tonight, it was so easy to surrender to him. My body seemed to remember him, trusted him even.

And even though I might want to, I can't let myself march back out there and demand he fuck me again.

This is Jace, the man responsible for so much of my past hurt. *He's also JR*, an unhelpful voice reminds me. But I can't allow myself to think of him that way, to blur those lines. I'd be giving too much of myself away, exposing myself to even more potential heartbreak.

Instead, I clean myself up, brush my teeth, wash my face, and decide it's time to leave the bathroom.

Unlocking the door, I twist the knob and make my way back

into the bedroom. Jace is sitting on the bed, watching me as I climb in. I assume he'll get up and go into the bathroom, but he just stares at me.

"Aren't you going to clean yourself up?" I prompt after a moment when he doesn't move.

"I already did," he says easily. "I went into the other bathroom in the living area."

"You did what?" Does he not understand there are cameras all over the place out there?

"Don't worry, I got fully dressed to go out there, cleaned up, then came right back in here to change."

"Fine," I mutter, grateful he was careful and didn't walk out there butt ass naked with a used condom on his softening dick.

I pull the covers up to my chest and roll onto my side with my back to him. The sheets are cool against my skin, but it does nothing to slow the heat still burning in me.

He still doesn't move, but I can feel the weight of his gaze on me.

"You gonna sleep or just stare at me all night?" I mutter.

"Depends, what do you want me to do?"

God, he's infuriating. Why is he the only one who's ever given me attention like this in private?

"Go to sleep, Jace."

He shifts behind me, and I feel his body close to mine. My pulse jumps because I don't know if I want space or for him to pull me in close and wrap his big body around mine.

Instead, he seems to settle on a third option. He doesn't touch me, but it's close enough that if I just scoot back a little bit, I'll be pressed into him. He's leaving the choice up to me, and I am, once again, at war with myself.

As much as I love words of affirmation, I have to admit, physical touch might be climbing my love-language chart. At least when it's Jace who's touching me. I keep thinking about the way it felt to be surrounded by him. It didn't mean anything when it was for the camera. But when it's just the two of us, where no one else can see… I think I like it more than I want to admit.

But I don't scoot into him.

I already handed too much of myself to him tonight.

JACE

Producer: "Do you believe in fate?"

Jace: "I don't know if I'd call it fate, but I believe some people are meant to be in each other's lives."

The next morning, we wake up on opposite sides of the bed. As much as I wanted to wrap my arms around Kieran last night, to pull his body up against mine, especially after how rough our hookup was, to make sure he was okay and knows how perfect he is… I'm attempting to respect his boundaries. He was upset the other day after all the touching in our apartment for the cameras, and I'm still not sure where the line is. So, I'm being good.

For now.

Selfishly, I want more with him; I'm determined to follow through with my plan of somehow convincing him to turn this fake relationship into a real one. Am I confident that's going to happen? Absolutely not. But I've already spent the last thirteen years wishing I had done things differently back then, and I'd rather not spend the rest of my life regretting not taking advantage of the opportunity I've found myself in now.

If we had met outside of the show, and he'd immediately hated me the way he so clearly did during the reveal, I know I would've had no chance of earning his forgiveness. But, by some amazing twist of fate, we started falling for each other without even knowing who the other was during those blind dates. I just have to keep reminding myself of that because, if nothing else, the show proved we are a good match. We chose each other. He agreed to move in with me, hoping we would get married. I wasn't pretending to be anyone I'm not while we were talking during the blind portion of the show. So, I'm clinging to the hope that Kieran can remember that he chose me too. That I'm JR and not the Jace he remembers.

The blanket shifts as he moves in the bed beside me. "Do you want to talk about last night?" I immediately ask as I turn to face him.

"Nothing to talk about," he says quickly. "We should probably get a move on, go into the main space with cameras so that we don't get in trouble again after we ditched the party last night." He jumps out of bed and heads straight into the bathroom.

That's fine. I'm not going to let his frustration with our situation get to me. I'm going to focus on how excited I am to be here with him, to have this time together so that even if my plan doesn't work, I can look back and know I gave it everything I have.

When we make it into the living space full of cameras, I start making breakfast for us again. "So, what would you like to do today?" I ask.

He shrugs, pulling out the makeup the producers dropped off for him and the small camera-and-tripod setup. "While we were still in the blind dating portion of the show, I shot a special *Love*

Without Labels Get Ready With Me: Isolation Edition. I'll probably do another Get Ready With Me today," he says casually as he seems to be cataloging the new products they gave him.

"Holy shit." I beam, unable to mask my excitement. "Am I going to get to see you record a video?"

He squints at me before slowly asking, "Do you want to?"

He's obviously skeptical of my answer.

"Hell yeah," I rush to agree. "I love the behind-the-scenes videos. This'll be like that, only better."

"Wait, you actually watch my content?" He sounds completely shocked.

"Yeah, I told you I'm a fan."

"I thought you meant… like, you'd seen a video once or maybe one of your exes was into it or something and made you watch a few."

My stomach drops instantly. "Are you against being with a fan? Should I pretend like I haven't seen them all?" I check, suddenly afraid that something else will come between us.

"I'm not against dating someone who likes my videos," he answers with a short laugh. "I would hope that whoever I'm with would be supportive, and maybe even enjoy what I do, but I definitely wasn't expecting that from you."

I internally cringe at how that sounds, especially coming from him of all people. "I feel like we should clarify for the cameras that you're not expecting it from me, because when we first met, I was very much in the closet and afraid of anything that might open the door," I explain, looking around the apartment because I still have no idea where the cameras actually are.

"Back then, I wasn't supportive of you, not with how you basically showed up with your middle fingers in the air—metaphorically, of course—to every rule that had been shoved down my throat, and it's something I've regretted ever since. I basically hated you for it, because I wished I had the guts to stand up to people the way you did," I admit, looking right at him. "I really admire how much strength and courage you've continued to show over the years by embracing who you are. You've shown so many other people that it's possible to find happiness as exactly the version of themselves they are or that they'd like to be. I just don't want anyone to think that you're going against what you've always stood for. And for the record, you helped me find my strength too, K."

I look back around the apartment before continuing. "He's not judging me based on my appearance. He would never look at anyone and say they couldn't wear makeup. His surprise comes from our personal history, not any preconceived notion of the way I might come across to the people watching the show."

Kieran is staring at me, wide-eyed, with his jaw hanging open by the time I hurry to finish my long-winded explanation for the cameras. After a moment, he swallows, straightening up in his chair as he visually pulls himself together. "Thank you for clarifying that. I wasn't even thinking about how my comment might come across to the people who don't know us."

"I really have changed since back then. It's me you were talking to as JR," I remind him. "If you'd rather call me JR or JJ or something else, I'll answer."

"JJ?" he questions. "Do you go by that a lot?"

"Sometimes." I shrug, not wanting to get into my online presence under that name. "My middle name also starts with a J."

"I can still call you Jace," he says dismissively. "I've always kind of liked your name."

"Come on, you have a way cooler name than me."

We smile at each other for a moment, and it feels like I've won something, like we might be back to building something more between us this morning. As much as I would love to spend the day lost in his gaze, I have to finish making breakfast, and he goes back to separating all the makeup products he has until we move to the table to eat.

"So, what kind of video are you planning for today?" I ask.

"I'm not sure yet. Sometimes I just wait until I'm opening new pallets to see what inspiration strikes."

"Well, I can't wait to see."

"Would you…" he starts, then cuts himself off with a laugh. "Never mind."

"Would I what?" I push, leaning toward him.

He sighs. "Well, if you really are a fan, then I was going to see if you might want to be in the video. But I don't want to pressure you. It's one thing to support me and enjoy my content. I shouldn't assume that you'd want me to actually do your makeup."

"You can do my makeup!" I blurt before he can talk himself out of the idea completely.

He blinks a few times, staring at me out of the corner of his eye before he responds. "You really don't have to. I'm sorry, I shouldn't have asked you on camera."

"Don't apologize. I want you to," I insist, grinning now. "You can't dangle something like that then take it back."

He looks at me skeptically, brows furrowed as he tries to find anything other than excitement in my expression. "Seriously? You actually want me to?"

"Hell yeah."

Finally, he shrugs. "Alright… if you're sure."

The smile on my face is huge. "Very sure."

He sits up a bit straighter. I think he's slipping into his professional mode. "I'll do a quick look off camera for myself after breakfast. Then we can get set up to film something. But if you change your mind before we start, no big deal."

"I won't change my mind," I promise. This is perfect. Not just because the fan in me is screaming, but because it's the best chance I'll ever get to prove I'm not the guy Kieran remembers. High school Jace wouldn't have touched eyeliner in private, let alone allow someone to put it on him in front of a national audience.

God, I hope my dad sees the pictures. I doubt he will, but if they end up plastered all over social media or promo graphics, maybe he won't be able to avoid them.

Daddy issues? Apparently still front and center.

I'm not excited about the makeup right now because I think I'll get the same thing out of it that Kieran does. I don't think I'll feel better about my appearance or feel more confident or creative, or any of the positive impacts he talks about in his videos with finding his inner strength and projecting his truest self to the world.

But I do think it will be a fun opportunity for us and our fake relationship that I'm determined to solidify into a real one. I'm thrilled to have the chance to show him firsthand who I actually am now. That's what his whole channel is about, isn't it? Presenting your true self to the world.

Maybe, once he finishes my look, he'll see me a little more clearly too.

"HEY EVERYONE, welcome back to another special episode of *Sparkles' Tutorials Love Without Labels:* Not-So-Isolated Edition! Today I have a very special guest with me, my… partner? Jace." He motions to me next to him, and I wave at the camera.

We're sitting at the kitchen island because apparently it has the best lighting in our small apartment. Kieran even set up a ring light he packed, positioning it behind the camera. I've seen him use one in his behind-the-scenes videos, but I didn't expect he'd bring one here, to a show where we're already filmed all day. But it feels more like I'm in one of his real videos, so I'm glad he did.

"Okay, Jace, I guess we haven't really talked about labels so I'm not sure what to call you. Are you my boyfriend? Are we sticking with partner? Are we waiting to see where things go?" he asks in his confident camera voice. *This is all fake for him,* I remind myself.

"I really hope you're my boyfriend. And I'm hoping to upgrade that title soon," I say with a cheeky grin at the camera. He probably thinks I'm talking about getting engaged for the show, and I am, but I'm also hoping to solidify the title so he no longer adds the word "fake" when he thinks it. Kieran smiles at me and then gives a knowing look to the camera. Hopefully he thought my response to his question was alright.

"Well, you heard it here first! This is my boyfriend, Jace, who I knew growing up and was unexpectedly reunited with on the show," he says casually. "But, we're not going to get into the details of that here. Right now, I'm going to do my boyfriend's makeup for the first time."

This isn't real.

This isn't real.

This isn't real.

Yet.

But my god, hearing those words—my boyfriend—with cameras rolling, knowing it's permanently out there with everyone else in the world about to hear him call me that too? I'll never recover. I'll replay it a thousand times in my head. My pulse is pounding because there will forever be evidence of this moment, and even if it's fake, I get to be what I've always wanted in this moment: his.

"I'm so excited," I can't help but comment, earning an amused grin from Kieran.

"Alright, Jace, what are you hoping for with your look today?

Are you wanting full glam drag queen with your eyebrows glued down, or are we embracing your facial hair and going with a more masculine look? Maybe somewhere in between?"

I think about it for a moment, weighing my options. "I definitely want you to do something that makes it obvious I'm wearing makeup," I answer. I already put my contacts in before we started so my glasses wouldn't distract from whatever he ends up doing. "But other than that, whatever you think would look best. Or just whatever you'll have fun doing."

Kieran gives me a small smile and nods before turning back to the makeup he's laid out on the counter. "Cool, that gives me a lot to work with. I'm going to have fun with it, which is kind of the whole point, for me at least." He takes a moment to assess my face, slowly focusing on each feature. I'd like to squirm in my seat and hide the evidence of what his full attention does to me. Thankfully my lap is out of the camera's shot—at least the one he's intentionally filming on—so moving around would only draw attention to the erection I'm sure is obvious in my grey sweatpants.

If Kieran does notice... *good*. I smirk to myself as I think about the possibility of making him squirm on camera knowing I'm hard just from being close to him.

"I think I'm going to do something in the middle," he finally says, completely unaware of the dirty turn my thoughts have taken. "I love your beard and strong features so I'm not going to hide any of those, but I would like to do something that's a little... traditionally more glam than my signature styles."

"That sounds great," I agree. "Do you need me to do anything?"

"No, just sit there and look pretty," he teases. I chuckle, wishing that he really meant that. *Maybe he does.* I shake out my shoulders, trying to relax, as he grabs the first product to put on my face. "Jace, is it safe to say that you don't have an elaborate skin-care routine?" he asks as he smears something on my cheek.

"Why? Is there something wrong with my skin?"

He laughs, and the genuine sound is a balm to my soul, replacing any doubts or worries I'm having with a feeling of comfort and joy. I think about every time we made each other laugh during the blind portion of this experience. To think it was him, and that perfect sound each time, is kind of mind blowing. I remind myself of my vow to earn as many laughs from him as I can for the rest of our time together.

"Everyone should have a good skin-care routine. Don't worry about it. I'll make sure to get one set up for you," he promises casually, like we're a real couple who would do things like look out for each other's skin.

I'm trying not to focus on how close he is to me, so I close my eyes, but it's impossible to ignore the feel of his breath fanning across my face or the way the air seems electrically charged between us. I don't need my eyes open to know exactly where he is. The connection that's always been between us is as strong as ever.

He moves through his routine with ease. I love experiencing him like this, so in his element, so happy, and so carefree. Even though it's obvious he's aware he's on camera with his perfect posture and witty remarks. It's also clear he was made for this.

"I'm going for a full-glam look here," he reminds the camera. "Jace already has amazing dark eyebrows, so I'm just going to brush them out a little bit. Do you mind if I bring out my tweezers?" He directs his question at me.

I shrug. "Whatever you'd like, darling." His eyes widen at the nickname, but he rolls with it, and it feels like another small victory.

Until he actually starts using them. "Oh shit! Oh my god! What the!" I whine, fully squirming now in my chair.

"It's just tiny little eyebrow hairs," he says with a laugh.

"Okay, well, I didn't realize you were a sadist," I tease. "You make this look painless in your videos."

"Beauty is pain," he jokes. "But for real, you do have great eyebrows. I'm only plucking a few... Okay, perfect." He turns back to the camera as he lifts an eyeshadow pallet and explains what it is. "So Jace has these gorgeous, warm brown eyes that remind me of melted chocolate with caramel, and I think a high pigment shiny gold eyeshadow is really going to make them sparkle," he says with a dramatic wink at me.

"Are you finally going to admit where you got that name?" I tease.

"I have no idea what you're talking about," he says innocently before turning back to the makeup, going on about the different shades of gold and browns that he's putting around my eyes. The smile on my face feels permanent. This really is fun. I've always had such a great time when it was just the two of us, but this is so much better than those stolen moments in the woods.

Even if there's still the layer of pretending, I feel like, in this moment, we're both the true versions of ourselves.

And I can't help but think about how perfectly we fit together.

KIERAN

Producer: "So, you admitted—or Jace admitted—that he hated you because of your self-expression when you were growing up. How did that impact you? Will you elaborate?"

Kieran: "No."

O f all the things I thought I might be doing on this show, hanging out in the kitchen, doing Jace's makeup, was not on the list. And yet he's sitting here, blindly trusting me to make him look good for millions of people to see while being so cool about it.

Everything he does seems to make it harder to merge the version of Jace in my mind from the past with the JR I was falling for last week *and* this new version of Jace before me now.

I can't help but think about how people always argue over whether or not someone can change. Some say people can't— that who they were when they were young, who they were in their worst moments, is who they really are. Maybe that's true for some people.

But—my very complicated feelings for Jace aside—I think most of us just don't know what we don't know, especially when we're young. We do the best we can with what's in front of us until life cracks the door open and shows us there's more. And once we've seen more, once we know more and actually want to do better, we can't go back to the narrow box we were stuck in before.

I grew up with supportive parents who I knew would always love me, and with Olivia, who—other than during our big fight—was there to hype me up and remind me that not everyone was as close-minded as the people who judged me. I even grew up with the internet to learn about makeup, being queer, and all the things I didn't know before.

I don't think Jace had any of those things.

His parents kicked him out for being attracted to men, and he never got into the details with me back then, but I don't think his home life was great. His dad was an asshole. His teammates were assholes. I think I even remember him saying something about not being able to look up anything about his sexuality because he couldn't risk his parents seeing it on their shared computer.

The Jace I'm looking at now has obviously changed. He's someone who's experienced more, seen more, *chosen* more than the scared teenager I used to know. He's someone who isn't locked inside that old version of himself because he's had the ability to freely explore who he is.

It's just so hard for me to move on when I've spent so many years hating *that* version.

I bring my attention back to the camera, trying to keep my voice light, keep my posture perfect, and keep my smile in place for the camera. But every time he laughs, or worse, calls me a sweet pet name, I feel myself slipping. Forgetting that we're supposed to be pretending because of my own rules.

Because Jace has always been the exception.

This feels more real and more intimate than anything I've ever done. Jace isn't polished, he doesn't have the perfectly curated online presence or practiced charm I usually surround myself with. He's honest in a way that makes me feel like he sees right through every layer of branding I've created under the nickname *he* gave me.

And instead of finding something to exploit, he genuinely likes what he sees. He's not sitting here thinking about his own gain or if this could help him gain followers for his own channel. He's simply doing this to bring some joy to our afternoon. It's fun, and that's disarming. Because, sadly, I can't remember the last time I did something purely for my own enjoyment that wasn't intended to be content.

I glance at him, with his head of curly brown hair tilted back, and his lips slightly parted as he waits for me to finish blending.

Today is showing me a whole new vulnerable side of Jace I didn't know existed—and it's adding another layer to the already conflicting feelings I have.

And hate isn't one of them. Not even close.

"Almost done," I mutter as my hand lingers at the corner of his jaw, and I stare at his now shiny lips. The urge to kiss him is getting stronger, but I shake that thought off.

I lean back and take in the finished look. The golden shimmer across his lids that makes his honey-brown eyes truly sparkle. It shouldn't work with his beard, the rough masculinity of him, but somehow it does.

I'd only brushed a light coat of mascara through his lashes to make them darker, and they frame the gold perfectly. I skipped liner because he doesn't need it—and because putting the mascara on was challenging enough for someone who's never worn it before. Instead, I smudged a little bronze at the corners to deepen the edges.

It's not overly dramatic, but you can tell he's wearing makeup and, God help me, it suits him well. Too well.

"Ready to see the final look?" I prompt him.

"Hell yeah."

I walk him toward the mirror, and his whole face lights up before he even steps in front of it.

Then he actually looks.

"Holy shit," he breathes, his grin stretching wide. He turns his head from side to side, leaning in close to the glass. "I look… good. Don't I?" He laughs almost in a bashful way, but he doesn't stop staring at himself.

There's no mockery in it, just genuine awe and a little surprise at his own reflection. His fingers hover near his eyes, careful not to smudge. "I can't believe that's me."

And maybe he's hamming it up, maybe this is another layer of his easy charm, but I don't think so. It feels real.

And I like it.

"You do look good. I kind of love this look on you. I think it might be one of my favorites I've ever done," I admit, smiling at him.

"Thank you, K. You're so talented; I'll never stop being impressed by you," he says in the most genuine voice, and my brain is trying to tell my stomach to stop doing somersaults at his words of affirmation, but that command is getting lost along the way.

I feel like I'm losing control. He's breaking my walls down so easily, and that can't happen. I have to protect myself here. I can't fall for someone who already broke my heart.

But I think I'm done pretending I hate him.

"Well, that's all for today, folks! Be sure to like and subscribe. I'm going to go enjoy my boyfriend's beautiful face now, bye!" I say before shutting off the only camera I'm allowed to touch.

Knowing we're still being recorded, I turn to Jace and smile. "Well, that was fun, huh?"

"Yeah," he says, his grin softening. "It was. I'm so happy you asked me. Getting to see you in action makes my heart feel… bigger or something, like it's bursting with how proud I am. I'm seeing the version of you that you were always meant to share with the world, and somehow, I get a front-row seat."

"Thanks, J. We can go take that off now if you want."

"What? No!" He practically shouts, and I'm shocked he actually wants to keep wearing it.

"Okay, okay, I guess tonight I'll have to introduce you to my skin-care routine before bed then." I laugh, and he just beams at me.

"I'd really like that."

The rest of the day goes by quickly. We attempt some more cross-stitching as I educate Jace on the other reality shows he's missed, and before I realize it, we're ready to wash our faces for bed. Jace is in the bathroom with me, watching as I take out my products for bed. The last few nights, I locked myself in here without him, but he's really about to see everything.

Though he's probably seen me go through this in my content before.

"You weren't kidding when you said skincare, huh?" He looks overwhelmed by the number of products I've set out for us, and I would never tell him, but his reluctance is kind of adorable.

"Nope, this face doesn't just happen, you know. It's a whole system."

"Guess I'm about to find out," he says with a laugh.

"You sure are." I hand him a gentle makeup remover to start. "Put this on, it'll help get the makeup off your skin first, then we'll cleanse next."

He does what I say, going through the same routine as me, following my lead.

"Now we apply a toner and serum. And of course, moisturize to hydrate and replenish your skin."

"Hydrate and replenish? You sound like you are talking about a sponsor right now." He laughs.

I roll my eyes, but I'm smiling. "Sometimes it just kind of comes out, but seriously, don't knock it until you try it. This'll have your skin glowing."

"Fine, fine, I want to glow too," he jokes as he rubs the serum across his cheeks. "How do I look now?" He props his chin on his hands and bats his lashes as he faces me.

I snort a laugh and swallow the lump in my throat at how good he does look. "Exactly like you're supposed to. Now come on, let's brush our teeth and go to bed."

We make our way into the bedroom, and each climb into bed on our sides. Jace turns to me the second we're under the covers.

"Today was a lot of fun," he says.

"Yeah," I agree, because it was.

He props himself up on his elbow, looking down at me. "So... did I do better today? Do I get a reward?"

I snort at the insinuation. "Hell no. Even if we were going to hook up again—which we're not—you succeeded in leaving me sore. Stay the hell away from my ass," I say with a small laugh and absolutely no heat.

"That's fine," he says casually. "I prefer to bottom anyway."

I whip my head toward him. "No, you don't."

"Uh, yeah, I do...?" His voice sounds convincing, but I don't get it because...

"There's no way you fucked me like *that,* and you're telling me you'd rather bottom?"

He chuckles, face breaking out into a huge grin. "I'm flattered you think I'm so good, and trust me, no complaints on my end, I had a fantastic time. But, yeah, that was my first time topping a man in a long time."

I shake my head again, feeling even more confused by all the layers of this man I'm trying to fit together. "I can't believe you're telling me you pulled that off like a pro and you haven't done it in years," I mutter, unable to hold back the compliment in my confusion.

He shrugs with a grin. "Guess I'm just naturally talented. But, I've always been a catcher, you know?"

"Oh, fuck you," I say playfully.

"You already did." He grins, and I roll my eyes, then he shifts a smidge closer, dropping the cocky edge in his voice. "But, yeah, after how great last night was, I'll acknowledge that I'm vers, but I do prefer to bottom. Is that a problem?"

"No. Of course not, because..." I trail off. I should say because this isn't real, because it's not. Or because it won't happen again.

But what I really want to say is, *we'll make it work.* I haven't topped in a long time either because bottoming is also my preference, but I'm not opposed to it. And there are plenty of ways we can both enjoy sex. So, instead, I swallow down both thoughts and give him another piece of truth. "Because I like knowing that about you."

"Yeah?" he asks, curiously, not even attempting to cover his smile.

"Yeah," I say softly. "It reminds me that the picture I have in my head of who you are might be different than who I'm getting to know—the real you, lying here with me."

"I am that person lying here with you," he says, voice full of conviction as he looks right into my eyes. "I'm the same person you started falling for behind all the voice alteration technology. I'm really hoping that I can keep proving that to you, K. I'm not the person you used to think you knew. I didn't even know that person, if I'm being honest."

"Fuck," I mutter, looking away. Because Jace is proving to be everything I've spent so long wanting in a partner, and as I sit here feeling like he's staring into my soul and saying things I'd never imagined him capable of, it's hard to believe he's making any of this up.

"Look, I know you're not agreeing to hook up again, but we are going to be spending a lot of time together with this plan, so I'd like to be very clear that I am very okay with having a physical relationship. And maybe I was too honest about preferring to bottom, and should've just kept my mouth shut, but trust me, we can make this work," he says, probably thinking I'm contemplating how we'll have sex—because I think we both know we're going to give in to the pull between us again—instead of how much this "relationship" is actually affecting me. "There's more than one way to enjoy sex, and I did really like fucking you. I think you can agree that we're compatible. I have some ideas."

"Compatible, huh?" I laugh at his implication.

He nods, head now on the pillow, inches away from my own. "Yeah, and not just for sex, either."

BETWEEN LIAM and Blake ditching the group meet up, then Jace and I sneaking out right after, production wasn't happy, and they're requiring us to do more group activities. I think they wanted more drama to unfold, but Liam assured Jace that what happened that night was a misunderstanding.

I'm still not sure why someone who thought they were straight would come on this show assuming they'd "know" if they were talking to a woman, but hey, that's not my relationship to concern myself with. If they worked it out and they're happy, then I'm happy for them.

The apartment building has an indoor pool, and we're all meeting up for a forced group hangout.

"I'm not planning to actually swim," I warn Jace as we walk into the humid space, and he nods in acknowledgement.

Luckily, there are cabanas, and Blake and Liam already claimed one and are waving us over. The pool area is nice with a large window wall that seems like it can fully open up in the summer. There's a smoothie and juice bar set up, and a table with snacks.

"Hey, guys!" Jace says excitedly as we make our way over to the empty chairs in their cabana.

"So good to see you again!" Liam smiles.

"Hey!" Blake adds. "Sorry about the other night, I'm excited to actually get the chance to hang out with you both today."

"Us too," Jace answers for me, and I realize I should say something.

"Yeah, can't wait to get to know you both."

We all grab some snacks, and then sit back down to eat with our smoothies and juice.

It's still kind of odd to me that Jace and Liam bonded so well *platonically* in the blind dating set up—and I'm totally chill and not at all jealous about it. Watching them interact as Liam tells Jace about a barn he'd like to renovate on his farm, it seems like they've known each other for years with how comfortable they already are with each other. *But they're talking construction, they aren't flirting.*

I hate that I feel so possessive of him. I don't want to be with Jace.

I just... also don't love the idea of him with anyone else.

How fucking mature of me, I know.

"That sounds like a really cool project, maybe we could come up for the weekend sometime and help out if it isn't done," Jace offers, pulling my focus back to the conversation.

Ugh. Why is Jace so naturally charming as he offers that we'll come help. *We*. As in me and him after we're married.

They don't know he's acting for the cameras.

But is he?

He's been friends with Liam for no reason other than emotional support. That's not something a complete asshole would do. I don't think he's making future plans for us to look good for the audience; it sounds like he just wants to visit his friend, and since that friend thinks we're dating, of course we'd come together.

Fuck, I think I've finally accepted that hate isn't the word I'd use to describe my feelings for Jace, but I don't think I'm emotionally prepared to admit how much I actually like him either.

In the short, post-blind-dating time we've shared together, we've maybe even become—I don't know that friends is the right word—something close to friends.

When I'm done eating, Jace picks it up without hesitation. "Do you want anything else?"

I stare up at him from my reclined position, assessing. There isn't a single sign that his offer, or his warm expression, are fake. He said he thought we were compatible last night in more ways than just sex. I'd brushed off the comment, but I think he might be right. He's everything I've dreamed about in a partner. "No thanks, I'm good," I finally reply.

"Just let me know if you change your mind," he responds easily before walking away.

"So, who wants to swim?" Liam asks when Jace returns.

We all have our swimsuits on, and I stripped down to mine when we got to the cabana, but it isn't until this moment that I realize Jace has kept his shirt on. He seems to hesitate for a moment, looking to me. "You already know I'm not swimming," I remind him with a short laugh. "But don't let me hold you back."

I'm not sure if his hesitation is about leaving me behind or if it's about being so exposed on camera, but either way, I don't want him to worry. At this moment, I think what he needs is encouragement and support from me, his partner. Real or not.

I get up and walk over to him. When I'm close enough, I reach out to grab hold of his hand and lean in so the cameras can't hear me.

"I don't know how you're feeling right now, but let me remind you, there's nothing about you that you need to hide," I whisper into his ear.

He squeezes my hand and smiles softly at me. "Thanks, K."

"I'll keep Kieran company, go have fun with Liam," Blake yells to us, assuring Jace I'll be just fine. Finally, Jace nods, lets go of my hand, and removes his shirt. I wasn't anticipating just how distracting it would be to have Jace half naked here in public with everyone else. Even though we've had sex, I still haven't seen his bare chest in broad daylight. And fuck, I had no idea how sexy he would be.

"Kieran," Blake says, clearing his throat. He probably said my name a few times if I had to guess based on the smirk he's aiming at me. I must've gotten lost in taking in Jace's broad, hairy chest and soft abdomen that clearly still covers a lot of muscle, plus his thick arms I want to be wrapped around me again.

"Shit, sorry." I laugh.

"No need to apologize, I get it."

I can't help but furrow my brows because didn't this guy think he was straight last week? Is he seriously checking out Jace now? "What is it that you get?" I clarify.

His smile doesn't falter. "I might be new at realizing how attractive men can be, but I've been pretty distracted by Liam in his bathing suit too."

Right. He's talking about his partner. That makes more sense. Fuck, when did I become such a jealous person?

"So, Kieran, what should I know about you?" Blake asks.

I blink at him, trying to process the question. "Like my job? Or…?" I trail off, not really sure what he's looking for.

Blake shrugs. "Yeah, that. But I also want to hear all about your likes and dislikes, and what your day-to-day life is like. Now that we're friends, I need to know all that."

A surprised laugh escapes my throat before I can stop it. "If you don't know any of that, are we actually friends yet?" I tease.

Blake pretends to look offended, dramatically covering his hand over his heart like I've wounded him. "Kieran, I hate to break it to you, but we're actually best friends now."

"And why is that?" I ask, playing along.

"Because our boyfriends are best friends. Look at them." He nods to where Liam and Jace are chatting on the edge of the pool. "Liam's only mentioned, like, one friend from back home, and I don't even think he lives there anymore. Jace has really been there for him during all this, and I don't want their friendship to end with the show," Blake says seriously.

I nod at him, his concern for his partner having a support system is not what I was expecting after the little bit I've heard about Blake so far, but it makes me warm up to him even more.

"So, like I was saying, since our boyfriends are best friends, we're best friends now too. I can go first if you'd like."

"Sure," I agree with a laugh.

There's something about Blake's positive energy that is really endearing. He goes on to tell me all about his life—his dog, Lucky, his best friend, Chad, his sports obsession—which now brings me back to the blind dating with BB—and how excited he is for Liam's farm. After his full report, I give him a similar one about me—my business, Freddie, how Jace and I picked up cross-stitching—leaving out the whole, *Jace was my bully and now we're only pretending to date except maybe I'm enjoying it more than I should be* part.

Eventually, Jace and Liam join us again and the show

provides dinner, forcing us all to sit around a giant table before finally allowing us to return to our apartments.

After showering—separately, unfortunately—Jace and I continue our cross-stitching attempts. I've made it my personal mission to become an amazing cross-stitcher.

"I feel like my artistic skills should be transferring more than they actually are," I complain, holding out the cactus I'm working on to look at it from another angle.

Jace looks over at my attempt. "I think you're doing an amazing job with that penis, but I personally would have chosen a different color," he deadpans.

I burst out laughing. "I thought I was finally getting the hang of it, too."

"Do you think it doesn't look realistic enough? I could offer myself up as a model, but we might need to move into the bedroom," he teases.

"Was that one of your ideas from last night?" Fuck, why is flirting with him so easy?

His gaze heats as it flickers between my eyes and my mouth. "Oh, I would love to tell you more about my ideas," he suggests, raising his eyebrows suggestively. "Have we been out here for long enough? Can we actually go into our room?"

I look at the clock, and sure, it's not exactly late yet, but after spending so much of my day around a half-naked Jace, I've been pretty excited about the possibility of a repeat. I'd intended to put up more of a fight, but after realizing that Jace and I might actually be friends now, I don't have it in me to protest. I want him.

"Follow me," I say, standing before I make my way into the bedroom out of the camera's view. With each step, my desperation seems to grow, blood rushing to my dick as I anticipate what we're about to do.

He hurries behind me, and the second he shuts the door, I push him back against it. We still have a lot to talk about when it comes to sex, especially since he surprised me with his preference to bottom, so I should probably start there, but once again, I'm desperate for him and am quickly losing my patience.

"Rapid fire, total honesty before we do anything else tonight. I love bottoming, definitely prefer something in my ass, am very into the taunting and praise combo you started last time, and I missed you calling me a cockslut like you did in high school. It's hot, and I like it rough."

He stares at me for a quick moment, and then nods as a smile spreads across his face.

"Uh… uh," he stutters. "Sorry, just trying to process what you said first. I wasn't prepared for all that. Okay, like I said last night, I really did enjoy topping you. I'm surprised by how much, to be honest, but I also really like bottoming. And yeah, I know, I'm a bigger guy so people expect me to want the opposite, but if I had to only choose one, then yeah, I'd rather you fuck me. I also love giving and receiving oral, as you might remember."

"Oh, I remember," I smirk. "I've been thinking about what you said last night all day. I agree that having a physical relationship would have its benefits."

"So many benefits," he quickly agrees. "Are you still sore? Do you want me to blow you again?"

As much as I really do want that, I like the push and pull of our dynamic even more. And I like knowing I'm the one driving my partner wild—driving Jace wild. Dropping to my knees, I look up at him. "I think it's my turn."

"Really? Fuck yes. My cock has missed you so much, K."

I waste no time unbuttoning his pants and pulling them down along with his boxer briefs. He's even more mouthwatering up close than I remember. His tip is wet with precum, and I lean forward to suck his straining cock into my mouth.

"Fuck, Kieran, you on your knees for me is a sight I'll never be tired of," he mutters, and my chest flutters because I never thought I'd be here again. I didn't think I'd ever want to be, but there's no denying it now that I do.

Instead of responding with words, I swirl my tongue around him, tasting the salt and heat and desperation. His thighs twitch, and his hands hover like he wants to grab my hair, but he's refraining.

"Don't hold back. Rough, remember?" I assure him before taking him back into my mouth.

He threads his fingers through my hair until he has a good grip on the back of my head, groaning as he starts fucking my face. "God, you already look so filthy, K. I wish you could see yourself like this." He pushes deeper, and I gag a little as I manage to hold him in my throat, spit leaking out the corners of my mouth.

"You love it, don't you?" he growls, hips rolling against my mouth as I suck him. "You've always been such a slut, so eager for me, even when you claim to hate me. You're so perfect like this, darling. Perfect for me."

The sting of the words and the sweetness of the praise collide in my chest, making me ache in the best way. My eyes water as I take him further, throat tightening around him. His breath hitches before he lets out a moan.

"Look at you, so fucking beautiful with your lips stretched around me, gagging on my dick. Are you always this much of a slut? Or is it just with me?" He frees one hand from my hair, moving it almost reverently to hold my face, wiping away an escaped tear with his thumb. "I'd like to pretend it's just for me, that you've always been *my* pretty little cockslut."

A shiver runs down my spine at the words no one has said to me in over a decade, and I groan around his cock, sucking him like it's the first time all over again. My own erection is begging to be freed, and I make a move to unbutton my pants, but he bumps my hand with his leg.

"What do you think you're doing? Good boys don't touch themselves, K."

I look up at him through my lashes with pleading eyes, desperate to do just that.

"Actually," he says with a smirk, "I think you've had enough. My turn."

51

JACE

Producer: "Are you sure your relationship with Liam is platonic?"

Jace: "One hundred percent. I'm all in with Kieran. And Liam is committed to Blake. But it's nice to have someone to talk to who understands how overwhelming this process has been."

"Your turn?" Kieran sounds offended when I pull out from his mouth. "I'm the one sucking your dick."

"Yeah, and I wasn't going to last much longer in that perfect mouth, and I'm not ready for this to be over," I explain. "You said you prefer to have something in your ass? How's my tongue sound?"

He sucks in a sharp breath, steps back and hesitates for a moment before finally nodding. His cheeks darken and he averts his gaze as he continues. "I wasn't necessarily planning for this to happen, but I showered thoroughly when we got back."

"Don't lie to me, K," I growl as I step up right into his

personal space, running a finger down the obvious bulge in his unbuckled pants. Kieran likes our taunting, and I know he isn't ready to admit how deep the connection between us really goes, so I lean in closer, until my mouth is right next to his ear. "I know you were thinking about me in the shower. Fantasizing about being with me again. What were you picturing?" I palm his erection. "Be a good boy. Tell me, and I might just do it."

He only glares at me in response, then bites his bottom lip, and I can tell how much he's enjoying this. "Fuck you."

I can't help but smirk as I shrug. "We'll get there. One day you'll admit how much you want me, and I'll make all your dirty fantasies come true."

"One day?" he scoffs. "You wish, hot shot."

"Whatever you say." I shrug again, playing along. "Do you want my tongue in your ass or not? Ditch the clothes and get on your hands and knees on the bed for me."

"Oh, so now I can undress myself?" he clarifies mockingly.

I grin in response. "Yes, because I said you could."

"God, you're lucky I'm so horny," he bites out as he takes off his shirt.

"My name is Jace, but 'God' works too if you insist," I tease, honestly impressed with myself for being able to speak at all as he slowly reveals more of his skin. He snorts a laugh, rolling his eyes before he notices how intently I'm staring. Then he really takes his time removing each item of clothing, but I'm not complaining about the free strip show.

When he's finally naked, he crawls onto the bed gracefully, arching his back in a way that makes his ass look so perfect that I'm frozen in place for a moment. Kieran is always gorgeous, but naked on *our* bed, waiting for me, he has to be the most beautiful thing I've ever seen. I've never been artistic, but suddenly I'm wishing I knew how to sculpt or paint, to somehow immortalize this moment where my dream man is presenting himself to me.

I shake my head, telling myself to focus and enjoy the

moment for the gift that it is. I need to make sure Kieran enjoys this as much as I do so he wants to keep doing it again and again. Maybe even forever.

I step up behind him, rubbing my hands over his perfect cheeks, squeezing before I spread him open even more for me. "Are you still sore?" I check before I do anything else.

"No, I should be good to go," he assures me, shifting his hips back a bit, as if he's seeking my touch.

So I lean in and slowly lick his hole, taking my time, really savoring the moment as I lap all around his entrance. I love the intimacy of this. Kieran might not want me to kiss his mouth, but I'm going to make out with his hole for as long as he'll let me.

The noises he makes at each swipe of my tongue are filthy. "I hope the cameras out there can hear you," I tell him. "I hope they catch you moaning and whimpering for me like the good little cockslut you are, and then I want a copy of the recording so if you decide you're done with me, I can listen to it and remember this moment," I say before diving back on him.

He lets out another loud moan as I play with his balls before I bring my hand up near my mouth, adding a finger into the mix as I continue to feast on him.

"More," he demands, so I pull back, getting another finger wet before I slowly add it as well. He's relaxed enough now for me to put my tongue inside of him, and when I do, his hips jerk. I reach my hand under him to his leaking cock, spreading his precum down his shaft as I work him slowly.

"Holy shit, that feels amazing," he mutters, his hips thrusting forward to move his dick through the channel my fist has created. "Jace, I'm so close already. Fuck—right there—oh my god."

I increase the speed of my motions. After another moment, Kieran's dick is jerking in my hold, his release painting our sheets. I work him through his orgasm, not wanting to miss a moment of his pleasure, knowing that I'm the one making him come.

"You're so fucking sexy," I can't stop myself from telling him. When he comes down from his post-orgasm high, I finally back off, intending to finish myself, but Kieran surprises me. He flips over in the bed, scooting down toward me until he's sitting on the edge of the bed right in front of me. His face is smug as he looks up at me through his dark lashes and says, "My turn." Without another word, he leans in, swallowing my cock right to the back of his throat.

"You really are a cockslut, huh?" I say, calling him the name he admitted he loves as he swallows, squeezing my dick even further. "You look so good below me. I wish I could have you like this always," I admit, running a hand through his flowy brown hair before giving it a tug.

He hums at the visual, and the vibration is too much. "Shit, K, gonna come—"

He doubles down on his efforts, and my release crashes into me. My cum shoots into his mouth as the euphoric feeling of my orgasm takes over for a few blissful moments. He doesn't pull off until he's sucked every last drop.

"That was amazing, K," I praise. The whole experience was so much hotter and more fun than I'm used to from a hookup.

"Yeah, it was." He smiles as we both lay on the bed, naked. "By the way, I couldn't take my eyes off you at the pool today."

I swallow the lump in my throat at his sincerity, and I wish I could kiss him, but since that's still a hard line, I think of the next best thing.

"How do you feel about some cuddle time after we clean up?"

"Fine." He rolls his eyes, I think in trying to hide just how much he wants me to hold him too.

I quickly pull him up, and we head into the bathroom to

freshen up and get ready for bed. When I finish, he's still brushing his teeth, so I crawl into bed to wait for him.

The moment he's in bed with me, I wrap my arms around him, and he settles against my chest. I love the way we fit together so perfectly. I'm six-two and he's probably five-eleven, and it works like we were made for this.

Hooking up with him again was amazing.

But this might be even better.

A perfect end to a perfect day.

KIERAN

Producer: "What's one thing Jace has done that surprised you since blind dating?"

Kieran: "Everything."

The last two weeks feel like they've lasted a lifetime. From meeting and falling for JR, to being heartbroken and pissed off when I found out JR was Jace, then agreeing to our fake relationship plan, hooking up multiple times, and realizing I don't actually hate him anymore—I actually kind of like him—it's been a lot mentally and emotionally.

We're finally back in New York City, and I'm on my way to my apartment. I can't wait to be there. I miss Freddie like crazy, and I'm grateful Liv's been taking care of him, but I want him curled up on my lap for the next two days. I forgot to ask Jace if he's allergic to cats, but he didn't say anything when I told him about Freddie so I'm just going to hope he's not.

Unfortunately, we can't just stay holed up at home with

Freddie though. I had to submit date ideas to production before the show, but it turns out I was asked to be a part of creator awards ceremony tonight.

I'm actually kind of surprised the show jumped at the chance to stick Jace and me in a publicized event. I thought the point of these reality shows was to keep your relationship hidden until it aired so nothing was spoiled. Maybe that's why they said for Jace to not walk the red carpet with me, but still, we *will* be there together and it'll be obvious he's my date. Nothing like throwing him straight into the madness that is my life.

I'm nervous to see if being in an unfamiliar environment where people treat *me* differently will make him act differently, but then again, he's been surprisingly consistent the whole time on the show.

Who knows, maybe he'll handle tonight better than I will.

Before we left this morning, Mitch and Jay handed us back our phones and ran us through the schedule. Even though we're both in the city, my visit is technically first. I'm supposed to meet up with Olivia, have some one-on-one time with her where we go over my new product samples that should be in while Jace gets dragged into interviews for the show. Then the three of us will go to the event together, smile for the cameras, and pretend this isn't awkward when I tell her I'm fake-dating her ex-boyfriend even though I know she won't care.

Tomorrow, he'll meet my parents—or re-meet them. But an awkward run-in at a Mexican restaurant fifteen years ago while Liv and I were fighting over him doesn't exactly count as a proper introduction. The fact that I still remember it at all is kind of embarrassing.

After the two nights at my place, we'll go to his place, and I'll finally get to meet his uncles.

To say I'm overwhelmed is an understatement.

I didn't even bother turning my phone on while we were at the airport, but I did finally give Jace my phone number and told him to text me. I figured I'd turn it on when Jace and I separated for the day because I didn't know what was going to be waiting for me, but I could only imagine a million notifications—and I was close.

I'm scrolling through everything at a very high level while I'm in the car being chauffeured to my house by the show, but nothing looks urgent, or even that important. Olivia was set to handle everything, and just like I expected, she seemed to have nailed it. If there was a fire while I was disconnected, I'd have no idea.

It's funny, when I first got to Atlanta and production took my phone, I felt like I was going to implode, but honestly, I've hardly thought about it since forming my connection with JR. I had a bit of anxiety about not being able to check in with Olivia, especially about Freddie, but I was so immersed in our new little world that it became far more of a distant thought. Especially because the show did give an emergency number to our immediate family in case anything happened and they truly did need to get ahold of me.

As soon we pull up to my building in Manhattan after what feels like hours of being stuck in traffic, I grab my bags and walk past my doorman who eyes me curiously as I'm being followed by a couple of the crew members. But all I can focus on is how good it feels good to be back here.

Jace and I never talked logistics, but it didn't seem that important since we never agreed to actually date after the show. We're only doing it *for* show, but maybe we should talk about a few of those things on these visits... just in case the producers ask us in an interview.

Fuck, I hope his interview goes well today.

I make it to my apartment and unlock the door, and the minute I'm inside, Freddie meows his way over to me. I pick him up and cuddle him in my arms.

"I missed you, little dude," I coo, giving him a kiss. "Did Liv take good care of you? I know she did."

I notice one of the two-man film crew that's here with me smiling from behind the lens, and I give Freddie another kiss before setting him back on the couch.

"Alright, time to get ready for this event and wait for Olivia to get here," I say out loud.

I have no idea if they'll use this footage of me wandering around my house, but once I'm showered, I start on my makeup, and when I look at the time, I realize we need to leave soon to get to the awards.

KIERAN

Where are you? I'm going to have to leave without you so I can be there to meet my boyfriend before he's thrown into the chaos without me.

A second later, my phone rings, and it's her.

"Hey, Liv."

"Kieran! Oh my god, today's been a mess." Her voice is breathless, like she's been running. "I'm late. I was hoping I'd still make it to you before, but I'll have to meet you at the event. I know, I know, I swore I'd be there to get ready with you, but the eyeliner samples got lost in the mail, and I had to go to the lab to pick them up since this is our only night together for another week or so. They were supposed to be ready hours ago, but of course, they weren't. I'm almost home, but I need to get ready there since I didn't bring my dress with me. I'll meet you as soon as I can. I can't wait to see you!"

"Breathe, Liv, it's okay. It'll all be fine." I laugh as I shake my head with a smile on my face at how fast she talks when she's stressed. "At least Freddie was here to greet me when I got home," I say, petting him in my lap.

"I made sure to bring him back this morning, thank god he

didn't get dragged into this mess. I promise I'll be quick. I can't wait to hear everything, and obviously I want to meet your new man! Just wait for me if you get there first, okay? I'm so close to home, and I'll get ready as fast as possible."

"I appreciate you. It'll all be okay!"

"Glad you're so calm. Ah, I'm excited to see you! Okay, love you, bye!"

I hang up and just sit here for a second, staring at my phone. Liv really has been the best friend and the best assistant I could've asked for. I was just really hoping to have a chance to talk to her today *before* she saw Jace again. I've really missed being able to talk to her about all the little details of my life, and navigating this situation with him has been so much more difficult without her there to talk me through everything I'm feeling.

I finish getting ready after a few final touches, and my phone vibrates again, but this time, it's Jace.

JACE

I'm on my way, can't wait to see you!

My stomach twists in that stupid, traitorous way it always does whenever he's involved. Nerves and… something else. Because the truth is, I missed him today. I kept wishing he was here to meet Freddie and see my house, just hang out and get ready with me, even when I tried to tell myself I didn't. I might've let it slip once to the cameras that I wished he was here with me, too.

It's only selling our fake relationship more, that's all.

When it's time to go, I head back down to the car that's waiting to drive me to the event. It's at a theater, and it seems like I beat both Olivia and Jace here. There's a small room set up for people to wait before walking the red carpet, so I find a spot off to the side and pull out my phone.

I text Jace to let me know when he arrives since I don't want him to go through this circus alone. Olivia walks up moments later, glowing in a red dress that looks absolutely stunning on her, and flashes a pass at the security guards. She spots me, and—as quickly as she can in heels and her dress—she sprints over and wraps around me the second she's within arm's reach.

"Oh my god, I missed you so much," she blurts into my shoulder. "Please don't ever leave me again. I swear, with the stress, I've aged years in the past few weeks—you owe me Botox."

I laugh, squeezing her in a hug. "Wow, I feel the same way myself, we can go together. You look perfect, as always, though. And thank you, seriously. For everything. I could not do this without you."

She waves me off. "Yeah, yeah, you can thank me later. So, let's get to the good stuff. Tell me everything. Who is he? What's the deal? I need the full download before he gets here."

I open my mouth, prepared to warn her that she actually already knows him. And dated him. But that's the moment I see Jace talking to the security guards, looking around, completely lost.

Shit, did he text me and I missed it? But I glance at my phone and confirm he didn't respond.

I swallow. "Well… that's actually him."

She turns to look, and her mouth drops open. "Wait a fucking minute. Is that who I think it is?"

I can't help the high-pitched chuckle that escapes. "Yep, now if you'll excuse me, I need to go save him."

Jace looks handsome as hell. His wide shoulders fill out his navy suit perfectly, his brown hair is curly and perfectly styled, and it even looks like he trimmed his short beard for tonight. I'm also *very* into the slutty little glasses he's currently wearing for this. He seems to only wear them some of the time, but I am a complete sucker for them.

"Hey, Jace, you look amazing," I say as I approach him.

Jace smiles that easy smile as he steps closer and pulls me into a hug.

My pulse feels like it just doubled as I think of all the ways this could unfold with Liv in a minute. I'd wanted to tell her before they saw each other because I have no idea how she'll react. She knows what happened in high school. She was there the last time I saw Jace; she knows how things ended and how heartbroken Jace left me. But as we walk back to where she's standing, she plasters on a smile of her own. "Hi, Jace. Good to see you."

"Hey, Liv," he greets. "You too."

"Uh, Kieran, can I have a word, please?" she says, not bothering to wait for an answer as she drags me away from him to the very back corner of this makeshift space, away from everyone else.

"Oh my god!" she squeals, eyes wide with her obvious confusion. "How the hell did you end up with Jace Ryan?"

"Shh, keep your voice down. I didn't know that's who I was talking to at first. Turns out, he was on the show too," I say, letting that hang, but I know she wants more. "He's not... he's not the same as he was when we were eighteen. I've told you about how different he was when we were alone back then, but now... he's different even from that. He's been—" I shake my head, trying not to sound too much like I'm defending him. "I don't know. He seems like he's changed."

Olivia grins, tilting her head like she's eating this up. "Holy shit, K! I am so happy for you! As long as he doesn't hurt you again. I will ruin him if needed," she threatens.

Her words make my cheeks heat, and I laugh, rubbing the back of my neck. "Yeah, well. I sort of told him this had to be fake..." My voice trails off at the admission.

Olivia raises a brow. "Fake?" she whispers, scrunching up her nose like the word tastes funny in her mouth.

"Yeah," I confirm. "I told him it had to be for the cameras. I couldn't risk breaking up with him immediately and then getting endless hate on the internet from people who don't know our history. I didn't know how they'd edit it, and you know my image affects everything. I hated him for all these years and that was my initial reaction, but now... I don't know, Liv. It's been horrible trying to figure this out on my own."

Her laugh is quick and sharp. "Oh, Kieran. You already sound like you're in deep."

I roll my eyes, but she's grinning, and that's worse because it means she sees something I'm still trying to hide from myself.

"I'm serious," I argue, but it comes out weaker than I mean it to. "I don't know what to do."

"What's the worst outcome if you see what happens and tell him you want to date him for real?"

The words hang there, heavy and terrifying, but I force myself to answer. "We don't work out and everyone hates me and my livelihood is ruined. You know how public breakups on social media are. It feels like a risk."

Olivia tilts her head, reading me the way she always has, her voice gentler now. "The world already thinks you're dating, or they will when the show airs, so the relationship being real or not wouldn't impact public opinion if you break up. You don't have to figure it out right this second. Just... maybe don't shove the possibility back in the box before you even know what's in there."

I think about what she's suggesting, and at this point, it really is about deciding if I'm willing to risk my heart again on someone who's already shattered it.

I'm not sure if I really have a choice though. Jace seems to have broken down every one of my carefully constructed walls, and I'm afraid my heart might already be his for the taking. "Okay," I finally agree.

"Now, let's go back and see your man! I can't wait to meet this new and improved Jace who's obviously stolen your heart."

Fuck. Is it really that obvious?

53

JACE

Producer: "When you're around Kieran, how do you feel?"

Jace: "Complete."

I can't believe I'm at this event right now *with* Kieran. I've admired him for years through my screen, and now this award show is probably going to honor him in some way. I actually don't know what it's for, but it feels like he should get an award. He deserves all the awards. My man is talented.

Okay, he might not officially be my man yet, but no one here knows that. Kieran and Liv have been gone for a few minutes now, and I'm sure they're talking about me. I hope my presence doesn't cause another fight. I know that's an egotistical thought, but I hated all those years ago when I came between them. Olivia was so sad, and Kieran obviously was too. It's been over a decade, though, and they are still best friends, so I'm sure they're fine. She's probably just surprised, that's all.

After what feels like an hour, but is more likely only another minute later, they finally walk back toward me, both smiling, and I feel like I can breathe again. I immediately reach for Kieran's hand, giving him a little squeeze. The production people that drove me here warned about avoiding PDA since the show hasn't aired yet, but we're in a room that seems pretty private, so I feel like this is fine and I really don't care. I need to touch him, so I do.

"How was your day? Did the interviews go okay?" he asks me.

"Yeah, it was fine, we can talk about that later though. I'm so excited to be here supporting you. Is there anything I should know?" I check. I want to make sure I can be the best boyfriend possible for him.

"Yeah—"

"Oh my god, Kieran Delaney? I can't believe it's you!" I turn my head, and Kieran drops my hand immediately. It looks like someone slipped past security into this private section. The man has his phone camera out, obviously taking pictures of everything around him, and is beaming at Kieran. He comes close enough to reach out to touch his shoulder, and Kieran's smile falters. It's like the light in his eyes flickers out as he glances down at the contact.

"Hi, yeah, it's me," he says with a smile I know is fake.

"Oh my god, we have to take a picture!" the man announces, grabbing Kieran's hand and pulling him in toward him, and jealousy flares through me. He flinches again, and it's so subtle that I'm sure this guy has no idea Kieran isn't enjoying this interaction. But I notice.

"Kieran isn't doing photos right now," I interrupt, turning him down in as polite a voice as I can manage for Kieran's sake. Kieran whips his head at me, eyes wide in surprise. But then he gives me a small smile, only lifting the corner of his mouth really, and the gratitude in his gaze is clear as day.

416

He pulls his hand back, placing it in his pants pocket, out of reach from the guy. "Thanks, babe," he whispers to me before turning to the other guy. "I'll do a selfie, let me see your phone." The guy eagerly hands Kieran the phone who takes one quick photo and hands it back.

"You need to go," a man in a security uniform says, escorting the man away.

"Does that happen a lot?" I ask when they're gone, and Kieran reaches for my hand again, lacing our fingers together. I guess I've known he was famous for years now—I'm in the fan groups, I see the comments. But it's one thing to participate in it behind a screen. Fame is such an abstract concept to apply to someone you already know, and seeing it firsthand is something else entirely.

"All the time," Liv answers.

"Usually, I don't mind it at all and am happy to do it. When I say I love my fans, I mean it. But every once in a while, someone gets grabby like that, and it feels... invasive." He bites his lip, like he's just putting the pieces together. "I think I'm realizing now that maybe I was so touch-averse because people only ever touched me in public. It always felt like it was for them— not for me—and every time, it took a little piece of me with it. I don't know..." He glances at me as he trails off at the vulnerable admission. "Thanks for stepping in, though. No one's ever done that for me before."

"Of course. I hope you know I'd do anything for you, K," I promise, giving his hand a quick squeeze.

I'd love to know what he told Liv about our arrangement, but I know better than to ask during this event full of cameras and strangers. Kieran suggests we get in the line for the red carpet, and while we're waiting, I ask Liv about her life, and we all catch up. Kieran handles the carpet like the professional that he is while Liv and I hang back. I'm relieved by how easy the conversation is; she doesn't seem to be holding onto any bad feelings from our past, and she even smiles as she looks between us, as if she likes the idea of us being together.

Kieran is presenting one award and is up for another. There's a catered meal before any of the awards begin as the host gives speeches about the evolution of influencers and content creators. It's wild to think about how early Kieran started posting things compared to so many other people here. The fact that he's stayed so popular and relevant for so long is a testament to how incredible he is. I can't believe I'm here right now as his date.

I can't get too in my head about that though. I do really think I could be a great *real* partner to him. I'd love to be the one at his side, protecting him and keeping him safe. Not that I think he really needs that. He's gotten himself here all on his own. But he shouldn't have to do it on his own if he doesn't want to.

I'm really hoping he doesn't want to.

He sneaks away to present, and when they forget to deliver his dessert in his absence, I give him mine, earning a smug smile from Liv. I don't know if she knows we're not actually together, but it definitely seems like she's a fan of us as a couple, so I'm counting that as a huge win.

Kieran doesn't win his award though, so apparently the judges are idiots, but he doesn't seem upset at all. I don't think he stops smiling the whole time. After the awards wrap up, there are a couple of other influencers who approach Kieran in a more respectful manner to introduce themselves, and a few more he already knows that he catches up with. He even introduces me as his partner to a few—asking them to hold off on saying anything publicly until after the show airs. He fills in gaps for me in stories I don't know, and looks to me during conversations with the people I've never met to see how I'm reacting to what they said.

None of it feels fake.

I know there are cameras everywhere, but I've seen the way

Kieran acts when he's in front of the cameras versus when we're alone, and this hasn't felt like he's putting on a show.

When the night wraps up, I'm thankful to be able to head out with him. I loved seeing him in his element, but I also want to get some alone time with him too.

"Are you sure you don't want to come back with us?" Kieran asks Liv as we're leaving the venue.

"No, it's been a long day, and I have to get up early. Let me know what you think of the eyeliner samples though." She gives me a hug goodbye, and I think she might only be going home in an attempt to give us privacy, but maybe that's more of a hope than anything. Either way, I'm grateful.

The camera crew from *Love Without Labels*, though, insists on filming me going to Kieran's house for the first time.

"Do you guys really need to film me seeing his place? That sounds like boring television," I point out on the drive back, eager to be alone with Kieran again.

"Trust us, once you see where he lives, you'll get it," the cameraman assures me.

"Plus, he's got the cat," the other person from the show adds. "He's cute."

I laugh at that. "I can't wait to meet Freddie." Kieran beams at me.

"I was hoping you weren't allergic."

"Not that I know of," I assure him, really hoping I'm not, but my lack of being around animals isn't very telling.

When we pull up to a swanky newer building on the east side of Manhattan, I realize why they wanted to film this. Kieran has money. Like, live in a fancy four-bedroom apartment in New York City kind of money. The doorman greets us as we enter, as does the person at the desk in the lobby, both of them addressing Kieran by name. He responds casually, and I attempt not to look completely awestruck by how nice this building is as we make our way up to his apartment.

This is by far the nicest home I've ever been in. I look around and take in all the details, the hardwood floors, the marble countertops in the kitchen that's probably the size of my entire apartment. *The four bedrooms.* I thought my place was nice because I have a bedroom and not a studio. I chuckle to myself as I have that thought. Kieran is going to be in for a rude awakening when we go stay at my place.

"K, this place is amazing," I tell him. "I'm so proud of everything you've built and earned."

He eyes me a little skeptically, but he also seems amused as he smirks. "Thanks."

"I mean it. You might not have won that award tonight because apparently, the judges have questionable taste, but I hope you know how spectacular you are."

Just then a cat appears, jumping right into Kieran's arms.

I don't think I've ever been jealous of an animal before, but it's definitely happening now.

"Freddie, I'd like you to meet Jace." Kieran is looking at me expectantly as he holds the cat in my direction. I have no idea what he's expecting though, I've never been this close to a cat in my life.

"Uh… hi, Freddie," I say, feeling awkward as I wave at the cat. I swear I hear one of the camera guys snicker behind me, but I'm not going to ruin their shot by glaring at him. They'd only insist on staying here even longer.

"You can pet him, he's friendly," Kieran suggests, so I hesitantly reach out my hand to stroke down his back. He's very soft, even more than I was expecting. I bet it'd be nice to cuddle up with him. He lets out a little meow when I pet him again.

"Holy shit, I don't think I've ever heard a meow in person before," I admit. "It's got to be the cutest thing I've ever heard."

"Have you never been around a cat?" Kieran clarifies.

"I've never been around any pets, really," I admit. "Freddie seems pretty cool though."

"Yeah, he's the best. It might seem kind of silly to admit, but spending time with him helps me so much. He's the perfect reminder that there's a whole world outside of my phone and social media."

I nod, loving how open Kieran is being with me as I continue to pet Freddie. "Thanks for looking out for my guy," I whisper to the cat, earning a chuckle from Kieran.

"Do you want me to show you around?" he offers, and I nod, eager to film whatever we have to. Hopefully after a quick tour, the people from the show can leave, and I can see if I have any shot of hooking up with Kieran tonight. There were a few times at the award ceremony that I caught him checking me out or staring at me with what I think was desire, so I'm really hoping that means he wants to do more tonight.

After pointing out some things in the main living space, he takes me around to each of the bedrooms. The first one is a guest room, but the second one isn't what I'm expecting.

"Holy shit, is this where you film?" I ask. I don't know why I didn't think about where he'd be doing that, but I immediately recognize the room from all his videos. "This is so fucking cool!" I look around at everything I've seen online. "Can you do my makeup in here next time?"

Kieran huffs a laugh. "I just can't get over that you're actually a fan."

I actually help run your biggest fan page. But now's not the time for that fun bit of trivia. "How could anyone not be a fan of you?" I say instead.

"Oh, the haters still exist, trust me."

"Those comments always piss me off," I can't help but add. "I wish that there was a better way to prevent those people from interacting."

"You and me both," he agrees.

The next bedroom has a lot of the behind-the-scenes equipment and products. I assume we're gonna go look at the last bedroom, but Kieran surprises me by leading us all back into the main living space. "Alright, everyone, you've got what you need. I'd rather you not be here when we go into my bedroom."

Fuck, if that wasn't one of the hottest things anyone's ever said. I really hope he means that and isn't just saying it for the cameras.

"You heard the man, we'll see you tomorrow. Byyye," I say, escorting them quickly to the door and locking it behind them the moment they're gone. I spin to face Kieran with a raised brow. "Is it time for the bedroom tour?" I ask in a suggestive tone.

Kieran is biting his lip and twisting one of his earrings as he looks up at me, heat shining in his eyes. "I've been thinking a lot since we mentioned our preferences. I have no idea if I'm going to like it, but ever since we talked about it, I haven't been able to shake the thought of what it would be like to fuck you," he says confidently.

Holy shit.

I definitely wasn't expecting that.

I feel like I'm frozen in place, unable to process what he just said to me, but I've never wanted anything more.

"Bedroom. Now," is all I can get out before I'm practically running there.

The second we're inside, I loosen my tie, yanking it off as I watch him strip off his jacket. I want to kiss him. Everything in me wants to kiss him. "Tonight was amazing. I'm endlessly impressed by you, K. You were so hot on that stage," I say as I walk toward him, leaving only a couple of inches of space between us.

He looks at my lips, then back to my eyes, and I can't tell if he's thinking the same thing I am, if he wants this as badly as I do. But there are no cameras on us, no reason for him to pretend. I want to just lean forward, but I can't break his rule without his approval. "Can I kiss you?" I ask softly.

He swallows, throat bobbing as he looks at me with a range of emotion in his eyes. If his answer isn't an enthusiastic "yes please" then I don't want to push him before he's ready. "Never mind, we don't have to," I assure him with a smile, hoping I didn't ruin the moment. "I want you to fuck me. What made you change your mind, darling?" I ask, brushing his hair back and out of his face because I can't stop myself from touching him.

I'm not sure if I imagine the flicker of disappointment on his face, but whatever his reaction, he quickly shakes it off as he reaches for my belt.

"Well, I was thinking about how surprised I was that you hadn't topped in so long, and still managed to fuck me like you did." He smirks before continuing. "I figured, if you could do that, then I'd probably be even better."

My face breaks out into a huge grin as I laugh at the cocky smile on his face. "Are we going to have some sort of competition to see who's the better top?"

"Bragging rights, baby, we've always done our best fucking through taunts." He winks.

My thoughts linger on the word baby, and for a second, it undoes me. I know it was just part of his taunt, but it makes something inside me feel like it's bursting open. The glass box I've tried to keep my feelings trapped inside—although I'm sure they're visible for all to see—is cracking, shattering open with that one simple word. I've stuck with calling him "darling" as much as I can because it felt more... common, I don't know. I've heard people use it more casually, even if that's never how I meant it. But fuck, do I want to be his baby, just like I want him to be mine. *Baby* feels more intimate, more real, and when I called him that last time, he never told me to stop. *Maybe I can try again.*

I want to tell him how I feel, how much I don't want this to end, but now isn't the time for that. Especially since *he* wants to fuck *me.* So I force myself to focus on what Kieran's saying.

"Let's see what you've got, *baby*," I taunt back, the word feeling wrong said like that, but I do it anyway.

"Get naked," he commands, snapping my belt open, and heat coils in my stomach. Kieran's always been a little bossy, but something about the way he's taking control now makes my body jolt with anticipation.

I oblige, stripping down. My skin prickles with the thrill of being under his gaze, and when I glance at him, he's already tugging his own clothes off. His cock strains against the fabric of his briefs, thick and obviously hard behind the thin fabric. He doesn't rush though. Instead, he turns to open his bedside drawer, pulling out lube and condoms, and setting them on the nightstand.

"Now," he says, smirking as he looks back at me, "I could bend you over the dresser like you did to me." His eyes rake over me before he tilts his chin toward the bed. "But I think I can do even better. I want to take my time. On the bed. Get on all fours. Ass up."

My mouth goes dry as I climb onto the mattress, the sheets cool against my palms as I spread my knees and arch my back, offering myself to him in a way I've fantasized about for years.

Behind me, I hear Kieran squirting lube on his fingers before the mattress dips as he kneels behind me, and then his hand slides over the curve of my ass, squeezing once before spreading me open. It feels so vulnerable to be positioned like this for him, but I want Kieran to see all of me.

"Fuck," he murmurs, more to himself than me, and I flush at the raw hunger in his tone. "Your ass has always been a fucking dream."

His slick fingers trace teasingly over my hole, circling and stroking, until I'm squirming. Then he pushes in, easing me open with steady pressure.

A shiver tears down my spine as he works me slowly. One

finger becomes two, stretching me until I'm panting and groaning, rocking back against his hand.

"You feel that?" His voice is low, taunting, almost smug. "You're opening up for me so easily. You're desperate to be full of me, aren't you? You always called me a slut, but you're just as bad."

I groan, clenching around his fingers, because he's right. Every thrust of his hand makes me burn with the need for more, and he knows it.

"God, you're perfect like this," he says, confidence dripping from every word as his thumb presses down, stroking right below my hole in rhythm with his fingers. "I could keep you here all night. Begging."

I would let him. I would do whatever he wanted me to. I love the way he talks when he's in control—I used to hate how much I wanted to give him everything, but now it feels right. I want to give him exactly what he's asking for.

"Actually, don't move," he says firmly. "And that means don't touch yourself. We're both going to get what we want tonight."

He jumps off the bed, his briefs clinging to his ass perfectly as I watch him go into the bathroom. He comes back out with a toy in his hand. "What is that?" I ask. It doesn't look like a dildo, but it's definitely not a butt plug, either.

"A prostate massager," he says, and my face must show my confusion because he laughs. "It's really intense, like that spine-tingling orgasm, basically does exactly what it says it will—massages your prostate. This way, we both get something in our ass. You can try it another night, but tonight, I'm gonna make sure you feel me every time you sit down tomorrow."

He strips out of his underwear and quickly lubes up his fingers before working himself open for just a minute or so. I'm mentally kicking myself for not being the one to prep him, but getting to watch him blows me away. He looks so sexy on his knees with his head back, reaching behind him to work the toy in. He's mesmerizing, especially with the way his dark blue eye shadow plays up the dramatic angles of his face, and the glint of silver jewelry on his eyebrow and his earrings somehow highlight his natural beauty.

"You gonna keep eye fucking me or you want me to actually fuck you, hot shot?" he asks as he rolls the condom on and lubes himself up.

"Show me what you've got, K," I taunt as he crawls up the bed behind me.

KIERAN

Producer: "Your friend at the event seemed to know Jace as well, and she was surprised to see you two together. Could you give us literally anything about why?"

Kieran: "I think most people would be surprised to run into someone they haven't seen in thirteen years."

It really has been a long time since I've topped, but I'm determined to fuck him just as well as he fucked me. Maybe better. My cock twitches with the reminder of what he did to me last time, and the anticipation in my ass from the untouched prostate massager only makes me harder.

Jace is spread out, waiting for me, arms braced on the mattress with his back arched just right. His ass is up, his hole flushed pink from my prepping and glistening with lube. He glances over his shoulder, eyes hooded, lips parted, and it knocks the breath out of me for a second. He looks wrecked already, and I've barely gotten started.

"Don't hold back on me," he dares.

I line myself up, one hand gripping his hip, the other wrapped around the base of my cock as I press forward. The first moment I'm inside him steals both our air, the tight heat pulls a groan out of me I can't swallow down. His knuckles go white where he grips the sheets, but then he exhales slowly, relaxing for me.

"That's it," I whisper, rocking shallowly, easing deeper with every slow and steady roll of my hips. "Fuck, you feel unreal." I praise him as I rub his back and continue to press into him.

Once I'm fully seated inside, I pause, taking a moment to enjoy just how amazing he feels, how fucking soft and warm and *tight* he is. I'm trying to let him adjust, but I can't help grinding against him, letting him feel me fill him. My fingers trail down his spine, then settle at his waist. "How does it feel to have all of me inside you?" I rasp, leaning close enough that my breath fans over his ear.

"Fuck me, and we'll find out."

I smirk. Challenge accepted.

I draw back slowly, then slam into him hard enough to shove him forward on the bed, my own moan tangling with his cry of pleasure. I set a rhythm that's punishing yet steady, each thrust testing the edge of his composure as I attempt to hold him in place with what's probably a bruising grip as I fuck into him.

Every breathless sound he makes winds me tighter. But underneath the lust, something else is gnawing at me, trying to demand my attention, even though now is not the time to get emotional.

I reach for the remote for my toy, thumb brushing over the smooth plastic before clicking it on. It hums to life inside of me, the sudden vibration combined with how amazing he feels around my cock punches a noise out of me I don't recognize, and Jace's head jerks toward the sound.

"Kieran..." His voice is gravelly, but there's wonder in it too.

I drive into him again, harder, and the toy pushes against that spot inside me with perfect timing. The dual sensation floods me, dizzying and pushing me closer to unraveling. I grip his hips even harder and fuck him like I've been waiting years to—because maybe I have.

The sheets are completely twisted in his grip, forehead pressed down, muscles trembling beneath me. "Fucking hell, you're good at this, baby," he pants—and not in that teasing tone he used earlier. Not at all. The way he says baby causes my thrusts to stutter.

He starts fucking himself back on my cock while I snap myself out of it, meeting me thrust for thrust, until he suddenly pants out, "Switch."

"What?"

"Switch with me, I want to fuck you now. I want to be the one pulling those filthy fucking moans out of your mouth, not some toy."

Before I can argue, he's moved off my dick and is on his knees, facing me on the bed. He reaches behind me, fingers brushing my ass, finding the base of the toy, and I grunt when he eases it out. He gasps when he sees it vibrating. I can't help but chuckle at the way his eyes widen.

"Yeah, I'm definitely trying that sometime, but right now, I need to be the one inside you."

"Please," I beg as he rolls a condom onto his leaking dick and slicks it up with lube. "Feel so empty right now, need you."

"On your back," he orders, and I grab a pillow, placing it under me. He settles between my hips, bringing my legs up to wrap around him as he lines himself up with my hole and guides his cock inside me, inch by glorious inch.

He pushes in slowly, and my back arches, a moan tearing out of me before I can stop it. The toy was good—better than good—but it doesn't compare.

"Fuck," I groan, clawing at the sheets. "I love that toy, but your cock feels so much better."

Jace groans above me, bracing himself as he bottoms out. His jaw's tight, sweat dripping down his temple. "Good," he grits out. "Don't forget that the next time you think about using it. You're mine, and I want you to say that every time I'm inside you."

I nod automatically because there's no room for anything else when he starts to move. My body clenches around him, wanting to keep him inside of me. He curses, his hips stuttering like he's already close.

"God, Kieran," he pants, one hand grabbing my thigh and shoving it higher. "You're so fucking tight. I could stay here forever."

"Then stay," I gasp, wrapping my arms around his shoulders, pulling him closer until his chest presses to mine. I try not to think about the double meaning behind the word as it leaves my mouth. "Stay. Just—please—don't stop."

He plows into me exactly the way I need him to, and it feels more intimate face-to-face like this. My legs flex, and all I can think about is how right this feels with him. How wrong I was to ever say things could be fake between us. I open my eyes—that I must have closed at some point—needing to see him as he fucks me so perfectly. He's looking right at me with such admiration and awe as I let out a gasp. His gaze flickers to my mouth, and I want to tell him to kiss me, to reach up and kiss him myself, but I can't breathe, can't move at all. I'm frozen in place as he drives me closer and closer to the edge with how amazing he's making me feel.

And just when I'm about to lose it, he pulls out suddenly, leaving me empty.

"Jace!" I shout in protest, but he's already flipping me, pressing me down onto my stomach and lifting my hips back up, only to push back inside of me. The angle has me crying out at how much deeper it feels.

"Couldn't stand not seeing your ass swallow my cock," he growls, smacking my ass with his palm. "You're so fucking pretty, baby, but I needed to see your slutty hole suck me in too."

The slap of his hips against mine echoes through the room, and every thrust makes me jolt forward, cheek pressed into the sheets. He drags a hand up my spine, tangling in my hair and yanking my head back just enough to hold me exactly how he wants me, to force me to feel the stretch of his cock with every pounding stroke.

"God, you make the filthiest sounds," he taunts, breath hot against my ear. "Like you'd do anything for me to keep filling you."

"I would," I gasp, pushing back against him, greedy for everything he's giving me. "Don't stop, Jace, please—fuck, don't stop."

He chuckles low and angles his hips just right to hit that spot that has me clenching around him. "Not until you're begging me to let you come. You think you're ready for that yet? Or do you need me to ruin you a little more first?"

I can't even form a reply. The only noise that leaves my mouth is a ragged breath that pulls another laugh out of him. His thrusts slow to a grind, forcing me to feel every inch sliding in and out until I'm trembling with frustration.

"Say it," he murmurs, biting at my shoulder. "Say how much you need *me*. Not your toy, or your hand, or anyone else— just me."

"Just you. Need you, Jace. Please."

"Good," he says, his thrusts slow, giving me the opposite of what I thought he'd do.

"What are you—?"

"If I come now, I'll be done. And I want to feel you inside me again before that."

When he finally does slip free, I roll onto my side, panting. He looks wrecked already—curly hair stuck to his forehead, pupils blown wide, cock still hard and dripping as he pulls off the condom. I drag him down with me, pressing him onto his back.

"Does that mean I'm the better top?" I tease. He smirks and watches me, chest heaving.

He flips over, giving me full access to his perfect ass once again, and I quickly reapply lube to my still-condom-covered shaft before I press inside. He curses under his breath. His hands clutch the pillows, and he groans as I fill him back up.

"God, Kieran," he moans, head turning to the side. "You feel… Fuck, you feel even better than I'd imagined when you take me like this."

I fuck him with everything I have. The power I feel while topping him is surprisingly addicting, watching this big, beautiful man wither beneath me. The sounds falling from his mouth while he takes my cock are enough to make me come.

He's meeting my thrusts once again, and I see his hand trying to stroke himself between his body and the mattress.

I push him down onto the mattress even more, so he has no choice but to rub his aching cock against the sheets. "You want to come? Go ahead, baby. Make a mess for me."

He gasps, body tightening all at once, and then he's spilling across the bed, groaning into the pillow as his ass clenches tighter around me. The pulsing drag of his release milking me is too much for me to fight, and I'm pulled over the edge with him, moaning his name against his damp skin as I fill the condom inside him.

The aftershocks roll through both of us until I collapse against him, panting as I catch my breath. He reaches back blindly, finding my hand and threading our fingers together as if he can't stand to let me go even when we're both wrung out and shaking.

"You're so perfect, K. I will never recover from this, from you," he whispers as we lie here, tangled in each other.

I can't respond aloud to that. Because I feel the exact same way. I don't think I ever truly recovered from him in the first place, just buried my feelings under my hurt and anger.

I know we'll have to talk about it soon, especially if I want this to be real. I just hope that conversation doesn't undo what we've built.

"Come on, let's go get cleaned up, then we can change the sheets," I say instead.

JACE

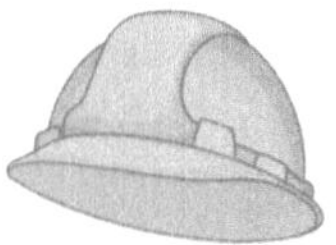

Producer: "Are you concerned at all about how different your lifestyle is from Kieran's?"

Jace: "Obviously Kieran has a lot more money than I do these days, but we're from the same place. I don't think he'll judge me for it. Besides, I'm proud of the life I've built for myself."

"I hope you're ready for the reminder of what life in New York City is like for us regular people," I tease as we pull up to my building.

Kieran rolls his eyes, smiling as he responds. "I think I'll manage."

Yesterday was great. Kieran had to do his solo interviews for the show in the morning, and I got to have some quality bonding time snuggling with Freddie. Then his parents came into the city for dinner. We met them at a fancy steakhouse, and unless he managed to call or text them beforehand, there hadn't been any time off camera, so I doubt he warned them our relationship was fake.

They seemed genuinely surprised when I introduced myself, obviously recognizing my name. Kieran gave them a quick explanation that, yes I was *that* Jace Ryan, and how, with the way the show was set up, we didn't know who we were talking to when we chose to move in together. They moved on from their initial confusion quickly, and were just as great as I remember. I'm trying my best not to read into why he didn't seem to have warned his parents that things between us aren't real.

After dinner, we attempted to watch a movie at Kieran's place, but ended up swapping blowjobs instead, taunting the other about who was better. He even cuddled up against me as we fell asleep together.

It was another perfect day with him that didn't feel fake at all.

Now we're doing my home visit. "Try not to be overwhelmed by how fancy my place is," I say with a wink as I punch in the code to unlock the main door to my building. He lets out a short laugh before we cram onto the elevator with the camera crew, because god forbid we have a moment alone.

"Home sweet home," I announce as I fit the key into the door then hold it open as I motion for everyone to enter.

When we're all inside, I stand in the middle of the space and clap my hands together. "Tour time, my kitchen is right there." I wave my right hand out toward the kitchen that's the size of Kieran's dining room table. "The living space." I nod to the couch that's set up in front of a TV without a coffee table because there isn't enough room. "Bathroom and bedroom." I motion with my other hand to the two doors in the small apartment. "So much easier than your place, darling," I tease, winking at Kieran.

"Hey, you have a bedroom." He shrugs with a big grin. "That's all I care about."

There's pounding at the door, and my stomach drops. I was hoping to have more time to warn them, so I sprint to answer it. I swing the door open, rush into the hallway, and slam it closed behind me, holding the handle so the camera people can't attempt to follow.

Joey and Patrick are standing in the hallway, looking amused by my dramatic appearance, but I rush to talk before they can say anything. "Hey, guys, so excited to see you. Listen. Real quick." My words are sort of blending together with how fast I'm talking, but they seem to be keeping up. I drop my tone so there's no chance I'll be heard through the door. "I didn't tell you on the phone because I didn't think you'd believe me, but I matched with Kieran Delaney on the show, and I need you guys to be chill and not embarrass me on camera. He is still pissed at me, or he was. I don't know anymore, honestly. But we agreed to fake date for the show, except it doesn't feel fake, and I'm trying to win him over for real."

They're both wearing the same shocked expression when one of the guys from the show knocks on the door. "Everything okay, Jace?"

"Great," I call back, giving my uncles a final warning look. They quickly nod, and I swing the door back open, pretending like nothing happened and that wasn't super weird. "Kieran, these are my uncles, Joey and Patrick."

Kieran arches a pierced brow in my direction but doesn't ask what that was all about. "Hey, great to meet you." He holds out a hand, which Joey quickly accepts, shaking it.

"It's nice to meet you, Kieran."

I should have known Patrick wouldn't blindly play along, though. He holds his arms open. "Handshakes are so damn formal, can I hug you instead?" Kieran looks at me again, laughing, probably at how red my cheeks feel, before accepting Patrick's offered embrace. I'm grateful it's a pretty normal hug that doesn't last long until Patrick steps back and opens his mouth again. "Wow, what are the chances Jace would meet his favorite YouTuber on a reality show!"

"Patrick," I scold. Trying to make it clear with my glare that we should drop that conversation immediately.

"He did mention he was a fan," Kieran responds with a smirk. "But we also met long before that."

"Oh good!" Patrick says, clapping as he sits down next to his husband on the couch. Neither of them are small men; Patrick is even taller than me with a similar build, yet they sit right next to each other on the couch like they couldn't possibly stand to have any space between them. "Do we get to talk about high school?" he asks with a giant smile that I know means trouble.

"No—"

"Absolutely not," Kieran and I answer at the same time, though mine is a bit firmer.

Patrick shrugs, grin still in place. "Are you sure? Because I've always wondered—"

"Behave," Joey interrupts, squeezing his husband's knee firmly as he does.

"Fine, fine. I'll save that for my wedding toast," Patrick says with a wink.

Joey shakes his head fondly. "Don't worry, I'll keep him away from microphones," he promises with a soft smile.

"That's why you're my favorite uncle."

"Come on, kid, after everything I've done for you?" Patrick asks in mock offense. "I take you into my home, this strange child I'd just met, get you a job, take you in under my wing at work and teach you everything I know, and this is the thanks I get?"

"I was eighteen when we met," I say with a laugh.

"A strange kid," Patrick repeats seriously.

"And you're barely twelve years older than me," I remind him with another laugh.

"Yes, so much older and wiser," he deadpans.

Kieran laughs beside me, and I turn to him. "I had planned for us to all go out together, but just say the word and I'll un-invite them," I offer, making him laugh again. The sound settles my nerves as I look into his blue eyes that are twinkling in amusement.

"Absolutely not, they're coming," Kieran confirms. "What are we doing?"

"A walking tour."

"Like a tourist?" he asks skeptically.

"Sort of." I shrug. "I thought it would be fun to walk around and point out some of the places we've helped build, and we can check out some of my favorite spots to eat on the way." I knew my apartment wouldn't be big enough for us to all hang out in, so I'd given the show some suggestions for the day, wanting to include my uncles because they really are my best friends.

Kieran gives me a warm smile. "That sounds perfect. I'd love to see what you've done."

And it is perfect. We have an amazing day. Kieran fits in with Joey and Patrick effortlessly, joking around and teasing like he's known them for years. He asks me questions about my job in a way that seems like he genuinely wants to know more. The food is great, which I expected, and everything is so easy, so right.

Joey pulls me aside when we fall behind the camera crew at the end of the day while walking back to our building, softly saying, "Doesn't seem fake to me."

My heart races at the confirmation that I'm not the only one thinking that, and I bite my lip to hold back all the things I want to blurt out about how perfect he is and how great I think we are together. Instead, I respond with a small smile and nod before I pick up my pace to hold hands with Kieran for the rest of the way.

"I think we've got enough for the day," one of the guys from the show says after we're all back, crammed into my apartment.

"Oh no, done already?" I ask sarcastically, already opening the door for them to leave.

"See you in the morning, Jace." They laugh on the way out. They seem like nice enough people, but being on camera all day every day is getting pretty old.

When I've shut the door behind them and turn back into my apartment, Kieran is standing in my kitchen across from the small counter island that's the only—sort of—table option. There's only room for two people to sit, and Joey and Patrick are both there, looking smug.

As soon as I make my way back over to them, they immediately start cracking up. Obnoxiously, uncontrollably, for far too long.

I cross my arms and glare at them, waiting for their outburst to end.

"Okay, we're done being good for the cameras," Joey finally gets out between laughs.

"Holy shit, it's really you!" Patrick says, turning his attention to Kieran. My stomach twists into knots. I have no idea what they're going to say to him, but I think it's too late for me to stop it. "He hasn't shut up about you the entire time since he moved in with us," Patrick continues.

Kieran squints at me. "Umm, really? Why?"

"It's not as weird as they're making it sound," I insist.

"Well, we were the ones who brought him to your house the day you turned him down after graduation," Patrick starts.

"He talked about you the whole drive here," Joey takes over. "He told us all about why he came out to his dad after he punched that kid who threatened you, and how he was worried about you because you stopped posting videos," he adds, and I feel like my blood drains right out of my body.

"Oh my god, shut up!" I hiss. *This can't be happening.*

KIERAN

Producer: "What are you most excited about for your life with Jace after the show ends?"

Kieran: "You not being around all the time."

*J*oey's words replay over and over again in my mind. *"Why he came out to his dad after he punched that kid who threatened you."*

He chose to come out to his dad? He punched David? Joey said it so casually, it must be true. I turn to give Jace my full attention, feeling like my world just shifted on its axis. Like everything I wholeheartedly believed was a lie.

My eyes are wide as I slowly blink, attempting to focus on the man in front of me, to not get lost in the memory of the one I thought I knew back then. I have to force my jaw to close as I try to process the thoughts flying through my head.

Finally, I remember how to speak. "You punched David?" I ask. Still completely confused by why he would've punched his best friend. *Joey said it was because of what David did to me.* But that doesn't make any sense at all when Jace was the one who sent him there.

Right?

"Uh, yeah. You didn't know that? I thought Liv would have told you about that," he mutters.

"We agreed to not talk about you," I admit. "And you came out to your dad voluntarily?" I'm unsure what to focus on when I apparently had so many details wrong.

"Wow, would you look at the time," Joey says. I hear their chairs scraping against the floor, but I can't look away from Jace.

"Yeah, so late. We'll just go back to our place now, byeeee," Patrick calls out before the front door closes.

Jace and I are still standing in his kitchen across from each other, gazes locked as I wait for him to elaborate on what I don't know.

"Yeah, I came out to my dad voluntarily." He finally answers my question, but I can tell there's more from the way he's cautiously eyeing me.

"Why?"

Jace bites his lip, staring at me for another long moment before finally taking in a deep breath. "Because he insulted you."

"I'm sure that wasn't the first time he insulted me, or other kids like me. So why did you decide to randomly come out to him after being so against it for so long? What am I missing? That's a huge jump."

Jace looks nervous, taking a steading breath before speaking. "My dad implied that you deserved to be attacked by David, to end up in the hospital, because you're attracted to other men," he admits. I knew Jace's father was an asshole. He'd made it clear that his dad was the one he was the most concerned about finding out that we'd been together. *So why would he suddenly come out to him?*

"I was a mess after not knowing why you weren't in school

the two days after I was held up at practice and showed up super late to our meeting," he continues. "I thought maybe you were mad at me for standing you up. But I didn't have your number to text you. I also knew you wouldn't have missed school for that, so I was concerned you were sick or something. Then I found out David hurt you, and I punched him in the school hallway. I would have done more but my dad pulled me off him. When he was lecturing me about staying out of trouble, he made that comment about you deserving it, and I snapped."

"What did you do?" I whisper, picturing the eighteen-year-old Jace in a whole new light.

"Said something about belonging in the hospital too, because I enjoyed having your dick in my mouth."

A shocked laugh escapes from my chest, breaking some of the tension between us. "You did not."

"I did." He laughs, posture relaxing a little bit. "I was done trying to live my life imitating such an awful man."

"And he kicked you out?"

"He told me he didn't have a gay son, so I wasn't his son anymore."

"Holy shit, Jace, I had no idea."

"You had a lot going on at the time," he reminds me gently. "Including a concussion."

I shake my head. "No, Jace, I mean I had no idea about… so many things. I thought you sent David to end things. That you had told him to threaten me, maybe even to beat me up."

His face immediately falls, he looks horrified, shaking his head as he responds. "No! Kieran, no. I had no idea for days that he'd even gone there that night. He said he followed us another time and had seen what we were doing. That he was looking out for me, but I swear I had no idea. Apparently, that's how he knew where to find you. He suggested my dad hold me late at practice that day. As soon as I found out, I punched him. I wish I could have done more," he insists.

Holy shit.

When we were eighteen, after all those times in the woods, I'd forgiven Jace for his past bullying even though he'd never apologized. I'd seen firsthand how confused and scared he was about his feelings for me, and I'd moved on from our negative past. I'd even started hoping we might have a future beyond baseball season. So, when I'd thought he sent David to hurt me, everything was made so much worse by the thought that I'd been such a fool to think he'd ever changed. It felt like I was an experiment for him, and he discarded me when he was done.

Now, thirteen years later, I'm finding out that I was wrong.

Jace has changed. He probably even tried to tell me. He'd wanted to talk to me, and I wouldn't let him.

But I believe him.

I fully and completely believe his side of the story. There isn't a single part of me that doubts this new-to-me version of the truth.

"Wait, what were you trying to apologize for when you showed up at my house that day if you didn't send David?"

"I felt horrible that David inserted himself between us, and that I hadn't realized he was on to us before it was too late. I felt like it was my fault that you got hurt because it was someone who I thought was my friend who'd caused it, but I never even considered that you would think I told him to go there." He sounds panicked trying to explain. "Holy shit, no wonder you wouldn't hear me out that day. I can't believe you talked to me at all once you realized who I was in Atlanta."

"Fuck, Jace. I'm sorry I didn't listen to what you had to say back then. At the time, I was so hurt, and I tried to rationalize what happened between us. In my mind, it made sense that, since it was your last baseball game, that you were done with me. Sending David to threaten me not to say anything made the most sense."

My chest feels like it's cracking wide open right now. I

wasted over a decade holding hate in my heart for Jace, and yeah, he did some really shitty things to me, but the man before me has proven he's become so much more than his teenage mistakes.

"No, you have nothing to apologize for. You were hurt, and we were so young. I should have just blurted it out. I even tried to get your number from Liv to text you, but she must've blocked me too."

"Uh, yeah. We both blocked you on everything," I say, which reminds me of something else I should admit to Jace in the name of honesty. "Also, I did tell her about us… after the hospital. I didn't know you'd come out to your dad at that point, obviously, but I was so hurt, and I just needed to talk about you with someone who'd get it."

He gives me a small smile, reaching for my hand, and I take his confidently.

"It's okay, darli—"

"Baby," I plead. "Call me baby."

"Fuck, baby, come here," Jace says, tugging me toward him and wrapping his big arms around me. I sink into his embrace, needing his comfort, and without my permission, tears start flowing down my cheeks.

"Jace, I'm so sorry."

"Me too, K. I'm so fucking sorry for all the pain I caused you, intended or not."

I press my face into his chest, tears soaking into his shirt as I shake my head. "We wasted so much time, Jace. Thirteen years. I hated you for something you didn't even do. And I don't know what to do with that. I don't know how to forgive myself for all the wasted years."

His arms tighten around me as he tries to hold me together. "I'd give anything to get those years back, but we can't. We probably needed that time to grow individually, and look, baby, we get a second chance. We can start over now."

I pull back just enough to see his face, his eyes shining with the same grief I feel.

"I've wanted you since I was sixteen, back when I first called you Sparkles. And I never fucking stopped, Kieran. Not once."

I'm pretty sure I've cycled through every human emotion since I stepped onto this show, but this one—the weight of hearing him say it out loud after all these years—feels like it might crack me open completely.

Wait.

Something else he said registers. "You said you were late that day? You still came?"

His shoulders sag, and he nods. "Yeah, I was so pissed off. Of course, the day I'd been planning to kiss you, I'd be almost two hours late."

That's the final crack.

His words shatter the final barrier I'd been hiding my heart behind.

He'd been planning to kiss me when we were eighteen? He showed up that night, and was upset, not that he'd missed out on a blowjob or his good luck charm before a game, but because he didn't get to kiss me?

I'm done holding back. I shift slightly, grab both sides of Jace's face in my hands, pull him down to me, and crash my lips to his.

JACE

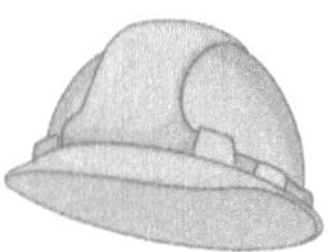

Producer: "What's the hardest thing about dating in this environment?"

Jace: "I think knowing that everything is being filmed makes it easier to second-guess yourself, to question what you should say or do."

*K*ieran is kissing me.
Holy fucking shit.
Kieran is kissing me!
Kieran! Is kissing! Me!

It takes a moment for my brain to restart after the initial moment of his lips landing on mine. All I'm aware of is how *right* it feels.

When I realize I'm a fully functioning person and can actually participate in this moment instead of being frozen in awe that it's happening, I remember to kiss him back. I bring my hands up to the sides of his face, revelling in the fact that Kieran is actually kissing me. A kiss that I've fantasized about for nearly half my life, but gave up on ever hoping would happen years ago.

I deepen the kiss, teasing the seam of his mouth with my tongue and groan when he opens up for me so willingly. He lets me explore his mouth for a moment before fighting me for control. It's sloppy and desperate and perfect as our tongues tangle together.

I shift one hand to thread my fingers into his hair, holding him to me and the other moves down his strong back until it settles on his firm ass. I use my hold there to pull his perfect body flush against mine. I'm overwhelmed by my desire for this man. Tender feelings, words like *mine* and *forever* and *love* fight for my attention. But right now, I give into my lust, let the burning need I feel for Kieran take over as I grind my erection against his through our pants, desperate for any friction I can find.

His lips on mine are everything I've ever fantasized about, but are somehow also so much more. I've never felt more connected to the person I'm kissing. Each moan that escapes his lips feels like it breathes new life into me. For the first time in my life, I feel whole.

Ever since I first noticed him, Kieran's been the center of my world.

I used to hate him for it—target him, blame him—for how distracting he was. For how confused his presence made me. When everything finally clicked and I realized I was attracted to him, he became all I could think about: when our next hookup would be, what makeup he'd wear the next day, if he'd ever think about me the way I thought about him.

After everything imploded at the end of senior year, I was left with so many regrets. I constantly thought about everything I'd say to him if I ever got the chance. I was heartbroken, hurt, grieving, and angry all at once.

His online presence let me feel like I was still part of his world, even if from a distance. It also meant I never really had to get over him, and I didn't try to. Instead, I leaned into it and embraced being a fan. I watched his growth, followed what he was doing, and cherished everything he posted online.

And now I know, really know, that Kieran will always be at the center of my world. This show brought us back together, gave us a second chance, and proved something I think I've known all along: he's it for me. It feels like we're connected on a soul level that I'm not strong enough to fight. Don't even want to attempt to fight. Because Kieran Delaney will forever hold my heart in his hands.

If this kiss is the start of something more, something real, I will spend every moment of the rest of our lives proving to Kieran that I deserve his forgiveness, that I will be the best damn partner he could ever imagine. I will spend every moment trying to make him as happy as he's making me right now.

He lets out another moan from deep in his throat and I can't ignore my aching cock for any longer. I let go of my hold on him while maintaining the kiss, moving to take off his pants as quickly as I can. As soon as he realizes what I'm doing, his hands are racing to undo mine, and in record time, we both have our pants and underwear shoved down our thighs so that our straining erections can line up with nothing between them.

Kieran pulls back and I shift to leave sloppy kisses down his neck, sucking hard when I remember the hickey that led to one of our first hookups all of those years ago. I want to cover him in my marks. I want him to always think of me when he looks in the mirror and sees the evidence of my feelings for him.

He pulls me away for a moment so that he can spit onto my dick, and if I wasn't already leaking from everything else that's happening, I'm sure that image would have done it. I take a moment to line up our cocks between us before wrapping my hand around us both. I add my own spit to the mix before using it to jerk us both off together in my large hand, loving the feel of his dick rubbing against my own.

We both stare at the visual of our cocks moving together in my fist for a moment before we seem to remember what we were doing at the same time, snapping our gazes back up to each other's swollen lips. With my hand occupied, Kieran brings his back up to my hair, tugging my face to his, and resumes kissing me like his life depends on it.

I feel like I could already come. My body is on fire from how hot making out with him is. Add in my bare cock rubbing against his in my tight fist, and I'm struggling to hold off at all. He's shifting his hips with my movements, fucking up into my fist, rubbing against my shaft in a way that's completely intoxicating.

And I know I won't last.

I wrap my other hand around his body, running my finger down his crease until I can tease his hole. He lets out a filthy moan when I do, so I increase my movements and do it again. Kieran lets out a strained cry as his cock jerks in my grip and it sends me immediately over the edge following him. That moment of bliss seems to stretch on and on as I work us through our orgasms, only stopping when he swats my hand away.

We both take a step back, and I try to commit this moment to memory. Kieran looks completely wrecked, lips swollen, cheeks flushed, his makeup smeared and his hair pointing in all different directions.

He's beautiful, and perfect, and *mine*.

"Well, tonight has been full of surprises," he chuckles, moving to wet some paper towels for us to get cleaned up.

"I love surprises," I add with a laugh.

I really hope we're not done surprising each other.

58

KIERAN

Producer: "Early on, you'd mentioned hoping to find someone you could be fully yourself around, someone who was there for you and not your online presence. Do you feel that way with Jace?"

Kieran: "I… yeah. Actually, I think I do."

e're walking through Central Park, hand in hand, filming the second day of Jace's visit, but I still feel like I'm waking up from a strange dream, trying to adjust to my surroundings after everything I thought I knew has changed.

I was confident Jace and I had no chance at a real future because of our past when we first reconnected on the show, but now? Now, I'm surrounded by more choices, and I don't know what's right.

Did last night confirm things could actually work out between us? And if they did, does that mean we should continue with the show as planned? Or should we quit and pursue a real relationship outside its structure without all the pressure to get engaged and married in a matter of days? I don't know if it's fair of me to go back on the plans we've made, or if I've just been swept up in the romance filming and maybe things will fall apart when it's over. We still have to navigate real life together, see how it works in our regular routines and schedules, so maybe the plan we have is still the best course of action.

I've always tried to remain confident and go after what I want, but today I could barely choose between the two outfits I'd packed. I'm in no shape to be contemplating major life decisions.

It's fine though, I remind myself. I don't have to make any changes today. The original plan is still in place; we don't need to break our show contracts or decide on forever right now. We're still filming as the perfect couple we've been presenting to the world.

Jace squeezes my hand, slowing our pace, and he pulls me off the side of the path we're walking on in the park. "Hey, can we stop here for a minute?"

I shrug. "Sure, are you finally going to tell me what we're doing here?" I ask with a laugh. When I'd tried to get details out of him on the drive over, he'd seemed nervous, not looking at me as he claimed we were just enjoying the outdoors.

"Yeah," he admits before taking a deep breath. "I was thinking about what we talked about last night. How you thought I sent David that day. I hate thinking that your final memory in our woods was such a horrible one."

"Hey, it's not your fault," I try to reassure him. "I know that now. I really am sorry I didn't listen to you back then."

"It's okay. You're here with me now, that's what really matters." He gives me a small smile as he squeezes my hand. "Those woods always felt special to me. They were the only place where I could truly be myself, could be with the person I wanted to be with. I was wondering if you might play along and give me a do-over. A chance to reclaim a different spot as ours and play out what I hoped would happen that day. This was the best I could think of in the city," he adds, gesturing to the trees surrounding us.

I think about what he said last night, about how he'd planned to kiss me that day if he'd been on time, and I can't help but wonder how different both of our lives might look today if that had gone like he'd hoped. I guess we'll never know.

But he's right. We're both here now, together, surrounded by different trees, and it's easy to forget the cameras and that so many people will see this moment play out on their screens. All that matters is the man standing before me, asking me to give him a second chance.

I might not be ready to make any real decisions about our future, but this choice is easy. "Jace, will you kiss me?"

His whole body relaxes as a huge smile lights up his face before he leans in to bring his lips to mine. He cups my jaw in his large hand to tilt my face up the way he wants it, moving his lips against mine in slow, sweet motions that leave my heart aching. It's nothing like last night's kiss that was full of desperation and lust. It's romantic and confident, and it feels like an admission of just how much he cares about me.

How does this man continue to break down walls I didn't even realize I'd built to protect myself?

He teases my mouth with his tongue but keeps the kiss mostly innocent. A moment worthy of the airtime I'm sure it will get across the country. When he pulls back, I'm not ready for it to be over, and find myself leaning toward him again without thought.

He chuckles and squeezes my hand again. "There is one more thing," he says slowly, reaching into his coat. He pulls out a sparkly notebook.

"What's that?" I ask, unable to shake the feeling that I've seen it before, but I'm not sure where.

He looks at it for a long moment, letting out a deep exhale

before glancing back up at me. "The first day of junior year, I took this from you," he admits, and I suck in a sharp breath as I remember that day. The first time he called me Sparkles.

There's no way that's actually the same notebook he's holding now.

But as I look more closely, I see how dull it actually is, how worn the edges appear. My heart is racing as I wait for him to explain why the hell he still has it and why he's giving it to me in front of the cameras.

"I should have thrown it away because we both know I was too big of an asshole to have returned it," he says with a chuckle. "But for some reason, I hid it instead—I couldn't risk my dad finding a sparkly journal in my things—and I had no idea why." He rubs his thumb across the cover, smiling fondly at it. "At first, I think I just liked having something that reminded me of you. But then when we stopped talking, I decided to write you an apology."

"When we were eighteen?" I manage to ask, voice barely a whisper as emotions threaten to close my throat.

"Yeah. I realized I might never get the chance to say it to you, but I needed to get the words out, and this felt like my best option." He hands me the journal, and I flip it open to the first page. At the top, in handwriting I distantly recognize as his, is the date

June 26th, 2012

and under that is a letter addressed to me, one that lasts for multiple pages. I try to make out some of the words, blinking away the tears that are attempting to fall. I know I'll need to read this in more detail when I'm not being filmed.

I flip past the letter and am shocked to see more entries. "What else is in here?"

"The things I wished I could say to you for the last thirteen years."

I swear my heart stops beating entirely.

How did I ever hate this man? How did I believe that he was the example of who I should protect my heart from?

I read the next entry, it's much shorter.

> *July 23rd 2012*
> *Kieran,*
> *You posted a video today. I'm so glad that you didn't let what happened break you. I'm proud of you.*
> *J*

I flip to another.

> *April 25th 2013,*
> *Kieran,*
> *1 million subscribers! Congrats on the gold creator award, I'm sure you'll earn the diamond in no time!*
> *J*

The next one.

> *August 25th 2014*
> *Kieran,*
> *You announced your first brand deal today. That's so amazing. I can't wait to see what else you accomplish.*
> *J*

There aren't a ton, but it seems like all of the major moments in my career are mentioned, spanning the years that we were apart.

> *November 1st, 2018*
> *Kieran,*
> *I bought the latest Sparkles' line of products that came out today. I'm going to give them to my sister. I always love seeing your face blown up on ads in makeup stores and thinking back to the one you worked in.*
> *J*

I should probably be creeped out or worried that he's a total stalker or something.

But I love it. I love that the man I've never been able to forget—even if I thought it was because I hated him—never forgot me either.

"I know you didn't feel the same way, but I've never felt like things were over between us, Sparkles," Jace says softly. "Read the most recent entry."

My hands are shaking as I turn to the page with today's date.

> *February 12th, 2025*
> *Kieran,*
> *I'm going to ask you to marry me today. I know that it's still not real and that's okay, but I'm really happy to have you back in my life. Thanks for giving me a second chance.*
> *J*

I look up to find Jace already down on one knee, smiling up at me. "Kieran, when we first met, I never imagined we'd end up here one day, but I'm so glad that we have. Every day that you're in my life is better because of it." He opens the ring box he's holding, revealing a platinum band that matches my other jewelry. "Will you make me the happiest man alive? Will you marry me?"

Jace's note might have said this isn't real, but as I nod, choking out, "Yes! Of course I'll marry you," through tears I can't stop, it doesn't feel fake. Especially not when his hands are shaking as he slips the ring onto my finger, and definitely not when he kisses me again like he's trying to memorize the moment.

I know the cameras are still pointed at us, but somehow this feels right. It feels real.

And I don't think I want it to be anything else.

JACE

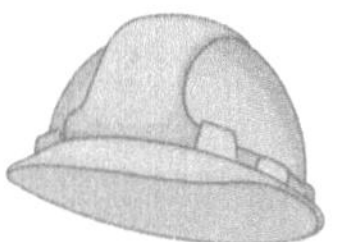

Producer: "Can you see yourself saying "I love you" soon? You did propose."

Jace: "Wait, have I not said that yet?"

$\mathcal{A}$ wedding when you aren't the one paying for anything is definitely the way to go. Not that Kieran would probably bat an eye at any of the prices, but I cannot imagine footing this bill with my own money; New York City prices are outrageous.

The proposal went even better than I'd hoped. I was a little worried about how Kieran would react to the park aspect after what David did to him in our old spot, but we talked about it afterwards, and he confirmed my hope that it was a reclaiming moment for us.

I also explained that I didn't think the producers would appreciate showing up in the morning and finding out that I had proposed the night before off camera like I'd really wanted to.

What we did was definitely better television, even if they've been begging to read what was in the journal ever since.

But Kieran and I are the only ones who ever need to know what it says.

I know our engagement isn't real and that Kieran would've said yes no matter how I asked, but it still felt like my one shot to propose to the man of my dreams. He deserves the best of everything, so I wanted to give it my all without making it a spectacle since so much of his life is already lived in the spotlight.

Things have been moving pretty quickly since the proposal. They've had everyone move back into the same hotel downtown where the ceremonies will take place at the end of the week. We've already gone tux shopping, picked out elaborate flower arrangements, confirmed our guest list, and last night they had us do a full tasting of the dinner menu options with the other couples on the show who are engaged. We've done countless interviews with Andy, talking to us individually and as couples, and even other pairings and groups that the producers hoped would make good television.

Now we're waiting to begin the thing I've been looking forward to the most: sampling all the wedding cake options.

"Hi, I'm Kayla." A woman with blonde hair pulled back and a white apron on comes to meet us while we wait at the table in the bakery.

"Hey, Kayla," I say with a small smile, trying to contain my excitement.

"Hi, I'm Kieran, and this is my fiancé, Jace, who forgot to introduce himself because he's already eyeing the cake."

"Sorry." I laugh, holding my hands up. "I'm just so excited about this part."

Kayla chuckles. "Good. That's what we like to hear. I've got six flavors for you to try today. Once you decide on your favorite, we'll talk fillings, frostings, and decorations."

Kayla sets down a tray with neat little squares of cake, each labeled with a tiny card with the flavors: chocolate ganache, lemon raspberry, vanilla bean, red velvet, strawberry, and carrot.

"Oh god," I groan. "How are we supposed to pick? I want them all already."

"I think I know what one I'll like the best, but let's try them," Kieran says, and that reminds me…

"Is red velvet still your favorite?" I ask, nudging the plate with red velvet toward him.

He turns to look at me, his fork hovering over the cake, and there's this small, surprised smile on his face. "You remember that?"

"Well, yeah," I say. "Bringing you that cupcake was my really smooth teenage excuse for us to spend more time together. I thought about that moment a lot, and I still always think of you whenever there's red velvet cake. Or cake in general. Or baked goods, really. I pretty much always think about you, and I'm not just saying that."

For a second, he doesn't move, just looks at me with that analytical expression that makes me feel like he's memorizing the moment. Then he finally takes a bite of the red velvet, and he smiles as he chews.

"Still my favorite," he says softly. "But this is the best red velvet ever because now you're here too."

My heart flutters the way it only ever does with him. I lean closer and whisper, "I really want to kiss you right now."

He doesn't bother whispering back, just steals the air from my lungs with a quick kiss that leaves Kayla politely pretending she's very invested in rearranging her sample tray.

Ever since our hometown visits, Kieran has been acting like we're in a real relationship, and it's given me hope that what we've built might last beyond the show.

I want to ask him if anything's changed so badly, but I don't want to burst this little bubble of happiness we're living in. Maybe I'll wait until after we're married because I really do want him to be my husband, and I can't risk us not making it to the altar.

I want to build a life with him. I want to support him, learn how to be a cat dad to Freddie, maybe even spend our nights cross-stitching on the couch together in our shared living room. Being with Kieran would give my life a sense of purpose I've never had before. I was always looking for the missing piece, but it's always been him.

I went along with the career Patrick offered me, and I was immensely grateful and surprised by how much I ended up enjoying it. I have a place where I live, but I chose it to be near my uncles; the only sense of home I feel there is when I'm spending time with them. I've spent so long going through the motions, taking what's handed to me instead of creating my own life.

I love building spaces where other people create their homes, their careers, their memories, but I've never had that for myself.

I will with Kieran, though, as long as he'll have me and keep me.

I want a partner and a home, and now I even want a cat. Having something real with Kieran feels like the first thing I've ever truly chosen for myself and I'm going to keep fighting for him… for us.

That's all I can think about as we go through the flavors one by one, trading bites. They're all so incredible, and I'd guess the chocolate ganache is a close second for Kieran. But he keeps sampling bites of red velvet and going back to it, so I know what we'll go with.

"Do you know what flavor you'd like for the cake?" Kayla asks.

"They're all great," I say, glancing at Kieran, "but I think we're going with red velvet."

Kieran blinks, surprised. "Really? I thought you liked the vanilla one best."

"I did," I admit, bumping my knee against his under the table. "But you love red velvet, and it was damn good. Plus, it reminds me of our woods. I want our wedding to have that one, baby."

His cheeks flush, and he shakes his head. "Thanks, Jace."

60

KIERAN

Producer: "If you had to sum up how you're feeling in three words today, what would you say?"

Kieran: "Three? There's no way. I'm feeling all the words."

*T*omorrow is our wedding day, and I'm freaking the fuck out.

Last night, we had drinks with Blake and Liam to celebrate us all getting married this weekend, and earlier today, their wedding... didn't happen.

And that's been eating away at me. I feel horrible for them, but I have to believe they'll work it out. We've spent a lot of time with them over the last two weeks, and I feel like we've all become friends. After the minor hurdle they had with Rachel, it seemed like they were inevitable.

Now, all I can think is "what if?"

What if Jace doesn't want to pretend to be married? What if he looks at me when I walk down the aisle and he realizes he can't do a fake forever? What if he breaks my heart at the altar? All because I didn't tell him how I really feel.

I've wanted to bring it up so many times since the proposal, but I'm so afraid of saying the wrong thing that I'd decided to wait until after the show was done filming to talk about everything since then there'd be no pressure or cameras. And we'd already be married.

But now I'm wishing I had been brave enough to have the conversation sooner. *There's still time,* my mind reminds me.

My life looks complete from the outside, but it's been missing someone to share it with. It's the reason I came on this show in the first place, and Jace makes my life feel full in a way nothing else ever has. He's everything I've wanted in a partner, even before I was ready to admit it.

Blake and Liam not making it to the altar is forcing me to face what it really means to stand in front of someone and promise forever. It shouldn't be fake. I shouldn't make light of the commitment because I'm scared. We've said all of this was pretend, but it's felt real for so long now, I don't even know when we stopped pretending. Or if we ever really did.

Jace feels like my forever, and I don't want to marry him while he's still thinking I'll hand him divorce papers the second the cameras stop rolling, like I said that first night together.

I don't want him walking down that aisle without knowing— really knowing—how fucking in love with him I am.

"K, what is going on with you? You've been so off all night." Liv's voice pulls me back into the moment. We're in my hotel room for the night since I'm supposed to be sleeping separately from Jace, but I keep zoning out on her.

"I need to talk to you," I say, standing from the bed and pulling her into the hotel bathroom with me. When the door is shut, and I confirm that there are no cameras in here, I turn to look right at her. "Liv, I can't do this."

Her brows lift in alarm. "Do what? Marry Jace?"

I drag my hands down my face. "Yes. No. I don't know. Blake and Liam didn't even make it into their ceremony, and all I can think is, what if that happens to us?" I'm unraveling, words spilling too fast from my panicking lips. "What if I walk down that aisle and he looks at me and decides he can't pretend anymore? What if he says no? What if I lose him in front of everyone?"

"Kieran."

"I keep thinking—what if he regrets all of this? What if—"

"Kieran," she says, much more seriously this time. She steps closer, putting her hands on my shoulders. "You're spiraling. And you're asking the wrong questions."

My throat feels tight. "What the hell does that mean?"

"It means you're so busy panicking about what Jace *might* feel that you're ignoring the truth."

I expect her to finish, but she just looks at me expectantly.

"Now is not the time for a dramatic pause, Liv! Spit it out!"

"I thought you might connect the dots there, but okay. K, that man has been in love with you since high school. And... I think you love him too."

The air fills back in my lungs at the realization that she's right. She's so fucking right. Jace has worn his heart on his sleeve the whole time we've been on this show. From night one, he said he wanted to do what I wanted, that he'd follow my lead. His proposal felt real. His journal entries were real. He remembered every little thing I shared, including my favorite cake.

Holy shit, I'm such an idiot.

He wants this to be as real as I do, I just haven't been ready to admit it to myself. I've been protecting myself, clinging to the plan, pretending that if it ended, I'd be fine.

But I absolutely wouldn't be.

The whole time, I've been guarding my heart from the one person I know would never break it again.

"What happened with Blake and Liam is because they kept

secrets," she continues softly. Everyone who's even peripherally aware of the show heard what went down by now.

"You know where silence gets people," she says pointedly. "So ask yourself, are you really about to walk down that aisle tomorrow and marry Jace without him knowing how you really feel?"

I swallow, letting all the pieces fall into place, acknowledging how right I know she is… especially when I think about how silence and refusing to talk to each other led me to hate him for thirteen years.

"You love him," she says knowingly. "And don't you dare stand there and try to deny it, because I've watched you fall. You're not panicking about losing him as a friend. He's it for you, and you know it."

Tears start falling down my cheeks as I nod in confirmation.

"So," she continues, crossing her arms, "you have two choices. Keep pretending it's just to protect your reputation. Something you're doing for the cameras and your brand. Or tell him the truth before you're at the altar tomorrow. Give him the chance to actually say yes to you."

I feel like I'm going to vomit, my past fears and anxieties of not being enough for other people, including him at one point, are popping up again.

"And what if he doesn't—"

"What if he does?" she shoots back instantly, shutting down the thought. "What if he's been waiting for you to stop being a coward and finally admit it? He's been obsessed with you since high school, Kieran. I think he's been trying to respect your boundaries this whole time."

Fuck.

I need to go and find him. I need to tell him how I feel, but even though I know that, I'm not moving. I'm frozen, terrified.

"You're scared? Good," Liv pushes, reading me so easily the way only a best friend can. "That means you care. But stop letting fear make your choices for you. Because if you stay silent and it all falls apart? That's on you. And we both know you'd never forgive yourself."

The room tilts around me, panic colliding with the clarity I'm finally feeling.

"Liv," I whisper.

She squeezes my shoulders. "Go find him. Say the words. You owe him the truth. I can't take another thirteen years of you waiting to find your way back to each other."

"This is why you're my best friend," I say, pulling her into a tight hug before running out of my room toward Jace's.

Just as I take off down the hall, Mitch starts storming after me. As predicted. He's probably cursing whoever cast me, but oh well.

"Kieran! I swear to God if you're about to cancel another ceremony! Where the hell are you running off to?" he yells.

"Don't worry, it's all good!" I yell back as the camera crew chases after me down the hallway, but they're still pretty far behind.

I pound on Jace's door, and when he opens it, he looks shocked to see me in such a panic. Joey and Patrick are in his room with him, as well as a couple of the camera crew, but they've all fallen silent at my sudden appearance.

"Jace, I need to talk to you," I demand, pushing my way into the room. I grab his hand and pull him into the bedroom of the suite he's in. I lock the door behind us but don't stop until I pull him into the bathroom, paranoid that even the bedroom might have cameras set up in it.

"What's going on?" he questions, worry written all over his face.

"Kieran! Get out of there! What is going on!" I hear Mitch yelling on the other side of the bedroom door, but I don't care. This is my moment.

"Jace, I can't do this—"

"What do you mean you can't?" he cuts in loudly, sounding completely panicked. "Are you backing out? Please don't—"

"No! Jace, no. You didn't let me finish." He looks heartbroken, and I need to get that look off his face immediately. "I can't do this if it's not real," I clarify, rushing to explain. "I can't stand out there tomorrow and say vows that you think are just for show when every single word I say to you in them is the truth."

Jace blinks, stunned, like my words don't compute. There's still so much commotion on the other side of the door. Patrick and Joey are yelling, probably attempting to drown out our conversation as they tell everyone to give us space. It's making the air between us feel even smaller, tighter, as he processes.

"I don't get it," he whispers, shaking his head. "What are you saying?"

"I'm saying—" My throat closes, and I have to force the words out over my fear. "I'm in love with you, Jace. I tried to pretend it was fake, tried to bury it, but I can't anymore. Not when I'm about to promise to love you forever on TV, and every cell in my body means it. I love you so much, and I want this to be real."

The world around us stops. The commotion outside seems to fade away and neither of us are breathing as his mouth falls open. For a moment, he looks like he's forgotten how to speak.

"I don't care about the cameras," I go on, my voice shaking. "I don't care about the show or what this does to my image or what people say. I don't care if my career disappears. I care about you. Only you. And if we're about to walk out there tomorrow and say our vows, then I want them to be real. I want this to be real. I love you, Jace. I need you to know how much I love you. I want to marry you, for real, with no end date. If you'll have me."

His hand trembles as he reaches out to grab mine. "Kieran…"

I sink to my knees on the cold bathroom floor, looking up at him. My heart is pounding so hard it feels like it's going to crack my ribs.

"Baby, now isn't the time for a blowjob," Jace whispers, his lips parted with surprise.

"Shut up, I'm trying to be romantic," I deadpan. *God, I love him so much.* I steady myself, looking up at him. "Jace, I might have dropped to my knees for you in a bathroom or two before, but this time, I want it to mean something. Will you marry me? Will you marry me for real? Will you be my husband?"

Jace's breath stutters, his whole body trembling as he stares at me on the floor. For a split second, he looks like he doesn't believe what I've just said. Then his eyes flood, and he drops down to his knees in front of me so fast we nearly knock heads.

"Yes," he breathes, voice cracking. He cups my face in both hands like he's terrified I'll take it back. "God, Kieran, yes! Yes, I'll marry you! For real. I've wanted this to be real the whole time. I love you. I've wanted this—wanted you—long before—"

I don't even let him finish before my lips crash into his. The kiss is desperate, messy, and perfect. His hands slide into my hair, my arms slide around his shoulders, and suddenly the world is just happiness and joy. The weight of the years we've wasted explode into this one moment where we finally, finally get it right.

Because he said yes.

For real.

The banging on the door comes back into focus. Mitch is shouting something about ruining the show with so much hiding, but when we stumble out of the bathroom, opening the bedroom door, flushed and holding hands, none of that matters.

Joey's eyes are wide and he looks like he's waiting for confirmation of *something*, so when Jace says "It's happening, it's *really* happening," Joey and Patrick absolutely lose it.

"Holy shit! It's happening!" Joey exclaims as he pumps his fist into the air, and I burst into laughter at how happy I am.

Patrick lets out this obnoxious cheer that even makes the camera crew laugh, and before I know it, the two of them are hugging us both like they've been waiting their whole lives for this too.

Jace and I are laughing, grinning so hard my cheeks hurt, and kissing again because I can't not kiss him.

We're really doing this.

We're choosing each other.

And it's the happiest I've ever been.

61

JACE

Producer: "What are you most excited for in the future with Kieran?"

Jace: "Everything. Absolutely everything."

I'm still not convinced this is actually happening.

But if it was only a dream, I'm pretty sure I'd be able to clearly see Kieran walking down the aisle instead of squinting through the blurred edges of my vision as I fight back tears.

Kieran's parents are walking him toward me in front of all our family, friends, and the *Love Without Labels* crew in this fancy ballroom that's decked out for our black-tie wedding.

I left all the decor options up to Kieran because I trust his creative vision way more than my own, and he chose black for almost everything. The room is dramatic and dark in a way that feels romantic and moody, making the pops of color that much more interesting. It's perfect for us and our love that started off so unconventionally but still managed to end up here.

Kieran is stunning in his all-black tux, the sparkly lapel pin a perfect nod to the clothes he used to wear that earned him his nickname. His makeup today is bold enough to make it obvious he's wearing it, to feel like *him,* without distracting from his naturally gorgeous features. And his smile as he approaches me lights up the entire room.

I've never been able to look away from Kieran; the pull I've always felt to him has only grown stronger as we've gotten to know each other again over the last month. And now, for the first time, I realize I won't ever have to stop. Kieran asked me to marry him, for real, for us, because he couldn't bear the thought of losing me. I'm still struggling to wrap my mind around the fact that my plan actually worked. That I somehow convinced Kieran that I'm good enough to be his husband *for real.*

When he finally gets to me at the front of the room, I can't hold back any longer and reach for his hands to hold in mine as we stand across from one another.

"Hey, Sparkles," I say quietly, only for him to hear.

His shoulders shake with his silent laughter before he mouths back, "Hey, hot shot."

The officiant launches into their speech about marriage and, the entire time, Kieran and I are lost in each other's gazes. I'm blown away by the warm affection, the love, the awe shining back at me. We didn't prepare custom vows because we hadn't planned to keep them, but as I have that thought, I realize between our two proposals, we've already said a lot of what would likely have been in them anyway.

We repeat back everything that we need to, and each promise we make is easy. I've loved Kieran for half of my life. We've already been through so much together, and I feel like we've learned from it all. I'm not saying I assume it will all be easy from here on out, but I'm confident that we've become a team, and can get through whatever life throws our way as long as we do it together.

The "I dos" are a blur, and as soon as I hear "You may now kiss—" my lips are already on his. It's just as amazing as every other kiss with Kieran has been, and it probably goes on for a little longer than appropriate, but it's our wedding day, so we can do what we want.

Everyone claps and cheers, and I really do feel like we're in a movie as we run out through the crowd holding hands.

We're whisked away to another room for pictures with Kieran's parents and my uncles and sister, while most of the guests get to enjoy cocktail hour, and then finally we're able to join the party. We cut our cake. Kieran shoves some in my face and even though I make it look like I do the same, I ensure it's a much smaller piece right into his mouth to avoid messing up his makeup.

We dance to a song that talks about slowing down time to adore their partner, even calling them "Darling," and it hits me that even though Kieran had been claiming this was fake up until last night, the wedding he planned for us is full of small details that are very specific to us and our relationship. I think we were both planning for a real future together long before then.

Kieran dances with his mom, and Joey surprises me when he asks me to share the next dance with him. By the time Patrick cuts in to finish out the second half of the song with me, the music changes from the sentimental slow song that had been playing to a much more upbeat pop hit, and he starts awkwardly dancing around me. The smile on my face feels permanent. Everyone laughs at Patrick's over-the-top attempt at dancing, and he effectively gets everyone to join us on the dance floor before the song ends.

Kieran and I find each other again, dancing and singing with all our friends, and when our gazes lock, and he smiles at me in a moment that is so full of joy, I have to fight back tears again.

When Kieran and I first met, my life was full of so much hatred. My dad hated that his dream didn't work out "because of me," so he spent every moment forcing it on me instead. Worse than that, he tried to teach me to hate anything and anyone that was different. I was never good enough for him, and I used the way he treated me as a model for how I should treat everyone else.

When I was that scared, misguided teenager, I was horrible to this man who I love, but he never let the hatred win. He has always let love and joy rule him. I am so fucking grateful that I was able to learn from his example, and that he forgave me, not once, but multiple times, and helped me to become the person I am today.

I take his hand, squeezing it as I nod away from the dance floor for him to follow. His smile never falters as I lead him away from the crowds and outside of the ballroom. "Are we sneaking away to our room?" he asks, tone full of amusement.

"We certainly can," I say with a laugh. "But I wanted to talk for a moment first if that's okay."

"Of course, husband." He smiles up at me.

I bite my lip at the title I don't think I'll ever get used to. "I know I apologized when we met on the show, and that you've now seen my apology that I wrote when I was eighteen. And we talked about what happened with David, but not really about all the shit I did before we ever hooked up. I'm so sorry."

"I love you, Jace. I forgave what you did a long time ago, even if it was nice to hear you say it."

I let out a big exhale. His continued acceptance lifts the smallest layer of my guilt away. "Well, I was thinking about how we didn't write vows, but I wanted to thank you for forgiving me, and I wanted to say that I don't think I'll ever truly deserve your forgiveness, but I promise to try. I promise to spend every day working to be a man worthy of you and your love."

"Baby, you already are," he assures me, and more tears start trickling down my face. He lifts his hand to cup my face, wiping them away with his thumb. "Come on, hot shot, I think we were at the party long enough. Let's go upstairs."

We sneak away and head up to the suite we're sharing tonight without anyone chasing us down a hallway.

The heat that's always been there is as strong as ever, but right now there's something more with it. The lust in Kieran's blue eyes is accompanied by so much love.

I know I haven't exactly been subtle about how much I care about him, but this still feels different. We've been together for weeks, yet somehow we've both been holding back the truth that it's more than just sex.

The teasing and taunting though, it's part of us, and I love it. But I'm also realizing we don't *need* it. I feel freer and more comfortable in our relationship as I acknowledge that we're choosing the dynamic that we both enjoy so much, but we aren't dependent on it.

I look at my husband, the man I've been obsessed with for half of my life, and take a moment to appreciate that this is our wedding night. Then I grin, because I know neither of us would ever settle for something as boring as quiet missionary sex in a dark room.

"What are you waiting for, baby?" I ask. "Just because you're my husband now doesn't mean you need to pretend like you're not desperate for my cock. The ring on your finger doesn't change the fact that you're still my filthy little cockslut, does it?"

His eyes flash with amusement and lust before Kieran starts to slowly undress. "I'm not the only one who's hard right now," he points out with a wink as he slowly walks toward the bed. "I think you've been hard all night." He pauses at the foot of the bed, leaning against it while working open each button of his shirt. "Have you been imagining what you wanted to do to me tonight?"

As he gets the final button open and shrugs off his shirt, my jaw practically hits the floor as I see what he's been hiding under his tux.

"Fuck me." I let out a deep groan as I take in my husband standing before me. Kieran is wearing a... harness? I'm not totally confident what to call it other than the hottest thing I've ever seen. It's made of black lace with straps that go across his chest and torso, highlighting his slim build and strong physique. It manages to look both masculine and delicate in a way that seems so perfect for him. I wonder briefly if he had it custom made.

It was completely hidden under his tux, which was definitely a good thing, because there is no way I could've gotten through today had I known what he was hiding underneath it. I've never seen anything like it.

My throat goes dry, my cock already straining against the front of my pants. "You're... you're going to kill me," I mutter, dragging a hand down my face, like that'll stop me from staring at every single strap hugging his body. "You've actually been sitting next to me eating cake, saying vows, and dancing while wearing that?"

Kieran's smirk takes over his whole face. "I wanted to do something special for my husband on our wedding night. I think I was making plans like things were real before I was ready to admit it, hoping we'd end up here."

I can't stay away any longer, I quickly close the space between us. The kiss is messy, full of teeth, clashing tongues, and hunger, because, fuck, he's mine now—officially mine. Kieran is my husband, with no plans to divorce, no end date. He's my forever.

Kieran gasps against me, fingers fisting the lapels of my jacket before shoving it off my shoulders. "You like it?" he asks. His chest is rising fast, nipples caught between thin lace and straps that make my hands itch to tear it all away.

"Like it?" I groan, sliding my palms down his torso, tracing every inch of fabric until my fingers are digging into his hips. "Baby, you're unreal. I can't decide if I should drop to my knees and worship you or pin you against the nearest surface so I can fuck you senseless. Jesus, Kieran, you're my goddamn fantasy."

His eyes flutter, and I know he's gone, just as wrecked as I am. "Good," he whispers, "because I bought it just for you. I'm yours."

"Mine," I repeat, sliding my fingers under the lowest straps, pulling back slightly so they snap back against his skin. His breath catches, and his pupils blow wider. "My pretty little slut, all dolled up for his husband."

He nods slowly, staring up at me with such need, like he would do anything I tell him to do in this moment.

I lean in, skimming my teeth down his neck before bringing my mouth up against his ear. "I've always been yours," I remind him. "I want you to fuck my face while I get that pretty little hole ready for my cock."

He shoves me back. "Well, what are you waiting for?"

I chuckle before I slowly drop to my knees before him. He runs his fingers through my hair as he steps in front of me so his erection is right in front of my mouth. "One more thing," I start.

"Oh my god, Jace, can't we talk after you've sucked my dick," he whines, thrusting his hips toward me.

I lightly slap his dick as I give him a warning glare. "No, this is important."

"Well, spit it out then."

"I don't want to use condoms," I say quickly, looking up at him. "We're married, I got tested just before the show started filming, it was all negative, and I obviously haven't been with anyone else. I don't want there to be anything between us if there doesn't have to be."

"I'm negative too," Kieran says as his small grin turns into a full-blown smile. "No condoms then. I've never not used them with anal."

"Me either," I admit. "Fuuuck, I can't wait to feel you." With that settled, I reach out to grip the base of his swollen cock as I wrap my lips around the head, slowly licking and teasing as I suck only the tip of him into my mouth. He lets out a deep groan, tightening his grip in my hair, shifting his hips and tugging my head toward him to try to force more of himself deeper inside me.

"Stop teasing me. You said that I could fuck your face," he growls, and I laugh around his cock as I give him what he wants, swallowing him down my throat in one go. I hold him there, showing off my lack of a gag reflex, and look up at Kieran through my lashes.

"Fuck, your glasses kill me. How are they so hot?" he murmurs. Then I wink and extend my arm up, holding two fingers out for him. I pull back enough to breathe before doubling my efforts on his cock.

He maintains eye contact as he grabs my wrist, brings my fingers to his face, and sucks them into his mouth in the filthiest display possible. When my fingers are nice and coated in his spit, I reach under him, seeking out his hole. The sound he makes as my finger teases around his opening sends a jolt of lust straight down my spine. He opens up for me easily as I slowly push inside of him with one finger, fucking him with it when he's ready.

In no time, he's rocking back to meet the motion, moaning "more" breathily as he meets each thrust. I add the second finger as slowly as I did the first, making sure to stretch and work him open as I do, all the while using my mouth and other hand to give his dick the attention he deserves. When he's effectively fucking himself on my finger with each thrust into my mouth, with the most addicting moans escaping his throat, I pull back from both.

"Fuck, what are you doing? Don't stop!" he scolds as I stand.

"I need lube," I remind him with a laugh as I walk to my bag to grab it, happily ignoring the condoms next to it. "And then I want my good little cockslut to ride my dick." I hand him the lube so that I can finally remove my tux. "Sorry, no surprises under mine."

"So boring," he teases, eyes locked on each movement I make to undress for him.

"Someone didn't give me much warning that today would be the real thing," I remind him. "But I'll happily wear anything you want me to, baby."

"Really?" He sounds surprised as he follows me to the small couch. "You'd wear something like this? With lace and sparkles and flowers?"

"I wouldn't look half as good as you do in it." I chuckle as I sit down. "But I think it's time you start believing me when I say that I'd do anything you ask me to."

He bites his lip as he moves to straddle me, sitting back on my thighs so he can coat my already leaking dick with lube. "Up," I command, slapping his ass until he's hovering over me. "I wasn't done prepping you."

"I'm ready," he insists, but I give him a warning look, and he sighs, handing over the lube.

I coat three fingers, starting with two again as I ease my way in, stretching him open before adding the third finger. He's gripping my shoulders as he kneels over me, sinking lower onto my fingers as he grinds and squirms. "Jesus, baby, you have such a greedy little hole. You're taking my fingers so well. You're desperate for the real thing, aren't you, darling? Need your husband's thick dick to split you open? Need me to fill you up with my cum and mark you as mine from the inside?"

"Yes, all of that," he pants. "Right now. Need you."

I finally remove my fingers, and he shifts his hips so that he's hovering right above me. I hold the base of my cock with one hand, and grip his hip with the other, trying to prevent him from slamming down onto me too quickly. As soon as the tip pushes in, I know that this is going to be unlike anything I've ever experienced. "Holy fucking shit," I exhale. "K, fuuuuck, this feels amazing."

I'm trying really hard not to thrust up into him with everything that I have, to let him control the pace as he lowers himself, but it's like I've lost all sense of rational thought as I use my hold on his hip to pull him down even harder as my hips raise up all on their own.

He lets out a cry, but it's laced with pleasure. "Yeah, just like that, Jace," he confirms between labored breaths. I set a punishing pace, both hands now digging into his waist, holding him in place as I fuck up into him. "Don't hold back," he reminds me, and thank god, because at this point, I don't think I could even if I wanted to. The only reason I can even remember my own name right now is because he's screaming it as he bounces on top of me. I'm completely lost in the feeling of being inside him with no barrier for the first time.

"So tight. So soft. So warm." I'm trying to explain how incredible this is, but sentences are hard.

I look up to meet my husband's gaze, and he grabs my face in his hands, leaning in for a sloppy kiss filled with so much passion and emotion. I can't believe I went so many years without kissing him. He wraps his hands around my shoulders, pulling me closer to him, but it still doesn't feel close enough.

"You still haven't... seen this... from the back..." he manages to get out between pants.

I immediately pull him off me and set him on the floor to spin him around. The straps that went around each thigh wrap around him, framing his perfect ass kind of like a jockstrap, but so much better because his dick is free in the front. The way the higher straps and lace show off his trim waist and strong back are just as sexy as it was from the front. "Hands and knees on the bed," I command, slapping his ass. "I need to watch my bare cock disappear into your perfect little hole while you're wearing this."

"So bossy tonight," he teases as he hurries to position himself as I said at the edge of the bed. I line myself back up and slam back in, knowing he won't want me to hold back.

"Still can't believe you're really mine," I admit as I shift my angle until he's crying out with each thrust. "Fuck, I don't know how much longer I'll last, baby, this is too good."

"Switch!" he shouts out, crawling away from me on the bed.

"What?" I ask, shocked he wants to stop now when I'm so close.

"I can't let you have all the condom-free fun," he explains, scrambling for the lube. "Swap positions so I can prep you."

I'm so torn right now because I am *so close,* and I need to come, need to fill my husband with my release for the first time more than I think I've ever needed anything. But I also really love the idea of having him inside me with no barrier. And if Kieran wants to fuck me, I know I'll never turn that down. So I crawl onto the bed.

"Your bubble butt is insane," he murmurs as he teases my hole with a lubed finger.

I rock back into the pressure. "You should already be inside me," I scold.

"And you say I'm the cockslut."

"Because you are," I remind him firmly. "My beautiful, perfect cockslut who needs to fuck me immediately."

He chuckles and preps me quickly, even if it isn't nearly as fast as I'd like him to. After a few more seconds, his tip is *finally* pushing in, and the feel of his bare cock sliding into me has my dick leaking all over the sheets.

"Oh my god, I thought you were overselling it, but, fuck, this is amazing," he groans, grinding into me once he's bottomed out. He pulls back, fucking me in an agonizingly slow rhythm that rubs against that perfect spot inside of me each time, and the noises coming from me are probably alerting half the hotel to how much I'm enjoying this.

"So glad this is real," Kieran says as he thrusts into me, rubbing a hand over the muscles in my back.

"It was always real," I answer through breathless pants, moving my hips back to meet his.

He moans, and I feel it throughout my body. "Your ass is so perfect, fuck, Jace. I wish you could see your hole swallow my cock."

Kieran's words make heat shoot straight through me, and I bury my face in the sheets with a groan. Every thrust of his hips feels like he's driving the air right out of me, but I don't want him to stop, not for a second.

"Fuck, Jace…" His voice is rough, like gravel dragged over fire. His hand slides down my side, holding me in place, and the mix of restraint and reverence in his touch makes me clench around him. "You have no idea what you do to me."

I want to tell him I do know, that I can feel it in the way he's shaking behind me. But all that comes out are broken moans as I push back against him, needing more.

He's perfect, and I'll never get enough.

I look over my shoulder at him as I push back against on his cock and see that fucking harness again. "Alright. You've had your fun," I say, pulling away from him. "Need to fill you up while I can look at you wearing that, baby."

He laughs but doesn't argue, moving to lay on the bed and putting a pillow under his hips. "I think I need to get more of these."

"Yes. All of them. All the colors and fabrics and designs," I ramble as I line myself up with his slick hole once more, groaning as I push in. Pleasure is building at the base of my spine and seems to spread throughout my entire body as his ass welcomes me like we were perfectly made for each other. He pulls me down so our bodies are flush together.

The rough edge of fabric against my sensitive nipples sends a shock through me, a rush that blurs everything until all I can focus on is the taste of his kiss and the ache building inside me. I move a hand between us to his cock. I won't last much longer, and I want to bring him over the edge with me, but he grabs my wrist and pulls away for the kiss. "Not yet, baby. Come inside me and then we're flipping one more time so I can finish in you too."

That does it. His words and the filthy picture he's painting with them send my orgasm slamming into me. The pleasure is so intense that the edges of my vision black out as I come inside Kieran, filling him with my release.

As soon as I come down from my high, he's rolling me onto my back. He quickly adds more lube to his straining dick and pushes my legs upwards to line himself up with my hole. I'm so sensitive that staying relaxed enough to let him in takes all the effort I can manage, but then he's inside me, looking down at me like I'm the greatest thing that ever happened to him.

He thrusts into me a few more times before he cries out my name with his release, I have to blink away happy tears. Tonight, all of today, really, was so perfect.

After we're cleaned up, and I have Kieran wrapped in my arms, head resting on my chest, in our bed, on our wedding night, I let my tears fall.

Kieran looks up at me, concern etched on his face. "Are you okay, baby?"

I smile down at my dream man, the person I've been obsessed with for half my life, my husband. "Happier than I ever thought I deserved to be," I admit softly.

He props himself up a bit, and it feels like his bright blue gaze is peering right into my soul. "We might have had a really rough start, but we both pushed the other to be who we are today, to be better," he says gently. "I love my life. I wouldn't change a thing about it. You make me so fucking happy, and you deserve to be happy too, Jace." He shifts to place a soft kiss on my lips. "You're my husband now, and I won't let anyone talk poorly of my husband, even you," he warns, managing to pull a laugh from deep in my chest.

"I love you, Sparkles," I whisper, pulling him closer, tucking him back into my chest.

"I love you too, hot shot." He places a soft kiss over my heart, and I feel like it's going to burst out of my chest with all the love I have for this man.

I never would've imagined me calling him Sparkles all those years ago as an intended insult to mask my attraction for him would lead us to this moment. But I know this life with Kieran is so much better than any other version I could've lived.

I signed up for *Love Without Labels* hoping to move on from my obsession with the very man I ended up falling for.

And I wouldn't change a damn thing.

EPILOGUE ONE

Kieran
August

*P*eople still complain about how little we gave away at the reunion taping, but I knew from day one I wasn't going to hand over everything when the stage wasn't mine.

I already give enough of myself to the internet, but the comments have been constant, and I've gotten so many podcast and interview requests. I figured if people want us to answer questions, we'd start with my audience because they're the ones who've been here the longest. We already handpicked some questions to answer that we keep seeing repeatedly and feel comfortable answering.

"Ready?" Jace asks from beside me, knees brushing mine under the table at my desk. He somehow manages to look too good in the plain T-shirt that shows off his thick arms and wide chest. If anything, I wish he'd wear something less flattering, so I'm not distracted the entire time we're filming.

I grin at the lens and hit record. "Hi, Sparkles fans. Today's the day you have been waiting for! My husband, Jace, is here with me, and we know you've got a lot of questions that we're excited to answer for you. Some of them are sweet, and some of them are nosy as hell." I laugh with a pointed stare at the camera.

"Hi, guys." Jace beams at the camera. It's adorable that he's still excited about the Sparkles stuff. "Alright, let's get into it," he prompts beside me with the list we made. "Do you live together?"

"Well, as you can see, I'm still in my same office studio. But Jace did move in with me. I offered to relocate, finding somewhere between us that we could make our own, but Jace told me there's no way I could change where I film. He's incredibly supportive, and I do love where I am. He's helped me add a few new things around the place to make it feel like ours."

"So many sarcastic cross-stitched throw pillows," Jace adds under his breath. He's also encouraged me to display some of my art, and when he went on and on about how happy looking at it makes him—how he used to always stop to find my art to admire in the hallway during high school, and he wants to be able to do that again—how could I say no to that?

He's smiling at me now with so much affection, not trying to speak over me or interject. He's been the biggest cheerleader for my work without trying to make it about him. It's been so refreshing compared to all the past partners I've had who've tried to ride the coattails off my success. I never really thought Jace would be like that, but the confirmation that he hasn't treated me any differently without cameras constantly being around was still a relief.

"Next question, what's it like working together now?"

I smirk at Jace as I consider. "Maybe you should answer this one, darling."

He turns to the camera again, huge smile still in place. "It's amazing," he answers confidently. "I loved the job I had before we got together as a structural iron and steel worker, but it was really physically demanding work with long hours. I enjoyed the overtime when I didn't have anyone to come home to, but after we got married, that quickly lost its appeal." He laughs, turning back to smile adoringly at me. I wonder if my stomach will ever stop doing flips when he looks at me like that. I hope it never does.

"I tried going part time at first," he continues. "But I saw how much Kieran and his assistant were juggling, so on my days off I offered to help wherever I could. I don't really feel like I'm working at all anymore. I tell people I'm a professional husband," he jokes.

I laugh too. "Come on, you do a ton of work. I honestly can't remember how we managed before you were here to run all the random errands that pop up, or to basically run my socials." I turn to the cameras. "He reminds me when to post and sifts through all the comments, showing me the positive ones, so I can focus on actually creating content and on my product lines."

"I have a feeling you skipped a lot of meals and literally never stopped working," he accurately guesses. I laugh thinking about the blind dating portion of the show and how neither one of us really had hobbies because all we did was work. Now, we spend so much time together, completely unplugged. I don't think I would have trusted anyone else to step in the way that Jace has, but somehow, we ended up with the work-life balance I used to only dream of.

"I love this next one." Jace smiles. "How do Freddie and Jace get along?"

I can't help but laugh at that even though I knew it was coming. "Why don't you take this one too, babe?" I prompt him.

"Well, I'd never been around a cat before, and the first time Kieran introduced us, I had no idea what to do, which I know sounds silly. But now, Freddie and I are best friends. He follows me everywhere and curls up in my lap whenever he can."

"It is super cute," I agree.

"Our favorite question is next," Jace prompts sarcastically. *I fucking hate this question.* "Can you tell us the details about your past?"

This has been the most asked question since we were so "secretive" during filming on the show. All the interviews we did, separately and together, we didn't give much about how we knew each other *before*, and I still don't plan to. All the audience has is that one kitchen conversation, where Jace admitted he'd been closeted "back then" and hadn't supported me—and that's how we plan to keep it.

"As we've said in the past on the show, we knew each other growing up. We went to high school together and we weren't friends. Reconnecting after all these years was great for us, it gave us each a chance to grow as individuals and understand what we really need, which is a healthy, supportive relationship. There's not much more to tell other than that," I say, completely comfortable with that half truth.

We go through a few more questions, but we keep everything truly personal close to our chests because this is still our life and we want some things to stay between us. Some people definitely want to know every little detail, but they're not getting it from us.

As expected, there were some rumors from people from our hometown that started circling, but nothing major. The big thing that happened, though, was David reached out to Jace on social media. He apologized for getting between us back then and asked if we could all ever "catch up." The real shocker was when he thanked Jace for being his own sexual awakening and said he wanted to introduce us to his partner.

Jace told me he hasn't spoken to David since high school,

and that he had no idea he was ever into him in that way. I fully believe him. But Jace needs more time to decide if he wants to reopen that door. That's kind of the theme of our life now. We choose what we let in. We choose what we share. We choose what gets our energy and what doesn't. People online might still speculate, and people from back home might still try to stir things up, but we're good. Better than good. We've got our work, our home, Freddie, and each other. That's more than enough. It's exactly what I dreamed I would find when I signed up for *Love Without Labels*, but somehow even better than I'd hoped.

As soon as we stop filming, Jace turns to me.

"There's one more question," Jace says, and I assume he's about to ask me to fuck him. "I heard you and Liv speculating about that fan account that used to help run your fan page but stopped posting. Do you know what happened to them?"

I scrunch my brows in confusion, but my mind goes immediately to JJ.

"What about it?" I ask, cautiously.

Jace smirks, but he's also blushing. "It wasn't some random fan."

I wait quietly for him to keep going.

"It was me."

My jaw literally drops. I don't even know what to do with that information at first. Jace—my husband, the person I used to think was too cool to ever watch my old videos—was running the biggest Kieran Delaney fan page on the internet?

"I probably should've told you before, but..." He shrugs as though he's trying to downplay this, but I can see the nerves in his eyes. "I didn't want you to think I was a stalker."

"You're telling me you're *the* JJ? The one who was always first to comment on my posts and defend me against all the negative ones? Who had 'New York' in his bio but never once showed up to an event?"

"Yeah…"

"Oh my god. Olivia and I used to sit around trying to figure you out. We had so many guesses. Entire elaborate theories. I can't believe it was you the whole time!"

"Are you mad?"

"No, of course not." I laugh. "I'm shocked and impressed. And honestly grateful. You kept me going some days. There were a lot of times when the negative comments would get to me or a post wouldn't do as well as I'd expected. When I felt like no one cared anymore, and when I wanted to quit, you'd come on my feed with a well-timed post about how great I was or something, and I'd feel like what I was doing did matter. You gave me the inspiration I'd need to keep going."

Jace grins. "I just wanted to help the world see you the way I did. Even when I couldn't be there in person."

For a second, I forget how to breathe. Jace was secretly the reason I made it through some of my hardest years, the reason I never stopped believing people cared what I had to say.

"You were my number-one fan before you were my number-one everything," I whisper.

He shrugs casually like he didn't just hand me the most romantic plot twist ever. "Guess I've always been playing the long game. There's one more thing, actually."

"What's that?" I ask curiously.

"I actually signed up for the show hoping to get over you. Seeing all your videos and being your biggest fan made it impossible for me to move on, but it doesn't seem like that was ever in the cards for us."

I move to straddle him, practically jumping into his arms as I kiss him with everything I have.

Because this man? This man who has been so many things to me, my bully, my crush, my first real heartbreak, apparently my biggest fan, my fake boyfriend, my real husband, the love of my life.

He's so much more than any one of them.
He's everything.
And I'm so fucking happy that he's my forever.

63

EPILOGUE TWO

This will include spoilers for book one!

Jace
October

"**W**ell, this is cute," Kieran says as we pull up to Liam's family farm. He invited us over to see the new setup they created for their pumpkin patch. It's our first time visiting his farm, but with all the videos Blake has sent us and posts online, I feel like we've been here already.

Liam must've heard us driving up because he's walking toward the car already as we exit. "Hey, guys, thank you so much for coming." He greets us each with a warm hug.

They've come back to the city a few times, so this isn't the first time we've seen them since the show stopped filming. We have a group chat where Blake sends regular updates about his latest animal adoptions, and pretty much every other farm-related idea that pops into his mind. I think it's safe to say we've become the kind of friend who'll remain in each other's lives for the long haul.

They opened last weekend for their Fall Fest and we thought about coming up for opening weekend, but Liam suggested we make the drive on a day they were closed so we could actually visit with each other.

"Where's the chicken daddy?" Kieran asks in a teasing tone.

Blake might not have Kieran's following, but he's definitely made a name for himself on social media with that viral clip of him introducing himself as "daddy" to the chickens. Kieran and I have thoroughly enjoy all his "chicken daddy" content. It's completely ridiculous and unhinged, which is perfect for Blake.

"Blake's friends Chad and Ash just got here, so I think the three of them are with the chickens," he explains. "You guys will also get to meet my buddy John today. He just moved back here and should be coming over shortly."

"Everything looks incredible," I comment, admiring what looks like a new barn as Liam leads us over to the chickens.

"Thanks," Liam responds. He seems so happy, so at ease here in a way that he never was during the filming. I'm thrilled that things worked out so well for my friend. "I know Blake likes to post about the funny stuff that happens around here," he continues. "But we really couldn't have done any of it without him. Who knew the city boy was what our farm was missing?"

Sure enough, when we arrive at the coop, Blake is on the ground surrounded by his babies. It looks like he's trying to show Chad and Ash how to properly hold them, although I think I hear him use the word "cuddle."

Blake looks our way, somehow growing even more excited. "Guys! Guys, hey, come look at my cock," he yells, as he holds up a chicken, and we can't help but laugh at his antics.

We've met Chad and Ash in the city before, so there's no need for introductions as we join them.

"This is amazing!" Chad says, staring at the chicken in his arms as if it holds the answers to all of life's questions. "I can totally see why you gave up life in the city to live here."

"You can?" Ash asks, tone full of disbelief as he completely ignores the chickens surrounding him. "Please don't tell me you're going to move away too. I swear all my friends are coupling up and ditching me."

"I don't know, Ash, Blake seems pretty happy out here. Maybe I should move to a farm," Chad says seriously.

"While you're at it, you should get married," Ash replies sarcastically. "Then I'll really be the only one who's still single."

Chad is nodding along seriously, and I don't know Blake's best friend well, but he doesn't seem to understand sarcasm. "Maybe I should," he agrees, as if Ash was making an actual suggestion.

"Hey, man, sorry I'm late," a deep voice calls out from behind us, and a large man I don't recognize approaches.

"No worries." Liam greets him with a warm smile. "Everybody, this is my best friend, John." He gives a short wave to the group, looking less than thrilled to be surrounded by strangers.

"Holy shit. How many tattoos do you have?" Chad blurts out.

"Uh, I'm not sure. I stopped counting a long time ago," John hesitantly answers.

"Alright. Everyone's here! Can we tell them?" Blake asks excitedly. Liam nods for him to go ahead, his indulgent smile and the love shining in his eyes making it clear how amused he is by his partner's boundless enthusiasm.

"We're going to Vegas!" Blake blurts out.

I glance at Kieran, confused about how I should react. "Congratulations?" Kieran shrugs.

Liam laughs again. "I think you forgot some of the details there, B."

"Right! Sorry, I'm just so excited. Okay, let me start from the beginning. We are officially engaged again!"

This time, everyone does congratulate them, confidently excited by the news. "So happy for you guys," I say quietly to Liam.

"Thanks." He smiles at me. "I know it took a little bit longer for us to get here, but it was the time we needed."

"Hey, I get it," I remind him. "Took us thirteen years to get it right."

There are plenty of things I wish I could change about those years, but looking at the easy smile on Kieran's face as we're surrounded by our friends, I'm reminded of what he always tells me: to not get lost in the past and to focus on our joy. We're here now, and I wouldn't change a single detail of the life we're building together.

Kieran really did make me the happiest man on earth when he married me.

"Yes, thank you, thank you," Blake is saying, so I force myself to focus and turn my attention back to him. "As I was saying, now that we are officially engaged again, we get to have a bachelor party. We want to do it together, so I would love to take all of you to Vegas to help us celebrate!"

"That makes a lot more sense," Kieran says quietly to me. We share an amused grin as he nods.

"We're in. Can't wait!"

THE END.

WANT TO READ THE INITIAL JOURNAL ENTRY?

Kieran skims over that first journal entry from back when they were eighteen during the proposal, if you would like to read it, check out our Patreon!

The Apology:
  https://tinyurl.com/4hjuajv2

ALSO BY

<u>Lexi Amber</u>

Chicago Awakenings

Accidentally Joining His Cult *contemporary MM romance*

Accidentally Falling For My Best Friend *contemporary MM romance*

Accidentally Falling for Her- The Girls *contemporary FF romance companion novella*

Accidentally Living With The Captain *contemporary MM romance February 2026*

<u>Bec Benson</u>

Straight To You *contemporary MM romantic suspense*

All In December *contemporary MM holiday romance*

<u>Co-authored</u>

Love Without Labels

The Reality of Wanting Him *contemporary MM romance*

The Reality of Wanting My Bully

The Reality of Ever After *LWL novella expected March 2026* The bachelor party in Vegas

Wanting My Husband *LWL spin-off expected mid 2026* not on the reality show

ABOUT LEXI

Lexi is an American author who is obsessed with queer happily ever afters. Most of her time is spent with her two kids, but if they're asleep then she is either reading, writing, or watching hockey.

Professionally trained as a nurse, Lexi decided to start writing when she became a stay at home mom and the characters in her head haven't stopped talking since.

Lexi also loves Diet Coke, traveling, and Halloween. Her house is probably obnoxiously decorated for whatever holiday is next because she thinks that little things that make people smile are important.

You can find her attempting to stay up to date with all of the social media below, as well as the MM wire and discord.

Signed copies of solo work and lots of fun merch at Lexi amber.com

ABOUT BEC

Bec Benson is based in the Northeast, lives for the first sip of hot coffee in the morning, genuinely believes emo music can make you happy, and is obsessed with mgk.

More about Bec and upcoming work at Becbenson.com

ACKNOWLEDGMENTS

Thank you so much to everyone who helped make this book possible!

Model Cover was created by the very talented Rebecca at Story Styling Cover Designs and the amazing cover image was done by Edd Banu who is a real life beauty influencer—check out his socials if you don't already follow! Copy edits were done by Raven at Raven Quill Editing, Proofreading was done by Lindsey Middlemiss.

Chapter images and character art drawn by Kierofoxen—thank you so much for all of the art you've already done for us, we can't wait to get more!

Sensitivity feedback was done by Jonathan Samuels—so happy to have all of your help and feedback with getting this story to where it needed to be! Thank you for everything!!!

The biggest shout out and thank you to our beta readers! Thank you for all of your feedback! The first version that you saw ended up being a very different one than this once again LOL

Our amazing PA Ash deserves a HUGE shoutout!!! So glad to have you on our team

Extra from just Lexi- I'd also like to thank my very supportive husband who believed in this dream before I did, and who's encouraged me every step of the way. I definitely couldn't have done any of this without you. Sorry this one kind of took over my life for a few months

Thanks to my parents who've been very supportive, even if I hope they never actually read any of my books.

And to my kids, why did we stop napping? LOL thanks for letting mommy work, even after I quit my nursing job to stay home with you guys. I'll love you forever and always no matter what.